# BERLIN WOLF

# BERLIN
# WOLF

## MARK
## FLORIDA-JAMES

Matador
9 Priory Business Park
Kibworth Beauchamp
Leicestershire LE8 0RX, UK
Tel: (+44) 116 279 2299
Fax: (+44) 116 279 2277
Email: books@troubador.co.uk
Web: www.troubador.co.uk/matador

ISBN 978 1783060 054

British Library Cataloguing in Publication Data.
A catalogue record for this book is available from the British Library.

Typeset in Book Antiqua by Troubador Publishing Ltd
Printed and bound in the UK by TJ International, Padstow, Cornwall

**Matador** is an imprint of Troubador Publishing Ltd

*Inspired by Maisie, our very own wolf and the best dog ever, and Ela Clark (15th May 1925 – 22nd May 2011), a dear friend who lived through those terrible times and courageously fought the Nazis.*

*With many thanks to Ela and Ann Clark for their feedback and encouragement.*

*In memory of my brother, Anthony (10th October 1984 – 1st October 1989).*

*Dedicated to my wonferful wife Jackie and our adorable dogs past and present, Maisie, Woody, Charlie and Gulliver.*

# CHAPTER ONE

## Bathing Beach, Lake Wannsee, Berlin
## 15th November 1941

'Good boy Wolfi! Good boy! Not long now.' Peter Stern stretched out his hand in the darkness and stroked Wolfi's head. 'Please come soon,' the young boy prayed.

They had been standing as still as possible for many hours. His feet and hands were numb from cold and he was hungry. His warm home with its larder full of food was just a short walk away. The fifteen-year-old and his dog were huddled together in a thick glade of trees alongside Lake Wannsee. Close by, his parents Isaac and Sara, were shivering, as much from fear as the biting cold. No-one had dared speak for over forty minutes. At last, it had turned dark and they could relax a little.

The plan had seemed so simple. They had walked from the family home on Schillerstrasse, around Lake Schlachtensee and then west to the woods surrounding Wannsee, Berlin's huge play park. To the casual observer they were a family on a picnic outing with hamper, knapsack and the family dog. They were dressed appropriately for the time of year with overcoats, hats and scarves. Even Wolfi had a coat of types. Possibly the most valuable dog coat ever, for sewn into the lining was Sara's

1

small, but precious collection of jewels, heirlooms handed down over many years. Had anyone listened closely they would have heard a slight rustle as she walked, causing the wads of Reich marks hidden in her petticoats to rub together. Papa had reckoned there was less chance that Wolfi or Sara would be searched if stopped. Each had their own identity card, just in case anything went wrong. There was no point hiding these. They were required to carry them by law. In his heart Papa knew that they were worthless so long as they were stamped with the red letter 'J'. 'J' for Jew.

As they had made their way by the familiar streets from their home to Lake Wannsee they were nervous of meeting neighbours. The sort of neighbour who might notice their sudden weight gain or, the excessive sweating caused by additional layers of clothes.

At least they had been lucky with the weather. Berlin winters were often very harsh and it was not unknown for there to be deep snow on the ground in the middle of November. A picnic on a dry, sunny, winter's day would not attract any undue attention. Berliners are a tough breed. A picnic in the snow might arouse suspicion. Had the weather been unfavourable the plan had been to pose as a family going sledging in the park. This had the disadvantage that there would be no reason to carry any sort of luggage.

Everything was fine until, rounding a corner from Fisherhüttenstrasse, they came across a mob of SS men.

'Pick it up! Pick it up! Faster you lazy pig!' one screamed hysterically.

The unfortunate victim was an elderly Jewish man. He

was easily identified by the yellow star on his lapel. Every time the old man bent over, one would kick him sharply in the backside and scream at him again. It was a sadly familiar scene in Berlin. The Stern family desperately wanted to help. They dare not jeopardise their escape. With a deep sense of shame they tried to avoid eye contact and continued their journey.

'Ahh!' the elderly Jew gasped and clutched his heart as he fell to the ground.

'Oh no!' Sara Stern cried out and stepped towards him. The leader of the mob of four SS men, more of a boy than a man, instantly turned towards her. He looked her up and down and then quickly surveyed the rest of the group.

'So you feel sorry for the Jew. Maybe you are also Jews. Show me your papers!' he demanded.

Isaac, Sara and Peter hesitated for just a second. If he had not noticed the faded patch on their clothes where the Jewish Star had once been sewn, their passes would betray them. The delay was unacceptable. Patience had long since deserted Germany. The SS man removed his revolver from its holster, pulled back the safety catch and cocked the hammer.

'Papers! Quickly!' he screeched. The gun was pointed at Sara's face, just a few terrifying centimetres away.

Before anyone could respond to the threat, Wolfi fell on one side, rolled over and put his paws in the air, as if dead. It was his best trick. The SS man fell into fits of laughter.

'All right you can go. No Jew could teach a fine German dog such a good trick.' He was still laughing as he put away his gun. He patted Wolfi on the head and, without waiting further, the family hurried on. To their relief the old man struggled to his feet. His tormentors were bored with their game and he was allowed to leave.

Once around the next corner Isaac stroked Wolfi warmly.

'I knew it was a good idea to bring you.' As he spoke he felt a pang of regret and guilt. He had not yet told Peter. His best friend Wolfi could not go with them.

During the daylight hours they had sat by the lake on a blanket, with picnic basket in view. Peter played with Wolfi and the rest of the family ate and drank in minute amounts. They had no idea how long their journey was to take. Periodically they had packed up and moved some distance away to try and avoid unwanted attention. That had worked quite well and had been relatively easy. They had even managed to sneak into the woods unnoticed.

Since then, the long hours standing in the dark and cold, remaining as silent as possible and encouraging Wolfi to do likewise, had been very trying. Even the sound of shuffling from one foot to the other to keep warm seemed to magnify and echo across the surface of the lake. Isaac thanked their luck that most other visitors had left early in the gloom of the November evening.

Now as he hugged himself for warmth, Isaac wondered how Peter would react when he realised that Wolfi must stay behind. Would it have been better to have left Wolfi at home? Someone, even a Nazi, might have adopted him.

He was after all a fine 'German dog'. Wolfi had more than served his purpose as he had been part of the cover story. Who attempts to flee in secret with a dog? This had to be the end of the line. The success of their escape would depend on remaining as inconspicuous as possible.

Oblivious to his father's dilemma, Peter rubbed Wolfi's furry black ears. He remembered the day five years ago when Wolfi arrived. As always an expectant son sat at the bottom of the staircase, waiting for his father to return from the city. On this occasion he was particularly impatient. It was his tenth birthday and he expected Papa to be clasping a large present of some sort. Maybe the kite he had seen in the toyshop or the model sailing boat? For some reason his father was even later than usual. Hopefully his work at the bank had not held him up? Not today of all days? To make matters worse, when Papa did finally push open the heavy wooden door he had nothing in his hand, only a snow-streaked umbrella.

The boy sat back on the step, trying to hide his disappointment. Surely Papa had not forgotten? And then he noticed it. Inside Papa's huge overcoat something was moving. The tightly woven, woollen material rippled in places, like the surface of the Berlin lakes in the wind. Peter was fascinated, following every movement. The ripple moved to Papa's lapel and out popped a black ball of fur. The fur ball grew two small pointy ears and a pink tongue that was clearly too long for its mouth. An ear flopped to one side, whilst the other stood very proud and erect. Two blue-grey pools reflected in the light of the hallway. The excited boy sprang from the step as a high–pitched bark confirmed that it was indeed a puppy.

When finally Papa was able to take off his hat and coat and remove the black bundle, Peter was surprised to discover that the rest of the animal was the same size as the head. He did not care. He had a puppy, the dog he had wanted for so long. He hugged it to his chest, almost smothering it. This was the best present ever. In spite of looking more like a little bear cub than a wolf, Peter had named it 'Wolfi' after one of his favourite stories. After all he had joked 'if I am Peter he must be the wolf'.

Within six months the small bundle of fluff that Papa could stretch out in one hand was now a medium-sized dog. Eighteen months later, at the age of two, he was a fully grown, entirely black, shaggy, long-haired dog. He had pointy ears that swivelled towards any noises, a long well-defined snout, sparkling grey eyes and a thick, bushy tail that was never still. His teeth, when exposed with a growl, struck fear into almost all who saw it. And indeed he looked very like a wolf. In appearance he was the shape of the famous German shepherd dog. Some thought he might in fact be a Belgian shepherd, cousin of the German variety. His breeding made no odds to Peter. He was his best friend.

Wolfi and his young master were seldom apart, except when Peter went to school or synagogue. Every school day morning he would rise early to take Wolfi for a walk in and around the lake and in the woods, even in the dark of winter. On his return from school he would greet Wolfi first, then acknowledge his mother (and father if present).

Once changed out of his school uniform, he would take his best friend out for another walk.

On weekends or holidays they would sometimes spend almost all morning and afternoon in the woods around Lake Schlachtensee making camps, swimming or fishing in the clear waters of the lake. If the severe Berlin winter was in full flow they would play together in the conservatory, with Peter teaching Wolfi tricks. How to sit, lie down, play dead and even sing along to Papa's opera records. The singing was for some reason not so popular with Mama or Papa.

At first Wolfi was restricted to the conservatory and the garden, then gradually, bit by bit, the boundaries were extended until he was allowed in virtually all the rooms of the house. He would sneak onto a comfortable chair next to Peter and lie across his legs; or slip into his bedroom having pushed open the door with his nose and then clamber onto Peter's bed, where he would sleep peacefully by his feet. He was even known on occasions to have found his way onto Papa's lap when he was snoozing after lunch in his favourite leather armchair. Papa had always claimed that 'the dog' as he referred to Wolfi, had jumped up without his knowing. No-one believed him.

As each boundary was pushed back a little further, the affection of all the family, Mama, Papa and Peter, grew for Wolfi, much though the adults tried to resist it.

As these happy memories filled Peter's thoughts, the gentle chugging of a motor launch was heard approaching the shore.

'Are you sure we can trust this man?' Sara whispered to her husband. She was clearly anxious. Their safety depended on the captain of the boat they were about to board and they knew so little about him.

'Yes, though in any case we have no choice.' Isaac was not entirely convinced by his own answer. He had only met the man the night before through an acquaintance at the bank where he worked. He was introduced to the Captain of a tug boat transporting coal along the waterways of Berlin to the west at Lübeck. For a smallish fortune he would convey them to the northwest coast where they should be able to buy a passage on a ship to safety.

The Captain, despite his rough demeanour, appeared trustworthy. He was no particular Jew lover, he just hated the Nazis. He had been interned for a while in the early years of the regime for his communist sympathies.

He had arranged to meet them on the eastern shore of the great Lake Wannsee, at the far end of the pleasure beach where once Isaac and his family had enjoyed long, care-free summer days. The same beach from which they were now banned. They were to meet at the pontoon at nine in the evening. No signal was to be given as the slightest unusual noise would travel far across the lake and even a single light would be readily visible in these times of routine blackouts.

All this had been agreed the previous evening. Any doubts Isaac had as to whether they should attempt to flee were dispelled by the Captain. When asked about the rumours of what happened in the East, the Captain had taken the pipe from his mouth, saying gravely,

'I have seen for myself what goes on. You need to get your family out of Germany.' Isaac had departed without delving further into what the Captain knew.

Without wasting any time they quickly gathered their few belongings and hurried out of the trees and towards the pontoon. Wolfi was on a short leather lead. He was excited to be moving again. Thankfully the only indication of this was a greater bounce to his step.

'What's this? This can't be our boat,' Isaac murmured and wondered whether they should retreat into the woods.

Only as he spotted the Captain at the tiller did he realise that it was indeed their boat. It was not, however, the canal boat or tug he had expected. This was a small pleasure cruiser, the type that would often be seen on Lake Wannsee, a type not so usual on the canals of the more industrial part of the city. Most worryingly this was a pleasure boat with all-round visibility. Passengers could sit in comfort and view the scenery, equally they could clearly be seen from the outside. Worst of all there was no below deck. At least it was an overcast night with little natural light. Isaac stepped on board and beckoned to his family.

'I thought you promised us a tug, not a pleasure boat for all to see.' The desperation was obvious in Isaac's voice.

'I can't bring a tug this far down the lake. There isn't any need for such a boat as that here. No-one will notice a tug on the canal at night time. They would at this end of the lake however. We'll change vessels when we get onto the narrower part of the river.'

'You should have told me that last night,' Isaac muttered, unhappy with the Captain's explanation. The sailor shrugged his shoulders.

Momentarily distracted, Isaac had forgotten about Wolfi who was now at the bow of the boat with his son.

'Hold on,' said the Captain, 'you can't bring that mutt.'

As Peter approached the Captain, Wolfi began a low growl, becoming unusually agitated.

'He's right,' said Isaac. 'You had better set him loose.' Even as the words left his mouth and, in spite of the darkness, Isaac could see the crestfallen look on his son's face.

'Quiet boy! Quiet!' Peter urged. Thankfully he managed to calm Wolfi, who stood head cocked to one side, wondering what was going on. 'Please Papa! Please!' Peter begged, 'I cannot leave him, I will not leave him.' He could not imagine any new life without his dog, even if it meant disobeying his dear Papa.

Once a vague fear, Isaac knew now for certain that he would lose his son if they did not take Wolfi. Isaac took hold of the Captain's arm and led him to the back of the boat. Soon the men were deep in a hushed conversation. The only word Peter could make out was 'money'. Eventually, after further negotiation and several thousand more Reich marks, the Captain agreed to take Wolfi.

'You keep him quiet, boy,' the Captain said sternly.

'Yes sir,' Peter replied, relieved, 'and thank you.' His thanks were directed at the Captain though clearly intended for his father.

'All right. We have wasted enough time. All on board,' the Captain ordered, eyeing the cause of the delay malevolently. At the rear of the boat Peter held the lead in one hand and pushed his face into the thick fur on the back of Wolfi's neck. Wolfi leaned against his young master's leg, just happy to be with him. Sara turned her face out of the wind and wondered what they might have done with those extra marks.

For the first half an hour they made good progress. They could not travel too fast to keep engine noise to a minimum. On the other hand they needed to push ahead quickly enough to break through the swell generated by the stiffening breeze. As the engine droned quietly, Peter held Wolfi tightly to him. He hardly noticed the scenery passing slowly by, as he wondered where they would end up.

Isaac was deep in thought and full of regrets. Try as he might, he could not help replay in his mind the series of events that had led them to this desperate situation. He, like so many others, had ignored the warnings when Hitler had first come to power in 1933. As Jews were forced out of official positions and banned from numerous professions; as their businesses were 'confiscated' and savings seized; as ever more restrictions were placed upon their daily lives, including where they could sit or bathe or go to school, he like most Jews had told himself that things would get better. They were German and he, Isaac, was the holder of the Iron Cross, a decorated war hero. He had even ignored the stark warning of 'Kristallnacht', 'The Night of Broken Glass'. The night of the 9th November 1938 when hundreds of synagogues were smashed and burned, Jewish businesses looted and destroyed and ninety-one Jews killed.

Even the advent of war had not stopped the persecution. Most of all Isaac blamed himself that they had not left Germany when they had the chance. They had relatives in America who had begged them to leave. And then it was too late. As the neighbours disappeared from around them, finally their turn to be transported had come. Thank heavens they had been warned by Herr Grüber, a colleague at the bank, that their names were on a list. That was just days ago and now they were escaping their homeland at night and in secret.

'Grrrrrr! Grrrrrr!' Wolfi's jowls were pulled back, baring his enormous fangs. He was straining forcefully on his lead, pulling in a way Peter had never seen. They were approaching the Spandauersee Bridge. Wolfi's vicious growl was directed at the Captain. It was a low, guttural growl that Peter knew would usually precede a blood-chilling bark.

'Keep quiet or I'll shut you up,' the Captain threatened, raising his hand to strike.

'No! Leave him!' Peter cried and instinctively jumped in front of the downward blow that was now aimed towards Wolfi's skull. The Captain's fist caught him on the side of his jaw with a sickening thud.

'Ow!' Peter's painful scream echoed under the bridge. Wolfi lunged at the Captain, snarling ferociously and pulling Peter with him.

No-one reacted more quickly than the Captain. He was old yet very agile. He jumped to one side and in one sweeping movement caught Wolfi by the scruff of the neck, heaved his torso and hind quarters over the side of the boat and dropped him into the water.

'Wolfi! Wolfi!' Peter cried. He was still clutching the loop on the end of the lead, half over the side of the boat and half in the boat. He was desperately trying to pull Wolfi towards him. The boat was too fast and Wolfi too heavy. Try as he might, he watched as if in slow motion, as the lead slid down his wrist and over his hand and Wolfi's black head slipped under the surface of the water. Seconds later the loop of the lead disappeared, still attached to the unfortunate animal.

'No Peter! No!' Peter could just hear his mother's anguished words as he hit the water. He had jumped in without any hesitation.

The icy cold water took his breath away. His chest tightened and he could taste the polluted water. Despite being a very good swimmer, he was struggling to keep his head above water. The heavy overcoat he was wearing and the extra layers of clothing were rapidly absorbing the freezing water, as was the school satchel with its strap looped over his shoulder. He felt his boots fill up and both they and his sodden socks were now acting like heavy diver's weights, dragging him down. The intense cold made breathing almost impossible.

In the distance he could just hear his father remonstrating with the Captain as the boat got further and further away and his mother's sobs carried through the air. While frenetically trying to kick his legs to keep above water, he was still looking in desperation for his dog. Wolfi was nowhere to be seen. With one hand he was trying to pull the strap of the satchel over his head, which only seemed to force him further towards the bottom as his hand became trapped, as if in a tourniquet.

He swallowed some of the foul tasting river as he disappeared beneath the surface for the third time and his nostrils sucked in even more of the freezing water. His eyes began to close and he sank deeper. The boat was out of sight.

'Uhh!' Peter groaned. He was still dropping to the bottom of the river when he felt the hard shove from behind, catapulting him momentarily above the water. Then he saw the leather woven loop of Wolfi's lead passing right in front of him. Just in time his free hand managed to stretch out and grab it. He felt a jolt as the lead became taut.

'He's alive! Wolfi's alive!' Wolfi's distinctive head was bobbing from side to side as the dog towed him towards the shore.

'Keep going boy. Keep going!' he encouraged. With all the strength left in his tired body Wolfi dragged Peter closer to safety.

After several minutes the exhausted dog and his owner were lying next to each other on the concrete foot of one of the massive bridge supports. Peter shuddered violently with the cold, aware of nothing else except the heavy panting of his canine companion.

'You saved me Wolfi. You saved me,' was all that he could manage to say.

With the last ounce of his energy, Wolfi stood up and flopped onto Peter. Lying across the boy's chest, with his face nuzzling his friend's, Wolfi licked Peter's face with his rough tongue, until boy and dog fell asleep.

Peter did not sleep for more than a few minutes as cold constantly reminded him of their plight. Wolfi was the only source of warmth he had.

'We must catch up with the boat,' he urged himself. As hard as he tried, he was too weak to raise his body from the ground. He cried as he thought of his parents, the salty tears warming his face.

After a while he heard a noise that he could not quite place. It gradually grew louder and closer. Then it became terrifyingly clear.

'Soldiers!'

It was the sound of jackboots on cobbles as soldiers jumped from the back of trucks. They were running just above them shouting to each other and shining torches into every nook and cranny. Bayonets were prodded into crevices and cracks as a shrill voice shouted,

'Look for the boy!'

Peter did not have to tell Wolfi to stay still. Neither had the energy to move. Even if they had been spotted they could not have fled. Fortunately they had landed on a pier supporting one of the longer bridges in Berlin and they were several metres out from the riverbank. He knew they would probably have to re-enter the icy cold water eventually. For the moment where they lay was in darkness and only visible from a particular part of the river. Any search boat would have to choose to come under the arch above them to have any chance of seeing them.

As boy and dog lay there, providing comfort and warmth to each other, Peter became aware of a conversation above them. He could clearly make out the shrill voice he had heard earlier. The sound seemed to be amplified by the structure of the bridge. It was clear that shrill voice was in charge.

'I delivered you two Jews didn't I?' a second voice was saying, 'You still owe me for them.'

'No! Please no!' Peter groaned. He was horrified. There was no doubt. The second voice was the Captain's.

'It is your duty to hand over *these* people, whether we pay you or not. And one of the parasites has escaped thanks to you.' Shrill voice was clearly agitated.

'That wasn't my fault. It was the damned dog. He must have sensed something was up and went for me. Anyway what does it matter, the boy and his dog have drowned. I saw them go under.'

'No! It's not true! It can't be true!' a female voice sobbed. It was Peter's mother.

'Oh Mama!' Peter cried, too quietly to be heard. An angry voice began shouting.

'Traitor! Traitor! I am a German war hero, holder of the Iron Cross, First Class and you have murdered my son.' The voice was unmistakable.

'It's Papa!' Peter moaned.

'Don't worry about that,' shrill voice retorted. 'Your war record will be given its proper recognition where you are going.'

On hearing his parents' voices, Peter longed to cry out. 'I'm not dead! I'm not dead!' He knew he could not make a sound.

As footsteps echoed in the distance and he knew his

parents had gone, the boy's crying turned into violent sobs. Wolfi's ears pricked up. The dog angled his head to one side, lay back down on top of Peter, comforting him again. For the second time that day Wolfi had saved Peter's life.

# CHAPTER TWO

Peter drifted in and out of consciousness, barely aware of the warm body beside him. The temptation simply to lie there and fall into a deeper sleep was almost overwhelming. He scarcely had the energy to grieve, let alone contemplate survival. His rest was disturbed by images of his mother and father back in their house, listening to the gramophone whilst he played with Wolfi, or on holiday in the mountains with Papa in his Lederhosen, the leather shorts favoured by the Bavarians. In all these pictures flashing through his mind they were always smiling, always there to comfort him. Papa and Wolfi snoring together in the armchair, Mama trying to persuade him away from the door of the oven where Wolfi would so often like to sleep. Mama pretending to be angry with both of them though still smiling.

As this last image drifted from his mind, Peter became aware of a pressure on his back, nudging him. He wearily lifted his head. In his dazed state he could see the reassuring outline of Wolfi's head. He was prodding him from behind, forcing him back to consciousness. Peter's hand reached out and gently tickled the dog's favourite spot on his head, right between his ears.

'I know boy. I know. We have to go. In a minute.' With that he placed his head once more on the cold ground.

Seconds later he felt another shove, much harder this time.

'Soon Wolfi, soon.' Peter fell asleep once more.

Moments later he felt a new pressure underneath his head as the faithful dog attempted to raise his master from the ground. Using all the strength he could muster, Peter propped himself on one elbow and then onto his knee and finally he stood up. From his saturated satchel he took out a piece of cheese wrapped in cloth. He broke it in two, gave one half to Wolfi and the other he devoured. It was wet, yet comforting nonetheless.

'Papa would be annoyed if he saw me giving you titbits,' he thought.

Though a tiny ration, the effect of the cheese was almost instantaneous, giving a feeling of warmth and some optimism. Following the cheese with a few wet crackers, Peter felt his strength renewing. He looked all around them and weighed up the options.

'We can't stay here for long Wolfi,' he said. He knew that in a few hours the waterway would be teeming with river traffic. They would not avoid detection for long. There was also the unwelcome possibility of an overnight canal boat heading towards the busy ports with essential cargo for the war effort.

It had now been some time since they had last heard any sign of movement above. Peter felt as sure as he could that they were no longer being hunted.

'Looks like we'll have to swim back to the bank.' He shivered as he resigned himself to the unpleasant prospect.

The thought of re-entering the icy water was

daunting. There was no other option. This time however he would ensure that his clothing would not drag him under. He stripped to his underwear, rolled his clothing in a tight bundle and with one sleeve tied the makeshift knapsack to his satchel.

'Sit Wolfi!' Peter ordered. His voice tremored with cold and anticipation.

The dog sat obediently whilst Peter removed Wolfi's homemade coat. Being waterproof it had absorbed little water. The only additional weight was from the jewels sewn into the lining. He tied the coat to the sizeable bundle and began swinging his arm behind him.

'Here goes,' Peter said, mostly in hope, and with a mighty throw, launched it towards the far bank. His heart in his mouth, he watched it land just centimetres from the water's edge, though stay where it was.

'Good. Now our turn,' he said and taking Wolfi's lead in his hand, for the second time that evening, he jumped into the river. Wolfi did not hesitate and followed his young master into the water.

'Ahhh! It's freezing!' Peter cried out, instantly regretting his carelessness.

To his relief he discovered at this point closer to the bank the river was not so deep, nor so fast flowing. It was still limb-numbingly cold. He soon appreciated the decision to remove his clothing, as in spite of the cold and the current, he was able to make good progress through the water. Soon they were safely on the riverbank.

This time they did not dawdle. Peter put on his clothes. The wet layers clung stubbornly to his skin. He was not helped by his natural reluctance to don the sodden clothing. He dressed Wolfi in his coat hoping it would provide some protection from the chill. Wolfi's fur was so thick Peter doubted he would feel the cold.

From their position on the riverbank he surveyed the area. Rusted iron rungs formed a ladder up onto the bridge.

`I could never haul you up there, Wolfi,' he said.

In any event it might attract some attention if anyone did happen to pass by. Where they stood was in effect a concrete tow path used in days gone by. The path widened under the bridge. Now it was an ideal walkway on which to travel further along the canal and for much of it out of sight.

'Mama and Papa must be long gone by now Wolfi. And who knows where? If they ever get away I am sure they will return home to look for me.'

And so, with the certain knowledge that his parents had been captured, Peter made the agonising decision that it was foolish and dangerous to try and find them.

The word 'home' was one Wolfi had heard many times. His body and tail shook with excitement at the mention of it. Peter knew that he had to fend for himself and Wolfi. That would be so much easier in a location familiar to him, somewhere they had spent many happy hours exploring.

Reluctantly he turned around. With his back to the north and the last sighting of his parents, he began the long walk back to Schlachtensee.

As Peter started his arduous trudge homewards, in a dark

and airless cattle truck, Isaac and Sara were crammed with so many other desolate souls, too many to count. There was so little space that they were compelled to stand with bodies pressing against them in a forced degree of intimacy. Sara was crying as she had done constantly from the time of their arrest and the pronouncement that Peter was drowned. Isaac lovingly held her hand, wracked with guilt that his inaction had brought them to this.

'Why did I ignore the warnings? Why did I wait so long? Why did I trust that scoundrel of a captain?' he said over and over.

Most of all he felt guilty about Sara. For whilst his wife grieved for the loss of their son, he had knowledge that would have relieved her suffering. Knowledge he had kept to himself: 'Peter is alive'. He repeated the words in his head.

Seconds after he had argued with the Captain on the boat and bright searchlights ahead had almost dazzled him, he had turned away to shield his eyes, just in time to see the familiar bobbing head of Wolfi. Not only Wolfi, but the shape of a young boy behind being towed to shore. He had almost shouted for joy and demanded the Captain turn the boat around, when the orders 'this is the Gestapo. You are under arrest. Bring the boat to shore' reached his ears.

The shocking realisation of the impending events and their certain capture, was softened only by the knowledge that his son had escaped, for now. He could not give the game away. Peter needed every chance. Wolfi had twice done his bit to save Peter today, now he must do his.

Much though he ached to, he could not tell Sara as they were roughly pulled from the boat. Nor could he break his silence as they were searched.

All the time the soldiers, assisted by the Gestapo, searched the riverbank for Peter, he dared not tell Sara that he knew their son was alive. Even in the agonising moment when the Captain had vouched that he had seen him drown, he could not relieve her pain. As they prodded bayonets into crevices he could say nothing.

Now, some hours later in the stinking dusty cattle wagon on a train siding at Anhalter Bahnhof he could at last break his silence. Certain that the enemy was not around, he leaned forward the few centimetres to his wife's ear and whispered, 'Sara my darling, our boy is alive. I saw the dog tow him from the water.' She did not react. He repeated it a little louder this time.

'Our boy is alive. I saw Wolfi tow him from the water. Our boy has survived.'

Finally the news registered. Sara's body shook as her sobs worsened. Tears of mingled grief and gratitude snaked down her face.

'He will be all right Sara. Wolfi will look after him and he will look after Wolfi. Together they *will* survive.' He emphasised 'will' more in prayer than firm belief.

As soon as he could Peter left the concrete path running alongside the river. He had found it difficult to prevent the sound of his footsteps echoing and the surface was hard on Wolfi's paws.

'Only ten kilometres to home, Wolfi, so a nice long walk for both of us,' he said.

Where possible it was better for both to walk on soft ground. They were less likely to come across any other pedestrians if they avoided the paths. The combination of the blackout and the blackness of the night allowed them to cover ground rapidly. Whereas a man might struggle across rough terrain in the darkness, Wolfi's instincts enabled him to lead Peter around the various bushes and shrubbery that might otherwise have been an obstacle.

Peter's navigation technique was quite simple: he would retrace their route and stay as far as possible next to the river. This admirable approach was successful to a point; however he knew that in parts the river opened into lakes and tributaries making for tiring detours. In normal circumstances he would have relished a long walk with Wolfi. He was exhausted from the two recent duckings, he was cold and still very wet and most of all, apart from Wolfi, he was alone and scared.

As he walked he still wondered about the wisdom of returning home. He knew, in spite of Papa keeping it from him, that they were on a list to be deported. He had heard Papa telling Mama the night before their flight. Perhaps the Nazis would be waiting for him?

'Where else can we go?' he thought. With no obvious alternative, they continued their journey, only stopping to try and regain their bearings.

After some time he noted that they were approaching the more densely built-up part of the river. He knew at some point he would have to brave the streets.

He tried to guess the time, estimating that it was

somewhere between eleven and midnight. At some stage he hoped to hear the chime of one of the many clocks on public buildings or even to see the face of a clock. At least when he got home he could retrieve his wristwatch. He had cursed himself when he had earlier realised he had left it behind. Why hadn't he listened to Papa? All the times he had chastised him for arriving home late for the evening meal when Peter's excuse was always the same – he had forgotten to wear his watch. He could easily spend hours with Wolfi in Grünewald and on Schlachtensee shutting out the outside world, losing all track of time. Often it was the realisation that he was hungry that made him return.

Now he was free of any restraints as to where he went, what he did and when he returned, Peter yearned to be chastised by Papa once more.

'Ah well, let's just get home first,' Peter sighed.

His thoughts abruptly returned to their current predicament. A distant rumble like approaching thunder was getting closer and closer. Then the air raid siren started wailing and the bombs began to fall. The explosions were still some way from them. Wolfi cowered with fear nonetheless.

'If only you were a gun dog,' Peter said, only half in joke.

Wolfi, fearless in nearly all situations had, like many civilians, not overcome his terror of the air raids. Peter knelt down and began scratching Wolfi's ears. Usually both dog and boy would hide under the oak table in the drawing room. Papa had often found them there, comforting each other. Here they were in the open air some distance from home with only a few sparse bushes for shelter.

Peter knew that, frightening though it may be, this was their best opportunity to cover a large distance quickly. The only persons on the streets would be the anti-aircraft battalions, the air raid wardens and fire-fighters trying to limit the damage. None of them would have the time or the desire to concern themselves with a boy and a dog.

'I'm sorry boy, we must go,' he whispered in Wolfi's ear. Peter got up and began walking briskly. Wolfi did not move. He was still trembling. Tugging the lead harder, Peter moved off. Wolfi took a few hesitant steps. He was shaking uncontrollably.

'We have to go boy,' Peter urged.

He knew the air raid shelter was not safe for them. He bent down and stroked Wolfi's large fluffy ears whilst whispering words of comfort at the same time.

'There boy, it will be all right. Those bombs will save us one day.'

Little comforted, Wolfi licked Peter's face and began to walk. Within an hour they had travelled a distance of almost six kilometres. For the most part they were able to take the most direct route, always keeping the river in view. Everywhere there was the chaotic noise of sirens and the sound of bombs falling. Usually these raids were over quite quickly. This one seemed more prolonged. For once Peter welcomed the raid, even though it terrified Wolfi. By now they had reached the suburbs of Wilmersdorf. It was an area Peter knew well. He had once gone to school there. They could take a more direct route, temporarily leaving the river behind. Soon they rounded the corner into Kleiststrasse, in the borough of Zehlendorf and Peter's pace quickened.

'Almost home,' he thought. At the speed they were travelling they might make it within the next hour.

It was the sound of buildings on fire and collapsing timbers that Peter noticed at first. Then the calls of rescue workers digging amongst rubble adjacent to the same building, as volunteer fire-fighters sought to put out the flames. A soldier in the grey uniform of the Wehrmacht was barking orders. Turning to retrace their steps, Peter heard a shout from behind.

'You boy, over here! We need as much help as we can get.' Peter ignored the shout.

'You, with the dog, come here now!'

Peter looked back, then reluctantly he and Wolfi walked towards the soldier. As they approached he could see that he was an officer, a major he guessed from his insignia. Whilst Peter deliberated whether to salute, the Major reached out his hand to stroke Wolfi who obligingly turned his head to accommodate him. Wolfi clearly had no fear of the Major.

'Great dog!' the Major shouted above the din. 'Now bring him over and let's see if he can sniff out any survivors.'

Peter wanted to say that he was a sheep dog, not a sniffer dog. Instead they followed dutifully. The Major came to a stop by a mass of entangled concrete and metal. He stooped down and, caressing Wolfi under his chin, whispered into the dog's ear. Peter did not hear what was

27

said. Whatever it was it had an effect. Wolfi clambered over the pile of smoking rubble, sniffing as he went. After some ten minutes, when all hope seemed lost, the dog began digging frantically. Loose masonry and half bricks were sent flying by the dog's powerful paws. Just seconds later Wolfi suddenly sat down and began to bark loudly.

'Over here!' the Major yelled, beckoning the auxillary firemen to the spot where Wolfi sat.

The firemen were tired and hungry. They had seen so much death and destruction that they longed to return home. Their faces were black with smoke and grime, yet even that could not hide their disbelief that a mere dog was dictating the rescue effort.

In spite of their concerns, after almost an hour of careful digging a wounded and bedraggled man in his fifties was pulled free of the ruins.

'Thank you! Thank you so much!' he spluttered, seized by a coughing fit. He was covered from head to foot in dust. The only object clearly visible was his lapel badge with the Nazi Party emblem still prominent.

Even though not trained in this work, the three rescuers, Wolfi, Peter and the Major spent the next two hours climbing over the rubble and then digging when Wolfi barked to indicate the presence of life. In this unsophisticated way they located three survivors, all grateful to be rescued.

When eventually it became clear that it was hopeless to continue, they switched their efforts to dousing the flames. As there was little either the Major or Peter and Wolfi could do, the three of them stood back at a distance.

'What is your name boy?' the Major asked.

'Peter.' Peter was about to say his surname when the Major, raising his right hand, signalled him to stop.

'You have a fine animal there Peter. Look after him well.'

He reached into the breast pocket of his tunic, took out a slab of chocolate and broke off two pieces. One he gave to Peter, the other he ate. Peter quickly devoured the small square of delicious chocolate. The Major laughed and handed the rest of the slab to the young boy. Peter hesitated.

'Go on take it.'

'Thank you,' Peter politely replied, as he took the chocolate and placed it carefully in a wet coat pocket.

'Now get out of here quickly Peter Stern,' the Major urged.

'But how..?' Peter stammered. His face was white. He was about to speak further when the Major took Wolfi by the collar and pointed to his dog tag.

'Be more careful Peter. These are dangerous times.'

Peter thanked the Major once more and, a little shaken, walked away. He did not look behind him.

# CHAPTER THREE

'Idiots! Bloody idiots!' Peter seldom swore, and never in the house. And never when his mother was around. This time he could not help it.

He was pleased to be home at last. Except it was not the home he had left less than twenty-four hours ago. In his hand he held a piece of broken crockery. It was Mama's fine china. There was barely a cup or saucer left on the large oak dresser that stood against the wall by the kitchen door. The shards of fine bone china were scattered wantonly all over the floor. Several chairs were broken and fragments of glass lay everywhere. There was no doubt that someone had come looking for them.

'Careful boy! Stay there! We don't want you to cut yourself.' Peter was anxious. A bleeding dog was the last thing he needed.

Wolfi sat patiently watching as he swept up the debris. In a few minutes the task was finished and it was safe for Wolfi to move freely around the room. Peter filled a bowl with water and placed it in front of Wolfi. The dog lapped the water noisily.

The sight of the mound of broken china and glass upset Peter. He recalled clearly the events not so many hours earlier when Mama and Papa had argued over that china.

'You can't take it,' Papa had said forcefully.

'But it was my mother's and her mother's and her mother before her,' Mama had replied.

'I know my darling. We have to take only the essentials. If we are stopped with precious china it will be obvious that we are escaping,' Papa responded less harshly.

'What is more essential than our history? Our past? This is our identity,' she said and looking away, started to cry. Papa had taken her in his arms and kissed her gently for several minutes. In the end she packed two particularly beautiful matching egg cups. Now the rest of Mama's family history lay in pieces on the floor.

The house was in semi-darkness. It was a few hours until dawn. Peter had remembered the advice from the kind Major and had sneaked into the house. Luckily the spare key was still under the plant pot outside the door. Wolfi did not understand the need for caution. As far as he was concerned he was home and ready for breakfast. Peter knew he could not risk a light in the kitchen. Gradually his eyes accustomed to the half-light. Wolfi was sitting hopefully in front of the tall cupboard where his food was kept.

'Poor boy! You haven't eaten since that bit of cheese and cracker,' he said. Wolfi's ears pricked at the word 'cheese' and his tail wagged vigorously. Peter could not help smiling. It was almost like any other morning as far as Wolfi was concerned.

He opened a can of Wolfi's favourite dog food and spooned a generous portion into his bowl. Still sitting, his dog shuffled from one paw to the other, licking his lips at the same time. In just a few gulps his breakfast disappeared. Wolfi stared at his master, hopeful for more.

'All right then,' Peter said. He picked up the clean bowl and emptied the rest of the tin into it, then placed it on the floor. After a few more seconds the bowl was empty. On seeing the dog's clear satisfaction Peter was hit by the realisation that he too was extremely hungry.

'My turn,' he said and walked across to the larder in the corner. He was cold and half-starved. As he opened the door a dreadful thought entered his head.

'Whoever did this will have taken all the food.' With a heavy heart he passed through the larder door.

'Cheese! A whole round! And a whole joint of salt beef!' he cried out. The joint hung invitingly from the ceiling.

He could have jumped for joy. Not as full as in pre-war times, there was still a treasure trove of food. Tins of meat, fruit, soups and vegetables as well as flour, powdered milk, sugar, coffee and tea, a large bag of salt and a bottle of vinegar. Several jars of homemade jams and pickles as well as a large tin of syrup and a tin of molasses were neatly stacked on the shelf above his head. On the floor in the corner were stored a variety of vegetables in hessian sacks: potatoes, beets, turnips, cabbages and carrots as well as a sizeable quantity of onions.

Apart from the items Mama had removed for their picnic, virtually everything else of their wartime larder remained. Mama had been keen to take as much food as possible or at least give it away. Papa had persuaded her not to. It would be too suspicious.

'Strange,' he thought, `why smash Mama's china and leave all this food?' Peter blessed their stupidity and the wisdom of his Mama.

He had never understood how she had managed to accumulate such a range of foodstuffs when the whole of the city was chasing smaller and smaller supplies. It was even more surprising as the authorities' restrictions on the Jews prevented them exploiting the opportunities presented to their fellow Germans. Yet until the previous evening Peter had never known real hunger. In spite of the general shortage of metal, Mama had even been able to get hold of Wolfi's tins of dog food.

He took two eggs from a bowl and a generous slice of the cheese, and went back into the kitchen. He felt the old cast iron stove. It was still warm after all this time. Peter recalled how they smiled when Mama had stoked the fire and placed several more logs in the stove just before they had left. Living so close to Grünewald they had a good supply of wood.

'We can't let the stove go out,' she had said. 'A cold kitchen is a miserable kitchen. And a miserable kitchen makes a miserable home.' She had even gone to the trouble of tidying the kitchen. 'For when we return,' she had said.

Within minutes Peter was voraciously forking pieces of cheese omelette into his mouth. It was delicious. Mama had taught him well. Papa could not understand why his son should learn to cook, but Mama was adamant.

'What for?' Papa had joked. 'Men don't cook. He will be a banker like his father!' As he swallowed the last piece of omelette Peter noticed Wolfi looking intently at him. He was clearly disappointed.

'Still hungry? Don't worry you can have some beef.' This seemed to satisfy Wolfi, who sat patiently, his tail wagging noisily as it swept across the floor. Peter cut two slices from the joint and gave one to the hungry dog. As always Wolfi was very gentle, taking the meat from his friend with the softest of touches. Both licked their lips with satisfaction.

'Coffee time, Wolfi!' Peter declared.

Minutes later the water began to gurgle in the percolator on the stove and the delicious aroma of fresh coffee filled the air. He blessed both his aunt in America for sending the precious coffee beans and Mama for showing him how to eke out the supplies by reusing half of the old coffee grounds.

Whilst the coffee brewed he removed all his clothing and hung as much as he could over the metal rail at the front of the stove. The rest he hung over the back of the kitchen chairs.

In the dark he went silently around the rest of the house. From each room he took items useful for his survival: clothing from his bedroom, as well as his best leather boots and overcoat and a warm woolly blanket; camping equipment from under the stairs, including an old alcohol burner, camping pots and pans, a tin mug and plate and a bed roll; his fishing rod, his penknife, his torch, his compass and of course his watch all from the study; a tin and bottle opener and knife, fork and spoon from the pantry; a small towel and soap from the bathroom, as well as some razor blades; wirecutters and twine from the garden shed. All were stashed carefully in the old rucksack he had left behind. To avoid suspicion he had been forced to use his school satchel instead.

After an hour he returned to the kitchen. Wolfi was snoring gently in front of the stove. His ears pricked as Peter entered the room. He stroked Wolfi, running his hand from the centre of his head, between his ears, all the way down his back to his thick tail. With a seemingly effortless movement Wolfi flipped onto his back, front legs folded at the elbow joint, his belly exposed. His head was raised from the ground and to one side and his tail wagged back and forth.

As he had done so many times, Peter bent over and rubbed his dog's tummy. Wolfi started snoring again. After a few minutes Peter stood up, took the coffee pot in his hand and poured the steaming black liquid into a cup. Adding a spoonful of sugar, he stirred the coffee rapidly and then took a sip. In his eagerness he burnt his tongue. He didn't mind. He was dry and warm and, for the moment, in his own house. He finished the last of the coffee, then gathered the tins and all the perishable items onto the kitchen table.

'I'll have to come back for the rest,' he said out loud. There was so much it was impossible to carry everything. Wolfi snored.

Once packed, he felt the weight of the bulging rucksack. It was reassuringly heavy. The remainder of the tins and vegetables he placed in a sack, along with the salt beef and cheese round. He kept a piece of the salt beef to one side to eat later.

'One more thing,' he thought and went into Papa's study. On the wall was a framed map of Berlin. He took the map out of the frame and carefully rolled it up. As he rolled, he spotted Papa's framed Iron Cross, First Class. He carefully took it off the wall and removing it from the wooden frame, he placed it in his jacket pocket.

'It might be useful one day,' he said, wistfully.

He pulled open the left hand drawer of his father's large oak desk and felt inside. His hands soon found what he had been looking for: a silver hip flask with leather carry strap. He smelt the remnants of the liquid inside, Papa's favourite cognac. It would be a small, yet useful water canteen.

Back in the kitchen he emptied his damp school satchel and wiping it dry with a towel, began to fill it with the few remaining tins of dog food and Wolfi's enamelled bowl. Once he had squeezed everything into the satchel, he turned around and saw Wolfi, sitting expectantly with his ball in his mouth.

'We can't boy,' Peter said, looking out the kitchen window at the same time. 'Damn!' He had been so engaged in his search that he had failed to notice that it was now daylight and getting lighter. His plan to sneak off in darkness would either have to be abandoned or postponed. He couldn't be seen with a rucksack heading into the woods in broad daylight. On the other hand he knew it was only a matter of time until a spacious empty house in an affluent area would attract the attention of the authorities. Or looters.

'We can't hang around here,' Peter said aloud.

It was a real dilemma. Instinct told him to get out of there as soon as possible; emotion told him that waiting for darkness in these surroundings, surroundings that he knew so well, would be so much more pleasant. After some thought, emotion won the day and he determined to wait until darkness. The decision made, he was once more aware of Wolfi, still sitting patiently with a ball in his mouth.

'All right then. But only in the garden. And quietly.'

The borders of the well-kept garden were planted with tall trees, mainly evergreens. It was a secluded spot in which he could let Wolfi run around. What he could not risk was throwing his ball, as this was bound to cause him to bark. Wolfi, unaware of any danger, kept dropping the ball on his foot and then sitting with a longing look on his face. Peter relented. It was daytime and most people would be engaged in essential wartime work. In any case the house was still theirs, at least for the time being. Perhaps it would never be taken over. For a brief moment, as he threw the ball and watched as Wolfi retrieved it again and again, he forgot the troubles of the past few days.

After some twenty minutes of playing, his mind inevitably came back to their current situation. He had resolved to leave by the back garden. As a precaution he decided to place his rucksack in the garden shed along with his satchel and sack of food. The shed was at the end of the garden and was shielded from the house by a row of mature conifers. He opened the door and placed the rucksack and satchel under a hessian sack. As he closed the door Peter spotted the shiny bell.

'A bicycle!' His bicycle had long ago been confiscated 'for the war effort'. This bicycle had never been used. Papa had bought it some years ago for Ilse. She had been their part-time housekeeper and cook. It was a birthday present so that her journey home would be easier. Unfortunately she never received it. Ilse had left their employ. She had no choice. She was an Aryan female under the age of forty-five and therefore by law could no longer work for a Jew.

Then the bicycle was simply too big for Peter. In any event Papa forbade anyone to ride it. It was a painful reminder of what had become of his beloved Germany. A brand new chain and padlock with key hung from the handlebars.

'I'm sure Papa will understand,' Peter thought.

Sitting astride the bicycle, he began to ride it up and down the garden. It had been many years since he had ridden, for once Wolfi was fully grown the faithful dog went almost everywhere with Peter, trotting or walking as if glued to his side. It had somehow seemed unfair to make the poor animal run after him while he cycled, depriving him of the regular smells along the way. In their current predicament that would have to change.

Having made several trips from one end of the lawn to the other, Peter stopped and called Wolfi over to him. He gave the command to sit. Wolfi instantly responded. He attached the lead to the dog's collar, looped the other end around one handlebar and then cycled off, encouraging Wolfi to come with him. Wolfi remained firmly seated on the ground. Peter crashed to the earth.

'Bad dog! Bad dog!' His anger quickly turned to laughter as he realised he had not given the release command. Wolfi would not leave his sit position unless told.

He repeated the experiment, this time giving the appropriate instruction. He and his dog happily rode and ran together in circles. He tried this several times with Wolfi off the lead. Wolfi complied perfectly.

'At least now I know you will follow the bicycle,' Peter said. Wolfi gave a knowing look in reply.

He took the bicycle to the very end of the garden and hid it in the shrubbery behind the vegetable patch. This was a spot he was very familiar with. There was a gap in the fence that he had often squeezed through unnoticed on the occasions when he had come home very late. The sack of food was tied to the basket on the handlebars.

It was now several hours since they had last eaten. Peter was hungry again. Using the salt beef and some vegetables he created a tasty stew which he shared with Wolfi.

By now the daylight hours had almost passed and it would soon be possible for them to leave. It was a bitter sweet moment. It was not safe to stay and Peter was understandably nervous. On the other hand this was his home. Reluctantly he decided to carry out one final sweep of the house.

He climbed the stairs for almost the seventh or eighth time that day, and went into each bedroom, leaving his own until last. As he turned to leave his room a furry head popped up above the metal bedstead. Wolfi had taken up his usual place and was expecting Peter to join him.

'I know boy, I know. I am tired too, but we have to leave.' As he said these words he sat on the bed next to Wolfi, placing his head on his flank. He began patting the dog's side. In a few minutes, the exhaustion and strain of the last thirty-six hours overtook him and Peter fell asleep.

'Stand up or I'll shoot!' a loud voice thundered. 'I mean it. Stand up immediately!' the same voice repeated, this time with more irritation. It was not the man's voice that finally woke Peter, rather it was Wolfi's very fierce barking. 'And shut the dog up or I'll shoot it! Now get up and get out of my son's bedroom.'

Peter sat upright and as he did so saw the hazy outline of a man of about his father's age in a uniform of some kind. Even though the room was in semi-darkness, Peter could see that he was pointing a pistol at him. From behind he heard another voice, less mature, egging the man on.

'Shoot him Papa!' the boy screamed. 'I know him. He is a Jew boy.'

Peter was now very alert. Behind the man he glimpsed a boy of similar age to him in the uniform of the Hitler Youth. A boy of about fifteen, with blonde hair and a look of hatred in his eyes. Peter vaguely recognised the young intruder, although in his panic he could not place him.

'Shoot him Papa!' the boy screamed again.

The hatred in the boy's face triggered a memory for Peter. It was the face of the boy from school who had taunted him so badly in the past. A boy who had once called himself a friend and even been to a birthday party at this house. A boy also called Peter. A boy who had shunned him then bullied him. It was clear he and his father had deliberately chosen this property. Why smash the china in the kitchen? Why not just leave it there? Few things made sense any more. That one act enraged Peter so much his fear was momentarily replaced by anger and defiance, until Wolfi brought him back to their current danger.

Wolfi was barking uncontrollably and pacing backwards and forwards towards the two intruders. He did not accept the Reich's law which allowed these two to take over his house.

'Up! Now! Or I will shoot!' The man's face was contorted in anger. He swung his hand at Peter's face catching him a hard blow to the jaw with the muzzle of the pistol. As Peter fell backwards onto the bed, Wolfi sprang through the air, knocking father and son to the ground in one movement. The surprise of the attack caused the father to drop his pistol and he was dazed as his head hit the bedroom wall. In considerable pain, Peter sprang to his feet and rushed to the end of the bed.

'Wolfi! Come boy!' Peter called out, whistling at the same time. Wolfi moved away from the man and his son. The boy was pinned to the floor by the weight of his unconscious father. The gun was nowhere to be seen.

A frightened Peter and his dog ran from the room, pulling the door behind them. He grabbed the sides of a large wardrobe at the top of the stairs and began to rock it from side to side. Using all the force he could summon, he managed to topple the wardrobe so that it barricaded the door.

He rushed downstairs, jumping several steps at a time. He was relieved to hear Wolfi's noisy footsteps behind. They passed through the kitchen and into the garden, removing the key from the door as they went. With shaking hands he tried locking the door.

'Come on! Come on!' The key would not turn in the lock. Anxiously he tried again. Finally the key turned and he heard the bolt of the lock slide into place.

'At last! Oh!' he gasped. The face of the Hitler Youth was pressed against the glass pane in the door.

'It can't be,' Peter thought. The gun was in his hand. He was pointing it at Wolfi. Peter was rooted to the spot with fear.

'No!' Peter managed to shout and stepped in front of his dog.

'Click! Click!' The pistol had misfired. The noise brought Peter back to the present danger. He grabbed Wolfi and both ran down the garden path. Fortunately, this was their garden and they easily found their way in spite of the dark. As they ran behind the trees shielding the garden shed, a shot whistled past them and cracked the woodwork.

Looking over his shoulder, Peter could see the silhouette of the boy still in the kitchen, his outline visible in the artificial light. The glass pane in the kitchen door was shattered where he had shot through it. His hand was reaching through the broken pane and feeling for the door key.

'Fool! Why did I leave it there?' Peter cursed himself.

He wrenched the shed door open and fumbled in the darkness for his rucksack and satchel and ran to the hole in the hedge where he had hidden the bicycle. Wolfi was running ahead of him, apparently aware of the urgency of the situation. The bicycle was heavy and awkward. The handlebars twisted with the weight of the sack. With a tremendous effort he lifted the bicycle through the gap in the hedge and encouraged Wolfi to jump. Wolfi easily cleared the hedge in one effortless leap. Peter stepped through the same gap and balanced the bicycle against the hedge.

With trembling hands he pulled the straps of the rucksack over his shoulder and hung the satchel round his neck, then mounted the bicycle. He began to pedal as hard as he could with Wolfi running alongside. The weight of the satchel almost pulled him over, however fear and determination drove him on.

'Come back you thief! You can't get away!' He did not look round though he heard the angry shout from behind. It was his old class mate.

'*Peeeong!*' A bullet screeched past his ear.

'Faster Wolfi! Faster!' Peter screamed. Wolfi did not need any more encouragement and soon he was ahead.

After ten minutes furious cycling they were a safe distance from the house and Peter stopped to allow both of them to catch their breath. His heart was pounding from fear and exertion. There was no sign of pursuit. They were close to Schlachtensee. It was early evening. Not wishing to hang around he cycled into the woods and began to search for a hiding place.

# CHAPTER FOUR

Peter's plan was to hide out in the woods around Schlachtensee or Wannsee. He had spent many happy holidays camping with his father throughout the mountains and forests of Germany. A successful middle-class banker, Papa's first love had always been the great outdoors. From an early age he had taught his only son how to hunt, snare rabbits and fish. Peter had learnt which mushrooms and berries were edible, all of which were plentiful in the woods at certain times of the year. He was very familiar with these surroundings and knew many places where few people, if any, ever ventured.

This had seemed a reasonable plan in the comfort of his own home. As the reality of the situation began to dawn on him, doubt crept in. It was one thing to survive in the wild in the summer or even autumn months, but this was Berlin. Winter temperatures would often be well below freezing, with lakes too frozen to fish and very few rabbits to snare. He had packed a good supply of food. That would inevitably run out and he could not return to his house. Even if he could manage to feed himself, he had Wolfi to look after. Worst of all, he wondered, 'can we survive the freezing temperatures?'

He climbed off his bike and walked along the western edge of Schlachtensee, Wolfi next to him. He thought about where to camp as he walked. This side of Schlachtensee was closest to Wannsee with a vast area of forest in between. It was criss-crossed by paths and roads. One such major thoroughfare was Kronprinzessin Weg, a place he was keen to avoid as it was almost always busy. He knew Schlachtensee and the immediate vicinity very well as it was so close to home. Wannsee might be safer as it was a much vaster area of water, lying next to the huge forest, Grünewald. On the other hand, Wannsee was an important tourist destination for all Berliners and seldom free of visitors. He could not risk staying in the area close to home as his former school friend, from the Hitler Youth, also knew Schlachtensee well. He had played there with Peter's friends many times and was aware of the best hiding places. It began to snow.

'We need to find shelter, and soon,' Peter thought.

For tonight, at least, it would have to be the more familiar woods of Schlachtensee. As the snow fell in soft flakes, the cold temperatures brought one benefit: there was no-one around and hardly anyone had witnessed his furious cycle ride.

He travelled further along the western side of the lake and stopped by a bench on the water's edge. It had the now too common sign 'Aryans only' attached to it. It was only just visible in the small amount of moonlight breaking through the clouds.

Facing away from the bench and into the trees, he began walking up a slope. He carried the bicycle for the first few hundred metres to avoid tracks in the mud. Fortunately the snow was now falling thick and fast and was already lying several centimetres deep, covering both paw and footprints. After a distance of a few hundred metres they stopped. He picked up the bicycle and placed it in the middle of a thick thorn bush. From this point he walked to his left and stopped in front of a huge oak tree. With his hands he felt around the base and soon found a gap between the large roots. He began digging away at the snow and leaves.

Fifteen minutes later he had created a fox hole big enough for him, Wolfi and his baggage. He took his hat, gloves and scarf and sleeping roll from the rucksack and dressed warmly for bed. He lay next to Wolfi and placed an overcoat over them to cover the gap above their heads.

'Good night Wolfi.' As he lay there he remembered what Papa always said, 'there is no such thing as bad weather, just inappropriate clothing.' With one arm around his dog, he tried to sleep. All the while he was hoping they would not be buried in snow.

In spite of the freezing temperatures, they both slept. Wolfi's body provided heat without which Peter knew he probably would not have survived. Whilst he dreamt of happier days with Mama and Papa, Wolfi dreamt of rabbits, his legs occasionally twitching as he chased his prey. Peter's dreams moved from pleasant thoughts, through disturbing images, until once more he was either fighting to the surface in the River Havel desperately gasping for air, or running from the Hitler Youth as he fired at Wolfi.

As a shot rang out in his head, Peter sat bolt upright, waking Wolfi and dislodging the layer of snow on his coat. It was the period just prior to dawn which is neither completely dark nor light. Drawing his coat back fully, he scrambled out of the hole and stretched his arms in a yawn. Wolfi also stretched, as if readying himself for a race.

Peter's jaw ached where he had been struck with the pistol. He moved his lower jaw from side to side and was content that nothing was broken.

However desperate he was to light a fire, he knew that this was not the place to do it. The ex-school friend Peter (or Hans Peter as he had been known), would certainly alert the authorities that a Jew had assaulted him and his father and, Peter smiled wryly as he thought, stolen food from 'their house'. He hoped they had not noticed the camping equipment he had taken from home, otherwise Peter's plans would be all too clear to them. This spot was one of the places he had played with Hans Peter and other school friends in the past, even pretending to hole out in the same enormous tree roots. It was not nearly far enough away from the closest path and the prospect of a stranger coming across them by accident would always be present.

Peter munched on some bread and cheese, while Wolfi ate the remainder of half a tin of dog food. He found himself unusually envious of the unknown meat in the tin. It certainly looked more appetising than his frozen breakfast. How he wished he could make a hot drink. That would have to wait.

With the empty tin of dog food packed in his rucksack, he walked over to the thorn bush where his bicycle was hidden. He lifted the bicycle and shook the snow from it, dusting Wolfi in the process. As always Wolfi was close by.

'We'd better hide the food for now.' As he spoke it dawned on him that he had not talked to anyone other than Wolfi for some time.

As he made to leave the woods he struggled to wheel the bicycle across the rough terrain. The deep snow hampered his progress even more. After a few frustrating minutes he laid the bicycle on its side and walked back to the oak tree where he had sheltered for the night. He attempted a few times to climb the massive trunk. The ice that had formed in the soles of his boots and the frost on the bark, made progress impossible. Each time he simply fell backwards onto the icy ground. All the while Wolfi simply sat and observed this strange game, only once approaching his master to check he was all right.

From the base of the oak he paced towards the thorn bush where he had hidden the bicycle the previous night. Further behind this was a similar bush, except slightly taller and broader. He measured the distance between this new hiding place and the giant oak. It was 170 paces from the base of the tree.

Forcing his way into the centre of the bush, he reached as high as he could, and with his pen knife cut away a few smaller branches. This allowed him to sling the rucksack over a branch higher up the trunk. He tied the sack of food to the same branch. He gathered up the cut branches and retraced his steps, smoothing the snow as he went. Back at the tree trunk he cut a gash in the base of the tree to mark the direction of the thorn bush. Underneath this, with some difficulty, he carved the single word *'Prokofiev'*.

Peter stopped to admire his handiwork and noticed Wolfi's paw prints in the snow. Luckily these crossed over so frequently it was impossible to say in which direction they were heading. With a branch tied to the rear wheel of the bicycle and trailing behind him, he walked the cycle back to the path with the satchel over his shoulder. Wolfi was just in front. The trailing branch hid their footprints just as Peter intended.

Once on the path, he mounted the bicycle and began cycling slowly. Occasionally the wheels skidded on the frozen snow, although for the most part he was able to make good progress.

Concentrating hard on avoiding a fall, it was only as he rounded a bend that he noticed Wolfi was no longer with him. He was some distance behind at the side of the track. He was lying down and biting at his paws in turn. Peter wheeled the bicycle back to Wolfi and leaned over to see what was wrong. Lumps of ice had formed from the snow compacting in the gaps between Wolfi's pads. Each step was painful for the poor dog.

'It's all right boy, we'll soon clear that for you,' Peter said, as he examined each paw.

With a hoof pick on his pocket knife he scraped out the icy lumps as best he could, knowing that it would not be long until more ice formed. He rummaged around in his rucksack and eventually found the two pairs of socks he had been looking for. He wrapped one sock around each paw and tied them in place with the twine he had taken from the garden shed. For a little while this prevented the buildup of ice until one sock, then another, came off. Peter grew worried. He could not leave Wolfi nor could he carry him.

He scanned the terrain about him. Spotting a gap in

the trees, he whistled to Wolfi to follow. He wheeled the bicycle into the gap. It was some sort of firebreak. They followed it for about 100 metres. Peter struggled to carry the heavy bicycle short distances at a time and Wolfi limped alongside.

Their progress was difficult and slow. They eventually slid into a ditch going off to one side. At this point the vegetation was so thick that the snow had not penetrated to the dry ground beneath. Peter heaved the bicycle under some low branches and covered it with greenery cut from a fir tree. He crawled on for another 150 metres under the branches, until they came to a clearing, surrounded on all sides by thick foliage. For the time being this was where they would camp.

Peter cleared the snow from a patch of ground and built a temporary kennel out of branches, angled against a tree. He was pleased he had thought to bring the small axe from the woodshed. The makeshift shelter completed, he took Wolfi and with a bit of the twine and his lead tied him to the tree.

'Sorry boy, you'll have to wait there while I fetch our things.'

Peter hated tying up Wolfi. In the circumstances it was all he could do. It was now reaching the time of day when there would be more people about, some using Schlachtensee as a shortcut. The best approach with strangers was to keep moving and give the appearance of going about everyday life. This could be difficult if Wolfi was suffering problems with his paws. Even in these troubled times, in the midst of a war, there were still those who would stop to admire a handsome dog.

50

He kissed Wolfi on the forehead and prayed that he would not bark as he had done the first time that Peter had ever left him on his own. Settling down with his head between his front legs, Wolfi looked dolefully after his master as he left the clearing. Minutes later Peter was by his bicycle, debating whether he should cycle or continue on foot.

'The bike is quicker,' he thought. He did not want to leave Wolfi for long. In the back of his mind he knew he might have to make a getaway. He rode off as quickly as he could. Without the breaks to clear Wolfi's paws, he made rapid progress and less than half an hour later he was back at the oak tree. His journey had been uneventful. The few people that he had passed had hardly given him a glance, either dwelling on their own problems or assuming he was just a rather lucky schoolboy with a bicycle.

Thankfully no more snow had fallen and he quickly retrieved his rucksack and sack of food. As best he could he obliterated the tracks that showed he had been there and then carried the bike and precious belongings back to the path. The weight of both was such that even in these temperatures he began to sweat.

On leaving the trees he ditched the bicycle and peered in both directions. Confident that the coast was clear he returned, picked up the bicycle and carried it back to the path and mounting it, pedalled as fast as he could. He nearly crashed into the only person he came across, a pedestrian who swore at him and demanded that he stop and apologise. Peter carried on regardless and in even less time than his outward journey he was almost back at the clearing.

As he crawled out of the trees he was relieved to see Wolfi, straining at his tether, tail wagging and apart from the odd low whine, completely silent.

'Good boy Wolfi! Good boy!' Peter was as pleased to see his dog again as Wolfi was to see him.

He spent the next few hours erecting and concealing the old tent he had brought from home. He disguised it from aerial view as best he could with more tree branches. Inside he spread out his sleeping roll and any spare clothes that he was not going to wear. These he placed over a layer of dry pine needles and moss for insulation.

Removing the food items he needed for that evening, he placed the rucksack inside the tent to use as a pillow. He pinned back the flaps at the front of the tent and took out a small oil burner and saucepan with its fitted lid. He started to prepare a stew of vegetables and salt beef with clean snow as a stock. He cut everything into small chunks to save his precious fuel, a trick his Papa had taught him.

'Enough for about a week,' he thought, as he examined his fuel bottle.

Taking his father's gold lighter he lit the burner. As the purple flame glowed underneath the pot he turned the lighter over and over in his hand.

'I hope you and Mama are safe,' he said.

After dinner, Peter and Wolfi crawled into their bed and went to sleep. Once darkness fell there was little else to do. He was reassured by Wolfi curled up next to him.

They were awakened by the early morning sunlight shining into his tent. Peter's sleep had been broken, not so much by the bitter cold, more by the horrific memories that haunted him. Each time he woke Wolfi's deep breathing calmed him and he would lie down once more.

When he crawled out of the tent he was pleased to find that no more snow had fallen in the night. He whistled to Wolfi and both of them disappeared into the trees to answer nature's call.

After feeding Wolfi on a smaller portion of dog food than usual, Peter quickly munched on a few paltry crackers and an even more paltry portion of cheese. He knew that with careful rationing he might eke out his supplies for three, maybe even four weeks, perhaps longer if the snares he planned to make were successful. After that he had no idea what he would do.

He took off his upper layers of clothing, scooped a handful of the looser snow and gave himself a snow bath. It was more important than ever that he did not attract attention. This he would do if he were smelly and dirty, like a vagrant living rough. Ignoring the unpleasant cold, he even gave his hair a type of wash with the snow, brushing it afterwards with a pine cone.

'Time to sort out your paws, Wolfi.' Wolfi looked on, disinterested. Peter sat down and set to work. It took him some time. Four pieces of cloth were threaded around the top with string that could be pulled tight. Wolfi was in his customary place next to Peter, lying on top of the map of Berlin. He held out one hand and on cue Wolfi held up his front right paw as Peter tied the first snow shoe to it. Looking very unimpressed, Wolfi stood up and walked around the tent, with his snow shoe making a padding noise.

After a little experimentation he pierced four holes at the front to allow Wolfi's claws to poke through. This was more to Wolfi's liking and he stopped trying to remove the boot with his mouth. All the while a basic stew was simmering above the oil burner and, as Peter finished the last boot, the stew was ready.

Whilst Peter ate a new problem occurred to him. His current camp was too close to the path. When the better weather arrived more people would venture further into the woods. He needed to find a more remote site. He had already decided on a location from the map. It was on the western side of Wannsee in the woods. He would scout the area soon.

Even though not particularly optimistic about catching anything, he made a number of snares from the wire he had taken from the shed. This skill his father had taught him in the summer of 1932 when he was just six. They were due to camp out in the mountains later that year and Papa had insisted, much to everyone's amusement, that they 'practise' in the woods around Schlachtensee. Hence, only a short walk from their comfortable suburban home they had snared rabbits, trapped wood pigeon and water fowl and caught fish. They had been so successful they ended up taking some of their haul home to Mama.

As each trap was set, Wolfi offered his assistance by sniffing the ground and showing his approval in the usual dog fashion. Making his way from their original hideaway, he laid traps as he went, until he was on the shores of Wannsee.

'Not much fishing here,' he thought and returned to his camp. The edges of the lake were frozen solid.

The following day Peter breakfasted, finishing a cold meal with his first cup of coffee in days. He had remembered to bring coffee beans. Unfortunately the coffee percolator remained forgotten and missed back at his house. Instead he created a coffee pot out of two old cans that he washed, then squeezed one inside the other. Folding the rim inwards, he pierced the bottom of the inner can to form a filter. Apart from granules in the liquid this worked very well. Taking a sip, he toasted the American relations who had supplied the coffee.

He disciplined himself that each time he left the campsite he must hide all traces of his existence. With this in mind he cut more branches with the axe, taking care to minimise the noise. These he used to completely hide the tent. His food he stored in a makeshift larder in the ditch, always ensuring that it was adequately wrapped in a sack. The rest of his equipment, apart from his fishing rod, was left in his rucksack and satchel which were hidden separately under a thick bush. By this means he hoped that, if discovered, they would not lose everything.

Unless it was impossible he had resolved to take Wolfi with him on each trip. On this, his fifth day since separating from his parents he was determined to find another secure hideout. Following the line of his snares he checked each one and with each was disappointed. As he approached the shores of Wannsee he thought back to the evening when they had hidden in the trees awaiting the Captain.

'Stop thinking about it,' Peter chastised himself. 'We have work to do.'

After a while he came across a thicker copse of trees with low-hanging branches. As he crawled on his hands and knees he discovered it was dry underneath the thickest branches. As he anticipated he soon came to a spot where they were much higher above his head, so high that he could stand comfortably. In all the area under the trees was almost three metres in diameter. Beyond the trees and barely visible when standing was a clearing, three or four metres across. He used the small axe to cut a tunnel through the undergrowth, lowering the height as he went. When finished only a small gap remained at the edge of the copse, about the height of Wolfi.

In the middle of the copse Peter made a mud wall from the pine needles and earth, supported with wooden stakes. Over the top he spread an interwoven layer of fir tree branches. He left a small entrance for a door. Once complete he was able to sit in his shelter but not stand upright. Stepping back to admire his labour he was pleased with his efforts. He would be sheltered from the very worst weather and no-one would stumble across this site accidentally. With his old tent and other equipment, the new den was well-protected from the elements.

'No-one will ever find us here Wolfi,' Peter boasted.

The young boy was now so confident in navigating through the woods that he moved everything to this one camp in the darkness. The real danger lay in crossing the footpaths. When in the trees he saw no-one, mainly because of the inhospitable weather.

By minimising their movements and carefully rationing their food, they survived in this way for the next few months. As expected, the oil for the burner ran out. Peter built a type of oven using large rocks. At night he would burn wood underneath when there was nobody about. The warm food would produce tantalising smells. His greatest fear was that the flames would act as a beacon or that the fire might ignite the dried pine needles all around him. By half burying the oven in the ground and creating air holes he hoped to reduce the danger. During the day they would largely sleep, only attending to necessary tasks requiring full light. They would eat lightly and at night consume their one hot meal of the day. His traps were largely unsuccessful, nonetheless their infrequent haul of just a few rabbits was enough to feed them for three or four days at a time. With the added protection of the trees and the warmth from Wolfi, Peter found this new camp really quite comfortable. Only the frequent thoughts of his parents interrupted the tranquility. Each morning they would venture out of the copse simply to alleviate the boredom of trees all around. For the moment life was a mixture of routine with the odd adventure, but at least they were together.

One morning, towards the middle of December, Peter looked in his homemade larder. He knew there was nothing inside, yet he still looked. They had not caught anything for over a week and the previous day they had finished the last of their tins. The only remaining supplies were of salt, vinegar and some flour. It was time to go hunting again. For a brief moment he had contemplated returning to his own house. He had been fortunate the last time. In truth he was reluctant to risk another visit. It had been dangerous for him. The pervading memory was the evil look on a young boy's face as he had pointed his father's gun at Wolfi.

'They'll have changed the locks on the door and blocked the gap in the fence,' he argued, more for his own benefit.

Having rejected that idea he was now underway at night-time under the cover of the trees of Grünewald. Wolfi was trotting along by his side. Living wild, both he and his dog had lost weight and gained some fitness in the last few months. Peter was unsure exactly what they were looking for. He hoped and prayed that some opportunity to obtain supplies would arise. This was the third night in a row they had been out searching. Neither had eaten for several days, other than a few solitary tasteless flat breads and both were starving. Peter trusted in his good luck whilst Wolfi trusted in his friend and master.

'What's that?' Peter whispered. Wolfi looked up at him, barely visible.

Peter had been on the verge of giving up when he spotted dim lights in the distance. At night-time it was unusual to see any sort of lights other than the blue flash from the S-bahn trains. The blackout was so effective. Even the smallest glow of light could lead to a report or reprimand by the air raid wardens.

His fear, overcome by curiosity and extreme hunger, drew him towards the source. As he neared he could see that it was a large building set in its own grounds. They were in the Gatow district not far from the western side of Wannsee. As a rule he did not venture out of the woods.

On this occasion necessity drove them forward. As he crept towards a fence he could just decipher a sign beneath a large swastika. 'Auslandshaus der Hitlerjugend'. Peter's first instinct was to turn and run. He did not.

'So this is where the Hitler Youth train,' he said very quietly. He had heard of this place. What little he knew did not reassure him.

From inside the building he could just make out the distant strains of the Nazi anthem, the Horst Wessel song. Horst Wessel, a hero of the Nazi party who had been killed in the struggle before the war and personally honoured by Hitler. The very nature of the occupants of this building chilled Peter's blood and enraged him at the same time. He had no choice in the matter. *He* could fast for another day, he simply could not bear the longing look in Wolfi's face when his usual mealtime came around. They moved along the fence to their right hoping to find a side entrance. After several hundred metres they were out of sight of the main door.

'Sit boy! Wait here!' Peter said in a whisper and proceeded to climb over the fence. Fortunately it was not electrified. No doubt here in Berlin at the heart of the Reich they felt totally safe. As he looked behind him the only thing he could discern was the light reflected in Wolfi's eyes. His deep black fur camouflaged him perfectly.

Approaching silently over the frosty grass, Peter came to the edge of the building. He could see chinks of light from inside where the blackout curtains did not quite cover the whole window.

He hauled himself onto a drain pipe and peered carefully through the gap. Instinctively he recoiled in terror. He could see a long hall with two rows of connected refectory style tables running lengthways and with benches either side. At the front was a stage with a huge picture of Hitler suspended above, next to a slightly smaller flag of the Hitler Youth consisting of a swastika on a red background. On the stage in an array of uniforms were four males, facing the flags at an angle of forty-five degrees, right arm raised in the Nazi salute. Alongside each bench was standing a boy about his age in the uniform of the Hitler Youth. They stood feet perfectly together, straight-backed and arm raised towards the flags. They were now singing a different song, the Hitler Youth anthem. On the tables next to each boy was a plate and goblet. Most plates were empty, except for a few where he could make out the remnants of a ham hock. He had never eaten pork, and in spite of that, the sight of the hock bones made his mouth water.

Peter stepped off the drain pipe and looked around him. He could not enter the main building, he must try an outbuilding. Further to his right he could make out a brick construction with wooden, barn style doors. He crept across the lawn and tried the door. It was unlocked. Pressing through the gap in the doors, he looked around nervously.

'Boom!' In the half-light Peter's foot kicked a large wooden tub with a wash board protruding from one side. The noise echoed in the roof spaces, seeming to announce his presence. Wincing, he remained completely still, the rapid beat of his heart seeming to mimic the noise of the wash tub. He waited. Thankfully no-one came. He looked cautiously about him. To his great disappointment it was a laundry block with not a scrap of food anywhere. He turned to leave.

'Get off! Get off me!' Peter cried out. Someone had grabbed him around the neck and was strangling him. As he struggled the grip tightened. The more he fought the worse it seemed to get, until finally he realised the true nature of his assailant. He had walked into something hanging from a washing line. In anger he pulled it to one side. 'What's this?' he wondered, his anger subsiding.

On closer inspection he could just see that it was the brown shirt of the Hitler Youth. Not only that, there were at least half a dozen shirts and the accompanying shorts and ties, with socks to match. On a table on the side were the dark leather belts and straps that they wore across their chest and around their waists. In a pile next to these were the badges presented to them by the SS and the accompanying armbands with the Hitler Youth emblem. These were clearly uniforms for new recruits.

Taking as little time as possible, Peter selected a shirt and shorts and gathered up two belts, an armband and the insignia badge, which he stuffed into his rucksack. The only thing missing was a pair of boots. He may not have found anything to eat, but with this uniform he might be able to venture further afield. Best of all, the uniform was clean and dry. In the few months living wild he had discovered that cleaning and drying clothes was virtually impossible in winter.

Next to a row of large porcelain sinks he spotted an almost whole bar of carbolic soap which he stashed in a trouser pocket. He carefully closed the barn door behind him and tiptoed across the lawn and back to Wolfi. He could just make out Wolfi's thick tail wagging in anticipation. Hopping over the fence, he patted Wolfi on the head. Wolfi sniffed the rucksack and turned with an air of disappointment. Still nothing to eat!

On the way back to their hideaway Peter was deep in thought about the possibilities of the uniform.

'Wolfi! Wolfi! Come on boy!' Distracted by the uses he might make of his find, he had not noticed that Wolfi had vanished. Desperately he searched around in the darkness, without success, until his only course was to whistle.

'Wolfi!' he called out, and whistled again. It was a chance he had to take. After a few minutes there was still no response. It was useless to search in this light and Peter knew from experience that retracing his steps would only confuse the scent for Wolfi. With a sigh he looked around him once more and began his journey again.

Try as he might, he could not dispel the agonising thought of what he would do without his dog. More than an hour later, he crawled through the tunnel he had cut out of the copse and emerged into the centre of their den.

'Wolfi! You're back! And what's that you have got?' Peter could just see Wolfi's outline in the dark. His thick tail was wagging even more vigorously than usual and in his mouth he gripped the limp body of a rabbit. They would eat that night after all.

# CHAPTER FIVE

For the next few days and nights, Peter and Wolfi stayed close to their hideaway. Secretly hoping that the uniform would not be missed, Peter was nonetheless quite aware of the German obsession for proper accounting. They might search the woods far and wide if they discovered that a theft had occurred. The fanatical youths would delight in the hunt, especially if they had any inkling of their quarry. It was too dangerous to appear in public dressed as a Hitler Youth just yet. Indeed for the time being he did not wish to venture far from the camp. Better to let the dust settle.

What was now evident was that he had to find other sources of food or they would starve. Their supply of wild game was irregular and unreliable. Even though he had never actually seen anyone else when hunting, he suspected there were others who had the same idea. The supply of meat in wartime was especially scarce and he may not be the only refugee in these vast woods. The rabbit would feed them for up to three, maybe even four days if he was careful. None of the animal was wasted with the less palatable innards roasted and then devoured by Wolfi. As far as Wolfi was concerned his master loved him very much, always letting him have the best parts of the animal. The carcass was boiled for many hours until it reduced into a stock which Peter would drink like soup.

Their den was quite comfortable, though Peter would often wear several layers of clothing at night to keep warm. After a while the clothes had started to smell and washing them in winter was impractical. To avoid suspicion they had to maintain the highest levels of cleanliness. Even though the shortages of war had forced many Berliners to wash both themselves and their clothing less often, more would be expected of a member of the Hitler Youth and his dog. This meant regularly brushing Wolfi's coat to avoid knotting. For Peter it was a case of scraping the mud off his boots and always being careful not to sit in the dirt so as to avoid muddying his clothes.

None of these tasks was objectionable and helped pass the time. For apart from the Nazis and the fight against cold and hunger, their greatest enemy was boredom. Wolfi was happy to lie next to Peter and sleep for long periods, awaiting their next adventure in the woods. The moments of inactivity for Peter were filled with both painful and happy memories, occasionally tinged with regret that he had separated from his family. Often he wondered where they were and what they were doing at that exact time. In his heart he kindled the desperate hope that they were safe, whilst in his head he could not expel the last images of them being captured.

Some four days having elapsed since his foray into the laundry block, Peter figured it was now safe to make his first appearance as a member of the Hitler Youth. He had carefully stored the uniform so as to avoid creasing. The belts, straps and insignias he polished with rabbit fur. His best synagogue boots were likewise buffed until they reflected the sunlight. Stripping to his underwear, he assembled the outfit one piece at a time, knotting the tie beneath his Adam's apple as the finishing touch. A flattened tin can served as a mirror. His first reaction was one of disgust and shame, the swastika armband reminding him of why they were here in the woods, eking out an existence. Apart from the fact that he was an escaped Jew in the uniform of the enemy, something else was not quite right.

'It's the hair,' he said. Wolfi looked baffled, tipping his head to one side.

In the months in the woods, Peter's hair had grown until it now touched his shirt collar. No member of the Hitler Youth would ever appear like this. He took a razor blade from his rucksack and wedged one side into a piece of wood. With the wood end in his hand and with extreme care, he managed to trim the hair back from his collar. He could do nothing about the thickness. Instead he wet his hair and combed it backwards so that it stuck to his head. The desired effect was achieved. He had inherited his mother's blonde hair and blue eyes and looked every bit the poster version of Aryan youth. Finally, he cleaned his fingernails with his pocket knife and held his hands out to Wolfi.

'What do you think Wolfi?' Wolfi barked his approval.

Before leaving their camp he brushed Wolfi's coat as best he could. As he did so the dog's metal identity tag glistened in the winter sunshine. The single word 'Wolf' now adorned the metal disc. Peter had remembered the warning from the Major and with the skill and patience of an engraver he had smoothed away the inscription 'Stern' and the address in Schillerstrasse. He had contemplated trying to carve a new address and surname, then abandoned it as each attempt looked more amateurish than the next.

This was one of the very few journeys they had made in daytime since they had been living in the woods. He was extremely nervous and could hear the sound of his own heavy breathing. He had brought Wolfi with him. Only the privileged few could afford to keep a large dog in wartime and this added to Peter's air of importance. Likewise, many bicycles having been requisitioned for the war effort, anyone so fortunate to own one must have powerful connections, especially a foreign bicycle. The uniform also provoked the desired response. Germans responded to authority and that usually meant someone in uniform or with an impressive title. Even caretakers had grandiose names. No-one stopped to question why Peter was not wearing an overcoat, normally obligatory at this time of year. One man even saluted as he cycled past.

Some thirty minutes later Peter came across his first prospect of success. He had left the environs of the lake and was in a residential suburb. There were pedestrians and the odd motor vehicle passing by, otherwise it was quiet. Most adults these days were either on war duty at the front, or on night-time patrols, or required in essential war work, sometimes next to the slave labourers in the many factories.

The object of Peter's interest however was a building in a side street that was almost completely flattened. One side wall was still partially erect and in the middle, a lone fireplace and chimney breast gave away the identity of the ruins as a former dwelling house. In front of the fireplace was a huge pile of rubble that was still smouldering, telling everyone that this was a casualty of the previous night's bombing. He knew that as a private dwelling it was unlikely that there would be any food under the rubble. Most 'legitimate' residents in Berlin queued with their ration cards on an almost daily basis. This was not possible for Peter. New regulations stipulated that tins had to be opened by shopkeepers as they were sold in order to prevent hoarding. Hardly anyone save the elite was able to stockpile rations. For the majority of Berlin, as for Peter and Wolfi, each day was a struggle to survive.

Peter was not interested in the ruined house. What had caused him to stop quite abruptly was the adjoining building that rounded the corner of the street. This had a large advertising sign on the side that indicated it was a grocer's specialising in fruit, vegetables, meat and fish. Below the sign and largely obscured by the rubble, he could see a gap in the bricks, small enough that a grown man would not get through, but large enough for a boy his age. In front of the hole someone had placed a large sheet of wood. At the front of the shop he could see a row of people waiting patiently to enter.

It was approaching midday and he guessed that the shop would soon shut for lunch or shut completely as it had nothing else to sell. As there were restricted provisions many shops opened for limited periods only. He had a choice: either he continue his journey and return to this spot if nothing else presented itself or he could stay here and wait for the right moment. As he was some distance from his camp, he was already feeling uncomfortable and concluded that he would stay where he was.

'Come on boy,' Peter whistled to his dog. Lifting his bicycle onto the rubble, he clambered over the ruins with Wolfi gingerly following him. As he had done with the kind Major, he would search for survivors, except this time it would be pretend only.

He looked at his watch and hoped that this charade would not have to last too long. He was aware of the great risk he was taking, as looters, whatever their background, were liable to be shot at the scene of their crime.

For half an hour he moved bricks from one spot to another. No-one disturbed him. In a built up area such as this looting in plain view was not suspected and the uniform deterred anyone from querying his motives.

'Let's hope the owners don't return.' As he said this a dreadful thought came to him. The owners were probably somewhere under this mound of bricks and cement.

One useful item he found was a pair of scissors, slightly bent though working. He stored them in his satchel, taking care not to be observed.

At a few minutes after one o'clock, Peter descended from the ruins and walked to the front of the grocer's. The blinds were pulled down and the queue had dispersed. Upstairs he detected movement and assumed the shopkeepers were having their own midday meal. He walked back to the pile of rubble at the rear of the building, and chaining his bicycle to some railings, left Wolfi standing guard, his lead loosely knotted around the front wheel. He was reluctant to leave Wolfi. The piles of bricks had proved to be quite rough and uneven. With so many pieces of broken glass strewn amongst the rubble he would not risk cuts to Wolfi's pads.

Clambering over the rubble pile once more, Peter neared the gap in the bricks. Cautiously he pulled back the wooden sheet and peered inside. Visible from the top floors of certain buildings when at the front, on the street, here at the rear, there were fewer windows. With the bricks that he had earlier been moving around he had gradually increased the height of the pile. The result was that the temporary repair to the wall was only visible from close range. Once through the hole in the wall, he found himself in a storeroom.

'Jackpot!' he said excitedly under his breath.

Wooden shelves stretched across each wall and from floor to ceiling. Most of the shelves were empty, save for one bearing tins of processed meat and fish. On the ground in small barrels were salt, vinegar and oil. He quickly removed two tins of meat and two tins of fish and hid them in his satchel. This was all he would take for now. He was uncomfortable stealing, for that was how he regarded it. He was desperate. To disguise the theft he rearranged the mound of tins, creating gaps at the back. Leaving by the same hole, he replaced the board and rushed back to Wolfi. As he rounded the corner he stopped dead in his tracks.

'Damn!' He was about to pirouette on the spot. It was too late. The Wehrmacht officer leaning over Wolfi and examining his tag had spotted him. 'I can't leave Wolfi,' Peter thought. He would have to brazen it out.

Approaching the officer in a confident manner, he clicked his heels together, raised his hand and arm in salute, shouting 'Heil Hitler!'

'Heil Hitler! Is this your dog?' the officer said. The enthusiasm and the sincerity of the Hitler salute convinced Peter that this officer was not at all like the Major. He should be particularly on guard. Wolfi was gyrating his body and wagging his tail rapidly in his normal fashion. There could be little doubt that Wolfi was his dog.

'Yes,' Peter replied. 'The bicycle is mine too.'

'Wolf. A good name for a dog. You know that our Führer has a dog with the exact same name?'

'Yes,' Peter responded, 'that is why I gave him the name. To honour our Führer.'

'Good. You also know that Adolf means 'noble Wolf' and the Führer's command centre is called 'Wolf's Lair?'

'Of course,' Peter said with more confidence, 'we are taught all of these things in the Hitler Youth.'

'Good, good. With future soldiers like you, and Wolf of course, Germany cannot lose the war.' With this parting remark the officer saluted in the conventional style, hand raised to his temple, and left.

'Phew! That was close.' Peter unchained the bicycle, mounted it and rode off with Wolfi, not looking back once.

Back at the camp, Peter changed from his uniform, ensuring he avoided dirtying it in any way. He unloaded his small bounty from his satchel and taking one of the tins of sardines, opened it. He ate half himself and gave the other half to Wolfi. The remaining three tins he stashed in his outdoor larder.

With his axe he split a medium sized log and using his knife spent the next hour carving a sign on the flat face of one half. He smiled as he showed it to Wolfi.

'Welcome to the Wolf's Lair.' Wolfi barked.

That same day, in the dark, Peter rode back to the shop. It was after curfew and a bitterly cold evening. There were very few people out and about. As a precaution he had dressed in his uniform. Wolfi had been left at the camp as he could travel faster alone. He hated leaving Wolfi behind, but the close call with the officer earlier that day had settled the matter.

By using the various paths and bridleways in Grünewald, he was able to avoid the checkpoints that would mean certain detection, until he reached the point at which he had to leave the woods. If confronted he would have to cycle away as fast as he could.

He blessed his good fortune constantly for it was a dark night with no moonlight. With the strict enforcement of the blackout regulations, Berlin was in complete darkness and in reality he was in greater danger of colliding with pedestrians or other road users or even lampposts, than encountering a checkpoint. Helpfully the edge of the pavements, street corners, crossings and obstacles were marked with a stripe in luminous paint. Likewise red-filtered lights identified scaffolding or excavations in the ground. Some pedestrians marked their clothing with phosphorescent symbols such as horseshoes to avoid being struck. Nonetheless any journey at night in wartime Berlin was hazardous for all travellers, whether by cycle, on foot, in a private motor vehicle or on public transport. Peter cycled hard, concentrating all the time. His eyes were fixed ahead, searching in the tiny amount of rose-tinted light cast by the obligatory red handkerchief tied around his bicycle lamp.

At his destination, he jumped from the saddle and wheeled the bicycle down the side street. He leaned the bicycle against the same railings, this time without locking it. It was a gamble leaving it unsecured, a necessary gamble, as he might need to make a quick getaway. Fortunately there were very few people around, and none in this area. Checking in all directions, he began to climb over the mound of bricks and debris and was ecstatic to find that the hole in the wall was still unrepaired. He pulled aside the wooden cover. As it scraped across the uneven ground the noise seemed deafening. Hesitating for a moment, he watched for any sign of movement inside the building. Satisfied the occupants were sound asleep, he squeezed his slight frame through the gap. He switched on his small torch and began to fill his rucksack with tins of meat and fish.

'What would Mama and Papa think? What would the Rabbi think?' he wondered, as he carefully placed each tin inside the canvas rucksack. In spite of his extreme care, each tin seemed to clink more noisily than the first. With each clink Peter stopped and waited for the inevitable challenge. None came.

Picking up a small barrel of salt, he exited through the hole, this time quietly sliding the board into place.

With the salt barrel stowed in the wicker basket on the handle bars, he mounted the bicycle and rode off into the night. As he turned the corner he took one last look at the shop front. His earlier guilt disappeared as he noticed the sign in the window. *'Jews not allowed.'* Above this the partially defaced shop sign with the word *'Neuberger'*, the name of the previous owner, was still legible.

# CHAPTER SIX

With his larder replenished, Peter had a new optimism that they would make it to the spring and summer months. Once the snows had melted and the ice thawed there would be a plentiful supply of fish. Game would be much easier to trap and nature would supply berries and wild mushrooms, as well as wild garlic and some herbs. The bland diet of the winter would be replaced with a true feast. He would not need to pursue his overnight raids, placing himself in terrible danger. With a sizeable quantity of salt he hoped to preserve the excess meat and fish for the harsher winter months. With any luck the war would be over by then. All of these advantages comforted him, even though he knew that with the passing of winter, the woods and lakes would attract families and walkers, lovers and friends, all of whom might stray into the *Wolf's Lair*.

Throughout these months he kept his own form of calendar. From the first he had notched each passing day on a stick, making sure to remember what day of the week it was. Although a Christian festival he celebrated Christmas with an extra portion of meat for both of them. New Year came and went with little to mark it, save the catching of a rabbit. Since the early weeks his skills as a trapper had improved enormously and what little game there was he seemed to bag. With each rabbit caught or wood pigeon snared, Peter's confidence grew that they could survive.

Apart from their physical well-being, he tried to obtain information wherever he could. Very occasionally he would find a discarded newspaper in a bin. As a Jew this was something he could not legally buy. Most of the 'news' was propaganda. Nevertheless he hoped to glean some inkling of how the war was progressing. It might also help locate the best bomb sites for his occasional sortie for provisions, provided the raids were properly reported. In the months leading up to their attempted flight Papa had insisted that they should listen to the BBC radio broadcasts, a dangerous business as it was punishable with hard labour. Anyone caught spreading the news from foreign broadcasters was liable to be executed.

At first Papa as a law-abiding citizen had reluctantly retuned the radio set. As the war progressed and the official news bulletins did not match the reality in Berlin, Papa, like so many other Germans, had insisted on listening as one of the few means to find out the truth. How Peter wished he still had a radio set. He was getting used to the constant dangers he faced, always being on guard, sometimes having to take risks he wished he could avoid. A radio, he reasoned would have helped him minimise those risks.

The greatest hardship was not the uncertainty of whether they would be caught or whether they would eat; the greatest hardship was when would it all end or even would it end? What if, as seemed highly probable, the war was won by Germany? In spite of the persecution he had suffered in recent years, he still felt guilt when he found himself hoping that Germany would not be victorious.

On a day in January, Peter determined to make another excursion. He still had a number of supplies. He faced a new problem. He was bored. Several uneventful days had passed. It was some time since they had journeyed far from the camp.

'Time for a long walk.' Wolfi jumped up and down enthusiastically as Peter announced his intentions.

It was customary when they left to scout for food outside the woods that he wore his uniform. He hated what it represented, even though it gave him a measure of confidence. On this occasion he decided not to wear it. The value of his simple disguise had proved itself over and over and he was now concerned that it would not survive the constant wear and tear.

'I should have taken two uniforms,' he repeatedly berated himself

If absolutely necessary, he supposed, he could always return to the same laundry block to obtain another. The image of all those ardent young Nazis, arms in the air and voices singing fervently, gave him such an icy feeling inside that he preferred not to think about it.

They walked for hours, through the trees and along the lakeside. Wolfi seemed to sniff every possible smell and jumped in the air eagerly when Peter took his ball from a trouser pocket. Boy and dog wandered together, forgetting their predicament for the time being and for a while they could almost have been back in the days before the war. For Peter it was therapeutic that there was no purpose to this walk, no hunt for supplies, no advance reconnaissance; it was simply a walk. He had calculated earlier in the day that it was the 20th January 1942, almost two and a half months since their ill-fated escape attempt.

As he was about to turn for home, he heard a noise in the distance. They were close to a gravel track leading down to the lakeside. Instantly he recognised the sound as that of a car.

'Wolfi! Here!' he called to his dog, whistling at as low a volume as he could. Wolfi ran to his side and both hurried into the trees.

Within seconds of reaching the cover of the trees, a convoy of vehicles whooshed down the gravel track, spraying pebbles everywhere. At the front was a long black staff car with elegant runner boards and a swastika flag on the bonnet. This was followed by several more such vehicles, four motorcycle outriders in army uniform and a truck full of soldiers with rifles. As this disappeared into the distance a similar convoy drove past.

Scared, but curious, Peter made his way through the trees in the direction of travel of the convoys. Ahead he saw the large wrought iron gates of a villa. Wolfi was by his side.

'Quiet boy,' he whispered to Wolfi, as he crept towards the perimeter. The villa was surrounded by a large whitewashed wall. Trying various trees, Peter finally found one that he could climb, and pulling himself ever higher into the branches he eventually secured a comfortable viewpoint. Wolfi waited at the foot of the tree anxiously. Fortunately he did not bark.

Behind the whitewashed walls, Peter could see a large gravel drive which swept around in front of the villa's main doors. The doors were set back in a grand covered archway. On the drive were the staff cars he had seen and many more vehicles, all with various flags and insignias on the front. Either side of the entrance to the villa there was stationed an SS sentry. On seeing them, he recoiled slightly, then leaned forward again.

From the last in the row of cars he watched as a tall distinguished man in a black uniform with a black attaché case under his arm exited the back of the vehicle. The door was held open by another soldier. The soldier was saluting. On the other side, another man in black SS uniform was also leaving the vehicle. From their demeanour it was clear that the taller of the two passengers was the higher in rank and by the exaggerated way that the others nodded to him, Peter guessed he was someone of great importance. As he looked more closely, the face jumped out from various newspapers and newsreels.

'It's Heydrich,' he murmured and leaned away. In his mind he could now see the photograph with the typed words underneath. '*Heydrich: Reinhard Heydrich, Head of SS Intelligence*'. The man responsible for Jewish '*emigration*'.

Heydrich and his entourage entered the building. Peter scrabbled down the trunk of the tree.

'Let's go boy. I don't know what they are up to, but I don't think it will help us in any way.' With that Peter and

Wolfi walked back to their camp, whilst inside the villa, for just one and a half hours, the top Nazis debated the fate of the Jews in Europe.

Gradually the blanket of winter lifted from Berlin. The trees were in bud and the sound of wildlife was all around. New life sprouted everywhere. For Peter a new opportunity arose. He could fish in the lakes and supplement their bland diet. Not only did fishing provide a practical benefit to them both, it lifted Peter's morale and occupied many hours. He still had to be careful and try to stay in those spots where fewer passers-by were likely to appear. Of these passers-by, many would simply ignore him, some would try and give advice as to how to cast and from time to time, some would try and barter or steal his catch.

On one such occasion he sold a pair of catfish for the princely sum of twenty marks. He had no idea what he would do with the money; without identification and a ration card he could not purchase anything in the shops. In the back of his mind he thought that it would improve his Hitler Youth disguise if at least he had some money with him when he travelled about. Whether he used the money or not, it was worth the loss of two fish for the feeling of normality that it brought to him, even for a brief period.

Apart from fishing with his rod, he arranged lines of hooks baited with worms. These he would leave in the water and check with Wolfi on a daily basis. Often there would be nothing at all, yet on a rare wonderful occasion he would find seven or eight fish in a row. As a result, after just a few weeks of the less harsh weather they had a healthy stock of fish. With the precious barrel of salt he was able to preserve the excess. Some he would smoke. The milder weather also allowed both he and Wolfi to bathe regularly and swim from time to time. It was even possible to wash and dry clothing if the weather was suited. No longer did they need to rely on cold snow to remain clean or wash with rationed water supplies from the lake or melted ice. All in all, life generally became that much easier and relaxed.

With the excess provided by nature, Peter was grateful that his trips into the city had grown much less frequent. His physical hunger was more than catered for, but his lack of any news began to play on his mind. After some deliberation he decided that another excursion was necessary. He dressed in his uniform, ensuring that his hair was neatly combed to one side, his boots were polished and with his twenty marks in his trouser pocket, he cycled into the centre of Berlin. It was daytime and about four in the afternoon. He had reluctantly left Wolfi behind as he intended to travel further than ever from their camp.

The weather was clear and bright and he made good speed through the woods and onto the streets. In a short time he was on the Kurfürstendamm. In the pre-war years this was Berlin's premier shopping district and the centre of much of the night life. Even now in wartime it was still a hive of activity. People were everywhere. There were sweethearts wandering arm in arm, soldiers with young girls at tables that sprawled out from pavement cafes. Trams travelled up and down, interspersed with the less frequent sight of a motorcar, usually occupied by some high-ranking official. It was a beautiful spring day with sunshine and warmth temporarily dispelling any thoughts of war.

Peter dismounted. The crowds were now so heavy that he was in danger of colliding with a pedestrian. No matter how good his disguise that was not a chance he could take. Chaining the bicycle to a lamppost he crossed the street and stood in front of a cinema. A queue of mainly schoolboys and a few girls and boys in their Hitler Youth uniforms and Union of German Maidens had gathered outside. There were a few soldiers, each with their arms intertwined with a pretty girl and a courting couple, the man in an expensive looking suit with Nazi party armband. Peter stood at the back of the queue looking nonchalantly around him.

'One please,' Peter said confidently, looking the kiosk attendant directly in the eye and handing over his twenty mark note. He ignored the sign declaring that Jews were forbidden admission. She simply smiled back handing him a ticket and some change. As he crossed the foyer he noticed a group of schoolchildren crowding around an usherette.

'Ice cream!' Peter could scarcely believe his eyes. She was selling a small quantity of ice creams. Even better, she was not asking for ration cards! He joined the throng and some five minutes later came away with a much-appreciated, if small, ice cream cone. Greatly to the annoyance of a mother with a child of about eleven, the very last one. In other circumstances Peter might have given the cone away.

'Sorry!' he said and shrugged his shoulders in a form of apology. He was not sorry. The ice cream was lovely and the angry mother was wearing a Nazi Party badge. He mounted the staircase to the upper level, licking the ice cream as he went. It was somehow not quite the same as he remembered, still it was the most delicious thing he had tasted since the beginning of the war.

At the door he handed over his ticket and eagerly took back the stub handed to him by the door attendant.

'Follow me.' The usherette began to show him to the front until Peter whispered, 'Better stay at the back in case I have urgent war duties to attend to.' As he said this he pointed to his armband. The usherette winked at him. With a broad smile on her face she guided him to a seat near the aisle, in the third row from the back.

The lights dimmed and a wave of excitement spread through the audience. It was many years since Peter had attended the cinema. Once it had been a common occurrence, with Papa especially enjoying the 'foreign films'. They had on special occasions come to this very cinema. Often there was the added treat of dinner in one of the many cafes, usually Cafe Kurfürstendamm, where the speciality was spätzle, a type of Bavarian doughy pasta. This little pleasure along with so many others had been denied them for some time.

Peter settled back in the seat. It was a long time since he had sat on a chair of any kind. He watched as triumphant music accompanied the 'German Weekly Newsreel'. Hundreds of Wehrmacht soldiers marched in formation, goose-stepping towards the audience. Stuka fighters were shown shooting down Allied planes as panzers rolled into battle, their huge canons firing. Russian partisans were rounded up and fire-fights between the Germans and Russian soldiers flashed across the screen. A headline appeared 'the Siege of Leningrad is approaching its end with a famous victory for our glorious troops'.

'What nonsense! We have been close to winning the siege of Leningrad ever since it started last September!' The voice was male and right next to Peter. In the dark another voice, that of a young woman cautioned the man.

'Careful! Talk of that sort is treason, and you don't know who is listening.' In the dark Peter could just make out the face of a pretty young woman, looking in his direction.

The newsreel switched to show Propaganda and Enlightenment Minister, Goebbels, delivering an impassioned speech to row upon row of uniformed men and women. The camera panned across their faces as they responded feverishly to his rousing words. To one side of Goebbels sat Adolf Hitler, head bobbing in approval. In another scene, Grand Admiral Dönitz was addressing a large gathering of newly qualified U-boat mariners. Reich's Marshall Göring, head of the Luftwaffe, dressed in his famous white uniform with long white coat, white baton and iron cross at his neck, visited a town in the East which remained 'untouched by the war'. A peasant man and woman smiling to the camera, greeted him warmly and a young peasant girl presented him with a bouquet.

As Peter had anticipated, nothing in the newsreels had provided him with any useful information. It was he suspected, the usual Nazi propaganda, carefully orchestrated, with Goebbels as conductor. Just as he was beginning to regret the great risk he had taken another headline appeared. He had not paid much attention until the words 'evil intention of Western democracy' were accompanied by footage of a grey-haired man in a large office, posing in front of an American flag. This was followed by scenes of planes crashing into warships and then a tribute 'to our allies in Japan'.

'America is in the war!' Peter wanted to scream it out. In the months since he had gone into hiding, both America and Japan had joined the war. 'Surely with America involved the fighting would soon be over?' he thought.

Almost unable to conceal his joy, he settled back to watch the main feature. He was to be sorely disappointed. It was a propaganda film called '*Jud Süss*' or '*Sweet Jew*'. He had heard of the film but never been allowed to see it. The prologue declared that it was 'based on actual historical events'. At this point Peter, who knew the truth about the film, was tempted to leave in protest. He dare not attract attention. Set in 1733, the film depicted how the Duke of Württemberg was deceived by a conniving Jew, who cleverly lent him money, making more and more outrageous demands. The Jew compounded his crime in that he forced his attentions on an Aryan woman. The brave German citizens had just begun a revolt against the evil Jew, when to Peter's surprise and some relief, the film stopped abruptly and the lights came on.

An SS officer, about forty years old, stood in front of the screen on the raised stage. He was accompanied by Gestapo officers, two of them. Peter sank back into his seat contemplating his escape. Looking around, he could not see any other Gestapo officers. His fear that this was a random search for undesirables, was momentarily dispelled.

One of the Gestapo men held out a piece of paper and began to read solemnly:

'It is with great regret that Reichs Minister Goebbels informs the people of the Greater German Reich, that today the 27th May 1942 the Reich has suffered an attack on one of its founders and greatest heroes. Reinhard Heydrich, Head of SS Intelligence was severely wounded in a cowardly act in Czechoslovakia. It is feared he will not survive. The perpetrator has already been dealt with and his collaborators are being met with swift and bloody retribution. The Reich's Minister will address the German people this evening at eight o'clock. As a mark of respect the cinema will now close. Heil Hitler!'

In unison, all except Peter responded with 'Heil Hitler'. Remembering himself he feigned a Hitler salute. Some in the audience were openly weeping, others were debating with each other as to what the 'bloody retribution' might be. Unsure as to whether this news was a good or bad thing, Peter stood up and greeting the usherette as he went, speedily made his way from the cinema.

# CHAPTER SEVEN

Spring ran into summer and life for Wolfi and Peter mirrored in many ways the old life they had once known. Only, at the end of a long day fishing or swimming or walking in the woods, they did not return to their comfortable home with the certainty of something hot and delicious and the warmth of family life. Apart from that, compared to the winter, their day to day existence was filled with more little moments of joy and triumph. It had been some months since Peter had felt the need to don his uniform and mix with the rest of civilisation.

As the different varieties of wild fruits appeared he would gather them and either eat some there and then, or dry them, or mash them into a type of jam. He wished so much that he had some real syrup or even alcohol to help preserve the fruit. The best he could manage was boiled rosehip which produced an acceptable syrup, although not as effective as the real thing. From his experience of the previous winter he knew how much a taste of the summer months would help to lift his spirits. He was always careful not to pick anything growing near to the large networks of paths as often there were other starving Berliners who were supplementing their diet in the same fashion.

He was now so familiar with a large area of the woods that he knew most of the secluded copses and clearings where few others went. Though he was scarcely recognisable as the young boy who had narrowly avoided drowning almost a year ago, he did not wish to gamble upon being spotted by a former neighbour or school friend who might denounce him. He was still only a short distance from his old home and, as he constantly had to remind himself, this was the main area of recreation for the whole of Berlin. In spite of the longing to visit his home, he managed to resist.

One of the most productive areas for wild fruit was the villa at Wannsee where he had spied into the garden. Blackberries and loganberries as well as wild cherries all grew near the walls that surrounded the huge mansion. He guessed that the inhabitants were so immune from the ravages of the war that they did not need to seek the riches on their doorstep. The building was so imposing, with a regular stream of military and official vehicles, no-one else dared to venture near its perimeter.

Peter was as wary as the next Berliner. He simply could not ignore what nature had to offer. He had devised a route to approach the villa which avoided the front gates completely. As far as he could tell there was no patrol around the outside. When he did cross the path of anyone else he simply kept walking as if there was nothing more natural in the world than a fifteen-year-old boy walking his dog. Sometimes it seemed that those he encountered were as keen to avoid eye contact as he was and he wondered whether they too were illegal. Often he sensed repulsion at the sight of his uniform, repulsion that might one day spell their downfall. The most important lesson he had learnt in his months alone was that an arrogant demeanour and an air of confidence would often deflect suspicion.

Thus it was that the summer passed by. He avoided travelling far on the weekends and public holidays. Most movements were restricted to early morning or late evening when the woods were largely deserted. By these means they avoided unwanted attention. By the time autumn approached and the trees began to shed their leaves and colour, Peter and his canine companion had built up a healthy stock of provisions, well hidden in the depths of the forest.

One October night a strong wind began to howl eventually turning to a gale, with rain lashing his camp. Wolfi was unsettled as thunder claps bellowed from above and lightning streaked across the sky. Wolfi had grown more accustomed to the noise and flashes of the air raids, yet they still frightened him. He sensed a fear in Peter that Peter did not wish to confront: one day a plane might crash into their hiding place or a bomb land in their precious woods. These fears were not unfounded. When the aerial battles took place over the city many stricken pilots would try and avoid crashing in to the heavily populated urban areas. Their clearest option was to crash land on Wannsee or Muggelsee or another of the large lakes. This applied to German and enemy pilots alike, for regardless that one had come to bomb the population and the other to defend, neither desired to be personally responsible for civilian casualties by crashing into a house. The result of these noble sentiments was that many planes were seen to plummet into the waters of Wannsee and disappear.

On this particular night the weather was so poor that Peter knew that no planes would be in the air, but he could not convey this to Wolfi.

'It's all right boy,' he whispered over and over, stroking Wolfi's head. The wind shook the trees above and around them and the rain fell in sheets to the floor of the forest, thankfully not into their den. With each clap of thunder and each bolt of lightning, Wolfi crept closer and closer to Peter, seeking reassurance from his friend.

At long last, after many hours of constant rain, the storm broke and they drifted into sleep. When they awoke it was a beautiful sunny day. They left the den and walked through the trees to the quietest spot on the side of the lake where they could bathe without fear of interference. As Peter approached the water's edge, Wolfi was already in the water, drinking and bathing at the same time. Peter bent over and, scooping some water in his hands, splashed his face, then rubbed the back of his neck and behind his ears. It had been many months since his meagre bar of soap had dwindled to nothing. He looked cautiously around and was about to undress further when, in the corner of his eye, he caught sight of a wooden object. It was to his left, protruding from some willow trees, on the bank of the lake. It was a varnished piece of wood. He waded through the shallow water, accompanied by Wolfi.

'A boat! It's a boat!' Peter was ecstatic.

It was one of the small sailing dinghies about five metres in length and two metres wide with a single mast and sail near the centre and tiller at the back. Towards the middle was a small cabin, no more than a metre tall and a metre and a half deep, for sheltering from the elements. It had clearly broken free of its mooring in the middle of the night. There was no clue as to how far it had travelled. The mast was broken about a third of the way up from the deck of the boat. Peter jumped on board. Wolfi hesitated briefly, then sprang in the air, landing cat-like on the deck. Unfortunately Wolfi was not a cat and as a result his claws slipped on the wet deck and he lay spread-eagled on his belly. He let out a groan, more of embarrassment than pain. Peter laughed.

Having checked Wolfi was not injured, he began to examine his find. Apart from the broken mast the rest of the boat was undamaged.

He slid into the water from the bow and pulled the front of the boat. It did not budge.

'Wolfi. Here boy!' he called out. Wolfi jumped into the water next to him, this time landing noisily without any mishap. He took the bowline in his hand and tied it to form a harness around Wolfi's back.

'Mush! Mush!' Peter said. Wolfi looked back lovingly, remaining stationary. `Here Wolfi! Here!' he beckoned with his hand and whistled. This time Wolfi understood and began swimming towards him.

With the dog's added power they had soon heaved the boat into the water. Once in the water fully the boat was easy to manoeuvre. Peter unhitched Wolfi and, taking the bowline in both hands, dragged the boat along the shore for about 100 metres.

'Look Wolfi, it floats!' The keel of the boat was undamaged and floated perfectly. As he held the front line in his hand he noted the name *Kaiser Wilhelm* written neatly on its side. This was a boat that had been loved and no doubt its owners would come looking for it.

After a search Peter located a spot where the shoreline was quite steep and sheltered from view by thick trees. The path around the lake veered back from the water's edge and was some 150 metres away. Below the trees the lake flowed into a culvert forming an inlet. By now he was waist deep in water with Wolfi swimming by his side. He guided the boat into the gap in the bank and moored it securely to a thick tree trunk, looping the rope around both the bow and the stern. From the boat's deck he checked that it was not visible from the lake and likewise not visible from the riverbank. Only someone swimming in this precise location or on a small rowing boat would discover his secret.

Peter waded back to the shore to the point where he had first entered the water. Various ideas as to how he might use the boat came into his head. First he would have to wait. He determined that he would allow a period of one week exactly to see if the boat had been discovered.

'Breakfast time Wolfi.' Wolfi did not need a second invitation and trotted back to camp with Peter, who was more excited than he had been for a long time.

The week passed very slowly for Peter. He was tempted many times to go back and admire the *Kaiser Wilhelm*, but wisely resisted. He even avoided washing at his usual place for fear the temptation would prove too great.

Finally the day came that he had been waiting for. First thing in the morning they walked back to their usual bathing spot. Stripping to his underwear and hiding his clothes in some bushes, Peter and Wolfi entered the water. As they rounded the bend in the lake's edge, he spotted the varnished wooden sides. It was still there! He pulled himself out of the water onto the deck, then reached back into the water and hauled Wolfi up until he was safely on board. All the while Wolfi had a look of horrified indignity on his face.

Other than repairing the mast and removing the name from the side, there was little to do to make the boat seaworthy. Ideally he would have liked to change the boat's entire appearance, but it was impractical.

The following morning Peter and Wolfi arrived with a rucksack full of all the tools they might need. After a long day's work the boat was seaworthy again. The mast was splinted with the straightest branch Peter could find. The wood was stripped and smoothed. The old sail was replaced by the canvas tent which he did not use any more. He had even created proper eyelets to thread the rope through. Best of all he had scraped off the original name from the side of the boat and carved a new one: *Seawolf*. The *Kaiser Wilhelm* had a new name and a different colour sail.

'Even the owner will not recognise it,' he said hopefully.

Content with the day's work they returned to their camp.

In calculating the many advantages that *Seawolf* would bring, Peter had overlooked one of the most important.

They now had a hobby. Although safest to remain hidden in the trees, the middle of Wannsee was almost as good a hiding place as any. Most visitors to the lake would either bathe from the beach or wander around the edge. Some would take pleasure trips on the lake itself, though for the most part their activities were confined to the shore or close to it and Peter knew the routes the commercial pleasure boats used. It was not as a hiding place that Peter and Wolfi relished the *Seawolf*. For the first time in a year they were simply having fun. They spent many hours on the water, tacking this way then that, always steering away from other boats. He even taught Wolfi to move from one side to the other when he tacked to change direction. Wolfi never quite understood why he had to move so frequently, he was just pleased with the praise each time he did. The tension and fear that had been so prevalent in many waking moments seemed to leave Peter just as soon as he launched the boat.

From time to time there would be a period of brief panic as the infrequent patrol boat came alongside. On these occasions Peter would simply salute and continue sailing. Fortunately, so far, no-one had bothered to question him. He was to their eyes simply a blonde-haired Aryan boy enjoying the water with his faithful dog.

Whilst sailing he would sometimes trail a fishing line behind the boat. He had already proved a successful angler from the shores of the lake. The moving vessel enabled him to catch a broader variety of fish. By fishing in this way, he no longer needed to restrict his hours as casual encounters with others were less likely.

His favourite trips were those that had no purpose to them. He was simply a youth living his childhood as best he could. The claustrophobia of the camp was for them both, a thing of the past. It was even better when there was a bit of bad weather so that often he felt as if they had the whole lake to themselves. On these bad weather trips Wolfi would lie in the shelter of the small cabin, while Peter manned the tiller.

In the early days of his sailing he stayed closer to the shoreline. He had previously sailed just once with his father and uncle when he was quite young. Luckily the design of this boat was so simple that he soon mastered the basics. With the knowledge that he was not heading out to sea, he rapidly became a competent mariner.

One day in early November, when winter had not properly arrived, Peter and Wolfi set off on another trip. Beforehand Peter had completed his 'housework' as he called it. He had cleaned off his cutlery and his pans and dishes. His many traps were set and his lines baited. Anything in his camp that would give away its location or purpose was hidden away. Now he was preparing for what he supposed may be one of his last sails that year, with bad weather approaching.

The winter of 1941 had been harsh yet bearable, unlike 1940. If those conditions arrived, life would be very tough. Winter 1940 had been the worst in Berlin for one hundred years. Lakes and canals had frozen, buses, trams and motorcars were stopped in their tracks. The city had come to a complete standstill, with coal and staples, such as potatoes in very short supply as transport routes had closed. In spite of the danger of frostbite, the authorities had decreed that domestic boilers were only to be lit at weekends, leading to a number of deaths. Some public buildings such as schools and hospitals had even been required to hand back some of their fuel.

'Let's hope we don't have another winter like that,' Peter hoped.

As possibly one of their last trips that year he wanted to travel further afield than ever. He headed north from Wannsee into Havelsee, passing as he did the field centre for the Hitler Youth at Gatow. He kept as far from the shore as possible because even now the memory of his night time raid made him nervous.

As he neared the centre of Berlin the sides of the lake became more and more built up. Swinging the rudder to one side and telling Wolfi to move, he hauled on the sail and having tacked successfully, the boat was soon speeding in the opposite direction.

As the wind hit his face and the waves lapped along the side of the vessel, his thoughts drifted onto the sombre subject of his parents. How his mother would have enjoyed today. His father would have come along to be sociable. One of the few clear memories of his first sailing adventure, when he was just five years old, was how keen Papa had been to return to dry land. And even more keen to find excuses if Peter ever asked about their next boat trip.

'Oh hell!' With the picture of his father clinging to the side of the boat still in his imagination, he had failed to notice the obstruction in the water ahead. The bow struck the unknown object and he fell to one side, jerking the tiller from his hand. As he hit the deck, Wolfi sprang to his feet and was sniffing to satisfy himself that everything was as it should be.

His instant fear was that he may have damaged the bow. He tied the tiller in position, loosened the sail, and fastening it around the mast, edged towards the front of the boat. As best as he could tell the bow of the boat appeared intact. Leaning over the side, he tried to see what had caused the collision.

A metal tail fin was just sticking out of the water by no more than thirty centimetres. Below the surface of the water he could see the black cross emblem of the Luftwaffe and a serial number.

'It's a plane!' Peter was unusually excited. He and Papa were very interested in aviation.

He moored the boat to the piece of the tail fin visible above the water and tried to get a closer look. It was a smaller aircraft, not a bomber, not a fighter either. It appeared similar to the aircraft he had seen on newsreels in the days when he could freely go to the cinema. It was the type of plane that high ranking officials or dignitaries, or even film stars were seen climbing from at private airstrips.

The main body of the craft was angled into the water at about forty five degrees with the metal fuselage still attached. The wings were missing with only short stubs of plywood covering indicating where they had once been.

Usually planes that crash landed into the lake were retrieved by the authorities, keen to reuse instruments and materials and repatriate the dead war heroes. Or if it was an enemy plane it might give them vital secrets for future use in the war. Wannsee, in particular, despite its size, was not especially deep, dropping down to about nine metres at the deepest point. As a result most crashed planes could be salvaged quite easily. The day after heavy aerial battles in the area Peter would avoid the lake for that very reason. The previous night had been very peaceful and so, he concluded, this plane must be from an earlier battle. For some reason it had been missed by the salvagers.

He stripped off his outer clothing. 'Stay there Wolfi,' he ordered, and dived into the clear water. It was cold and took his breath away.

By following the line of the fuselage he began to dive deeper into the lake. With each extra metre, the pressure on his ears intensified until he wondered whether he should give up his search. By pinching his nose and blowing gently the pressure was relieved. Once he had become accustomed to the extreme cold, he looked around for clues.

'Siebel FH104 *Hallore*,' he read. The name was in small lettering on the side of the fuselage. The last word was written in Gothic script. This was not a standard war plane. His first thoughts as to its usage were correct. He *had* seen this type of plane in a newsreel. In 1938 it had won a long-distance flying competition and in 1939 had flown 40,000 km around Africa. In spite of its heritage, few had been manufactured and so he surmised that this one had belonged to someone quite wealthy or important. He recalled how excited he and his father had been when they had heard of its achievements and had discussed the possibilities for future air travel. Now here it lay, broken and unwanted in Wannsee.

Peter came to the surface, his lungs screaming for air. He knew this type of plane was normally used to carry passengers. If that were the case he was anxious as to what he might find. The war had brought death to Berlin on an almost daily basis. The prospect of confronting it in the water was something he did not relish.

Bracing himself, he dived under the surface once more. Whatever his fears, he had to insure that there was nothing of practical use on board. Secretly he hoped he might find a radio set or a pair of binoculars. He was almost disappointed when he reached the cockpit. The single pilot's seat was empty.

'He must have bailed out,' he thought. There was no sign of any fire. He wondered whether he had been shot down or crashed for other reasons. Many planes crashed without help from the air defences.

Coming back up for air, he passed the mid-section where the five passengers would normally sit. Instead of two rows of seats there was a number of wooden crates, all stamped with a black swastika, about twenty centimetres tall. He broke the surface, took one more deep breath and descended again, the last thing he saw being Wolfi's large face, peering anxiously into the water.

The door to the rear of the aircraft was ajar, where the hinges had been damaged. The pressure of the water was such that Peter had great difficulty in opening it. The door finally moved to one side and he swam deftly through the opening. Tugging at one of the crates, he managed to dislodge it by a few centimetres. There were loops of string on each end and by pulling on one he managed to drag the crate through the open door and then followed as it bobbed to the surface. Treading water, he passed the string handle on one end through a mooring ring and fastened it with a knot. He hoisted himself onto the side of the boat in a continuous athletic movement, then exhausted, wriggled over the side and onto the deck where Wolfi greeted him with excited licks to the face. Peter quickly put on his vest for warmth and then, untying the knot, he hauled the crate into the boat.

'Let's see what we've got here,' he said aloud. Wolfi was sniffing the wooden box. With some difficulty Peter prised open the crate with his pen knife. There was straw inside. Rummaging around, his hand felt the familiar touch of cold glass.

'Cheers!' he shouted, as he pulled out a bottle of champagne and held it up for Wolfi to admire. He pulled out another, then yet another and another. There were six bottles in total in the crate. Wolfi was unimpressed.

Peter took off his damp vest, and slid from the side of the boat into the water. It felt much colder this time. Diving again and again, he retrieved another nine crates. There were at least another six crates and he was now completely exhausted, cold and hungry. This was a valuable cargo and if the pilot had survived he was bound to search for it. He could not stay here for too long.

In spite of this concern, he forced himself to dive just one last time. Wolfi looked somewhat uncertain as Peter rose out of the water wearing a life jacket and with a gas mask held aloft in his hand. With the life jacket he would resemble an amateur sailor even more; the gas mask would be the final touch in his Hitler Youth disguise. Peter was thrilled.

He stowed as many of the crates in the small cabin as possible and covered the rest with the original canvas sail he had taken off the rigging. He dressed without drying himself off, and only when he had put on his hat and gloves did any warmth flow back into his body. Without stopping or detouring he sailed back to his regular mooring on the side of the lake.

Instead of carrying his haul straight back to camp, Peter decided to open each crate. 'More champagne,' he said disappointed as he opened the first of the crates.

The next two crates were similarly disappointing. They contained cognac. He had sampled the odd glass of wine or champagne on special holidays, and like most children had wondered why adults were so keen on the taste. 'Ah well, we can always cook with it,' he thought.

The other crates were more interesting. In one there were small tins of something labelled 'caviar', forty all told. Peter had heard of it, though never tried it. He knew from the movies that it was something that was eaten with toast and champagne. Another crate had jars of preserved fruits in brandy and Armagnac. Gradually he began to fear that all the crates contained alcohol of some kind, or caviar. Then they struck gold.

'Look Wolfi, meat!' Peter held aloft tins of paté and cured meats. Wolfi barked. Most things he liked came from tins. Peter was pleased to find that there were another three crates that contained meats of some sort, either dried or tinned.

As he began prising open the last of the wooden boxes he tried guessing what this one might hold.

'Probably more wine,' he thought. As the last of the nails lifted out of the wood he looked inside hopefully. As with all the others there was a layer of straw on top. He pushed the straw to one side and felt around the box with his hands.

'Coffee! It's Coffee!' he shrieked. It had been many months since he had tasted even the horrendous ersatz coffee. 'And chocolates!' Wolfi looked at him, wondering what all the fuss was about.

It was not just slabs of ordinary chocolate. These were handmade chocolates from Bruges just like those Papa had brought back from a business trip. Eight boxes of chocolates and four large sacks of coffee beans.

He filled his rucksack with the most valuable of the commodities and took them back to camp. The remainder, the bottles of champagne, the cognac and most of the caviar he replaced in the boxes, and nailing down the lids, hid them near the boat. No chocolates or coffee were left behind. One of the bottles of champagne he suspended in the water from the side of the boat, something he had seen done in a film.

That evening they dined like kings. Instead of their usual diet of fish or meat stew, man and dog enjoyed several courses. The first course was the caviar. They had no toast to accompany it and as the tins seemed very small Peter had selected two. With a spoon he scooped out a generous portion and placed it in his mouth. The caviar burst on his tongue releasing an overwhelmingly salty flavour and not much else.

'Yuck!' The look on his face instantly told Wolfi that something was wrong. This was confirmed when Peter spat out the tiny black eggs. 'Disgusting!' he exclaimed, looking at the tin for signs that it had been damaged. 'Perhaps it needs the champagne and toast, Wolfi,' he joked.

For once Wolfi was oblivious to Peter. He had gobbled down the caviar on the ground and was leaning over with his tongue licking out the small tin.

'Well, well. At least one of us likes it.' Peter took the tin away from Wolfi and scraped the remainder of the contents into his bowl. Within seconds it had disappeared and Wolfi sat down, eyeing up the other tin.

'Okay, okay!' Peter proceeded to open the second tin. That disappeared more rapidly than the first.

The second course was savoured by both Wolfi and Peter, consisting of a tin of compressed meat with a wild berry jam. This was followed by some apricots in brandy. The final course comprised four of the delicious chocolates accompanied by fresh coffee. The simple task of grinding the beans on a stone and then brewing the coffee in his homemade percolator, brought immense pleasure. It was not that he had drunk much coffee in the past. It was the association with his family, particularly Papa who had often declared that 'dinner without good coffee is a meal not a feast.'

'Mama and Papa,' he toasted, as he drained the last mouthful of coffee from his cup and washed it down with a swig of the cognac as he had so often seen his father do.

The following day Peter returned to the wreck of the Siebel aircraft, this time early in the morning. He had worn his Hitler Youth outfit, just in case he was disturbed. He was not, and after twenty minutes of diving he had retrieved another four cases. Two he had been unable to budge as they were wedged in a damaged part of the plane. He resolved to try one last time.

'Last two cases Wolfi,' Peter cried and dived into the icy cold water. His eyes were now accustomed to the light under the water and he soon found his way to the rear of the cockpit. He tugged as hard as he could on the rope handles. They did not budge. A combination of tiredness and cold had weakened him.

'Better leave it,' he thought and started the swim to the surface. He was now almost completely out of breath as a result of his exertions. He pulled himself through the open door of the cockpit, kicking his legs at the same time. He was half way through the opening when he could move no more.

'I'm stuck! I'm stuck!' Panic began to take hold. He knew he could not hold his breath much longer. He wriggled as hard as he could, aware of Wolfi staring into the water above him.

Desperately he reached behind to find the cause of his distress. His underpants were snagged on the door handle. A few more seconds passed and his wriggling ceased. His eyes began to close. His mouthful of air had gone and he knew he could not keep his lips closed any longer as the instinct to breathe would overcome him. His mind returned to the terrible day when he had almost drowned rescuing Wolfi from the River Spree. The traitorous Captain's face appeared and seemed to be laughing at him until the even more terrible vision of his parents swept the image away.

Though terrible, the sight of his parents was somehow comforting and he held on to the image as a permanent sleep began to overwhelm him.

`Uhhh!' he groaned, exhaling the last remnants of air from his lungs, as suddenly he lurched forward. He was freed! He shot out of the water, gasping for breath. His underpants were half-ripped and still on the door handle. Wolfi paced up and down the boat whining. Peter hung onto the side of the boat for several minutes. His breathing was heavy and noisy. He was glad to be alive, even if cold and naked.

Back at his mooring point he forced open the crates, one after the other. The day had not been completely wasted for, apart from the disappointment of two cases containing more cognac and champagne, the remaining two had a mixture of the finest sugar, flour, herbs, spices, condiments and dried pasta. The pasta was particularly welcome as for the last few months they had survived on fish, meat and fruit. The straw from the crates was not wasted as he used it to stuff a pillow for himself and a bed for Wolfi. The wooden crates were used either for storage or fashioned into a small table. Some were broken up for kindling. The string handles he tied together into a small net. The collection of tins he had accumulated were used as additional pots, or tied to a string and stretched across the front of the camp as an intruder alarm.

As he sat in his hideaway that evening, the moon illuminating the clearing and reflecting in Wolfi's blue-grey eyes, Peter reviewed his current situation. It was the 4th November 1942. That day he had almost drowned. On the other hand his countryside larder was bulging with a variety of delicious foods, both those he had salvaged and those he had foraged. There was enough caviar to feed Wolfi for a month. Their den was warm and dry and well-hidden. They had a boat to sail and fish from and as yet the winter was still fairly mild. With any luck the war would be over in the New Year and he could begin the hunt for his parents and go home.

That night he had eaten his best meal for many weeks. He had allowed himself an extra portion of meat and double the quantity of coffee and chocolates.

'Happy Birthday to me Wolfi,' he said, raising his cup. As a final celebration of his sixteenth birthday, he popped the cork on a bottle of champagne and drank it straight from the neck of the bottle. It was better than the cognac, but he still preferred coffee.

Having emptied the bottle, he crawled into his bed, his movement a little clumsier and uncertain than normal. He pulled the covers over him. Wolfi lumbered slowly alongside and flopped to the ground in his special place, next to Peter's head. Within minutes both were snoring contentedly

# CHAPTER EIGHT

After the initial euphoria of his discovery in the water, and having experienced his first hangover, Peter made two resolutions: he would not drink alcohol and he would ration the supplies. The non-perishable items he stored separately for when the climate worsened. Rather than depend on the meat and fish he had preserved, he went hunting as usual. Only in the event of returning empty handed did he turn to his larder. As the winter deepened, this became a more and more frequent occurrence.

It was mid-December. Peter and Wolfi had gone foraging as had become their routine. They checked all their snares and traps and then the fishing lines dangling in the water. Often there was ice on the edges of the lake and no matter how much Peter longed to take out his boat, he resisted the temptation. He did not want to attract attention, a situation that was inevitable if he was the only one on the water. To his dismay, as he pulled each of his fishing lines out of the water, it was the same story as had greeted him with the traps. Nothing! At best his larder would last him three months, and then only if he carefully restricted what they ate. He was already worried. In spite of the relative boon in recent weeks, Wolfi looked thinner.

He dropped the last of his fishing lines in the water

and trudged back along the bank to the den. Wolfi, sensing his dejection, picked up a stick which he hurled to one side with a swing of his head. Peter took the hint and began a tug of war with his dog.

Still wrestling Wolfi for the stick, he walked to the entrance of the tunnel he had carved in the trees so long ago. Suddenly Wolfi dropped the stick and bounded ahead into the centre of the camp.

'Wolfi! Wolfi stay!' It was no use. His dog was already out of sight. For once he had ignored Peter's instruction.

Peter crawled along behind as fast as he could. He was still midway along the tunnel when he heard Wolfi's fierce bark followed by a long, low growl. Whatever it was he had no choice but to follow. He could not desert Wolfi. Terrified at what he might find, he rushed from the end of the tunnel to be greeted by the vision of Wolfi crouched in the attack position, intermittently barking and growling.

'Oh please! Please!' A boy, little more than twelve or thirteen was shuddering with fear and retreating from the angry dog. His hands were raised in front of his face as he repeated the same words again and again.

He seemed to be dressed in striped pyjama bottoms with an overcoat over his top half, many sizes too big. On his head was a thin, round cloth cap, also striped. His feet were wrapped in nothing more than sack cloth. He had not even noticed Peter, he was watching Wolfi so intently. Each time the dog moved or barked, the young boy recoiled in absolute terror.

'Down Wolfi! Down!' Peter commanded. Wolfi immediately obeyed, sitting back on his hind quarters, never removing his eyes from the boy. Peter walked across to his dog and, as a measure of reassurance for the boy, clipped Wolfi's collar onto the lead.

Any anger Peter initially felt at the intrusion dissolved almost instantly. The boy was still shivering from cold and fear. He looked about twelve, yet he was so incredibly thin with sunken cheeks and the outline of his jaw protruding, it was hard to say. Under the cap Peter could see that his hair was shaved off.

'Who are you? What do you want?' Peter asked.

He instantly regretted adding the second part of the question. It was obvious what he wanted and what he needed. He was starving and very cold. Without waiting for a reply, Peter lifted the cover to his underground hideaway and taking his only spare coat, gave it to the boy. The boy hesitated, still staring at Wolfi, rather than Peter.

'Don't be scared,' Peter said. 'He won't bite, honestly. He is a friendly dog. He was only protecting our home.' Slowly the boy reached out and took the coat from Peter and, slipping his arms into the sleeves, placed it over the clothes he was wearing.

'You must be hungry,' Peter said by means of encouragement. At the word 'hungry' the boy's eyes left Wolfi for the first time. Peter went to his larder in the ground and removed a piece of dried meat. With his pocket knife he cut off a thin slice and handed it to the boy. The boy snatched at it greedily and within seconds it had gone. Peter cut another slice, thicker this time. This was dispatched with the same speed. He handed the remainder of the meat to the boy.

'Thank you,' the boy said and this time ate the meat more slowly.

'So you speak German,' Peter said, 'but are you German?' Since the outbreak of war there were thousands of foreigners in forced labour in Berlin.

'Yes,' came the reply, 'I am German. I come from Berlin.'

'Are you a Jew?' Peter asked, wondering at how such a question would have been irrelevant before the war.

'No,' the boy replied. 'I am an enemy of the state.'

Peter almost laughed. The look on the young boy's face told him he was serious. With some encouragement the boy sat in Peter's hideaway, even allowing Wolfi to sit next to him. Peter would normally avoid lighting fires in the middle of the day. On this occasion he knew that he had to feed his visitor with something warm. With a mixture of some of his smoked rabbit and apples in brandy he prepared a stew. He even added an extra cupful of cognac. As each ingredient was added, the boy gave an approving look.

They ate in silence, the boy so rapidly, he hardly seemed to breathe between mouthfuls. In spite of giving him the largest portion of the stew, it was clear that the boy was still hungry. Peter took out the last box of chocolates and offered them to the boy. The look of delight on his face softened any doubts that Peter had. He removed one and popped it in his mouth motioning to the boy to do the same. Once the chocolate had dissolved on his tongue, Peter offered him another. He took it once more saying 'thank you' as he did.

'It looks like you'll have to stay here for a while,' Peter

was saying, as he placed the box of chocolates back in its hiding place. 'What did you say your name was?'

He turned to face both Wolfi and the boy. The boy was lying on his back, asleep. Peter lifted the blanket to cover him. Taking his arm and slipping it under the blanket, he noticed a red cloth triangle sewn onto his jacket and on the other side a six digit serial number.

'I wonder what that is?' Peter thought. He pulled his coat tighter around the neck and lay down next to the boy, with Wolfi squashed between them.

The next morning Peter was awakened by the break of dawn. Next to him Wolfi was asleep. The boy was not there.

'He's gone!' Peter said to himself. Hurriedly he checked his provisions. Everything was as he had left it. He felt a moment's shame for his unfounded suspicions. He walked from under the tree branches into the small clearing, where the boy stood looking at the sun.

'The sun never seemed to shine in the camp,' the boy said.

'What camp? You mean a camp like this?'

'No,' the boy said sadly.

Peter said no more and proceeded to make breakfast, feeding the young guest more than he would ordinarily consume in a day. After they had eaten and were enjoying a cup of coffee, he tried to encourage him to tell his story.

At first the boy was reluctant. Peter tried to wean information from him, bit by bit. Noticing that the boy still followed Wolfi's every move, Peter asked 'Why are you so afraid of Wolfi? Have you been bitten in the past?'

The boy simply shook his head. After a pause he said, 'They use dogs like him in the camp. They make them attack people for fun or when they do not work hard enough.'

On hearing this Peter persuaded the boy to stroke Wolfi's ears.

Next he made his dog sit and then roll over dead as he had been taught. For his encore he rolled onto his back waiting for his tummy to be tickled. Clearly reassured, the boy began to tell his story.

Peter listened intently, scarcely believing what he was hearing. As each new horror was revealed, he fought back the tears, wondering if this was what Mama and Papa were suffering.

'My name is Franz. I am fifteen years old. My father was an industrialist and a politician. He was very wealthy. When the Nazis seized power in 1933 he opposed them. He refused to allow his factory to be used for their 'evil' purposes as he described it. For years he fought with the authorities, always managing to politely yet firmly decline their demands. One evening the police came and arrested him for 'undermining the resistance of the people'. He was taken to Prinz Albrecht Strasse, the Gestapo headquarters and kept in 'protective custody'. My mother went to the station every day for a month, with an expensive lawyer. Each time they were told only that they were continuing their enquiries.

'On one particular day my mother attended as usual and was told he was no longer there. They would not tell her where he was. After bribing one of the policeman the equivalent of three months wages, she found out that he

111

had been taken to a camp in Oranienburg, north of Berlin, called 'Sachsenhausen'. Nothing that the police did dissuaded my mother from seeking his release and undeterred she had gone to Sachsenhausen. She took me with her.

'Yet again it was the same story. At the gates of the camp we were politely refused entry. The guards told us they would find out what they could. 'Come back tomorrow,' they said. The next day we arrived at the front gates and were met with the same response. Each day for several weeks we went to the front gates and each time we were sent away with no news. The guards became increasingly hostile in their attitude, demanding bribes in return for information. Determined to see my father, she just ignored their insults and paid the bribes.

'After about three weeks of the same wearying routine, we finally met with a different response. A senior SS officer came to the front gates and looked us up and down. He asked my father's name. Mother repeated it again. She could not hide the irritation in her voice. He asked her if we really wanted to come in and see him. She replied, 'Of course, why did he think we were there?' The guards on the gate smiled. They opened the gates and let us inside.

It was horrible. The people were like skeletons, men, women and children. We were taken to a wooden barrack where we were introduced to a jaundiced looking man in what we thought were pyjamas. His head was shaved. It was my father we had failed to recognise. In the few months of his incarceration he had already lost a lot of weight.'

At this point in his tale Franz had tears welling in his eyes, but stubbornly refused to cry. He continued his narration. Peter blocked as many of the details from his mind as thoughts that he simply could not bear.

'We were allowed just fifteen minutes together, until he was taken away. When we got up to leave the SS officer stood in our way, asking where we were going. We had wanted to come inside, now we had to stay, he said. My mother was taken away shouting her protests all the time. I never saw her again. I was deloused and forced to wear this striped outfit, the one I am still wearing. At least I got to share a hut with my father.'

Franz went on to tell of the hard labour he endured, the cruelty of the guards and the starvation rations, mainly consisting of turnip soup and mouldy potatoes. If they were too slow in their work they were whipped or beaten with rifles. Sometimes an inmate was shot 'as an example'.

'On one work detail outside the camp,' he continued, 'two of the guards had gone off into the woods, leaving just one guard behind. Whilst they were gone my father whispered to me to sneak away and escape. I did not want to. I did not want to leave my father. I knew that the whole work party would be punished. But as a dutiful son I could not ignore the pleading in my father's eyes and reluctantly I obeyed. The last words I heard father speak were to tell me that I should go to the Weiss family, to Uncle Willy and Aunt Berta. They would look after me.'

Franz paused. He stared at the ground for several minutes then continued. 'I have been on the run for days, scavenging whatever food I can find. I hid on a freight train and arrived in the outskirts of Berlin. I was making my way to the Weiss family, though I do not know exactly where they live. Yesterday I ducked into the bushes to avoid some pedestrians and I found this camp.'

That was his story. There were some details missing, such as the significance of the red triangle and serial number on his jacket. Franz would tell him when he was ready. He put his arm around his guest and neither moved for a number of minutes.

'We can look after each other and Wolfi can look after both of us,' Peter said.

'I would like that,' Franz said smiling. Reaching out his hand he stroked Wolfi's ears. Wolfi barked his agreement.

Franz's story had taken several hours to tell and by now all three were hungry again. Normally Peter and Wolfi would have little for lunch, usually surviving on breakfast and a larger dinner. Franz's tale of deprivation and hardship was still very much in his mind and Peter determined that here, at least for the next few weeks, he would not go hungry. Fifteen years old, Franz's size and weight suggested he was much younger. Peter prepared a luxurious feast of meat and preserves followed by hot coffee for Franz and himself. Wolfi was to enjoy his now regular treat of caviar, supplemented with preserved offal. As Peter began opening the tin, Franz's eyes bulged in wonderment.

'You know caviar?' Peter asked.

'Of course, of course,' Franz confirmed enthusiastically. 'My father served it to important guests at many banquets.'

'And you actually like it?' Peter said, questioning the sanity of his visitor.

'Oh yes. I love it. But it is so expensive I was seldom allowed any. Only on special occasions.'

Until this moment Peter had simply regarded these fishy eggs as a bizarre foreign food that came in impractically small tins. How expensive could it be? Franz, guessing what was in Peter's thoughts, leaned over and whispered in his ear.

'How much?' Peter shrieked. 'Wolfi is the most valuable dog in all Germany!'

For the first time in over a year, Peter and Franz laughed, really laughed. Wolfi stared at them both. He was still waiting for his lunch.

Once they had regained their composure, Franz explained that whilst thin toast was important, champagne was the essential companion to caviar. In honour of his guest, Peter chilled a bottle of champagne and a tin of caviar to sample that evening. When the moment came he watched as Franz closed his eyes and spooned an indecent amount of the fish eggs into his mouth, followed closely by a swig of the champagne. Franz licked his lips in rapture. With this encouragement Peter followed suit. To Wolfi's approval he spat the lot out.

Once more, in the space of one day, both boys laughed and laughed until their sides hurt. Any concerns Peter harboured about this unexpected extra mouth to feed were now long forgotten. Even though he had used almost three days' rations in just one day, he and Wolfi had something much more precious: a new friend.

That first full day Franz spent with Peter and Wolfi had been occupied with Franz's tale and caviar sampling in the evening. In the hours between, Peter had recounted his own story and his adventures since separation from his mother and father. Not wishing to embarrass himself in front of the younger boy, Peter struggled not to cry. Luckily, each time he felt that he was about to give in and weep, Franz appeared to look away, allowing him to gather his thoughts. Whenever Wolfi's heroic deeds were mentioned, Franz looked in amazement at him and then patted Wolfi approvingly, saying 'You are not like the dogs in the camp.' When Peter had finished and was silent again, Franz simply put his hand on Peter's, saying nothing.

After this moment of silence, Peter showed Franz the layout of his camp and the supplies that he had gathered. He told him the geography of their location and a few basic rules to ensure their safety. At the end of the friendly lecture, Peter removed his prized uniform from its hiding place. In spite having heard about it when Peter recounted his night time raid to the Hitler Youth centre, Franz was nonetheless stunned when he actually saw it. It was the genuine article and awe inspiring.

On seeing Franz's reaction, Peter gestured to him to follow and taking him to the edge of the lake, he proudly showed him the *Seawolf*. Any doubts that Franz still retained, disappeared in an instant.

'So it's all true!' Franz said. He was impressed. 'The night time visits to the bomb site, the spying over the wall at the villa, the aircraft with its sunken treasure. So many adventures Peter!'

Franz had heeded his father's parting words and he would obey them, eventually. For the moment he was not only content, he was positively enthusiastic to stay with Peter and Wolfi.

# CHAPTER NINE

Within days of their first meeting the two boys had become close friends, united by their past suffering and common struggle. Franz's initial fear of Wolfi had completely vanished. In the short time they had been together, he had become as fond of Wolfi, as Wolfi was of him. Indeed, when Franz thought Peter was not looking, he would often slip a morsel of his own share of food to Wolfi. Peter simply pretended not to notice.

Even though their provisions were now required to feed an extra mouth, neither Peter nor Wolfi bore any resentment. In little time at all, even though the rations were meagre, Franz started to regain some weight, so that his face was less sallow and his eyes less sunken in appearance. The times Peter would see Franz staring into space with a deep sadness in his eyes became thankfully less frequent.

Franz was not as skilled in trapping or cooking as Peter. It turned out he was a talented artist and wood carver. Borrowing Peter's knife one day, he took a section of wood from an empty crate. It was about fifty centimetres long and fifteen centimetres wide. For two ~urs he hid from Peter's gaze, whittling and carving the ᴿy the time he had finished he had carved ~erfect Gothic writing. After a further two hours he had cut each of the letters from the original piece of wood, so that they were now individual characters. Charred in the fire, they turned black and would be perfectly visible when affixed to the side of the boat.

On another day, when the weather was too poor to venture out, Franz carved a wooden spoon with a fork and knife to match. This was appreciated by both, as hitherto one had eaten with a spoon and the other a fork. Peter did not assist in any way at Franz's request, he simply marvelled at the skill involved.

Of even greater use was the simple wooden trap that Franz fashioned from a crate, with some guidance from Peter. Peter's own rope or wire snares were quite efficient except often the quarry could struggle free. Either that or they had been taken by someone else, something he had grown more concerned about lately. This latest invention, when properly sprung, would prevent escape. In return, he taught Franz the essential skill of how to start a fire with a lighter flint, dried moss and sedges. Franz was intelligent and a quick learner. His contribution was immense and greatly appreciated.

When Christmas Eve arrived they celebrated as if they had not a care in the world. Jew, gentile and canine shared a sumptuous meal and afterwards, to each other's surprise, they exchanged gifts. Peter's present from Franz was a walking stick carved from a hazel branch. On the top the handle was shaped to resemble a wolf or as Peter soon realised, Wolfi! There was even a leather strap to loop it over his hand. Nor did Franz forget Wolfi. His present was his own wooden bowl to drink from.

Peter was a little embarrassed when he handed over his Christmas offering. It was a tin of the caviar and a bottle of champagne. Franz was delighted. Just a few months ago he could not have imagined dining so well and with such excellent company. He only wished his parents could have shared the evening with him. Thanking Peter and Wolfi profusely, for in reality the sacrifice was Wolfi's, he went to bed that evening happier than he had felt in a long while.

As the days became weeks, the nights became shorter and colder. Their success rate in hunting and fishing had dropped completely. Apart from a decent supply of coffee beans, champagne and cognac, there was little to eat. Peter had insisted on only turning to their larder when the hunt had been unsuccessful. This strategy had stretched their stocks for much longer than he ever thought possible, but now things had reached rock bottom. It was six weeks since Franz had first arrived in the Wolf's Lair.

In that time Peter had not ventured into the city to scavenge bomb sites. It had not really been necessary. One of the attractions had been the chance to mingle with others, not necessarily speaking to anyone, enjoying the knowledge that he and Wolfi were not alone. Franz had satisfied this craving for human companionship. The knowledge of how Franz and his family had been treated, even as non-Jews, brought home the fear that he had previously managed to suppress.

Reluctantly and with some foreboding, Peter began to don his uniform. He struggled to button the shirt and the shorts were even worse. In spite of his sparse diet he had grown from a boy into a young man and the clothes no longer fitted. He had been aware of this problem more and more in recent weeks, as the boots he wore were much too tight and walking was becoming increasingly painful. He must find new boots soon. But how could he acquire them without the disguise?

Franz had watched as Peter had tried each piece of clothing and quickly guessed the truth. 'I can look for food. Let me wear it,' he begged.

'No,' came the single word answer, more harshly than intended. Peter would not enter into further discussion. It was not that he lacked faith in Franz, he simply could not bear the idea that anything should happen to him.

Instead they checked the traps once more and hauled out the fishing lines from the icy water. Nothing. That evening Peter made a thin soup of water and some of the sedges he hoped were edible, along with the few dried fungi that were in the larder. The resulting mixture was barely drinkable, though neither wished to show the other their disappointment. Wolfi was scarcely any more fortunate, only having a half-gnawed bone to chew on.

The next day Peter decided that regardless of the hazards, they would have to launch the boat. At least it would distract them from their hunger. There was a slight breeze, just about enough to sail. Franz was visibly excited at the prospect of their first excursion, hardly listening to Peter's safety advice. With Franz in the only life jacket and Wolfi between them, they cast off.

It was a pleasant enough trip. As expected at this time of year and in this bitter weather there was no-one else on their part of the lake. Trailing a line of hooks with feathers knotted together as bait, they sailed the lake for almost an hour. By now they were both turning blue with cold. They had caught nothing. At least it had been a break from the camp.

Back in their den, the two boys sat pensively. To keep the cold at bay they had opened a bottle of cognac. At first the smell and taste were off-putting, although the warming sensation in their throats and chest made the effort worthwhile. After a long period of silence Franz said: 'It is because of me that you two are starving. It is time for me to go.'

'I will not allow that,' Peter said.

'I must obey what my father said,' Franz replied firmly.

'You don't even know where they live, this Weiss family.' Peter was adamant.

'Then let me go into the city to scavenge. I can wear the uniform,' Franz begged once more. The dialogue between the two boys went back and forward in this manner, until Peter gave in and agreed that Franz should go into the city.

'Only if I go with you,' Peter said. Franz knew from his tone that any further debate was useless.

And so that night the two boys, accompanied by Wolfi, crossed the woods and entered the blacked out city. They could have left Wolfi behind. Their attachment to him and his attachment to them was so strong, that neither wished to contemplate it. For two hours they nervously moved in convoy around the city, looking for suitable targets. As usual the threat of collision with others was always present. They found a row of bombed out houses with the stark warning sign *'looters will be shot'*. They spent an hour looking through the rubble with no success. It had already been picked over many times. Two other sites produced similar results. One yielded a tablecloth, but nothing to eat.

'At least we can dine in style,' Peter joked, trying to hide his increasing concern. It was now the middle of the night and the three were tired and hungry, and a little discouraged. 'It's no use. Let's go home,' Peter said.

They had been looking for almost three hours. Since the first RAF 'terror' attacks in the early part of the war, Berlin in 1942 had been largely ignored and as a result there were fewer bomb sites. The Allies had been concentrating on the Battle of the Atlantic. In recent months enemy planes were more likely to drop propaganda leaflets than explosives.

'Just one more site, then we can go home,' Franz replied.

They were desperate. They walked along the darkened streets, one behind the other, and as far away from the pavement edge as possible. From previous experience, Peter had discovered that this was the best means to avoid accidents or unwanted lights being shone in their faces.

They had decided that they would not travel beyond Schöneberg, a small district directly adjoining Tiergarten, the area near the centre of the city, with Berlin Zoo at its heart. They had reached the point at which they had previously agreed to turn back when Wolfi stopped in his tracks and began to nudge Peter's side. The dog was trembling.

'What is it, boy? What is wrong?' he asked, stroking Wolfi's ears.

The wailing of the air raid siren disturbed Wolfi even more. It was a noise that had not been heard for many months. Within minutes the low rumble of the bombers could be heard. And then the dreadful whining as their payloads descended to earth, preceded by parachute flares to light the way, followed by the awful explosions. Tracer fire from the anti-aircraft battery lit up the sky closely pursued by the rat-a-tat-tat as real bullets sought their aerial targets and sixteen pound shells were thrust into the heavens. Soon the large metal shards of flak would fall back to earth, posing as much danger as the bombs themselves.

'We have got to find cover,' Peter shouted to Franz.

They were in an exposed area of the city with few residential buildings. Peter was in a quandary. They could not hang around as the danger from the bombs and flak was too great. They dare not risk using a public shelter as neither of them had identification and Peter was by now almost crippled in the boots that had seemed to shrink around his toes. His overall appearance might raise a few eyebrows. Above all, with shelters being so crowded already, it was uncertain whether Wolfi would be allowed in. Neither Peter nor Franz would leave him outside. Wolfi had grown more used to the terror of the air raids, but even in the security of their den, he was always unsettled. They could not stay where they were.

In the panic of the moment any caution was put to one side. It was the middle of the night and it was unlikely that many people would be out and about, however that could soon change as public shelters filled. The illuminated sky provided some light by which they could navigate.

'Over there!' Peter shouted, struggling to be heard above the noise of the air raid. He was pointing at a half-demolished building surrounded by a high wooden fence. A poster pasted on the outside indicated that this was not the work of the RAF, rather it was another of Hitler's grand designs for the capital of the Reich. Inspired by Hitler's favourite architect, Albert Speer, many buildings were being laid low to make way for huge boulevards and new public buildings on a scale never seen. It was Hitler's vision of 'Germania', a city that would outshine Paris or Rome. Before taking flight with his parents, Peter had admired the ambition in the plan. With Berlin crumbling under Allied bombardments, further demolition seemed a little crazy.

Peter grabbed the top of a fence plank and pulled as hard as he could. It did not budge. Taking the other side of the plank, Franz wrestled to free the nails and gradually, first the top half and then the bottom of the plank came away. They repeated this with two further planks until there was a space large enough for all three to squeeze through.

Franz had not stopped to question Peter as to why they were entering a building site. Soon it became clear. This building, like virtually all in Berlin, had a cellar. As this was a building demolished by man rather than by a bomb, the cellar was still intact.

'From the air the bomber pilots will assume it has already been hit and ignore it as a target,' Peter explained.

A short while later, Peter, Franz and Wolfi were squashed together in the basement. With each explosion, Wolfi crept closer to Peter. After an hour the noise grew more distant. The all clear had not been sounded. They could not wait any longer. It was close to dawn and the site would soon be busy with construction workers.

'We'll have to go if we want to get back to the camp in darkness,' said Peter. He led the way out of the basement and back towards the fence. Wolfi was a little way behind with Franz, both struggling over rough bricks and debris. As Peter approached the gap in the fence he heard a clicking noise.

'Halt! You are under arrest!' Behind him and to one side, was standing a policeman and a soldier. Not a Gestapo officer, a regular policeman from the 'Kripo', or Criminal Police. The soldier was pointing his rifle at him. The noise Peter had heard was a rifle bolt being pulled back. He was so hungry and tired he had failed to connect the sound with any danger.

'Down Wolfi! Down!' Franz spoke under his breath, ducking and pulling Wolfi to the ground at the same time. In the darkness the men had failed to see Franz and Wolfi in the background. Fortunately Franz had recognised the sound.

'You are under arrest on suspicion of looting. Hand over your bag! At once!' the policeman ordered. Peter passed the loop of the satchel strap over his head and handed the satchel to the policeman. Opening the buckle, the policeman searched inside and with a satisfied grin and a dramatic flourish, held a tablecloth aloft. Peter had forgotten about it. Franz groaned. Useful as it might be, it was not worth being shot for.

'You know the penalty for looting. Dr. Freisler and his colleagues at the People's Court have given us authority to carry out that penalty. You will now be shot.'

Franz was torn. He could try and overwhelm them, but with what? He could bluff it out claiming Peter was his prisoner, although why should they believe that? He had no weapon and Peter was obviously stronger than him.

'What shall I do?' he murmured. Frightened and hesitant, Franz watched as the two men frog-marched Peter towards the perimeter fence. Peter was placed against the fence and the two men moved back a distance of twenty paces. The soldier raised his rifle and took aim.

Franz stood up. He was holding Wolfi back by his lead.

'Boom!'

Just as Franz was about to cry out, a thunderous bang reverberated around the building site, knocking him to the ground. It was not the sound of a gunshot, it was much louder. It was a bomb! In the excitement and noise, none of them had noticed the stray plane overhead jettisoning the last of its deadly cargo. Franz stood up. He could see the policeman and the soldier prostrate on the ground, still moving. Wolfi struggled to free himself from Franz's grip, and having wriggled loose, was sprinting towards the hole in the fence. As he leapt through, Franz could just make out something ahead of Wolfi.

'It's Peter! He's got away!' It was the back of Peter's head he could see. About thirty seconds later he was being pursued by the two men.

While Franz was watching Peter and Wolfi disappear from view, chased by the soldier and the policeman, Peter was sprinting as fast as he could. He was encouraged by Wolfi at his side, although by now his feet were almost bleeding. In spite of the agonising pain in his feet, fear and youth carried him a long way from his pursuers. He ran for almost twenty minutes. Stopping to catch his breath, he looked around him.

'I hope Franz will be okay,' he thought. He felt a pang of guilt that he had left Franz behind, even though there was nothing he could do just then. Dejected and with sore feet he decided it was time to return home. Limping badly, he started on the long journey back to Grünewald.

Meanwhile, Franz had sneaked out through the hole in the fence and was searching for signs of Peter. Ten minutes later he decided that it was hopeless and began his long hike back to the camp. The journey was agonisingly slow as Franz feared the worst. He knew Peter was suffering with tight boots and both were very hungry. How could he possibly outrun the well-nourished men, especially if they were shooting at him?

Some hours later Franz was at the entrance to the camp, where he hesitated. He wanted to know if Peter and Wolfi were safe, though he dreaded what he might find.

Crawling on his hands and knees he approached with heavy heart. Hunger and starvation were dreadful. To be left alone after all this time would be unbearable.

He was within a few metres of the clearing when suddenly he was knocked onto his front by a weight on his back. All he could feel was Wolfi's rough tongue licking excitedly at his face as the large dog pinned him to the ground.

'What kept you?' Peter laughed, his concern still noticeable.

'Peter! Peter!' Franz replied, overwhelmed by relief.

When the fuss died down and Wolfi had finally released Franz, each boy apologised repeatedly for abandoning the other. In the end they agreed that neither was to blame, and satisfied, but hungry, they crawled into bed.

When Peter awoke the next morning he was cold and hungry and concerned for the future. His sleep had been broken by the dreams of the past and images of what might become of them. It was just after dawn and Franz was already brewing coffee, fortified with brandy. Peter rubbed his eyes and stared.

'It's a good fit, isn't it?' Franz said. He was in Peter's old Hitler Youth uniform. It fitted almost perfectly. He passed Peter some coffee and began to outline his plan.

'I don't know the address of the Weiss family. I have been there when I was much younger. I am sure I could recognise it again.'

'So how will you find out where they live?' Peter wondered, unconvinced.

'He is an aristocrat of some sort and is listed in some book or other. It lists all the most important men in Germany. In this uniform I can gain access to a library where I can look for the address.'

Peter leaned back and thought about the idea. The Nazis certainly did not expect fugitives to attend libraries. That part of the plan should be fairly safe. The greater risk was getting to the library.

'Even with the address, why are you so certain that this family will help even if they can?' Peter's query was quite reasonable. Franz was confident.

'Herr Weiss was in my father's regiment in 1914. He was his commanding officer. My father saved his life and was decorated as a result. After the war Herr Weiss supported my father financially to enable his business to get off the ground. When it became very successful, netting him millions, Herr Weiss became a director. The two men were business partners and closer than anyone could have imagined possible. I even called his wife 'Aunt Berta'. They are good people. They owe a lot to my father. They will help us.'

'They may help you Franz. What about a Jew? And his dog?'

'They will help both of us and Wolfi,' Franz replied. 'I promise you.' Peter hesitatingly agreed. There really was little alternative.

The first stage of the plan went very smoothly. As with Peter, no-one suspected a young member of the Hitler Youth riding a bicycle. His greatest fear was a daytime air raid. The RAF bombed at night time, the American air force during the day. He had no desire to be ushered into a shelter by a warden with the possibility of being trapped there for hours and with Peter fearing the worst.

Thankfully the skies remained clear and without hitch he arrived at his destination. At the library he had been shown to the reference section and quickly found the address he needed, which he then memorised. It was in the district of Charlottenburg, closer to the city centre and only two districts north of their camp. It was still quite a way on foot, though at least it was not in one of the districts far to the north or east. He had returned as fast as possible stopping only to listen to a public broadcast from loudspeakers on the outside of a row of shops. The broadcast told him nothing new. It repeated the propaganda of how the war would soon be won, how many British and American planes had been shot down. It finished with the rousing message often displayed in placards that 'no-one shall hunger; no-one shall freeze'.

'If only!' Franz remarked, more loudly than was wise.

Back at camp Peter and Franz sat down with Wolfi to talk through the next step. Peter was about to start speaking when Franz reached inside the satchel and took out a loaf of rye bread and a small salami.

'But, but how?' Peter stammered.

'I bartered a bottle of cognac on the black market,' Franz said with a grin.

Peter's initial anger subsided as he savoured the meat and bread. The black market was highly illegal and carried severe penalties for those who were caught.

'I told the man who gave me this that my father was an alcoholic and my mother had sent me out to sell his last bottle of cognac,' Franz explained proudly.

'Thank you. Never again Franz. It is too dangerous.'

As he said this, as earnestly as he could, a cheeky grin appeared on Franz's face. 'So I better take these back!' Franz pulled a pair of black lace up boots from the satchel, like a conjuror pulling a rabbit from a hat.

'How on earth?'

'Best not to know,' Franz said, tapping his nose conspiratorially as he spoke.

For Peter the new boots were more welcome than the bread and meat. His feet had become so cramped that he could barely walk without stooping or limping. As the aim of his disguise was to avoid attention, that could prove fatal. They were a little too big, which was heavenly compared to his old pair, and he had not yet stopped growing.

They made the bread and meat last for another day until once more they faced the age-old dilemma. So far Franz's plan had worked. Peter still retained his nagging doubts.

'You go alone Franz,' Peter suggested. 'If everything works out you can come and get me.'

'I am not going to leave you on your own,' Franz replied. 'It will work out, I am sure of it.'

Eventually Franz's warm and enthused description of Aunt Berta and Uncle Willy persuaded Peter that they would help them both. It was time to leave their camp. They had no choice.

The next day Peter secured the *Seawolf*, hiding it in the usual spot with extra foliage to cover it. As he touched the boat with his hand he recalled the many happy trips it had afforded him. He sincerely hoped he would be able to make use of it again.

Back at their camp, the two boys set to work hiding any signs of its existence. The old crates were stowed in the underground larder, along with the empty tins and bottles. Remnants of the many fires were carefully buried under pine needles and earth. Peter packed a few of his homemade snares and fishing lines, just in case. He left behind the fishing rod, carefully secreted. Anyone who happened across the clearing now would have little idea that it had once been a home.

With his new boots, the journey was much more comfortable than either of them had expected. Peter rode the bicycle to take the pressure off his feet. Franz walked alongside, holding Wolfi's lead in one hand and Peter's hand-carved walking stick in the other. Wolfi cantered happily next to them.

They had left at night as they were carrying as much of their reserves as possible. In all this was eight bottles of champagne, six bottles of cognac and the last precious sack of coffee beans. They had wrapped each bottle separately in clothing to stop the clink of bottles, a happy sound that most Berliners had not heard for some time. As their luggage was quite substantial they had decided to travel under cover of darkness. In daytime someone was bound to wonder what was in their backpacks.

And so it was that the three friends trekked from their forest hideaway to the suburbs of Charlottenburg.

# CHAPTER TEN

After journeying for two hours, hiding in the shadows when anyone approached, the three travellers arrived at their destination. Charlottenburger Chausee was a wide, tree-lined avenue with carriageways on two sides of the street. It was similar in appearance to Schillerstrasse only much more grand. Peter's neighbours had been the wealthy middle classes of Berlin, the bureaucrats, the civil servants, the doctors and lawyers. This street consisted of large town houses or mansions each surrounded by its own substantial garden and driveway. These were the homes of the idle rich, the aristocracy or the business tycoons and industrialists. Or they had been the homes of such people. Many of the original occupants remained, yet Peter suspected that some of the homes had been confiscated by party officials. Probably the homes of the Jewish industrialists or newspaper owners. The prospect of bumping into a member of Hitler's war cabinet chilled Peter to the bone.

None of these concerns appeared to trouble Franz, who it was quite clear, felt entirely at ease in these surroundings. Whereas Peter had grown up with the services of a part-time cook and housekeeper, Franz was accustomed to the fawning attention of a myriad of household staff: butlers, chauffeurs, maids and nannies.

'Houses like these will still have servants,' Peter worried. He had been quite prepared to trust in the loyalty of close family friends. It was an entirely different matter to trust in the loyalty of their servants. Germany had seen many changes. The Nazi State thrived on betrayal and denunciation.

'This is a bad idea,' Peter murmured, but Franz was already half way through the imposing gates of the Weiss family mansion. Peter held back behind a tree with Wolfi sitting by his side.

The 'plan' as they had laughingly called it, seemed quite brazen now. Franz was to knock at the door wearing his uniform. He would ask to see Herr Weiss, saying that he bore a message from a friend, his 'nephew' Franz. If he was denied access they would call an end to their plan. It was that simple.

Peter watched nervously as Franz crunched along the gravel drive to the large front door. On reaching it he put his hand on a metal ring and pulled it towards him. A bell rang inside. Peter shrank back out of view. It was almost dawn and one way or another he would have to hide from prying eyes.

There was no response, so after a delay of some thirty seconds, Franz pulled the bell cord once more. This time the door swung open and an elderly man in evening dress appeared in the doorway. He appeared to grimace at seeing Franz's uniform.

'May I help you?'

Peter could hear very little of Franz's response and the ensuing conversation. The butler, for that was what he assumed he was, disappeared, closing the door behind him. Franz waited patiently outside. A minute or so later the door opened in a fast, sweeping motion, almost hitting Franz. A large lady in her late fifties or early sixties in a silk dressing gown and fur slippers had pulled Franz to her chest and was almost hugging him to death.

'My little Franz! Oh my poor boy!' she said over and over. She looked carefully around before they went inside, closing the door behind.

Peter remained stationary for a few minutes. He was on the verge of leaving when Franz rushed out of the door saying, 'Peter! Wolfi! Come! It's safe.'

Peter held back. Wolfi did not and dragged him towards the open door. Eventually Peter's fear of what might meet him inside was overcome by his desire not to separate from his friends.

Thirty minutes later, they were sitting at a large, mahogany table eating powdered eggs with slices of meat and bread and ersatz coffee. Wolfi was chewing happily on a mutton bone with scraps of meat attached.

The house was enormous inside. Despite its size, it appeared that there was only the one servant, Albert the butler and more recently, cook. Aunt Berta had welcomed Peter as if he were her own child. An animal lover to the core, she had happily allowed Wolfi into her fine dining room.

Once they had eaten Franz recounted how he had met Peter and the sad events relating to his father and mother. Aunt Berta wiped away a tear and taking both boys to her chest, hugged them until they could barely breathe.

'These are the terrible times we live in,' she said. 'Even my boy Kurt has been taken from me.'

Franz was curious at this remark as he had not remembered any children. Seeing his puzzled look, Aunt Berta enlightened them.

'Kurt is the son of an old servant. Sadly he was orphaned before the war so we adopted him. Presently he is at a KLV camp in Elgersburg, Thuringia.'

Seeing Franz's consternation she quickly added, 'It's not that sort of camp. Lots of children under the age of fourteen have been evacuated to the countryside to avoid the bombings. Officially of course the phrase 'evacuation' is forbidden. The KLV camps are staffed by teachers and senior members of the Hitler Youth who educate the boys in all things necessary for the 'future well-being of the Reich'. This includes sports, war games and many other types of physical education. I did not want him to go, but unfortunately we had little choice.'

Aunt Berta did not sound very convinced by the official propaganda that she had heard so often. It clearly saddened her to think about it.

The phrase for the 'future well-being of the Reich' unsettled the boys when they heard it. It seemed somehow completely meaningless in their current environment.

'As for Albert the butler,' Aunt Berta whispered, 'don't worry about him. He is a Jew.'

Peter marvelled at this news. Here right next door to some of the top brass of the Nazi party, a Jew was hiding under their very noses.

'Better than that, he has even served drinks to some of them,' she giggled.

That first night in Aunt Berta's house was idyllic. Her enormous wealth enabled her to buy many of the everyday essentials such as potatoes, powdered milk, bread, eggs and butter that few other Germans could afford or even find, as they were so severely rationed. As well as the staples of everyday life she could purchase some luxuries, but even the wealthy Aunt Berta struggled to find real coffee. On hearing this, Peter took great delight in producing the last sack of the beans that he had rescued from the water. Her face was a picture of shock and delight. Her face lit up even more when between them they unloaded their haul of champagne and cognac. She kissed both of them repeatedly on their cheeks, saying 'You are my angels, my darlings.'

After dinner they sat in front of a real fire, with real coal, sipping coffee and cognac. Normally such pleasures were denied the young generation in Aunt Berta's household, until at least eighteen. After all the trials and tribulations that these two had gone through she did not have the heart to scold them. At Peter's request Albert joined them, and for three hours or so, the war seemed just a dream.

When they retired to bed each had their own room with an adjoining door between them. Without hesitation or inquiry, Aunt Berta said that of course, Wolfi must sleep on Peter's bed. In the event he slept on the floor by the door of the bedrooms, keeping a watchful eye on both boys.

Peter and Franz slept like never before. The sheets were crisp white cotton and lemon-scented. The pillows and mattresses were stuffed with goose feathers and were so soft the boys sank into them as if in the lake. For the first time in many months, neither boy suffered from the recurring dreams that had so often haunted them. Both slept soundly with full stomachs and a goodnight kiss from Aunt Berta.

In the morning Peter soaked in a hot bath. He could scarcely believe it. Hot water and soap! The bath was so large that Peter, Wolfi and Franz could have bathed at the same time, without ever bumping into each other. As he relaxed in the soapy water, Wolfi lay next to the tub, only looking up when some of the contents splashed onto him.

For the next few days life continued in the same wonderful vein. By the standards of the war, there was plenty to eat and drink, only the coffee being rationed to after dinner. There was always coal for the fire and, so it seemed to Peter, always hot water. The boys were kitted out in new clothing, some left behind by their servants. Peter even got a second new pair of boots. They had been bought for Kurt, a detail Aunt Berta withheld when she presented them to him.

'You are very kind Frau Weiss,' Peter said. 'And very brave, harbouring three 'enemies' of the Reich.'

'Nonsense. This is my house I will have whomever I like to stay. And please call me Aunt Berta,' she replied.

He was pleased to call her 'Aunt'. In spite of her defiance, Peter knew the penalty for a woman of her age would be fatal. Such was Aunt Berta's nature that she did not allow any discussion about such matters.

'Don't worry about me,' she said, 'let me show you something.' Aunt Berta stood up and they followed her into the dining room.

'By the time any unwanted visitors get from the front door to the drawing room, you will be hidden in here.' She pressed an oak panel which opened to reveal a secret cupboard.

The greatest pleasure for all concerned was to sit after dinner, listening to the radio. In defiance of the regulations, and in common with most of Berlin, they would listen to BBC news bulletins.

'It will all be over soon, my darlings,' Aunt Berta would announce optimistically as each British success was reported.

After these bulletins, Albert would turn the dial to a music channel, where symphonies and concertos were the order of the day. On hearing one particular piece of music, Aunt Berta sprang from her chair. 'Dance with me,' she implored and danced a waltz with each in turn. Even Wolfi joined in.

The joy of life at Aunt Berta's continued for almost two weeks, following the same routine. One morning, after breakfast, Aunt Berta became unusually serious.

'My husband has been away on business for some time. He has visited Kurt at the KLV camp and he is bringing him home for a visit. I am sure you will all become good friends. Until I can be certain of Kurt's reaction, it is best that Peter and Wolfi hide somewhere else.'

The news was an unwelcome shock. They knew that their stay could not last forever, but the idea that they might separate was completely unexpected.

'We shall stay together, the three of us,' Franz declared angrily.

'No, no, you misunderstand, my darlings. No-one will have to go away. Peter and Wolfi will stay in a summer house next to the lake until we are sure it is safe. There is a heater in there and he will have plenty to eat.'

Franz was still indignant. Aunt Berta managed to calm him.

'Kurt was a sweet, harmless boy when he left. He has changed. He seems hardened in his attitudes by all the indoctrination and full of hate. He did not even want to come home for Christmas or New Year. That was why we have decided to 'bring' him back for a while. To recover the old Kurt, if it is not too late. As yet he does not know anything about the two of you or even Albert.'

'Then I cannot remain here either,' Franz replied to Berta's explanation.

'You will stay as my nephew. I know you are an enemy of the state, but with the war and Hitler's obsession with the Jews, no-one is likely to devote much time looking for you, my darling.'

As she made this observation she took a card from her silk purse and handed it to Franz. Franz gazed at it in disbelief, for on the front was his photograph. An old picture, yet unmistakeably a picture of him.

'It's an identity card. It describes you as my nephew,' Berta explained. 'It took me some time to get it. It was all done through a church. The congregation is opposed to the Nazis. It is quite clever. One of them leaves their genuine identity card in a basket outside the church. Someone, known only as 'the forger', takes the genuine card and returns it altered with a new photograph. Luckily I had an old photo of Franz which he used.'

Aunt Berta stopped whilst Franz absorbed the news. The significance of the moment was not lost on Peter or Franz. Franz had been 'legalised' by forgery and could come out of hiding.

'Kurt will not suspect anything,' she said. 'Prior to his adoption I often spoke of my wonderful nephew Franz.' Franz blushed.

'I had intended obtaining papers for Peter as well. Understandably the church members are nervous as so many have reported lost papers. I will find another way,' she said apologetically, 'although it will have to wait for now.'

Peter rose from the table and kissed Aunt Berta tenderly on the cheek. She placed her hand on his and held it there for a few minutes.


And so Peter and Wolfi moved into the summer house by the lake, forty minutes away from the house that had become so comfortable to them, awaiting the arrival of the adopted son. The summer house was less luxurious than the main house, and still, a great deal more comfortable than Peter's previous hideouts. To describe it simply as a 'summer house' did not do it justice. It was more spacious and well-equipped than the dwellings occupied by most Berliners, and was very secluded, set within its own grounds of several acres, with a huge lawn fronting directly onto the water. It even had an old Blaupunkt valve radio. It was a small miracle that the property had not been requisitioned or confiscated by some Nazi official or other, especially as the Weiss family had not used it for years. It was to them just another of their many houses.

'Aunt Berta must have really powerful friends,' he thought.

Once again Peter was living with Wolfi by the side of a great lake, this time the Havelsee, and on his own, fending for himself. In the few weeks in the Weiss mansion he had grown fond of the conversation and shared moments of laughter. Hopefully it would only be for a short while until they could be sure of Kurt's attitude. At least each day he would be visited by Franz and Aunt Berta when she could manage it, he comforted himself. And he was well-fed.

So Peter remained in the summer house taking advantage of its many books. He had forgotten how much he had missed simple pleasures such as reading. For some reason he had found himself drawn to *Robinson Crusoe*, a book he had once rejected as too childish. With reading, listening to the radio and exercising Wolfi, the hours and days passed quite quickly.

It had been almost five days since he had moved to the summer house. Kurt had returned three days ago and yet there was no indication as to when or whether they would be able to move back to the house with Aunt Berta, Franz and Albert. Since Kurt's homecoming, Franz had only managed to sneak away and see Peter and Wolfi once.

Meanwhile at the Weiss house, Franz was unhappy and deeply concerned. Herr Weiss had briefly deposited Kurt at the house, shaken hands enthusiastically with Franz and wishing both well, departed on his war duties once more, only stopping to whisper in Aunt Berta's ear.

From the very first Franz had taken an instant dislike to Kurt. He tried not to show his feelings. He just did not trust him. As always Aunt Berta saw the best in everyone and encouraged them all to get along, as they were now related.

Kurt was a boy of fifteen. He had striking blonde hair with deep blue eyes. He was tall and thin, but athletic. He looked like the perfect image of the Nazi youth.

However when he disliked or disapproved of anything his face took on a hideous sneer that transformed an otherwise normal countenance into something resembling a gargoyle. Worst of all he talked as if he were Goebbels himself, constantly referring to 'hideous Jews', 'filthy communists' and 'enemies of the state'. Great Britain and her Allies were the 'Western terrorists'. Not yet a fully fledged member of the Hitler Youth (Berta had prevented him being press-ganged), he nonetheless always wore the emblems and badges of the movement. Whenever a senior party leader such as Goebbels or Göring or Hitler spoke on the radio, he would stand right arm raised in the Nazi salute, paying homage to the wireless set. Often when a broadcast finished he would sing the 'Flag Song' of the Hitler Youth, or worse still the hated 'Horst Wessel Song'. His prized possession was an authentic Luger pistol with real bullets.

'This weapon was presented to me by an officer of the SS. It was a prize for my brilliant recital of the Nazi ideology. It has already been put to good use against our enemies,' he boasted. 'The Oberleutnant told me himself.'

Often, ignoring Aunt Berta's pleas, he would wave the gun about, pointing it at Franz and screaming 'Are you an enemy of the Reich?'

In the midst of conversation, Kurt would interject with tit-bits of 'important detail'. 'The Führer is a hero. He was wounded in the First World War. At his birthday parade in 1938 the Führer stood arm aloft for five hours without any break whatsoever; the Führer is an animal lover who has decreed humane conditions for transporting cattle by railway; only the Führer foresaw the betrayal of the Reich by the November Criminals in 1918.'

Worst of all, Kurt, who enjoyed all the comforts that Aunt Berta could bestow on him, repaid her kindness by berating her for 'undermining the war effort'.

'Don't you know how the heroes at the front are making sacrifices for all Germans? All you do is complain about shortages of this and that. It will be different when we are victorious.'

For Franz disguising his repulsion was impossible. He winced whenever Kurt railed against the 'enemies of the state' and clenched his fist when the Jews were similarly denounced.

The main reason Franz detested Kurt was that he seemed to spy on him wherever he went. He could not leave the room to go to the toilet without finding Kurt waiting for him at the door. And though he had no proof, Franz was certain that he had been into his room and searched through his property. His precious new ID card was moved from where he had left it.

It was soon obvious to Aunt Berta and Franz that with Kurt in the house they could never divulge Peter or Albert's religion. In fact Franz was quite clear that Peter must never meet Kurt. As yet he had not had the heart to mention any of these fears to his friend.

It was near the end of February and for Kurt the only topic of conversation was the impending victory for the Greater German Reich and how it would be great to celebrate it on the Führer's birthday. Berta, Franz and Kurt were in the drawing room after dinner. Music was playing in the background, Berta was embroidering a tapestry, Franz was reading and Kurt was dispensing his wisdom on why Germany would inevitably win the war.

'We Germans are the master race. The lesser nations of the world cannot possibly hope to overcome us.'

Franz bit his tongue. 'The master race lost the last war. Goebbels has a club foot and Himmler is short, fat and virtually blind. Some master race!' he thought. Casting a quick glance at Aunt Berta, Franz got up.

'I feel a little unwell. I think I will go to bed,' he said.

Kurt looked at him with contempt. The new German superman was not permitted to feel unwell.

Once in his room, Franz peaked through the gap in the door. As suspected, Kurt was at the top of the stairs. He waited for fifteen minutes and then looked again. This time the sneak was gone so he locked the door to the bedroom and proceeded to climb out the window, over the large balcony and down the ivy onto the drive.

It was many days since he had seen his friends and tonight more than ever he wanted sane company. On tiptoe, and as silently as possible, he crept from the drive out into the street. It was a little after nine o'clock. It was dangerous to go out at night, although he was comforted by his new identity papers. Within half an hour he was at the summer house. He gave the signal of his arrival by hooting like an owl and waited for Peter to open the door onto the verandah.

'Franz!' Peter was thrilled, if surprised to see him.

Inside they talked for hours with Wolfi lying at Franz's feet. He missed both of his friends so much. The house was wonderful, yet occasionally he thought they would be better off in the woods.

Finally, Franz came to the real purpose of his visit.

'I'm afraid with Kurt around it is not safe for you at the house.' As Franz told his friend about the detestable Kurt, Peter was not surprised. He had suspected as much when he had heard nothing about his return.

Shrugging his shoulders and with a heavy sigh he said, 'Ah well I shall have to stay here or go back to our den'.

Franz was pleased when he referred to it as 'our den'. At about eleven o'clock the two boys said their goodbyes.

'Best if you stay here, for the time being,' Franz said, with a tinge of envy. He stepped off the verandah and into the woods. As he did so the noise of a twig snapping in the bushes caused him to stop. He stood absolutely still for several minutes. Nothing. Just silence.

'You're getting paranoid,' he castigated himself, and continued his journey back to the house.

CHAPTER ELEVEN

The following day, whilst Peter and Wolfi shared breakfast, at the house Aunt Berta and Franz were finishing their ersatz coffee. With Franz's agreement, they had reverted to drinking this artificial sludge as, to use Berta's words, 'Why waste it on Kurt? He only disapproves of our luxuries?' A more important consideration was that Kurt might query where she had obtained such a precious commodity.

Kurt was not with them. He had left earlier that morning, muttering under his breath about some parade or other. Neither Aunt Berta, nor Franz really cared what he was doing. Franz was free to visit Peter for the second time in two days and Aunt Berta was free from the constant Nazi propaganda. She regretted that she could not accompany Franz. She had become very attached to Peter in their short time together and secretly wished Kurt was more like him. Only one more week and Kurt would be gone. That was the news that had greeted them that morning. He was to go into a specialist training camp for future leaders of the Reich.

'Soon I will be able to do my bit in the East, upholding the honour of the Fatherland,' he announced, then left.

Aunt Berta had wanted to argue with him and deny permission to go, but it was futile. He would soon be sixteen and she was unlikely to be able to stop him. And if she was being entirely truthful with herself, he had become so obnoxious she could hardly stand to look at him, let alone listen to the constant nonsense that he spouted.

Rising from the breakfast table, Aunt Berta went to her writing desk and began to scribble a letter to Peter. In it she wished him well and looked forward to the approaching day when she could entertain him once more. She signed it 'your loving Aunt Berta'. In a post script she wrote 'Have patience my darling. Germany will come to its senses and we will rid ourselves of these idiots.' She handed the letter to Franz.

'Take this to my poor Peter along with a food parcel from the kitchen.'

As Franz was filling a bag in the kitchen with Albert's assistance, a loud knock came at the door. It sounded like a boot against timber not a normal rap. Albert had been in service so long now that he instinctively knew the difference between a friendly knock, a curious tap and an aggressive arrogant banging.

'It's the Gestapo!' he said under his breath.

Most people rang the bell, they always banged the door angrily. Sometimes they did not wait for a reply. Albert hurriedly left the kitchen to greet the visitors. As he approached the front door he looked anxiously behind him.

'Hide Franz! Quickly! I don't like this,' he whispered.

From behind the kitchen door Franz could see the hallway. He watched as Albert slowly opened the door. Kurt barged rudely past him followed by two Gestapo men, easily identified by their long black leather overcoats.

'Where is he? Where is that traitor Franz? I know he has been hiding a Jew. He will take me to him.' Grabbing Albert by his lapels he bawled into his face 'Where is he? Where is he?'

One of the Gestapo agents pulled Kurt away from Albert and began searching the house. Fortunately he went straight upstairs.

'I must warn Peter,' Franz thought and crept out of the kitchen.

He ran as quietly as he could along the adjoining corridor towards the rear of the house. Through the window he could see more Gestapo men stationed outside.

'Trapped!' Franz was desperate to leave the house. For the moment his only way out was guarded. He had to hide in the secret compartment between the dining room and the drawing room. Luckily all the Gestapo agents inside the house were already upstairs with Kurt and he was able to slip into the space without fear of being caught. He remained still and waited. His breathing seemed almost as noisy as the footsteps on the stairs.

'Where's Aunt Berta?' he wondered.

As he stood there in the dusty secret compartment, his question was soon answered. In the drawing room he could hear raised voices. He could just discern Aunt Berta's incensed tone.

'This is an outrage! Do you know who my husband is? You will pay for this.'

Placing his eye to a tiny hole in the oak panels, Franz was just able to see into the room. He touched the letter in his pocket. It was gone!

'I have dropped it,' he thought anxiously. 'If they find it Aunt Berta will be arrested!'

The thought of this kindly lady in the custody of these thugs was too much for him to bear. After what seemed an eternity he heard another voice well known to him. It was Kurt.

'I know you have a summer house and there is a Jew hiding there with his filthy Jewish dog. You have betrayed your country and your people. When we find him, and we will, he will tell us everything you have done.'

'Kurt, my little Kurt, I am your mother why do you speak to me like this?' Aunt Berta pleaded more softly.

'My mother is dead. I have no mother and no father. The Party and my country are the only family I have.'

With this parting remark, Kurt stormed out of the room followed by the two agents. The front door slammed violently. Franz left the secret compartment and rushed to Aunt Berta. They hugged each other briefly.

'I'm all right. I'm all right,' she reassured him. 'Go quickly! You must warn Peter and Wolfi! If you cut through the woods you might get there first.'

'What about the letter? I have lost it and they may come back,' Franz replied, unsure what to do.

'You mean the letter I have been standing on for the last ten minutes?' Albert smiled. 'One of those thugs kicked it by accident and didn't notice. I couldn't pick it up in full view.'

'Well done Albert,' Franz said, relieved and rushed from the house.

He ran as fast as he could, taking parallel streets rather than the most direct route to avoid being caught, but he was on foot and they were in a staff car. He knew he could never possibly get there first.

'If I can at least get close enough to shout a warning,' he thought.

Out of breath and chest pounding, Franz ran and ran and in half the usual time, emerged from the woods into the garden of the summer house. He vaulted the fence and sprinted across the rear lawn. He was about to shout to Peter when he halted on the spot.

'No. No! I was too slow!'

From his position he could see Peter held on either side by the Gestapo agents, with Kurt grinning behind. To the side of the house was an army lorry with a canvas back. There were at least five or six soldiers by the front of the house. They had grabbed Peter even as Kurt had been in the house.

One of the soldiers was struggling to hold back Wolfi who was fighting to get to Peter. He was muzzled and clearly distressed. Kurt walked over to Wolfi and kicked him viciously in the side. Wolfi yelped in pain, causing Peter to turn round.

'I will teach you to be a proper German dog, not a Jew lover!' Kurt screamed.

'Leave him alone!' Peter shouted and tried to wrestle free.

Peter's anger only served to encourage Kurt even more. He swung his foot to kick Wolfi once more. Wolfi reared up on his hind legs, pulled over the soldier who let go of the lead, then ran towards Peter.

'Run away boy! Run!' Peter shouted.

Wolfi understood this command. It was against his

natural instinct, but he had practised it with Peter and Franz. He turned reluctantly away from Peter and ran towards the fence.

'Shoot it! Shoot it!' Kurt's voice was high pitched and screaming. The soldier took aim with his rifle.

'No!' Peter called out, echoed less loudly by Franz, some distance away.

The soldier fired into the air just above Wolfi's head. Wolfi raced at the fence, springing high above, cleared it easily and disappeared into the trees, his lead dangling behind him. Peter mouthed the words 'thank you' to the soldier who, embarrassed, turned away.

The last thing Franz saw was Peter being loaded into the back of the open lorry, surrounded by soldiers. His head was bowed and he appeared to be smiling.

'He is pleased that Wolfi got away,' Franz said out loud.

Franz sat for a few minutes. He was wracked with guilt. He was now certain that the previous night he had led Kurt to Peter. There was no time for recriminations. He had to think quickly. He must formulate a plan. He walked back to Aunt Berta's house as briskly as possible. Some distance from the house he checked for signs of any more unwelcome visitors. The coast was clear. As he walked towards the front door a low whining noise came from the hedge at one side. A black furry head and two ears came into view.

'Wolfi! Wolfi!' Franz shouted and ran towards him.

He undid the buckle on the leather muzzle and leaned over to comfort the dog. Wolfi licked his face all over with his rough tongue. 'Don't worry boy. We'll get Peter back.

I promise.' As Franz said Peter's name, Wolfi stopped licking, looked at Franz and whined.

Inside the house Aunt Berta was distraught. Her influence and wealth were such that without firm evidence, even the lawless Gestapo would not arrest her, much to Kurt's annoyance. She was deeply shocked, not just by Kurt's attitude, so much as the fact that a fifteen-year-old boy had been given so much credence and authority by grown men. It was just a matter of time before they came back to look for Franz.

While Aunt Berta was grieving at Peter's capture, Franz had gone upstairs to his bedroom. He took out the Hitler Youth uniform and quickly put it on, expressing his gratitude that they had kept it 'just in case'. In Kurt's room he searched the bedside cabinet and in the wardrobe. At last he found the pistol brandished at him so often by Kurt. He placed the Luger in its leather pouch and attached it to his belt. He brushed his hair, cleaned his face and checked his appearance in the mirror. He made one final detour into Peter's old bedroom and removed an object wrapped in a cloth from within a bedside cabinet.

Downstairs in the kitchen he polished his boots and the Nazi badges on his shirt. With some wax, he cleaned the two leather belts he wore, one diagonally across his chest. By the time he had finished he looked like the perfect model Nazi. When Aunt Berta saw Franz she was horrified.

'What are you going to do? You will be taken again. You must flee,' she begged.

Franz touched her arm gently and in a soft voice said: 'Dear Aunt Berta. Peter saved me, now I must try and save him. If not I must join him. I cannot desert him.'

'B-b,…but what can you do?' she pleaded.

'I can try,' he said, 'I must try.'

'Then wait here just a few minutes longer, I want to help too,' and wiping her tears dry, she left the room.

Franz shifted impatiently from one foot to another. Aunt Berta had been gone for almost twenty minutes and every second was vital. When she reappeared she was clutching a velvet bag. It was stuffed with banknotes, more than Franz had ever seen. In a separate bag inside were four or five white diamonds.

'Take these,' she said. 'You may need to bribe a few people. There is a car waiting outside.'

'A car?' Even resourceful Franz had not expected this.

'Yes. Take Albert as your driver,' Aunt Berta replied.

She so wanted to travel with him. She knew she could not. She was too well known and the authorities must be aware of the earlier visit to her house. There was also the problem of Kurt. He could return at any moment.

Franz was concentrating so much on his immediate plan that he did not question where Aunt Berta had found a car, and not just any car. Outside a large silver limousine was waiting. Inside sat a fur-clad lady, in her thirties with ruby red lipstick. She was at the wheel.

'Aunt Berta told me you need a favour,' she said nonchalantly. 'Take my car. There is enough petrol for about three or four hours driving. I would quite like the car back, if you can.' With that she got out of the driver's seat. 'Oh and it might be an idea to put this on the front.'

She handed Albert a small red and black swastika flag.

Adjusting Franz's knotted cravat, she bent over and kissed him on the lips, swivelled elegantly and walked towards the house. As she sashayed in her ankle length dress, high heels and fur coat across the lawn, the door opened and Wolfi ran towards Franz.

'Not this time Wolfi,' Franz said. 'You'll have to stay here.'

Wolfi would have none of it and seconds later he was sat upright on the back seat looking out the window, his claws digging into the expensive green leather.

In the back of the limousine, Franz could not quite believe what was happening. Just a few weeks ago he was living wild off game and fish and now he was being chauffeured in luxury. If his mission had not been so serious he might have enjoyed himself.

The swastika-bedecked limousine with Albert the chauffeur, resplendent in morning suit, proved invaluable. Very few outside the ruling elite were able to travel in this style and the message sent was that this was someone very wealthy, or very powerful indeed. The young boy in uniform must be the son of someone special. As a consequence they were not stopped at any checkpoints, until they arrived at Prince Albrecht Strasse. This was the infamous headquarters of the Gestapo where many detainees simply vanished.

As they pulled up to the barrier, a sentry leaned forward to speak through the open driver's window.

'Papers!' he demanded.

'Papers always papers. What an outrage! If my father were here you would be sent to the Russian front,' Franz sneered, waving his new identity card about. His privileged upbringing had given him many examples of the rudeness of the aristocracy. 'Your father? Who, who is your father?' the soldier stammered.

Franz was about to reply, when Albert leaned over and said calmly, 'Put it this way if anything happens to the Führer, he will be the new Führer.'

The sentry went white and ordered the gate to be opened, saluting at the same time. Albert drove under the raised barrier, outwardly a model of composure. Inside, however, he and Franz were now extremely nervous. They had to hope that they would not be challenged, also that they did not encounter Kurt. For the moment they had decided that Wolfi was safer in the car.

Once inside, Franz strode towards a reception desk manned by a single official. Albert was a few paces behind as befitted the dutiful servant. As the official glanced ever so briefly towards him, Franz stopped.

'He knows me. He has seen me before,' he thought.

Franz was certain the clerk would recognise him. He knew this face well from the many times he had accompanied his mother on her daily visits, as she desperately sought information about his father. He need not have worried. Then he was just the insignificant son of a nuisance woman who just would not go away. Now he was a boy in uniform with a servant. And as with so many in Nazi Germany, the official saw the uniform, not the person wearing it.

'Heil Hitler!' Franz saluted and clicked his heels ostentatiously. The official responded less enthusiastically. He continued to read the document on his desk.

'I presume it is all right to leave my limousine parked at the front door?' Franz said, emphasising the word limousine.

The official looked up. He was surprised at the confidence of a boy so young.

'Of course. You are…?'

Franz cut him short. He wanted to control the conversation.

'Back to the car and wait for me,' he dismissively waved Albert out the door. The official was impressed, more so when Albert bowed and left without delay.

'Earlier today you arrested a Jew boy at a summer house on Havelsee. This Jew stole a precious item from my father's house. My father has personally instructed me to retrieve that item and deal with the thief. Where is the boy now?' Franz's tone was aloof and arrogant.

'We deal with so many Jews here. And anyway who is your father?' the official retorted.

'I believe the thief is called Peter, Peter Stern. He is about sixteen. My father is irrelevant. This is my task and I promised my father and Uncle Heini that I would succeed without relying on their help,' Franz stated confidently.

As he spoke the name 'Uncle Heini', Franz feigned an adoring look at the autographed and framed picture of Himmler on the wall behind. 'I hope he doesn't know him personally,' he prayed.

'Uncle Heini? You don't mean…' The official was now stuttering badly as he eyed up this young boy.

'The same. Now where is the boy? Uncle Heini is waiting for me.' Franz stood back as he said this and looked at his bare wrist, one hand covering it so that the absence of a wristwatch would not be noticed.

'I will find out straight away,' the official replied and scurried off down the corridor, leaving a single secretary behind the desk.

The time passed agonisingly slowly as Franz waited. The hands of the clock on the wall appeared stubbornly still. Dreadful thoughts raced around his head.

'Maybe I have been discovered? Maybe he's trying to ring 'Uncle Heini'?'

He rocked from one foot to the other nervously. Suddenly he stopped, and was absolutely motionless. He had spotted something, or rather someone.

'Kurt!' He was at the far end of a corridor coming towards him. Franz turned his back.

He noticed the reception desk was now empty. The secretary had gone. On her desk was a telephone. He leaned over, picked up the receiver and looked over his shoulder. Kurt was climbing the stairs behind him. He was with one of the Gestapo officers.

'Please don't let him enquire about Peter. Not now,' Franz muttered under his breath. Thankfully Kurt disappeared out of view. At the same moment the official came through a door and was walking towards Franz. With the receiver to his ear Franz began a very loud conversation with his 'Uncle Heini'.

'Yes Uncle I am still waiting.'

He hoped that his 'uncle' was not actually in the building. All the time his little finger placed strategically on the phone prevented any possible connection being made. When the official was just a few steps away Franz said into the phone, 'Do you want to speak to him or shall I just have him arrested, Uncle?' He held out the receiver as he spoke. The official went ashen faced.

'I am afraid you are out of luck. The boy in question is not here. He is at Anhalter Bahnhof ready for transportation,' he said. 'The train departs in half an hour.' The official looked apprehensively as he conveyed the unwelcome news. Franz picked up a sheet of letter-headed paper from the secretary's desk.

'I presume you can type?'

'No, but we have a secretary who can,' the official replied, 'I will go and find her'.

'Stay there! I will type!' Franz said as he sat down behind the desk.

The official was now so scared of the consequences of upsetting this boy, he did not question the order. Nor did he question the words.

*'Please give the bearer of this letter all assistance in finding the Jew Peter Stern and release the said Jew into his custody.*

*By order of the Head of the Gestapo and Reichsführer SS, Heinrich Himmler.'*

'Sign it!' Franz ordered. The official hesitated. Franz picked up the telephone and started to dial. The terrified official grabbed the phone. 'All right, I'll sign it.'

Not only did he sign it, underneath it was dated and stamped with the seal of the Gestapo and countersigned with an indecipherable signature.

'Many thanks, you have been of great service. My

father and uncle shall be told. Heil Hitler.' Franz saluted, turned and marched from the building.

Just twenty-five minutes after entering the headquarters of the Gestapo, Franz and Albert were back in the limousine speeding towards Anhalter Bahnhof. They had to hurry. Anhalter Bahnhof, once the largest railway station in Europe, was literally just around the corner, and they had to get there in time to stop the transport. In his hand Franz held the valuable sheet of paper with the address at Prinz Albrecht Strasse on top.

Albert brought the car to an abrupt stop outside the station. Franz jumped from the vehicle, leaving the rear door open and allowing Wolfi to leap out after him. There was no time to argue. Both ran into the main concourse followed by Albert, who was by now some way behind and out of breath.

Franz grabbed a train conductor by his sleeve.

'Where does the transport to the East leave from?' he demanded.

The guard, slightly taken aback, replied: 'Platform four. And we are not supposed to call it a transport. It is a 'resettlement'. You had better hurry it leaves in a few minutes.'

Franz dashed across the concourse and down the stairs onto the platform, with Wolfi running beside him. At the bottom of the stairs a metal railing had been placed across the platform, attended by a train guard.

'Sorry my boy. You can't go through,' he said.

'Don't call me 'my boy'. You will address me as 'sir'. I have a personal order here from Himmler to remove a passenger from the train. Now let me pass.'

The guard looked very briefly at the letter. The name Himmler was enough to persuade him to move back the metal railing. Some distance along the platform an SS Captain was standing with his sergeant, smoking a cigarette. Franz ran towards them and thrust the letter into the Captain's hand. He glanced at it and handed it straight back.

'You are too late. The train is departing. I do not have time to search for one Jew.'

'That is a direct order from Heinrich Himmler himself. Now obey it or I will shoot you for insubordination!' Franz removed the pistol from its holster, released the safety catch and pointed the gun at the Captain's head. He was shaking. The Captain was unperturbed. He stamped out his cigarette with his boot, smiled and said: 'I like your nerve boy. I tell you what, I am a fair man. If you can find him in under three minutes you may have him.'

At this both he and the Sergeant smiled.

'It's a deal,' Franz replied to their obvious surprise. He turned and began walking up and down the platform shouting: 'Peter Stern! Peter Stern!'

At the front of the train were a mixture of passenger carriages, mainly third class. In the middle and to the rear were cattle wagons with horizontal boards. Franz hurried back the way he had just come. Wolfi meanwhile rose onto his hind legs and started pawing frantically at the side of one of the cattle wagons, whining all the time. Long scratches appeared in the wood from the dog's furious, if futile attempts to open the doors.

'Leave it Wolfi! Leave it! We have no time for cattle.'

On saying this Franz turned away, and still ignoring Wolfi, he ran back and forward along the platform The three minutes were almost up. The Captain and his Sergeant grinned smugly at each other. Wolfi barked loudly, still pawing at the side of the cattle truck. Franz did not understand. Wolfi rushed at him and bit on his sleeve dragging him towards the wagon.

'Not now Wolfi! Not now!' He was irritated and pulling away as hard as he could. But Wolfi was too strong and too determined and the more Franz resisted the harder the dog pulled, until both were right next to the cattle wagons. It was only then that Franz noticed the human cargo.

'Peter! Peter Stern!' he cried.

No response. Wolfi let go of his friend's sleeve and desperately clawed at the side of the wagon.

'I have found him! He's in here!' Franz shouted. 'Open the doors!' Finally he had realised what Wolfi was telling him. Sergeant and Captain looked at each other bemused.

'Open the doors!' the Captain ordered. The Sergeant assisted by his corporal, slid back the heavy bolts and then the door. A number of people almost fell out.

'Peter Stern? Where is Peter Stern?' Franz shouted.

He did not need to for Wolfi was already licking at Peter's face as he bent down from inside the cramped cattle truck. As one of the last to be loaded he was near the front. Franz struggled to keep his emotions in check when he saw his friend.

'How do we know he is your Peter Stern?' the Captain said.

'This is why,' Franz said, and reaching across to Peter, he felt in his pocket.

After rummaging a little while, he took his hand from the pocket and triumphantly displayed the Iron Cross awarded to Peter's father. This was the object he had taken from the drawer in the bedside cabinet.

'He stole it from my father. That is why Uncle Heinrich authorised his release to me. I am to have the great honour of dealing with him personally,' Franz explained, snatching the black metal cross away from the scrutiny of the Captain.

'Ach the damned Gestapo, they never search anyone properly,' the Captain complained.

By now Peter was standing on the platform. He was in a daze struggling to believe the nerve of his young friend and the fact he was once more able to breathe.

'So you have your prisoner. What do I get for my trouble?' the Captain asked 'I could use a dog in my work. Why don't I keep it?'

'No, no,' Peter tried to say. Thankfully no words came out.

Franz managed to hide the worry he felt at the Captain's suggestion.

'That is not possible Captain. The dog belonged to this Jew here. He was part of a gang of partisans living in the wild. This dog will help us hunt them down. I have something much better for you,' and as he spoke he motioned to Albert to come forward. Franz took the cloth bag from Albert, reached deep inside and removed two small diamonds giving one to each soldier.

'I think you have been cheated, young master. Enjoy

taking care of the prisoner,' and as he said this, the Captain signalled for the wagon to be resealed.

Franz pointed the gun at Peter. 'Move!'

As they walked from the platform, neither could bear to look at the anxious souls still on the train.

# CHAPTER TWELVE

When they were safely back in the limousine, Franz put away the gun and placed an arm on Peter's shoulder.

'Thank you. Thank you,' was all that Peter could say. Wolfi was wedged between them on the back seat and lay with his head on Peter's thigh.

'Don't mention it. I only did what you would have done. I had a good teacher,' Franz said.

As the car motored through the streets of Berlin back towards Aunt Berta, Peter blessed the series of fortunate events that had helped rescue him: the Gestapo's decision to place him on the next available transport rather than spend days or weeks interrogating him; his decision to leave his father's Iron Cross at the house where it was safer and in the hope that his stay in the summer house would not be too prolonged; the Captain's failure to inspect the Iron Cross with its inscription that honoured the courage of his Jewish father. Most of all Peter gave thanks for the two friendships that had saved him so often, Wolfi and Franz.

Franz sat quietly during the journey. The magnitude of his daring and the real danger he had faced had only just begun to sink in. And they were in peril still. They were on their way back to Aunt Berta's, not knowing what awaited them. They could go back into hiding straight away, even if there were practical difficulties.

Nearly all their belongings were in the house, they needed to hand back the car to its glamorous owner and most crucially, they wanted to check on Aunt Berta.

'Pull over here please, Albert,' Franz directed. They were still half a kilometre from the house. 'We will wait here. Please go back to the house and check that the coast is clear.'

In the last twenty-four hours Franz had matured. He was quite willing and able to take charge of the situation. Peter was shell-shocked and grateful that for the moment, he was no longer required to make any decisions.

Albert walked from the car back to the house. He reappeared ten minutes later and almost jumped into the driver's seat. With skill and speed he quickly started the engine and drove back to Aunt Berta's house, pulling onto the gravel drive. Aunt Berta was already at the door of the car.

'Oh my poor boy! I was so worried about you.'

Her arms were flung around Peter's neck as he tried to get up. Wolfi's head was between the two of them washing both their faces. From Peter she went to Franz and clasped him close to her chest, crying tears of joy.

Inside the hallway Franz stopped and looked around cautiously for any sign of Kurt. Aunt Berta guessing his concerns spoke to reassure him. 'Kurt? Don't worry about Kurt. He is tied up in the cellar.'

Peter, Franz and Albert were relieved, though stunned by this news.

'What? But how?' Franz gasped.

'Oh I hit him with a champagne bottle. A good vintage too. Luckily the bottle didn't break.' These words were spoken by the glamorous limousine owner who was now leaning, one hand against the door frame, cigarette holder in her other hand.

'There's never been a man or a bottle that Lotte couldn't handle,' Aunt Berta joked. 'Maybe we should send her to sort out Herr Hitler.'

Everyone laughed.

After some minutes Berta explained how Kurt had been so encouraged by his success in capturing Peter, he had rushed from Gestapo Headquarters to Aunt Berta's to give her the bad news. Now he was the captive.

Once comfortably ensconced in the drawing room and refreshed with 'English tea' Franz modestly recounted how they had rescued Peter. Lotte and Aunt Berta were astounded.

'It sounds like one of my old film scripts,' Lotte commented. At this Peter and Franz looked at her admiringly, neither bold enough to ask any questions.

After the well-deserved praise for Franz subsided, they began to discuss the various difficulties they now faced. For Franz the principal concern was Kurt and what was going to happen to Aunt Berta. Aunt Berta was worried about Peter, Franz and Albert. If there was any investigation at Gestapo Headquarters Albert and Franz were sure to be identified. The registration number of the limousine might be traced back to Lotte if anyone had remembered it.

'Ah well,' Lotte declared, 'I didn't like the colour much anyway. I will abandon it and say it was stolen.' Seeing the upset look on the boys' faces she added, 'I'll just have to use one of the other two.' That at least was one matter resolved.

'The boys and Albert can stay with me for a while,' Lotte added.

'No it's too dangerous with your husband still around.'

Berta refused the generous offer without consultation. Lotte was an ex-film star whose career ended abruptly at her own choice when the Nazis took over film production. Her wealth came from her husband who had since evolved into an ardent Nazi. Berta was sure the risks were too great.

After an hour's discussion and much consternation, they were little further forward. Albert must leave Germany, they all agreed. He, however, would not leave his mistress. Berta was happy to leave her homeland with Albert, not without Peter and Franz however.

'Peter will you come with us to Switzerland? We can all live as a family in my chalet. You will be safe until the end of the war?' Aunt Berta pleaded.

'I cannot think of anything better than spending the rest of the war in safety with you Aunt Berta, but I must stay in Berlin for when my parents return,' Peter replied.

Lotte and Aunt Berta looked at each other knowingly. In many ways Peter had become a man, yet he displayed the untainted optimism of a child. How they both hoped his optimism would be rewarded.

Peter continued, 'Also, after today my survival is not enough, I want to help others survive. I want to fight the Nazis.'

'All right then. We shall all stay and fight the Nazis in our own little way,' Aunt Berta sighed unconvincingly.

'It is too risky for you, Aunt Berta. We still have Kurt to deal with,' Franz said, alarmed. He so wanted to go to Switzerland. He would not desert Peter and Wolfi.

'Kurt will not be a problem. I promise you that,' Aunt Berta said confidently. 'I will just have to tell him that he is a full Jew'.

No-one else spoke, shocked by this announcement.

'Oh yes. I know he looks like the perfect Aryan. He is not. Kurt is the son of my old gardener and his wife, both of whom were Jewish. Neither of them practised their faith. They worked for us even though they were Marxists.

'Months after the 'little corporal' seized power they were denounced by a neighbour as communists and agitators against the regime. One day they were just taken away. Even my husband's connections could not protect them. Kurt was very young at the time and so we adopted him. He knows nothing of his Jewish roots. The mood at the time was so plainly anti-semitic and in view of his parents' wishes, we decided to bring him up as our own son, with no particular religion.'

It was clear to the others Aunt Berta had agonised about Kurt ever since, and more so as he started to display such a fondness for the Nazis.

'So,' Aunt Berta finished, 'if he wants to hunt down Jews so much, he better hand himself in for transportation.'

At the end of their meeting nothing was firmly resolved. Aunt Berta and Lotte pleaded the case once more for all to escape to Switzerland, all meaning, the two boys, Wolfi, Albert and Aunt Berta.

'Please,' Berta begged, 'my husband will not mind. Every day he hates the Nazis more. He travels abroad regularly and sees the destruction and havoc they wreak. He can easily join us in Switzerland. The two of you can

170

fight the Nazis by telling the outside world of your experiences. Please, think about it?'

Peter and Franz found it hard to ignore Berta's plea. She had already done so much for them. In the end it was decided that they would think about their plans overnight. In spite of the threat, the two boys would spend the evening at the house and sleep in the summer house. Kurt would remain tied up in the cellar. They would reassemble the next morning at breakfast to hear Peter and Franz's decision as to whether they would escape to Switzerland or stay in Berlin.

A few days later, Lotte's two remaining limousines were parked at the roadside in the village of Wettin, some 150 kilometres south-west of Berlin. In one limousine was Aunt Berta with Franz in the back. Albert sat up front in his morning suit and top hat. In the other limousine, parked directly behind, was Lotte, perched next to Wolfi on the rear seat. In the driver's seat, was a young, handsome chauffeur in a pristine and expensive uniform in charcoal grey, made to measure and perfectly fitted to enhance his athletic physique. He wore a peaked cap with a motif and long shiny leather boots. In his inside breast pocket he had his obligatory identity card with the name 'Peter Müller', occupation 'chauffeur'. Not even the most suspicious of observers would have suspected that this was the fugitive Jew, Peter Stern. If anything were to betray them it was Peter's driving. He had learnt just a few days earlier.

Each limousine was loaded with many luxurious calf-leather suitcases and hat boxes. As Franz had his 'official papers', it was considered safer that he travel as Berta's nephew. Peter was to pose as the chauffeur with Lotte, as all agreed, she would distract any curious official. Wolfi chose his own place behind Peter, always keeping an eye on Franz.

Albert was the most nervous. None of them believed the Nazi racial stereotyping about Jews, but those that did would have cause to stare at him a little longer. Whereas Peter had inherited the blonde blue-eyed looks of his mother, Albert was dark in colouring and with the more prominent nose that the Nazis treated as so distinctive of the Jew.

'Maybe I should travel separately?' Albert had offered.

'Nonsense!' was Berta's response. 'My husband's 'Aryan nose' is much bigger than yours. Besides, the Romans, that the damned Nazis constantly compare themselves to, were famous for their noses!' In the end Albert gave way to his mistress's wishes.

Lotte was to accompany them to Switzerland where she would stay for a short holiday and then return to Berlin. She simply would not entertain the prospect of letting the others travel alone. She had used all her charm to persuade her husband that she needed both cars, especially after one had already been stolen. As always he gave in and agreed that for one week he would 'make do' with an official vehicle. Little did he know that one week would in fact be two or more. With her husband's contacts, Lotte had been able to arrange accommodation along the way. It was basic, but clean and comfortable she was assured.

Peter's identity card had proved a little more difficult. Selecting a badly bombed area of Berlin, in which both the police station and rationing office had been destroyed, Lotte had arrived at a temporary office in one of her limousines. Peter was at the wheel of the car in his newly-made chauffeur's garb. She had entered the office in one of her most glamorous outfits accompanied by her young chauffeur. Ignoring the queue of patiently waiting bomb victims, she had marched up to the desk.

'My driver needs new papers. His were destroyed by the bombing,' she demanded.

'Madam there is both a war on and a queue,' the civil servant said, not looking up.

'I cannot manage without my driver and I am not going to wait here all afternoon,' Lotte said in outrage.

The civil servant's attitude had changed as soon as he saw Lotte. As always Lotte had her own way and within a short time she and Peter were leaving the building with his new identity as 'Peter Müller'. For the first time since he had gone into in hiding Peter also had his own ration cards which he used to supplement their supplies for the journey.

For the moment, the convoy had stopped unexpectedly. Franz excused himself, left Aunt Berta and Albert and went to consult with Lotte and Peter. After a few minutes he returned.

'Everything's all right. We were just checking this is the right way to the inn,' Franz explained.

As each day went by, the party drew nearer and nearer to the Swiss border. For Aunt Berta and Franz the hardest thing was to remember to speak to Peter as a servant and not a dear friend. When in the inns, Lotte would clear her throat loudly if Berta seemed too close to Peter. Wolfi as always followed Peter everywhere. No-one paid any attention to this, assuming that as usual, the poor servants had to look after the spoilt pets.

The journey was thankfully largely uneventful. Peter's driving skills had improved immensely and even he began to relax. At times they admired the rolling countryside and laughed at the curious looks of impressed villagers. At lunchtimes they would picnic in the open air, forgetting the purpose of their journey completely. Occasionally they would come across bomb damage that was so familiar in the city.

Once they held their breath as they passed a convoy of soldiers marching on the side of the road. With their ostentatious display of wealth and power, they were left to continue, unhindered. Lotte had not appeared in film for almost eight years, yet there were those who recognised her. Her celebrity eased their path as if she were Hitler himself.

Their greatest obstacle was obtaining precious supplies of fuel. They had brought as much as they could in petrol containers, strapped to the runner boards. This had enabled them to travel a substantial part of the overall distance, until eventually they had required other sources. Once more Lotte had astonished all of them when having ordered a detour from the route, she brought them to an army fuel depot. There she had bribed and flattered the commander until he had replenished the tanks.

'Oh he was a fan from years back,' was all Lotte said by way of explanation.

Thus it was that some five days after their departure from Berlin the group of friends stood beside the cars on the edge of the Bodensee, looking at the Swiss border in the distance. They had a last look around them and Aunt Berta and Albert got back into their car. Peter, Franz and Lotte stood next to each other with Wolfi lying in front of them.

'Come on darlings. Time to leave,' she urged them. Neither Peter nor Franz moved, not daring to look at dear Aunt Berta. 'Come! We must go!' she implored.

Still no-one moved. Worse still Peter and Franz continued to avoid Aunt Berta's eye. Aunt Berta slid across the back seat and holding onto the door, pulled herself to her feet. As she looked at the faces of her closest friends the truth dawned.

'You are not coming! You are leaving me!' Swinging round on the spot, she yelled at Albert. 'Did you know about this?'

Albert shook his head, dumbfounded. For the first time Aunt Berta had lost her composure.

Lotte was the first to step forward and speak: 'Please don't blame Albert. He didn't know. The boys have made their decision. They must follow their conscience. They have done this because they love you and knew you would not leave them behind. This was the only way to save you and Albert. *Please* Berta, don't make this any harder.'

'I didn't need saving,' Aunt Berta retorted angrily. 'I was safe in Berlin.'

Lotte hesitated. 'I'm so sorry, dear Berta, I am afraid you did need saving. Kurt has some sort of evidence against you which he says he will hand over to the Gestapo.'

Berta's face fell, confirming that there must indeed be some sort of incriminating evidence.

'When we took food to Kurt in the cellar he boasted that 'soon he would dance on your grave'. He simply does not believe that he is a Jew and he is even more determined to prove his worth as a true Aryan, even if it means betraying his own family.' Lotte waited for Berta's reaction.

Berta was silent. She knew what the evidence must be. It was a collection of letters she had received and foolishly kept. Each was from abroad, hand delivered by her husband. In them she was thanked by the various 'enemies of the state' for her help in smuggling them out of the hands of tyranny. The news that Kurt intended to hand these over to the authorities distressed her. He must not have been able to find them when he had tried to have her arrested. Clearly they had since been found.

'Come Aunt Berta. Please go with Albert. Please!' Peter had stepped forward and was holding her hand. He knew how she loved to be called 'Aunt' by him.

Franz joined them and added, 'Please Aunt Berta. Peter and I have lost our parents. We do not even know if they are alive. You may be the only family we have left. Help us to fight on by staying safe. You can tell the world what is really happening in Germany.'

His earnest words recalled thoughts that all of them preferred to avoid, particularly Peter.

'I would hope that by now I am one of the family too,' Lotte joked, 'but call me cousin Lotte. I'm too young to be an aunt.' As so often, Lotte's constant good humour broke the gloom that had descended.

'Don't worry I'll look after your boys for you. I promise,' Lotte said, serious once more.

Peter and Franz shook Albert's hand and wished him luck. Aunt Berta threw her arms around Lotte's neck and kissed her over and over saying, 'Be careful darling. Please be careful.'

She released Lotte from her grip and then, taking a hand each from Franz and Peter, she looked at them, struggling to speak.

'With young men like you…' Her voice tailed off.

All the things she wanted to say remained unspoken. How proud she was, how she would see them again soon. Instead, she reached into her purse and gave each of them a wad of notes. They knew by now that they could not refuse. She embraced them both tightly to her, and gazed at each in turn, one last time.

Finally, she leaned over, kissed Wolfi on the head and stepped into the car. Without looking back, she and Albert drove to the border crossing.

'Right Franz. Back to the forests of Berlin,' Peter ordered, holding open the rear doors of the limousine. Lotte, Franz and Wolfi dutifully clambered onto the back seat and all three, expertly chauffeured by Peter, began the long trip home. It was the 1st of March 1943.

# CHAPTER THIRTEEN

Peter looked nervously around him.

'Where is he? He's late,' he muttered under his breath.

He was waiting for his contact to arrive. A contact that had been arranged by a friend of a friend of Lotte and whose trustworthiness was uncertain and untested. With so many unknown links in the chain they were taking an enormous gamble. The Gestapo had informers everywhere in their employ. Even for those opposed to the Nazis there were many temptations to denounce others, not least to save one's own life.

In spite of his impatience, the Berliners passing by did not give Peter a second glance. The heavy and sustained bombing over several days at the beginning of March 1943 had taken its toll. Their thoughts were on important matters such as where their next meal was coming from. Unknown to everyone except the individual in question, one man was simply walking. Hoping against hope that no-one would ask for his papers. He was a 'u-boat'. One of the many Jews who had gone underground to avoid detection.

About fifty metres away Franz kept lookout with Wolfi sitting patiently and obediently at his side. He was anxious too, though luckily managed to control his unease so much better than Peter.

'I should have met him,' Franz said quietly to Wolfi. He was worried that his friend's nerves would betray him as he was shaking so badly.

Peter's nerves were understandable. They were on the steps leading to Anhalter Bahnhof, the station where Peter had been shut in a cattle wagon waiting to be deported. The station where he had determined that he would no longer simply survive. He was going to save others.

'Perhaps this is a trap,' he said to himself, and felt the large brown envelope tucked under his arm. It was stuffed with cash for these days everything had its price, even amongst the resistance. He wished he could have used Mama's jewels. They had remained hidden in Wolfi's coat. Franz and Lotte had firmly refused. Neither said it, but both feared this could be all that remained of Peter's family history. Lotte had once more funded the purchase. She seemed determined to bankrupt her husband before the war was over.

'Never mind Peter,' Lotte had joked, 'when he divorces me I can always marry you.'

Peter had blushed deeply. Even now this wonderful woman was unaware of the depth of Peter and Franz's devotion.

As these thoughts passed in and out of Peter's head he failed to notice the gentleman walking purposefully towards him. When he finally spotted him, his instinct was to turn and hurry away. It was already too late. The man was almost upon him. He was about forty years old with a sun-tanned face and healthy appearance, dressed in the field-grey uniform of a lieutenant in the Wehrmacht. Peter shot a glance towards Franz and Wolfi.

'Get out of here Franz!' Peter muttered under his breath.

To his consternation Franz stayed put. Franz was in a dilemma. Any movement might be understood by Wolfi as an indication to go to Peter. He regretted their decision to bring Wolfi along. Once again Peter had been adamant.

'Wolfi can spot danger better than any of us,' he had argued.

'Ah my dear nephew. Here is the birthday present for my sister, Clara,' the officer said, much too loudly and melodramatically for Peter's liking. On saying this he handed over a manila brown package about the size of an attaché case.

'Do you have Grandpa's present for me?' the officer queried.

Still in a state of shock Peter removed the envelope from under his arm and gave it to the officer.

'What the hell?' To Peter's surprise and concern the officer opened the envelope in full view and looked inside for longer than was advisable.

The officer closed up the envelope and said, again much too loudly, 'Thank you. I hope that my sister enjoys her birthday. I am sure that Grandpa will have an excellent time.' With that the officer clicked his heels together and gave a half-hearted Nazi salute.

Composing himself, Peter walked off towards Franz and Wolfi. As arranged they made their way separately for the few kilometres towards their meeting point. At least they were separate for the first half a kilometre of their journey. Wolfi was constantly turning towards Peter.

'It's no use Peter,' Franz said exasperated. 'It's obvious that he is your dog. Let's just walk together. It will be less suspicious.'

After a journey of about half an hour during which neither spoke, they arrived at the steps to a large apartment block in the Luisenstrasse. At the large front door, Peter selected the lowest brass button of a long vertical line. He pushed it twice quickly in succession, then again for a longer period, followed once more by two short blasts.

The door buzzed and a click sounded as it unlocked. The three companions made their way across the lobby and through the now opened door of a large ground floor apartment.

Inside the apartment was typical of those inhabited by the upper middle classes of the city. The sitting room was large and spacious with huge bay windows framed by velvet curtains that rose from the wooden floor all the way to the white-plastered ceiling. There were two long leather sofas with accompanying winged, high backed, leather chairs. Behind one of the sofas was an oak desk inlaid with a green leather insert and a gold writing set on top. To one side of the desk there was the unusual sight of a black Bakelite telephone. On the floor lay an enormous Persian carpet several centimetres deep. One wall was dominated by a white marble fireplace with a mantelpiece above and covered with silver picture frames containing smiling faces, mainly of Lotte.

Lotte was standing by the fireplace as the two boys entered. She was chewing on the end of a cigarette holder. She put the cigarette holder down in an ashtray and rushed towards her friends. 'At last you're back. I was so worried.'

For possibly the first time in her life Lotte had been truly anxious. Since their parting with Berta at the Swiss border, she had promised herself that nothing would happen to Peter and Franz. Unknown to Lotte, Peter and Franz had made the exact same promise. Nothing would happen to Lotte.

'That was close. I would never have expected a soldier to be the contact. Or maybe he was not a soldier, just using the uniform as a disguise, exactly like us,' Franz blurted out.

'No he was definitely a soldier,' Peter replied and signalled with his hand for Franz to keep his voice down.

Peter's caution was necessary as even an apartment block such as this had its own 'Blockwart' or warden, the eyes and ears of the Nazis. These were minor Party members whose job it was to spy on their fellow residents and inform the authorities. Their other duties included lecturing the residents on blacking out properly and threatening punishments for infringements of other regulations.

In this magnificent building the warden was the not so magnificent caretaker, Herr Klein. A cabinet maker whose business had gone bust long before the war, not because of his uncontrolled drinking and reckless spending, no, it was all the fault of the Jews! The beloved Führer recognised the role of the Jews and that was why he, Herr Klein was now in such a trusted position. Lotte loathed him. Fortunately she knew exactly how to exploit his roving eye and thirst for schnaps.

'What soldier? No-one mentioned any soldier to me. I knew that I should have gone.' Lotte's consternation was obvious in her voice. The scenario of a soldier and his sweetheart saying goodbye was one which played out every day at Berlin's railway stations. It was a role she as a talented actress could easily have fulfilled.

As Wolfi lay peacefully on the rug, the three conspirators gathered around the coffee table in front of the largest sofa. 'Let's see what we have got,' Peter whispered and tipped the contents onto the table.

There was a pile of official papers which when examined disclosed four identity cards, four ration cards and four Party membership cards. The membership cards were very valuable as Party membership was essential in almost all aspects of life in wartime Berlin, even deciding who was allocated accommodation.

'Not a lot for such a large amount of money,' Lotte said aloud and then immediately reproached herself. Each document she realised might represent another life saved.

As they scrutinised each item carefully they stared at the black and white faces that stared back. There were several women. The majority were male. Thankfully the names were typically Christian German. That should make them easier to alter. They could not help but wonder what had happened to the unfortunate owners of these passes. Most likely dead, they surmised.

As Peter laid the last of the identity papers on the coffee table, he shook his head and said disconsolately, 'Look at the official stamp. How on earth are we going to replicate that? Without it the papers are useless.' As he said this he slumped onto the sofa and for the first time in many weeks Lotte and Franz sensed his disillusionment.

Franz made no reply. He left the room and moments later returned with a large cardboard box and placed it on the floor. As if in a conjuring trick, he thrust his hand inside and skilfully removed a wooden object, about the size of a corkscrew. It was not a corkscrew however. From close up his audience could see that it was a stamp with the swastika and eagle carved on the end. It was home-made, yet expertly executed.

Before anyone could comment, Franz reached into the box again and produced an ink pad in its metal case.

'Where… on earth?' Peter stammered.

Like an expert magician controlling the audience, Franz reached for a third time into the box. To everyone's great astonishment he pulled out a Leica camera and leather case.

'All very well,' Peter teased, 'but we can't exactly take photographs along to be developed.'

For his grand finale Franz placed his hand into the box for the last time and produced a number of glass bottles with brightly coloured liquids inside.

'We can develop them at home!' Franz said, grinning from ear to ear. Lotte and Peter sat dumbfounded by their friend's resourcefulness. He really was amazing. Their resistance had begun. It was a small start, but a welcome start nonetheless.

# CHAPTER FOURTEEN

It was another pleasant spring day in Berlin and Peter and Franz like many Berliners were enjoying the afternoon sunshine. Wolfi was running around in the gardens of the zoo. This was Wolfi's favourite time. He was with his two closest friends with no other purpose in life than to chase a stick. In spite of all the trials of his time in hiding, Peter had somehow managed to preserve a semblance of a routine for Wolfi. That included his daily walks and playtime. Today, for some reason, Peter was distracted and Wolfi had to keep tapping his foot with his large paw, just to remind him he was there.

Peter was very frustrated. It had been over a week since the rendezvous outside the train station and so far they had not achieved anything. He was aware there must be hundreds, maybe even thousands in desperate need of help. The problem was how to contact them. Most people were rightly wary of anyone who offered assistance.

He had even contemplated returning to the woods to look for fugitives. Often when he had checked his traps he had been certain that someone had got there first. Now that he was a little freer to roam the streets, he had noticed more and more the conspicuous individuals who always tried to avert their eyes and whose shabby condition, even by the standards of wartime shortages, suggested they might be living rough. Mostly though it was the look of panic in their faces that gave their true status away

'Wolfi. Where's Wolfi?' Peter's deep thoughts were suddenly interrupted by the realisation that his dog was nowhere to be seen.

He scanned the immediate vicinity and then beyond. After some moments his panic eased as his eyes lighted on Wolfi the other side of the park. He was seated in front of a park bench. On the bench a man was sitting who from the distance appeared about sixty years old. He was stroking Wolfi between the ears on the top of his head as the playful dog leaned further into the man's legs.

Peter's initial reaction was one of pride, which soon gave way to concern. Even the simple act of petting a dog could lead one into conversations that might betray too many secrets.

'Wolfi! Here boy!' Peter said and whistled.

Wolfi ignored him. He whistled again. Still there was no response. This was very unusual behaviour for Wolfi who was normally so obedient. There was nothing else to do so Peter reluctantly walked towards the stranger. As he approached the stranger stood up and began to hurry away in the opposite direction. Wolfi followed him.

Peter could see the man as he leaned towards Wolfi and said something to him. Frustratingly, he could not make out what. With Wolfi moving further away, he ran towards his dog and grabbed him by the collar. As he did so he was able to gain a close view of the stranger. He was wearing a grey wool suit that had clearly seen better days. It was frayed on the cuffs and the trouser ends were ragged and the whole suit looked very much as if it had been slept in many times. The man wore a pale, beige raincoat that was crumpled and dirty and seemed out of place on such a warm, sunny day. On his head he wore a brown Homburg hat, the only part of his appearance that was in any way respectable.

Most striking Peter thought were the soles of the once expensive leather shoes, for they were worn all the way through. Each time the man lifted his foot the holes seemed larger and larger. This was just the sort of person that he had been thinking of. He surely needed help.

'Please,' Peter said quietly, 'don't go away.'

The man looked backwards with fear in his eyes, still hurrying away.

'I must get home to my own menagerie,' the stranger said, and moved even further away.

'Menagerie! Menagerie!' Peter repeated.

By now he had taken the old man's sleeve in his hand. At close range he could see the stranger's face. The cheeks were thinner and the eyes a little sunken and sad, but he had no doubt as to their owner.

'Please. Don't be afraid. I can help. Please Professor Blumenthal!' Peter pleaded.

The mention of his name was like a blow from a truncheon to the Professor. He could not hide his surprise. His reaction confirmed to Peter what Wolfi had long since known. This was the same kind old man that Peter had once met virtually every day in the woods around Schlacthensee.

When Peter had struggled at first to train Wolfi, the Professor had helped. He had looked after dogs all his life. It was he that showed Peter how to recall Wolfi, how to get him to sit, to lie down and walk to heel. As a consequence, apart from Peter, there was no-one Wolfi responded to better than the Professor. Each day when they had parted the Professor had left with the words, 'I must return to my menagerie.'

'If you want to help, please just let me go,' the Professor replied sadly.

'But Professor it's me Peter Stern and this is Wolfi.' Peter spoke quietly, though firmly.

'We don't know who are friends and who are enemies these days,' the Professor lamented. 'And you should be careful where you give your name.' The Professor's caution was not unexpected, nor unusual.

'Professor we cannot trust everyone. We must trust someone. If we trust no-one then we have lost everything. We are no longer human,' Peter argued.

The Professor was impressed by Peter's sincerity. He had always had a soft spot for Peter, almost regarding him as an intellectual equal, even at the age of ten.

Peter continued to try and persuade his friend. 'I understand your caution, Professor. Please meet me at three this afternoon at the junction of Luisenstrasse and Invalidenstrasse. I have the means to get you off the streets. Please come, but be careful.'

The Professor did not respond. Something in his face said that he would be there. Peter walked back to Franz who was watching, extremely curiously. It seemed to Franz that he had a certain swagger in his gait and was happier than he had been for some time.

Franz was pacing up and down Lotte's appartment. At first he had been furious when Peter told him what had occurred. It was perhaps their first ever real disagreement. Once he realised the depth of Peter's feelings on the subject he gave in. Peter assured him the Professor was trustworthy, especially as he was a dog lover. Franz and Lotte were not so certain that a person's trustworthiness could be gauged by a love of dogs. After all Hitler loved dogs. Peter's final argument had been irrefutable.

'I trusted your judgment about Aunt Berta. You have to trust my judgment about the Professor,' he had said. 'I'll take Wolfi with me. He will know if there is any danger.'

So where were Peter and Wolfi? Why had they been gone so long? The truth was that they had not been gone for very long, Franz's anxiety making each minute drag on and on. At least the prying caretaker Herr Klein was out for the day.

At long last and to his relief, the doorbell rang. It was the agreed code, two short rings, one elongated, followed by a further two short rings.

Lotte raced to the bell and pushed the button that opened the door. Within seconds the door to the apartment opened and Wolfi, followed by Peter and a small, elderly man walked into the sitting room. The man stepped back when he spotted Franz and Lotte.

Peter feared he was about to run away and so moving nearer to his friends said, 'Don't worry Professor. These are my closest friends. They have both saved my life more than once.'

Lotte and Franz blushed simultaneously. The Professor appeared reassured by this bold statement and shuffled further into the room. With his shoes in such a state he found it difficult to walk any other way.

Lotte by now was right in front of him as he stood with his hat in his hand. The other hand he offered to Lotte to shake in greeting. She had already placed both arms around his shoulder and kissed him on the cheek. For this frail man the gesture was overwhelming and his eyes watered.

As always, Lotte knew exactly what to say: 'Where are my manners? You must be starving. Please, please take a seat.'

The Professor was hesitant, admiring the beauty of the sofas and how clean they were. Sensing his concern, Lotte put him at his ease.

'Don't worry about the furniture. The sofas are due to be cleaned soon.'

His concerns allayed, the Professor sat down, sinking into the luxurious leather so that his bottom and legs were almost completely enveloped.

Lotte disappeared into the kitchen only to reappear some few minutes later bearing a wooden board. On the board were some cheeses and smoked meats with a chunk of bread. In her other hand she carried a wine glass with a ruby red liquid inside. She placed everything carefully in front of the Professor.

'Please this is a feast. Will you not join me? I do not like to eat alone,' the Professor asked.

'No thank you Professor. That's just a snack. We shall all eat together later.' As Lotte said these words, Peter and Franz looked at each other. Their agreement was that any doubts and they would feed the Professor then send him away. Her reference to 'dinner' meant he had been accepted.

In spite of his recent deprivations, old habits died harder with the Professor than many others. Rather than simply attack the plate of food, he swirled the wine in the glass, took a long draw of its odour and took a sip. The wonderful liquid flirted with his taste buds as he swished it about his mouth, over his tongue and finally swallowed it. His eyes rolled with delight as he announced the verdict: '1910 Chateau Neuf du Pape! Excellent!'

'Very impressive, Professor. Enjoy your meal then you can go to bed for a while,' Lotte responded.

'Please call me Ernst. And sleep can wait,' the Professor said, as he sliced the first piece of cheese.

Having consumed the meal at a slow and deliberate pace, he wiped his lips with a white cotton napkin and began to speak. His voice was wavering, but firm, and everyone could see that he struggled to control his emotions.

'I was a Professor of Modern Languages at the Friederich Wilhelms University here in Berlin. In 1933 when the Nazis came to power I was forced to resign my post. Like many of my former colleagues we stayed in Germany, that is my wife and I. We foolishly believed that the situation could not get any worse. We are Germans and this is our country. For the first few years we managed to live off our savings until these were all spent. Then we were very lucky and we were sent parcels from friends abroad. They were difficult times, but at least Hilda and I were together. At the outbreak of war I was conscripted to work in an armaments factory, polishing shells. The work was dull and arduous. I was relatively happy as I had a purpose and was safe and we were still together. Then one day we received notification to attend the Lewetzovstrasse synagogue for 'resettlement'. A neighbour, back from the fighting on leave, warned us not to go. 'Whatever you do, do not get on the train,' he begged us. The same kind neighbour arranged a hiding place for us where we hid out in an attic for several months.

'It was early one morning not long after dawn when they came. Some in uniforms with machine guns. Some in their leather coats and hats, with shiny pistols and smirking faces. They brought vicious dogs with them to help in the hunt. At the front was a female, a Jewess I knew as the wife of a friend from the synagogue. Her name was Stella and she had become a Jew catcher. In return for her own freedom and that of her family she was hunting Jews. She is supposed to have caught fifty-three in one weekend.

'We were not the only Jews concealed in the house. They had almost reached the attic when we managed to squeeze through a skylight and escape over the rooftops. We had only the clothes we were wearing. For the last four months I have been living on the streets, scavenging for food where I can, sleeping rough at night or wherever I can find refuge with old friends. Sometimes even sleeping on the pavements. Normally I walk around trying to look busy.

'When Peter and Wolfi saw me, I had broken my golden rule and sat down for a while. It was so sunny and such a lovely day I simply forgot my troubles. When Wolfi came to me I thought I had been caught. Little did I know that Wolfi might be my salvation.'

The room was silent. The painful change from 'we' to 'I' stood out. Finally Lotte broached the question they had all wondered about. 'My dear Professor, what happened to your wife? What happened to Hilda?'

'She was too frail to live on the streets. She died in my arms of pneumonia and I couldn't even bury her!' The Professor's gaze fell to the floor. As he looked up, Lotte was once more in front of him. Her hands were on his shoulders and she leaned over and kissed him on the forehead.

For the second time in only a few hours he had experienced more affection than in the previous four months. Emotion overcame him and he began to weep, sobbing gently.

Lotte waited a while and then passing a handkerchief to the Professor, said, 'Now Professor, no arguments, you need some sleep.' With that she ushered him off to bed.

The following morning the group of friends assembled in the sitting room once more. Lotte looked stunning in a blue summer dress made of cotton and her long blonde hair tied up with a blue silk scarf. Her appearance could not fail to make a mark upon any man, as indeed it had with the little Professor.

The Professor was sitting on the largest of the two sofas draining the remains of his coffee from a fine bone china cup. He was wearing a white bath robe that was much too large for him. Some of the colour had returned to his cheeks and his eyes shone with a little more enthusiasm for life. He was warm and had savoured a hearty breakfast of powdered eggs with real meat and fresh bread. The coffee was substitute, but it was the first in a long while and he had eaten more food than he had seen in the previous week. Better even than the food and coffee was the hot bath he had just enjoyed. Nothing served to degrade a man more quickly than the inability to wash.

'Please forgive my rudeness, kind friends,' the Professor said, for the third or fourth time. For most of the morning the Professor had been apologising that he had been so rude as to sleep through dinner. The poor man had been so exhausted he had slept solidly for sixteen hours. No-one had the heart to wake him, still he was apologetic.

As usual Lotte made a joke of the matter. 'Don't worry Professor. We can go on a dinner date another time.'

'That's a promise,' the Professor responded. 'At the Hotel Adlon, when this damned war is over. And please call me Ernst.'

'No, Professor, I will not. I have been thinking about it. The Nazis took away your status when they forced you out of your job. I will not do the same. But you can be 'my' Professor.' The Professor's face reddened.

As they finished their coffee, first Peter then Franz told the Professor their own stories. He listened intently and was amazed at the resilience that each boy had shown. In his time surviving on the streets he had come across a few other 'u-boats' or 'submarines'. Naturally they were wary of who they trusted. None, as far as the Professor knew, had managed to survive undetected for any length of time without the assistance of friends or relatives, who could offer them temporary shelter and food. Peter's existence alone for so many months was quite remarkable. The fact that Franz had entered the lion's den, the Gestapo headquarters in Prinz Albrecht Strasse, he could hardly believe. As the successful outcome of each adventure was related, the Professor's resolve and determination increased.

When Lotte had finished telling the tale of their trip to the Swiss border, the Professor sat back on the sofa and let out a slow whistle. 'Unbelievable! Simply unbelievable!' he said. 'So what happens next?'

Lotte stood up and walked over to the Professor. 'Come with me Professor.' She took his hand and led him into her bedroom.

After an hour the two emerged. Not even the Professor's wife would have known him. More importantly none of his many former students would either. His wispy grey hair was much thicker and a subtle ginger colour, with patches of grey still on view. His unkempt beard was gone and he sported a handlebar moustache, also with a tinge of ginger, accompanied by impressive, neatly trimmed side-burns. Perched on his nose were round, gold-rimmed spectacles held in place with a lanyard. His teeth gleamed a healthy bright white and his cheeks were ruddy and somehow fuller in appearance. His dirty fingernails had been carefully manicured. He was resplendent in a green, tweed, three piece suit. He looked every bit the country gent. All that was missing was the pocket watch on a chain.

Peter and Franz were amazed at the quality and fit of the suit. The Professor was a small man, smaller than either of them and nothing that fitted Lotte's husband could possibly fit him. Lotte could read their thoughts and simply dismissed their enquiry with a 'best not to know expression'.

'Very impressive Lotte! What about the shoes?' Peter pointed to the soles of the brogues that had hardly any leather left. 'It is always the shoes that give people away.'

'I'll have them resoled along with a pair of my husband's. The cobbler will not care,' Lotte replied. It was a generous offer as leather was in demand and costly.

The final act in the Professor's remarkable rehabilitation was to photograph him and forge his papers. This would take some time and so whilst this was finalised and his shoes repaired, he spent several happy days with his new-found friends. He could not leave the apartment for fear he might be spotted by the caretaker. After months living outdoors that was not a hardship as he engrossed himself in different books and took advantage of his warm surroundings.

# CHAPTER FIFTEEN

Peter looked around his old camp. He was planning a reconstruction. The low branches of a tree rustled and Franz's head appeared in the clearing. Wolfi ran to greet him as usual, tail wagging energetically. Franz was struggling to carry the old Coventry bicycle from the summer house by the lake. In their haste to leave, Kurt and his Gestapo friends had left this valuable item behind when they had arrested Peter. It had lain out of view for all this time.

'Great you found it,' Peter greeted his friend. 'At least now we can save money on fares.'

He did not need to add that they would also be safer. True the two boys had their identity papers, yet they were always wary on public transport. As the war stumbled on there were fewer and fewer fit and healthy young men of their age still in the capital. Those that were to be seen were almost always in uniform as the age of conscripts was continually lowered. The chances of being challenged grew each day.

It was several weeks since the Professor had undergone his transformation. He was living in a small apartment about half an hour away by tram from Luisenstrasse. He was registered with the authorities in his new name and had received his own genuine ration cards. It transpired the owner of the original identity card had been recorded as dead and therefore when the Professor turned up to apply for new documents and accommodation, no-one queried his story that he had been pulled from the rubble of a building destroyed by Allied bombs. He had been concussed for some time, but was now much better, he had claimed. They even renewed his Party membership card. In view of his age and Party membership he was given priority status in the search for lodgings.

The two boys set to work transforming their old den. Five hours later, and after much hard work, they stood back to admire the results of their labour. It was greatly improved with a larger underground shelter, an expanded larder and a new stove lined with bricks as well as a proper funnel for a chimney. Wolfi gave his seal of approval as he lay down inside the new shelter.

'No boy. It's not for us. Not this time,' Peter said. Wolfi tilted his head to one side, curious to know who was to use the shelter.

'I have one more thing to do,' Peter said and walked off, Wolfi by his side as always.

After half an hour travelling in silence they came to a part of the woods neither had visited for some time. They left the path and walked a little way into the trees until they came upon a large oak tree. At the base was carved the word 'Prokofiev'. It was the hollow where Peter had hidden on his very first night in the woods. Beneath the word Prokofiev was carved a long number:

**3 9 14 35 7 24 18 21 26 11 20 8 1 24 13 11 24 24 1**

Taking out his pocket knife Peter carved another number below the old one.

**7 18 1 15 25 11 20 22 24 1 11**

When he had finished he stood back. Franz scratched his head, looking bemused. 'I know it's some sort of code,' Franz ventured, 'but what it means and who it is for, I can't work out.'

'It's quite simple,' Peter replied. 'I left a message under a flower pot at my house. When my parents return they hopefully will find it. It says 'summer 1932'. My father and I camped at this spot in summer 1932. When they get here he will see the word 'Prokofiev'. That will tell him that I have been here.'

'Of course 'Peter and the Wolf', Prokofiev's famous composition,' Franz interrupted.

'Yes, Wolfi is named after it,' Peter said, pleased that Franz understood the meaning.

'The word has another purpose too. It is a key to the code. It was a game we played, inventing codes and leaving messages for each other. Each letter of the alphabet is assigned a number from one to twenty-six, starting with 'A' at one. The first letter of the key word, 'P', is the sixteenth letter of the alphabet. The last letter 'V' is the twenty-second letter of the alphabet. The secret with this code is that the first letter of the key word is moved to the position of the last letter. So if we place 'P' where 'V' is and then number all the letters thereafter, we find that 'P' is twenty-two, 'Q' is twenty-three etc. and 'A' becomes the number seven, and so forth.'

With this knowledge Franz began to crack the code, each time stumbling over certain letters. 'I know it is an address, except some of the numbers are wrong,' he complained.

Peter laughed. 'I should have told you another feature is that the very first number is random and is nonsense. It also tells you the position of another random, nonsense number that you should ignore. In the first line of numbers it is the three and the thiry-five.'

Franz punched Peter playfully on the arm. 'Now you tell me!' he joked. With this new information he was able to work out that the two messages read 'Charlottenburger Rue' and 'Luisen Rue'.

'You can't spell,' Franz chastised his friend.

'That was deliberate, it makes the code harder to break,' Peter retorted, 'and I have used the French for street for the same reason.'

Satisfied with the explanation, Franz turned to leave and as he did so said to his good friend, 'I hope your parents see it one day, I really do.'

Before finally returning to the apartment the three friends went to the lakeside to check on the *Seawolf*, Peter's beloved boat. They were overjoyed when it was still there and they promised each other that they would come back to use it soon. Pleased with the accomplishments of the day, the two boys and Wolfi made their way back to Luisenstrasse.

The following day the first occupant of the newly

constructed camp was in residence. They nicknamed him 'Robin'. For security they had decided, where possible, not to use real names. The man was in his forties and very nervous. So nervous about his 'Jewish appearance' he had spent the last year concealed in a wardrobe, and looked after by friends. They had since been bombed out and he had been homeless again. Identity papers were no use to him as he was betrayed instantly by his constant nerves that made him shake uncontrollably.

Lotte read the letter to herself again. She had no need to do so. Its contents were firmly fixed in her mind and she was racking her brains as to what to do. At first she had been delighted on seeing the Swiss postmark and knew at once it could only be from Berta.

Berta had learnt her lesson about being too explicit in her writing. As a result the contents were of the seemingly dull, everyday type. It was not all dull however.

'So Kurt is returning to Berlin,' Lotte said out loud. Only Wolfi was with her. 'And he is to be given the great honour of attending a Napola School in recognition of his achievements in furthering the National Socialist ideals,' she read from the letter.

The Napola schools were for the most elite of Nazi children, the leaders of the future where the indoctrination exceeded anything ever imposed in the Hitler Youth. It appeared that the disclosure to Kurt of his Jewish origins had not harmed his prospects in any way, nor had it dampened his enthusiasm for the Nazi cause. From the elite school he would quickly enter the military to serve the Fatherland.

Lotte had witnessed Kurt's outright hatred towards Peter and Franz and his determination to catch them. His contempt for Berta had been all too evident. Berta who had done so much for him. It was little consolation to Lotte that Kurt did not know her name.

Placing the letter to one side, she resolved that by the end of the week she would have come up with a plan of action. The doorbell interrupted her thoughts. It was the coded ring and so she knew it must be the Professor. He had proved a real asset. In spite of being at risk himself he happily acted as courier. In his new disguise he attracted a lot less attention than Peter or Franz.

Soon the little Professor was inside the apartment. On the sofa sat a family of three: father, mother and twelve-year-old daughter. This was a problem as the remaining identity cards were for adult males only. Altering the sex as well as date of birth and names was too dangerous. Only the father could be given a new identity card. At least with new ration cards and money, he had some hope of feeding his family. In return the father, a skilled tailor would help with clothing repairs. So many of those in need had only the clothes they wore.

Whilst Lotte looked after the most recent guests, Peter and Franz were looking at the bathing beach at Lake Wannsee. Peter was holding the handlebars of his bicycle. They were close to the spot where he had hidden in the copse of trees with his mother and father and Wolfi, waiting for the arrival of the tugboat captain. Little had they known then that he was to betray them. The memory was painful and Peter tried hard to concentrate on the task at hand.

'Look Franz,' he said, pointing towards the bathing beach.

Franz had already noted what he was pointing at. It was a mild day in late April, yet colder than previous days. In spite of this the hardier residents of Berlin were bathing in the lake. For some this was their only real means of washing. What had attracted the boys' attention was the group of four sailors larking around at the edge of the water. None could have been much older than Peter or Franz.

They were in bathing costumes and their uniforms were neatly folded at the edge of the water. They had not paid the admission to the official bathing area and as such their clothing was unguarded. Neither Franz nor Peter relished the idea of stealing their clothes. The uniforms would be invaluable and they could see no other option. They waited patiently until the four young men were further out into the depths of the lake, one swimming ahead of the other three.

'Give me 200 marks,' Peter said.

Franz looked around him and took out a money belt hidden under his shirt, unfastened it and handed over the notes. He looked on as Peter reached down and picked up two stones. Each stone he wrapped in a 100 mark note.

'I'll see you at the other side of the lake, at our usual meeting point,' Peter said, mounting the bicycle. He rode to the edge of the lake.

Franz watched as he swooped down and gathered up one bundle and then a second bundle of clothing and dropped them into the basket on the front. He rode off as fast as he was able. Where each bundle had lain Peter deposited the banknotes, weighted with a stone in the middle.

Just as Peter gathered up the second bundle one of the young sailors turned to face the shore and spotting the theft shouted, 'Stop! Thief! He has stolen my uniform.'

The crowd of about twenty people on the bathing beach turned to see the cause of the commotion. Luckily for Peter he was already cycling furiously and was out of range of even the fastest pursuer. Franz walked in the opposite direction to Peter's flight.

About fifteen minutes later Franz met up with his friend, well out of view of the bathers. Peter was holding two identity cards in his hand and some small change. In the other hand he had a black leather wallet. 'We have to return these some how,' Peter said, not even taking time to greet Franz.

'Of course,' Franz agreed.

Both knew the sailors faced a severe penalty for losing their identity cards. They would be punished for the theft of their uniforms, yet the boys earnestly hoped it would not be so severe in light of the way it had happened.

Franz walked back towards the bathing beach. The young sailors were talking to a policeman. Two of the sailors were in bathing trunks, their arms flapping in the air. Clearly it was their uniforms that Peter had taken.

Franz approached the group surrounding the policeman. Not many months ago he would have been terrified, but after his success at the Gestapo headquarters his confidence had grown immensely.

'Excuse me officer. I found these by the side of the path just round the corner. Someone must have dropped them.' He held out the wallet and ID cards to the policeman.

The policeman was about to examine them, when one of the sailors snatched the wallet and opened it. His face gave away the immense relief that he felt.

Quickly the young sailors verified that the property was theirs. To avoid questions, Franz had turned and was about to go when a voice shouted: 'He was with the boy on the bike, the thief. I saw them talking to each other.'

The voice belonged to one of the other bathers, a middle-aged woman.

'Is that true?' the policeman said.

'Yes, but I was not with him. He stopped and asked me something about bathing in the lake. I did not really pay him any attention,' Franz replied.

The middle-aged bather was about to speak again. The policeman was mulling over Franz's answer. Franz acted quickly to back up his story.

'Look if I am with the thief, why would I bring back these items? Even the ID cards are valuable, let alone the money in the wallet. I would have to be a very stupid and an unusual thief to do that!' he said indignantly.

The policeman, the sailors and most of the other bathers nodded in agreement.

'Now please may I go? I have important factory work to go to.' Franz's indignation had by now increased.

'All right, you can go, just give me your name,' the policeman said, the matter settled in his mind.

Without waiting for the customary identity check,

Franz had begun walking away and simply shouted back, 'Franz, Franz Becker. Thank you constable.'

The policeman scratched his head as he wondered whether he should follow him and insist on seeing his identity card, but by now the two sailors were demanding he find them some clothes.

Half an hour later Peter and Franz were at the den in the woods handing over supplies to 'Robin', at that time still the only inhabitant. Having demonstrated how to use the traps and a few other basic tasks, Peter and Franz travelled back to Luisenstrasse. They chose a longer route than usual, one that kept them a safe distance from the bathing beach.

# CHAPTER SIXTEEN

Peter and Franz had barely spoken for almost half an hour. They were shivering and a little out of sorts. The weather was unseasonally cold for the time of year, as spring defied the approaching summer of 1943. The icy wind blowing through Berlin in the middle of the night penetrated their overcoats all too easily. The warming effect of Lotte's coffee laced with cognac had long since gone. If only Wolfi had come with them. With his thick fur coat they would have been cosy and warm. This was not an occasion for Wolfi's help, much though it would have been appreciated.

Apart from the cold they were cramped, having spent an hour in a hollow on the side of the railway embankment. It was a black night with little visibility as the normal blackout curtain had once more shrouded the city. In the near distance the dim glow of Lehrter railway station could just be seen as the workmen operated in the minimum light necessary. Other than the light of the station the only other illumination was the blue flash or spark as trains arrived and departed.

Many freight trains had come and gone. It was approaching four in the morning and no passengers had either arrived or left the station. The one train that they awaited was overdue and they were close to calling off their raid. The temptation was so much the greater with the knowledge that they were so close to Lotte's apartment, just minutes away. This was to be their most audacious escapade yet. A train was due with a valuable cargo: not coal, nor oil, nor weapons, nor even foodstuffs. It was carrying paper and not just any old paper. This was the same cardboard-like paper used for official documents such as identity and ration cards.

A few days ago the last of the 'official papers' had been distributed. It had been an extremely worthy gift, for the recipient was a former railway worker, who had worked at this very station. His job had been in the dispatch office, checking and counting consignments bound for destinations throughout the Reich or arriving at the station for distribution throughout Berlin.

Shortly before he was due to be arrested for 'anti-war sentiments' and 'sabotage', he had happened to see a 'special order' about which he knew nothing. Taking a great risk he had opened the document to discover that a train was due to arrive a week later and its cargo was paper for printing. The train was to be heavily guarded by an army escort. Luckily the man had been tipped off about his imminent arrest and had disappeared just as the Gestapo appeared to take him away.

Within a week of his disappearance he had come to the Professor's attention. Though not a fleeing Jew, he still needed help and all had agreed, without dissent, that he should receive their assistance. And so it was that a few days later, Peter and Franz were freezing in a ditch at the side of the tracks, awaiting a train.

'This is madness,' Peter whispered.

'Maybe it is, still we have to try. We need that paper,' Franz whispered back.

Peter knew he was right. With the correct paper they would no longer have to rely on altering stolen passes. They could print their own without regard to the sex or age of the recipient. It would save them a fortune and there would be no more dangerous liaisons at train stations.

'At least tell me your plan again,' Peter insisted.

Franz's plan was hardly that. They would await an opportunity to sneak onto the train. If no chance arose they would return home empty handed.

'Don't worry. It will work. At least we know when the shifts change.' Franz's optimism was often infectious. Not on this occasion.

They were about to concede defeat, when a locomotive approached the station. As soon as they saw it, they knew this had to be the one. As it slowed to enter the siding sheds they could just make out at least eight, possibly ten soldiers armed with machine guns and rifles.

'The train is too well guarded. We'll have to forget the whole thing.' Peter was disappointed, but looked forward to the warmth of the apartment.

Franz had other ideas. As soon as the convoy came to a standstill he began to creep across the tracks towards the rear of the train.

'Franz! Franz! Come back!' Peter said, as loudly as he dare. It was too late. He had to follow.

In the darkness of the night they were able to reach the end of the train undetected. Some of the soldiers walked towards the platform to use the toilets or purchase a sludgy substitute coffee. As one soldier left his post he was relieved by a different soldier.

Peter was about to drag Franz away when they noticed that the guard at the very back of the train had left and had not been replaced.

'Now's our chance Peter.' Peter nodded.

Moving alongside the rear wagon, Franz tried the lock on the sliding door. It was firmly shut and would not budge. With his pocket knife he attempted to pick the lock. Again it would not yield. He ducked under the compartment and tried to prize two floorboards apart. To Peter's amazement a section of one of the boards came away and then another. The carriage had seen much more use of late than was normal and much less maintenance than was required. Fortunately the creak of the boards splintering was drowned out by the sound of men working all around them. There was now a gap about seventy centimetres wide. It was too small for a full-grown man, or even Peter to climb through, but Franz was smaller and in seconds he disappeared completely into the darkness.

Inside Franz felt around him and then nervously switched on his small torch. There were reams of thick paper wrapped in polythene. With his pocketknife he cut open the wrapping and removed several reams. They were more cumbersome than he anticipated and it took a considerable effort to move them.

'Peter! Peter! Catch!' he said, as he dropped one onto the track through the hole in the floor. Peter just managed to catch it before it hit the metal rails.

'Careful! Not so much noise Franz.'

Peter opened the empty rucksack he was carrying and carefully placed the paper inside, rolling it first as much as possible.

'That's enough Franz. Let's get going,' Peter said quietly. He was anxious. Franz was already dragging more reams towards the hole.

'Halt! Don't move or I'll shoot! Step forward and identify yourself!' a voice shouted in the half-light. Peter could just discern the silhouette of a soldier with a rifle pointed towards him. He was nearly thirty metres away.

He stood completely still, more from fear than obedience, until a familiar voice whispered, 'Run Peter, run! There's no point both us getting caught!'

Peter responded instantly and, diving behind the train for cover, he ran away as fast as he could. The rucksack was quite heavy but fear sped him on. He did not look behind him. His body tensed as he awaited the inevitable shot. As a train approached the station he was just able to run in front of it, evading his pursuer and avoiding the bullet that whistled nearby and into the approaching train.

He had reached the embankment and was about to descend the other side, when he cast an anxious look behind.

'Over here! Over here!' he shouted as loudly as he could. It was pointless. His pursuer had given up and was trudging back to the platform. He was war-weary, tired and quite overweight. Above the noise of industry he could not hear Peter calling out.

'Good luck Franz! Good luck,' Peter said to himself and turned away. Once down the embankment, he sprinted the short distance home, hoping against hope that Franz would be safe.

Lotte was extremely distressed when Peter arrived in the apartment without Franz. He was out of breath and in between panting could only say, 'he's bound to be caught, he's bound to be caught.' Wolfi nuzzled his master's leg with his nose, but even that did not console him.

'What happened to him?' Lotte asked a little impatiently. Straight away she recognised the harshness of her tone. 'Don't worry Peter,' she said more gently, 'Franz is very resilient. If anyone can escape, he can. However I am going to give him the best chance possible.'

With that she disappeared into the bedroom, reappearing just five minutes later. She looked stunning in a figure-hugging black dress, its hem-line above the knee. On her feet she wore black stilettos, with silk stockings, a rare item for any Berliner. On her head was perched a wide-brimmed straw hat and around her shoulders hung a fur wrap. Her lips were painted with a deep ruby red lipstick.

She crossed the sitting room to the walnut drinks cabinet and opening the flap at the front, rummaged amongst the bottles. She pulled out two large bottles of vintage cognac.

'Pity,' she said, 'I was saving these for your birthday.'

She poured half the contents of one bottle into a silver hip-flask encased in leather. The other bottle she dropped into her handbag and marched towards the door.

'I'll be back soon. Wait here for me,' she said. Peter was not going to argue with Lotte as determined as this.

As Peter was running away from the train, Franz was considering what to do. It was clear that at least one of the soldiers had given chase, yet there were still many about. For the moment it was safer to stay there. He replaced the two pieces of board as best he could and sitting down on one of the large bundles of paper, he began to wait.

To his horror, having just sat down, he heard the sound of gunfire and worryingly in the vicinity of the rear of the train. He prayed that Peter would be all right. Outside the fat soldier had looked very cursorily under the compartment. He was too unfit and stiff to bend far. Franz held his breath as a bayonet clinked between the metal wheels of the train.

He still dared not breathe as the lock rattled. The soldier was checking the door. Franz exhaled quietly, relieved that the door remained shut. Satisfied, the guard returned to his post.

As he sat there in silence, Franz could not help recall all the events of the past year. He hated the Nazis for taking his parents away. On the other hand he had made some wonderful friends. Peter was now more like an older brother, than just a friend.

'Please let him be unharmed!' he murmured to himself.

Suddenly a single, beautiful voice trespassed upon his daydreams.

'Underneath the lamplight by the barrack square.' It was the familiar words of 'Lili Marlene', a favourite song of both Allied and German forces. The voice was soon joined by male voices and the haunting notes of a mouth organ. The soldiers were singing.

Franz forced his way through the bundles to the opposite side of the wagon. He placed his eye up to a tiny gap in the wooden wall of the compartment and peered out. His one eye confirmed what his ears had already suggested. It was Lotte!

She was on the train platform, swaying in time to the music as she sang, hip flask in one hand, a bottle of cognac in the other. She was surrounded by a group of about ten soldiers, all singing along. Each had their army issue tin mug with a generous splash of cognac inside.

Franz moved away from the spyhole. This was his chance. He prised open the hole in the floor and lowered himself onto the rails. Seconds later he crept away into the darkness and made his way over the tracks and down the embankment. As he did so he could still hear the distance strains of Lotte's voice. Somehow it seemed less mournful than earlier.

It was indeed less mournful, for Lotte had glimpsed the unmistakeable sight of Franz's boots as he clambered onto the track. As a professional performer she had maintained her composure and continued singing. Following one more rendition of the soldiers' favourite song and a further request, Lotte thanked them and left the station.

The next morning Peter, Franz and Lotte slept until much later than usual. The drama of the previous evening had frayed their nerves, with only Franz seemingly unaffected. When Lotte had returned home she had discovered him telling Peter what had been happening at the station. Peter was extremely happy to see his friend again and they were full of praise for Lotte's diversion. After embracing them, Lotte had retired to bed promising that she would tell the full story in the morning.

It was just after eleven when she recounted the events of the previous night.

'It was quite simple,' she began modestly. 'I told the officer in charge that I had just lost my husband at the front. The last time I had seen him was at Lehrter station on that very platform and I wanted to pay my respects by drinking a cognac and toasting him, as I couldn't very well do it on the front. I invited them to join me, which they did quite eagerly.'

'What about the singing?' Peter said.

'Oh that! Most of the soldiers were just boys, some about your age. I could tell they were homesick and wanted to cheer them up. It just seemed the right thing to do. Also I couldn't think of any other way of letting Franz know I was there,' she replied nonchalantly.

'Remarkable! Quite remarkable!' was all that the Professor could add. By now he was a regular and welcome visitor to Lotte's apartment. He was examining the printing paper very carefully and expressed his approval with a tilt of his head.

'It seems to me, however, that Lotte is taking all the risks. Everything operates through this apartment. The photographs are done here, the forgery and all the refugees come through here. If this place is discovered the whole operation fails,' the Professor added.

It was a thought that had occurred to each of them at various times. There was now a more pressing reason that they find a new venue. Lotte's husband had been on business for the Reich in the Eastern territories. He was due home in a week's time. She had been able to use her charms on him many times, although recently he had become less agreeable. He certainly would not look the other way if she harboured Jews in the apartment. At least it would be a short stay of just a few weeks before he would be off on his 'essential' travels.

'Peter and Franz can stay with me, along with the equipment,' the Professor offered.

'No. Your apartment is too small, Professor. Franz can stay with you. We can take the paper and photography equipment to your apartment today. I will go back to the woods for a few weeks,' Peter said in a voice that left no doubt that his mind was made up.

'Then I shall go with you, Peter,' Franz interjected. He was not willing to leave his friend now.

'No. You are the only one who has the skills to develop photographs and to forge papers,' Peter said, 'It is imperative that you have the right facilities to do that. You shall stay with the Professor and I will go back to my camp. I have been worried about 'Robin' as he is taking too many stupid risks. Anyway this is the best time of year. It is almost summer and I can replenish the stocks of meat and fish for the winter ahead. It will only be for a few weeks and then we can look for a new set of premises.'

'What about Wolfi?' Franz said. Wolfi lifted his head from the carpet when he heard mention of his name.

'Let's ask him,' Peter suggested. 'Wolfi do you want to stay with Franz or come with me to the woods?' Wolfi stood up, stretched, walked over to Peter and sat by his feet. No-one was surprised.

Later that day Peter, Franz, Wolfi and the Professor were walking together along Luisenstrasse towards Unter den Linden, perhaps the most famous avenue in Berlin. Peter had a rucksack on his back and Franz was carrying a large leather suitcase. Peter and Franz were attired in the naval uniforms they had recently acquired. With the expert help of the tailor they had rescued, they fitted them better than the original owners. For the moment they had left their precious bicycle behind as the Professor had agreed he would collect it later.

They had given some thought as to whether the three of them should travel together or separately. Lotte had settled the matter when she pointed out that, with the boys in their uniform and the Professor in his elegant suit, he looked like a grandfather escorting his two grandsons to the station. It was a sadly normal scene.

As the four companions walked along they did not talk about anything important. It was much too dangerous to debate their business on the streets. And so the conversation was generally meaningless. Until Franz halted abruptly.

'Quick Peter! Hide Wolfi and you as well!' Franz said under his breath. They were opposite some steps to a ground floor apartment and it was the best that Peter could do to disappear out of view. He stood with Wolfi in silence trying to remain hidden.

As he stood there Peter could see the cause of Franz's concern. Kurt! He was approaching on the pavement on the same side of the avenue. He was in his familiar Hitler Youth brown. Much worse he was with an SS officer in the distinctive black uniform, with a pistol holstered on his belt. Franz had positioned himself with his back facing outwards and his front towards the Professor and was apparently engaged in conversation with him. They were blocking the steps down to the apartment and any pedestrians would have to walk behind Franz. By this means they hoped that Kurt would not be able to see Franz's face.

It was a terrible risk. There was nothing else to do. Franz had spent much more time in Kurt's presence and he would surely recognise him if he even glimpsed his face.

'Quiet boy! Quiet!' Peter urged Wolfi. The last time they had encountered each other Kurt had kicked Wolfi and then tried to have him shot. Wolfi sensed the danger of the moment and remained perfectly still.

The seconds as Kurt passed by each seemed like a minute. Normally he did everything in a hurry. Not today. As they ambled past, the Professor raised his hat politely and the SS officer saluted. Kurt briefly interrupted his flow of conversation to utter a 'Sieg Heil!' and then continued his sentence.

When they were safely out of sight, Franz gestured to Peter and Wolfi that it was safe to move.

'That was a bit of luck,' Franz said to everyone's astonishment.

'What do you mean 'luck'?' Peter said.

'We were worried about Kurt's return to Berlin. I overheard him boasting that it is a great honour to serve the Führer and in the SS. And to be allowed to serve at the front at just sixteen. At least now we know that his stay in Berlin is only temporary.'

Peter was not entirely convinced. The weasel might still find time to search for Lotte and thereby track them down. It confirmed one thing that, for the moment, Wolfi was better off with him. Lotte's apartment was just one street away from the dreaded headquarters of the Gestapo. There was more than a chance that they would come across Kurt again. They continued on their journey and thankfully reached the Professor's accommodation without further incident.

Having helped Franz find a suitable hiding place for their equipment, the Professor left them alone and went back to Lotte. He collected the printing paper and rode back, balancing a large suitcase on the basket at the front. It was an odd sight, but luckily no-one challenged him. Safely back at his apartment, the Professor made tea for the three of them. Afterwards Peter left for his hideout in the woods.

# CHAPTER SEVENTEEN

Peter took a swig of coffee from his tin mug. It was only substitute. Still not a bad way to start the day. At Lotte's he had learnt to improve the taste with a dash of cognac or rum or whatever else was available. At that moment in time the best he could do was to sweeten it with a tiny spoonful of sugar.

It was now six days since he had left Luisenstrasse and returned to his old hideaway. He had looked forward to the outdoor existence, especially at this time of the year. April had given way to May and the milder summer was just around the corner. Unlike his previous stay in the camp, he now had a few books to occupy him and the prospect of visits from Franz and the Professor.

Even Lotte had managed to come and see him on one occasion. She was used to luxury and seemed awkward crouching on the dirty ground in her fine clothes or drinking from tin mugs. At Peter's request she had agreed that next time they would meet up somewhere half way between the two venues.

Franz managed to visit every second day. The work he had to undertake was so important Peter insisted that he devote most of his time to that. Still the day that Peter and Franz spent improving the facilities of the camp was very pleasant. Almost like the old days, except for 'Robin'.

Peter could understand the man's discomfort and the odd complaint. He was unlike anyone else they had ever tried to rescue. He really did not suit life in the woods. They needed to think of somewhere else to hide him.

As always Peter was determined to make the most of his few weeks back in camp. He decided to treat it as a holiday. Wolfi missed the company of Lotte, Franz and the Professor, and on the other hand loved the freedom of the woods. When he and Peter went fishing on the lake Wolfi could not have been happier. In the first few days Peter had already caught large numbers of water fowl, woodpigeons, rabbits and fish and the cupboard was almost bursting. With some valuable herbs and spices brought to him by Lotte, he was able to conjure up fabulous stews, appreciated by everyone.

A source of tension between Peter and Robin was the arrival of three more residents. There was a father with his son and daughter, one eleven, the other ten. They were very grateful for refuge. The father had declined the offer of new identity cards. He had been a concert violinist before the war and was concerned that he was too well-known to adopt a false identity. Recently they had been sheltered by friends. This happy situation ended upon the return of the eldest son from the war. Though badly wounded, he had lost none of his fanaticism for the Nazi cause. Until other arrangements could be made, the new arrivals were content to accept the offer of shelter in the woods. The son and daughter even seemed to enjoy the lifestyle, seeing it as something of an adventure. Both children were immediately befriended by Wolfi.

Peter drank the last few dregs of coffee and began to rinse out his cup. It was just after dawn. Once back in the woodland environment he had quickly adapted to the old routine of rising very early. The family of three were fast asleep and huddled together in the covered pit. Robin was asleep under a tarpaulin. As Peter dried out the tin mug Wolfi began to growl.

'What is it boy? What's up?' Wolfi growled again, only louder.

Peter knew not to ignore Wolfi in this mood. It was a warning. The growl grew in intensity and without waiting Peter shook the visitors.

'Wake up! Please wake up.' First the family and then Robin came to.

Peter's stomach knotted. A growing din was approaching and fast. The impression was of a large group of people, shouting, blowing whistles and beating drums, as if at a demonstration.

Wolfi had run to the entrance to the tunnel of branches that led into the clearing. His snarl was fierce and very menacing.

'We must leave and quickly,' Peter urged the visitors. The increasing wave of sound and Wolfi's demeanour terrified him. He did not know what was coming, he did know it was not good and they must not hang around. Robin grumbled something under his breath.

'No! No!' Peter screamed, as an enormous dog's head emerged from the tunnel.

It was a Doberman in full flight. Its head seemed so large because in fact there were two dogs together, with a third close behind. Their fangs were bared and their mouths drooling. It was a terrifying vision, made worse by the feverish shouting, somewhere just behind.

Only Wolfi reacted to the appearance of the slavering dogs. He bravely sprang into the air, fixing his teeth on the neck of the nearest Doberman, bringing it to the ground. The dog behind jumped on Wolfi as he defended his friends. Wolfi rolled swiftly on his flank, tossing his head from side to side. The thick fur on Wolfi's neck prevented the two Dobermans from getting a proper hold.

'Wolfi!' Peter screamed.

The third Doberman launched at Wolfi and to Peter's horror, ripped his sharp teeth into the poor animal's hindquarters. Peter's instinct was to defend his dog, but he knew he must not. In spite of the pain, Wolfi swiftly spun around, throwing the Doberman on his side into the path of the other two as they fought to get at him. There was a sickening dull thud as their powerful skulls collided.

Wolfi yelped in agony then struggled to his feet. With a last look at Peter, he ran away into the trees towards the shouts and whistles. He was chased at close quarters by the three vicious Dobermans, their sharp teeth snapping closer and closer as he disappeared into the undergrowth.

Soldiers were combing the woods with dogs and herding any wood dwellers together. Apart from the din of banging drums and whistle blasts the odd pistol shot could be heard. The combination of the cacophony of sound and the dogs was having its desired effect: all who heard it were panic-stricken. All except Peter. He was in turmoil. He wanted to go after his dog, but knew Wolfi was leading their hunters away. Quelling his anguish he signalled for the others to follow him.

'We're going to be caught! We'll all be killed!' Robin shrieked, again and again. He was hysterical and nothing Peter could say would calm him. Before anyone could stop the distressed man, he had run into the trees, in the same direction as Wolfi.

'Stop! Stop! You are running towards them!' Peter shouted.

Robin was so overcome with terror, he was simply running in blind panic, until soon he was out of sight. Moments later a shot rang out in the trees and the anguished cry of its victim was heard. Peter knew it was Robin.

'At least his torment is over,' he thought.

'Come we must hurry!' Peter urged again. It seemed heartless, but he was determined that Wolfi's sacrifice would not be in vain.

In his months in the woods Peter had learnt all the escape routes better than anyone. He circled around the back of the soldiers and made his way to the *Seawolf* by the side of the lake, stopping periodically to check on the others. As they came to the path around the lake Peter could see more soldiers, rifles pointed into the backs of grubby looking men, with straggly beards and filthy clothing. Their hands were held high up in the air. With the sun rising in the sky, the men were in silhouette. They looked like a row of crosses. In all there must have been at least ten of these men. One was just a boy, perhaps no more than thirteen.

It confirmed what he had always suspected. There were others hiding out in the woods. When the soldiers had lined up all their captives and marched to the other end of the lake, Peter crossed the path and scrambled down to the boat, followed by the others.

'Quick follow me! Don't stop until you are off the path.' Peter's words were unnecessary. The man and his children were too afraid to linger.

With shaking hands Peter managed to unhitch the mooring rope and cast off. He was not concerned for his own safety, he was worried about Wolfi. He grabbed the young girl and boy and placed them in the middle of the boat. The father took his hand as he helped him into the stern. Raising the sail, Peter began to cruise around the edge of the lake. There was some wind, not as much as he would have liked. Gradually the distance between the boat and the land increased and only the noise of the hunt hinted at what was happening in the woods. No-one spoke. Behind him Peter could see patrol boats on the water, no doubt trying to prevent any escapees into the lake. It was quite clear that they had spotted the *Seawolf* and if they wanted to catch up, the *Seawolf* could not outrun them. As they gradually increased the distance from both the shore and the patrol boats it was clear, that for now, they were not being chased.

'They probably don't believe that anyone in hiding has a boat,' Peter thought. Nonetheless he did not look back. 'Move under cover,' he ordered.

The man and his children obeyed without question. Close up they would easily be seen. From a distance the appearance was that of a young boy enjoying a day's sailing.

'Thank you, my son,' the violinist said, placing his

hand on Peter's shoulder, 'and I am sorry about your dog.' He moved to the front of the boat to comfort his children.

Peter could not respond. He felt grief and some shame. Grief for Wolfi who surely could not survive and shame that the grief felt was as real and deep as the day his parents had been captured.

They sailed further into the middle of the lake and turned towards the north. There was still no sign of any patrol boats. Peter could only think of one thing to do. They would make their way to Peacock Island in the middle part of the Havel River that formed the northern end of Lake Wannsee. There was an old chateau on the island which he believed was no longer inhabited. The name of the island promised an abundance of peacocks, although it was better known for its many rabbits. For the time being this would have to serve as their haven.

As Peter contemplated the loss of his faithful dog, the 'clearance' operation in the woods continued. Some of the wood dwellers simply surrendered and were taken captive. Others having survived much less ably than Peter, gave up hope and deliberately ran into a hail of bullets. It was the 20th May 1943, exactly one month since Adolf Hitler's birthday. Goebbels, always pleased to fulfil his master's wishes, had promised him a special birthday present. He would make sure that Berlin was finally Jew free. The terror of this day was just the latest fulfillment of that promise.

Peter had often passed Peacock Island on his many sailing trips. He had even contemplated using it as a permanent hideout. The uncertain nature of the sailing winds and the difficulty of escape had persuaded him that the side of the lake was a better choice. Besides, it was one of Berlin's most popular attractions, nicknamed 'The Pearl in the Havel Lake'. The chance of coming across day trippers or boaters was quite high. In spite of the drawbacks, they really had no choice.

Peter had no idea how long they sailed until they reached their destination. His mind was still on Wolfi. The man and his children respected his grief. When the island came into view, they circumnavigated the whole piece of land, checking for signs of human life. There were none. Choosing an appropriate landing point, they tied up the boat and went ashore.

After a brief look around, Peter identified a suitable spot in some trees where they could make a temporary camp. It was not perfect but would do for the moment. Though he desperately wanted to leave the others on the island and go in search of Wolfi, he knew he must wait for darkness. They had been lucky to reach the island unobserved. He could not jeopardise everyone's safety, not when the patrols were still around.

The remainder of the day Peter filled his time with practical tasks. He still had his pocket knife which he used to cut branches to create shelter. He had fishing lines on the boat which he used to catch lunch and dinner, all of which was grilled over a fire in a pit of earth. As he performed each little chore, he would recall how Wolfi used to observe him and sometimes help. The memories simply fuelled his growing impatience. All the while he worried about other visitors to the island.

Finally darkness arrived and Peter set off on his boat. His aim was threefold. He had to alert Franz and the others not to turn up at the camp. He needed to restock and look for alternative sites. Most urgently, he wanted to look for signs of Wolfi. He had to know whether his best friend was still alive.

Fortunately, his greatest fear had not been fulfilled. There was still enough breeze to sail back to the shore. It was difficult in the darkness and without lights, though his innate sense of direction served him well. After an agonising two hours, he was able to discern the shoreline closest to his old camp. He was still some distance from his secret mooring point, but mercifully he could tell where he was.

A quarter of an hour later and he had managed to find the exact spot where they had earlier left the side of the lake. He knew it was important to retrace his steps as Wolfi, if able to, would follow his scent as far as the bank where they had entered the water. Once he had tied up the boat, he jumped onto dry land.

'Wolfi!' he whispered. No response. He whistled quietly. No response. It was too much to hope that he would still be alive. He whistled again, loudly this time. Still no response.

From the bank of the lake, he made his way through the trees, following the route of their escape as carefully as possible. It was not easy, as tree branches caught him in the face and tree roots tripped him up.

A painful twenty five minutes later he was back at the camp. The soldiers had destroyed as much as possible.

They had not discovered the underground larder and that brought some small comfort, but still no sign of Wolfi.

'Wolfi!' he called out, and whistled louder than was wise. He did not care.

'Wolfi!' he repeated and whistled once more. Nothing. He tried in vain for a third time.

'Wolfi? Is that you boy? Where are you?'

On the third time of whistling he thought he could hear a slight, almost undetectable movement. He whistled again and listened carefully. A few metres away he could just discern a large black mound. Peter fell onto his knees and crawled towards it. He stretched out his hand and felt the familiar touch of his old jumper. Lying curled on the jumper was a fur bundle.

'It is you boy! It is you!' Peter's tears cascaded down his cheeks onto his collar.

He could scarcely believe it. His joy turned rapidly to anguish as he felt the sticky liquid on his hands. Blood! The jumper was saturated and Wolfi's breathing was very shallow. He had been badly injured. Owing to the poor light he could not tell how seriously.

'It's all right, boy. I'm here,' he said, caressing the dog's ears.

Wolfi moved his head as if to sit up. The effort was too much, and his head sank to the ground again.

'Why did I wait so long? Why?' Peter was furious with himself and now there was little he could do to help. It would be madness to try and move Wolfi in the dark without knowing the extent of his injuries. How he wished he had not gone to Peacock Island! If he had made for shore further up the lake he could have come back much sooner.

Now he faced a much greater dilemma. Wolfi was obviously seriously hurt and had been bleeding for some time. Even without the benefit of light Peter could tell that much. He could remain at his side and comfort him, possibly for his last few hours. Or he could try and save him. The only way of doing that was to seek help. But where and from whom?

After much soul-searching, he decided that he would have to try and fetch help. The only person he could think of was Lotte. She might have access to a car. With fuel being so scarce, her vehicle had become redundant, although with her husband so important in the Party, he still had his official limousine. There was no other way to move Wolfi safely, except by car. Peter hated leaving Wolfi in this state. He had no choice. He stroked the poor dog's ears once more and buried his face into the dog's fur.

'Don't worry boy. I'll be right back.' Wolfi's only response was to lick Peter's face and then close his eyes. Peter wrapped his jumper around the area of the wound hoping that it would prevent further injury.

In his many previous adventures, there had been times when Peter had to move fast to avoid detection and capture. Most recently it had been running across the railway tracks at Lehrter station with a rucksack on his back. Now, with his dog's life at stake, he ran faster than ever. He cared little for the dangers around. Every second was vital. As he sprinted through the woods away from Wannsee he caught the blue flash of a street car.

Normally both he and Franz avoided public transport. There were too many hazards and too many chances of being stopped and questioned. It was almost ten kilometres back to Lotte's apartment and Peter knew, even at full tilt, it would take too long. For the first time in many months he diverted towards the S-bahn station. Even though this took him south for a little while away from his final destination, ultimately he knew it would still be quicker. He felt the wallet in his trouser pocket. He was so glad he had taken the precaution of always keeping it with him, even when he slept. It contained money and his ID card. Soon he was at the steps into the S-bahn. It was still quite early. Most workers, other than evening and night shifts, had returned home. As such there were very few passengers about.

'A single to Tiergarten station, please,' Peter said impatiently and out of breath. He barely noticed the strange look the attendant gave him.

Walking towards the platform entrance, Peter spotted the telephone kiosk for the first time.

'Of course,' he thought, 'Lotte has a telephone. I could ring her first.' He could have kicked himself for forgetting. He was being very harsh with himself. As Lotte was the only one from their group to own a telephone, its uses were limited. And they could never be certain who was listening in. Both the Gestapo and the euphemistically named 'Research Bureau' of the Air Ministry routinely tapped or eavesdropped phone calls. They had tried using code on the phone on the rare occasions they called, until in the end their conversations became so nonsensical and confusing it was barely worth the trouble. It was unwise to underestimate the wit of the Gestapo and even an effective code might have been their undoing. As a result all of them had agreed that the telephone would be used only in an emergency.

'This is an emergency,' Peter told himself.

He walked over to the telephone kiosk and stepped in, closing the door behind him, under the watchful eye of the ticket booth attendant. He took out his wallet and searched for the few pfennig, the copper coins needed to make the call. He inserted the coins slowly and listened as they dropped into the phone. He dialled the operator. A female voice answered.

'Number please caller.'

'Berlin Tiergarten telephone number 4884. Quickly please it is urgent.'

After a brief silence a male voice spoke saying, 'Yes. Who is this please?' It was Lotte's husband. Peter had forgotten he was at home again.

'Very sorry. I must have the wrong number,' and with that Peter replaced the receiver. He could think of nothing else to say.

'Damn! Damn!' he said over and over. The phone call was a mistake. Who knew what problems it might cause Lotte. He hurried down the steps to the tunnel leading to the opposite platform. Behind him the telephone in the kiosk was ringing.

The next train was due in two minutes. Peter looked anxiously back up the steps. He sincerely hoped that no-one answered the phone that was still ringing. He resisted the temptation to pace up and down the platform. To distract his thoughts he retrieved an old newspaper from a bin. His concentration was such that he could not even have said what newspaper it was. As he stood pretending to read the paper, he caught his reflection in a pane of glass behind which a timetable was posted. As he looked closer he could see a blood smear on his cheek. He wiped his face as best he could. Traces of the blood remained. To hide his face he pulled the newspaper closer to him. His impatience grew at the sight of Wolfi's blood.

The train arrived and he grabbed at the door and leapt into the carriage. There were only two other passengers, one an elderly lady, the other a man in overalls. Thankfully there were no policemen. Or so he thought. He had not seen the police constable running down the stairs after him, followed by the ticket booth attendant, pointing at him. The train doors closed and pulled away. At the same time the constable had reached the compartment. He was out of breath, hands waving rapidly, trying to signal the driver.

Peter would never know the luck that he was to have that evening. For as the constable and the booth attendant were about to ring ahead to have him arrested, the air raid alarm sounded. Wannsee station was mainly above ground and so the staff and passengers hurried to the nearest shelter, accompanied by the police constable and the ticket booth attendant. Trains and train stations were a prime target for the bombers. They were not going to jeopardise their necks trying to apprehend a boy who most likely had not done anything. He surely had an innocent explanation for the blood on his collar. The constable was due to finish his shift soon. He did not want a lengthy, meaningless chase to eat into his rest time. By this means the two men justified their decision to leave the station and seek refuge.

Whilst they hid in the air raid shelter the train driver continued the journey. From experience he knew that a moving train was just as likely, or perhaps more likely to escape the bombs than one that was stationary. Hopefully the train drivers up ahead would take the same view. This driver hated abandoning his locomotive to the mercies of the Allies. Once more Peter's luck that evening had taken a turn for the better as the Allied planes headed towards the industrialised east of the city and the trains from Wannsee to Friedrichstrasse continued to run.

Oblivious to his narrow escape, Peter felt that the journey into the city would never end. In other circumstances he would have enjoyed his first train ride in many months, but he could only think of Wolfi.

On reaching his destination he walked as calmly as he could from the carriage. He stopped briefly at a public toilet to wash his face. He could do nothing about the blood that was now dried on his collar. There seemed to be so much and it only served to remind him of Wolfi's perilous condition.

From the station he ran the few streets to Lotte's apartment. Outside he was both pleased and a little concerned to see a large black car with the swastika at the front. It must belong to Lotte's husband. Up until now he had not thought through how he would get to see her without her husband knowing.

He walked up the steps and reached towards the bell, reminding himself of the secret ring as he did; two short rings, one longer ring and a further two short rings. It was their code and he hoped that tonight Lotte would appreciate its significance.

Just as he went to press the bell, the door opened. Peter was relieved to see Lotte's face. She had guessed when the caller had abruptly hung up the telephone that someone was in trouble and had been keeping watch as best she could at the door. She was anxious, though pleased to see him. As he stepped towards the light of the hallway she noticed the blood on his collar.

'What's wrong? You are hurt Peter.' She stepped out of the doorway as she said this, hoping to avoid prying eyes from behind her.

'It's Wolfi,' Peter said, tearfully, 'he's badly injured. They cleared the woods with soldiers and dogs. His side was ripped open by another dog as he defended us.'

'Tell me what you need, quickly,' Lotte replied, 'my husband is still here. I have persuaded him to take a bath. He is still soaking at the moment, but he will become suspicious if I am not there when he gets out.'

'I need to borrow the car and my old chauffeur's uniform. Please hurry! Wolfi can't last much longer.' Typically Lotte did not react when he said he needed to borrow her husband's car.

'I'll be back as soon as I can.' Turning away she closed the door behind her.

Minutes after disappearing Lotte opened the door. She handed him a parcel made up of a woollen blanket containing his old chauffeur's outfit, a set of car keys, a cognac bottle filled with water and a card with an address, inside an envelope. Next to the card lay an earring, pearl and gold.

'You can change in the car. The address is a vet that I know. Show him that earring and he will know I have sent you. He will look after Wolfi for you. I will try and telephone and warn him, if I can. Hurry! My husband's driver is due to come for the car early tomorrow.'

She kissed Peter and told him not to worry and then disappeared inside. In the cellar flat, Herr Klein, the block warden and caretaker, closed his window and sat back pondering what to do about the scene he had just witnessed.

# CHAPTER EIGHTEEN

It was after eleven o'clock and Peter was at the wheel of the powerful Daimler. He was in the chauffeur's uniform that he had last worn to escort Berta to the Swiss border. If stopped his identity card gave his work details as 'chauffeur'. He just hoped that the car would not be missed until he completed his task. The petrol gauge showed that there was still half a tank of fuel. That should be more than enough to get him to Wannsee and back.

The temptation to race through the streets was almost overwhelming. He resisted, knowing that car accidents in the blackout were much more common. Travelling at a steady forty kilometres an hour he soon left the central precincts of Berlin and was now motoring at greater speed along the Spanische Allee towards Wannsee. His journey was uninterrupted and he arrived at the closest point to his camp, still on the road. He pulled the Daimler into a lay-by and leapt out, blanket and cognac bottle in hand. In his haste he almost forgot to switch off the lights, such was his anxiety to see Wolfi again.

It was almost fifteen minutes walk to the camp. He covered it in less than ten. He crawled through the tunnel of branches and ran to Wolfi's side.

'It's all right Wolfi. I won't leave you now.'

Wolfi was not moving. Frantic, Peter placed his ear

towards his mouth. His breathing was very faint and just audible. He was still alive! He took the cognac bottle and poured a little water into Wolfi's mouth. The weakened animal drank a small amount and slowly licked his lips. He poured some more water into the dog's mouth.

'It's all right boy. It's all right,' he said, soothing his dog. Slowly he slipped the edges of the blanket under Wolfi, who moaned as it touched his hind quarters.

'Sorry boy,' he said. 'I'm going to have to lift you.' He wrapped the blanket completely around the injured animal, knotted the ends together and lifted the whole lot with the greatest care. Wolfi groaned at first then went silent. The distressed groans were upsetting, yet Peter preferred that to silence. Any noise or movement by Wolfi meant he was still alive.

Wolfi was a big dog, though in his time in the wild he had lost all excess fat. In the same time Peter had grown to be a strong, athletic adolescent. It was hard work nevertheless, as he carefully carried his dog in the blanket back to the car. All the time he spoke words of comfort. He opened the rear door and laid him gently on the more spacious back seat.

Peter drove away as smoothly as possible, aware that a rough journey might cause further injury. Carefully he navigated the many potholes avoiding any sudden jolts. He had a vague idea where the vet lived and as he neared his destination he had to slow down to read the street signs.

'It's so damn dark,' Peter complained, as he struggled to see ahead and read the directions Lotte had given him. At last forty-five minutes after lifting Wolfi in the blanket he was in the right street, just off Barbarossa Square, near Nollendorf Square.

Nollendorf was familiar to Peter as he had once had piano lessons in a small apartment in one of the side streets. That had stopped shortly after Kristall Nacht when his Jewish tutor had been forced out of the area.

The premises were easy to identify. It was a flat above a glass-fronted window with the inscription 'Dr. Gerhard Messner, Verterinary Surgeon'. Beneath this was engraved a list of qualifications and opening hours. The premises looked a little shabby, a poor shadow of their previous splendour. In wartime there was less call upon the services of a vet, as pets were often a luxury many civilians dispensed with first. Peter was pleased that the doctor lived above the shop. Had he been resident in an apartment block his visit would have been difficult to conceal. Next to the vet's premises were a number of businesses, each seemingly with accommodation above.

Peter parked adjacent to the kerb. There were few other vehicles around and so plenty of space outside the vet's surgery. He decided to leave Wolfi in the car for the moment. If the vet was unwilling to see him, there was little point increasing the poor animal's distress. He climbed out of the driver's seat and leaned into the back.

'Don't worry Wolfi. I'll be back soon.' Wolfi did not stir.

He closed the door softly. With mounting trepidation he approached the door of the surgery and pressed the buzzer marked 'Dr. Messner. Emergencies only'.

'I hope he's in,' Peter said, 'And I hope he agrees to treat Wolfi.' A full minute passed.

'Come on! Come on! Please be in.' Peter had no idea what to do should the vet be away. Wolfi could not survive much longer.

There was no sign of life. He pressed the buzzer again this time for longer and more impatiently. A light went on upstairs and he heard the sound of footsteps approaching the front door. The door opened a fraction and a handsome face looked back at him.

'What do you want? It's late. I don't know you do I?' the face enquired. The tone was hostile and unfriendly, as was common in wartime Berlin. Lotte had not been able to telephone him.

Peter had little time to waste. He held up the earring and said simply, 'Lotte.' The effect of the name was remarkable.

'Come in come in, don't just stand there,' the vet said, beckoning him inside.

'My dog is badly injured. Lotte, my friend, said that you would treat him,' Peter replied, knowing that every moment was precious. He emphasised Lotte's name and did not move.

The vet's face filled with disappointment as he realised his professional services were required. His passion for Lotte had not dwindled, even in the years since he had first presented her with the pair of earrings, one of which this stranger held in his hand. They had cost him almost three months income in the years before the war, but she was worth it.

'Please will you help my dog?' Peter pleaded, interrupting the vet's reminiscence.

'Where is the animal?' the vet said, adopting a professional manner.

'In the car. I will bring him to you,' Peter said, so overjoyed he was already running back to Wolfi.

At the passenger door he leaned into the vehicle and spoke encouragingly to his friend. 'It's all right boy. You will be all right.'

Wolfi lifted his head barely millimetres from the seat in acknowledgement. Peter winced at Wolfi's painful whimper as he placed his arms under the dog and lifted him out of the car.

It was not long until he had carried Wolfi from the car and into the doctor's surgery. They were in a room at the back of the building on the ground floor. The vet was unwrapping the blanket covering the wounded animal. Under the spotlight Peter could see for the first time the amount of blood that Wolfi had lost and the depth of the wound. He recoiled in horror at the sight.

'It may be worse than it looks,' the vet attempted to reassure him. He wiped around the affected area as Peter held Wolfi's head, comforting him.

Once cleaned, the wound, though still long and deep, did not appear quite so bad. They hardly spoke. Peter was not in a state to note the irony of the black and white poster on the wall behind the vet. It was entitled 'Law on Animal Protection 1933' which prohibited cruelty to animals and threatened severe penalties for their mistreatment.

The vet looked up. 'He has lost a lot of blood and is dehydrated. I shall do my best. Be prepared. He may not survive.'

Peter was not surprised, though reassured himself that Wolfi had survived a long time already. Now he was in the right hands he knew his dog would fight on.

'Come on boy. Don't leave me now,' Peter whispered close to the dog's ear. He cradled Wolfi's head in his arms.

He watched as the vet skilfully inserted a drip and suspended it from a stand. He shaved the fur around the hole in Wolfi's thigh. Next he sterilised the wound with iodine and began to stitch the flesh back together. Wolfi initially tried to bite at the area as each stitch caused pain, then settled as Peter calmed him, in spite of the discomfort.

'I'm sorry I don't have any pain relief,' the vet said.

Peter nodded his understanding and the vet continued stitching. As he finished the final stitch, the vet looked up and said what Peter had hoped not to hear: 'He'll have to remain here for a few days. He has to be completely rehydrated and he needs medicine to counteract any infection. The greatest danger is that the wound has been exposed for so long. Ideally I would like to give him a blood transfusion, but I have no supplies.'

So be it. This was clearly the best place for Wolfi and his best chance of survival. Peter would just have to trust the vet with his friend. Whatever hold Lotte had over him, it was a powerful influence.

'You look exhausted. Will you take a coffee with me? You can tell me all about Lotte,' the vet offered. For the first time Peter noticed the limp and the prosthetic leg as the vet stood upright.

'That would explain why he is not in the forces,' he thought. 'I would like to. I must get the car back. This is for the treatment.' Peter held out the earring to the vet.

The vet closed Peter's hand around the piece of jewellery and said, 'That was a gift to a special friend. Tell her a visit from her would be more than enough payment. It has been far too long.'

'I'm sure that can be arranged. I will bring you payment of my own. Thank you doctor. Thank you very much.' Peter reached out and shook the vet warmly by the hand.

The vet was impressed by the maturity of the young man in front of him and his quiet determination. Mostly though, he was excited about seeing Lotte again.

It was one thirty in the morning and Peter was at the wheel of the long black limousine again. He was very tired and regretted that he had not accepted the vet's offer of coffee. Even substitute coffee. Before he could return the car to Lotte's address he had one more thing to do. As Lotte's husband was still at home she would not have the opportunity to warn Franz that their camp had been raided. He would have to do it.

He was making his way as carefully as possible along the still dark streets. There was virtually no other traffic and although the kerbstones were identified by fluorescent paint, at times it was difficult to keep the car in the correct position.

His eyelids were heavy. A combination of mental and physical exhaustion began to take its toll and he struggled to stay awake. As he rounded a bend he jolted upright as the runner board scraped the pavement.

'Damn it!' he swore at himself and the dark. There was nothing for it he would have to go straight back to Luisenstrasse and deposit the car. He would pass the Professor's apartment on foot and alert them. With luck he would still make it early in the morning before anyone was up and about.

There were a few near misses as he drove through the dark streets, until eventually he pulled up outside Lotte's apartment. He was so tired he did not see Herr Klein pull back the curtains in his basement flat and observe as he got out of the car and locked the door. He bent over to examine the nearside runner board. It was badly scratched. He hoped that the car's official driver might not notice the difference in fuel level from the night before. He could not fail to spot the damage to the runner boards, certainly not in daylight. A near exhausted Peter pondered whether to ring the doorbell and warn Lotte. It was so late at night she would struggle to explain to her husband what was happening. He placed the keys into the envelope which had originally contained the card with the vet's address, and sealing it he was about to drop it into Lotte's postbox when the door opened. Lotte appeared in the gap.

'Your friend the vet has stitched Wolfi's side. He has to stay with him for a few days. I am really sorry, I have damaged the runner board.' Peter gave her the envelope and the earring. Lotte was completely calm and simply touched his arm.

'The main thing is that Wolfi gets better. Now take this parcel and go to the Professor's. I will visit Wolfi tomorrow and the day after,' she promised. 'We shall meet at the Professor's the day after tomorrow, at two in the afternoon.'

Peter took the parcel and peaking inside could see his naval uniform. His quizzical expression told Lotte he had not comprehended. He was obviously too tired to think straight.

'You can't turn up at the Professor's dressed as a chauffeur, when you have previously been seen as a sailor. You must change before you go,' she explained. She beckoned him into the lobby and kept watch as he switched outfits. He wrapped the chauffeur's uniform and his old clothes in the brown paper and wished Lotte good night.

As Peter descended the steps, Herr Klein moved away from behind the curtains. He did not notice the new uniform, nor had he heard any of the conversation between Lotte and Peter as they were speaking very quietly. Unluckily for him he was unable to observe the exchange on the steps, as they were out of the light. Nor had he been able to identify the young man, either from earlier that night or more recently. He suspected that they were one and the same. It might even have been someone he had seen at the apartment, except that young man was never without his dog and too young to be a chauffeur, for he was confident it was a chauffeur he had seen just now. He so wished he had heard and seen more. It was clear, however, that their meeting and the one earlier had not been innocent. He would do nothing at that precise moment. This was an opportunity and he would have to consider carefully how best to exploit it.

# CHAPTER NINETEEN

Peter made good progress on foot. The combination of the fresh, cold night air and the exercise helped to revive him. His eyes were by now quite accustomed to the darkness and he was able to avoid the many obstacles on the pavements.

He was in a much better frame of mind. Wolfi was far from saved, but he now stood a decent chance of recovery. His original decision to contact Lotte had proved to be the correct one. The vet had confirmed this. Without her name and his obvious devotion to her, Peter doubted whether he would even have spoken to him.

It was approaching four in the morning when Peter arrived outside the Professor's tenement block. It was much less grand than Lotte's residence, in the poorer working class district of Kreuzberg. As everywhere these days the buildings were half-standing, half-demolished. The great advantage of the Professor's residence was that the concierge did not live in the building itself. He was responsible for several buildings and lived in the next street. The Professor, like all residents of Berlin, had his own warden to enforce Party rules. In this building it was a man of almost seventy who seldom left his apartment on the top floor. He had deliberately chosen the top floor, in spite of the stairs, as he liked the view over Berlin. He was not particularly well-qualified to act as the official warden. Nobody complained as his son was a high-ranking Party member, and all assumed, rightly, that it was his son who got him the job. A warden who kept himself largely to himself was much more preferable than the snooping, prying Herr Klein.

Peter pushed open the front door into the foyer. It was not locked. He climbed the stairs to the second floor and gently tapped on the door to the Professor's lodgings. Two short taps, a single louder tap and then two further short taps. The noise was deliberately gentle, though sufficiently loud to be heard by Franz who was asleep on the sofa.

Franz was rubbing sleep from his eyes as he casually opened the door.

'For heaven's sake, Franz, ask who is there before opening up. I could have been anyone,' Peter said.

'Sorry. Why are you here?' Franz said, holding back a yawn.

'Wolfi's been hurt. The camp was raided by soldiers and he was mauled by their dogs.'

As soon as Franz heard the words 'Wolfi' and 'hurt' he woke up completely. Peter could see his distress and tried to reassure him. 'He's all right for now. It's touch and go, but at least he's with a vet.'

'What about the others?' Franz asked, fearful of the reply.

'Robin didn't make it. The others are safe for the moment on Peacock Island.'

'Robin has been caught?' Franz asked. The prospect of Lotte being arrested was uppermost in his mind.

'Not caught. Killed,' Peter replied. Both were aware that the poor man's tragedy had probably saved them. He could not have withstood questioning at the hands of the Gestapo.

Peter pushed back the blanket on the sofa and sat down on Franz's makeshift bed. He related the events of the previous few days. Franz winced when Peter described how the Doberman had torn Wolfi's flesh. He was on the verge of crying as Peter told how he found Wolfi curled up on his jumper half-dead. He smiled as he listened to Lotte's role and the effect that her name had on the vet.

When Peter had finished Franz paced up and down then announced, 'You are tired. You have been up half the night. I will look after our friends on Peacock Island.'

'No Franz. We shall go together,' Peter replied. 'We shall wait until midday.' That matter settled, Franz gave up his bed to his companion. Peter lay down and fell asleep instantly.

He did not sleep for long, no more than a few hours. Instinctively on waking his hand fell to the floor, looking for Wolfi. Then with some sadness he remembered.

It was after dawn. The Professor was awake and preparing breakfast. He had been updated about the previous days and night. His response was as so often, simply 'dear, dear'.

Peter took little persuading that he should stay with the Professor for a few days, at least until Wolfi had recovered. The last thing he wanted was to be stranded on Peacock Island with no news of Wolfi and no way of seeing him. He was desperate to know about Wolfi's condition, but accepted his friends' advice that it was better and safer to leave that to Lotte. At least for today. Similarly, for the time being his old camp was unusable and it was essential to avoid it for the next twenty-four hours.

'We will not make it to the island today.' Franz's words were unnecessary. It was obvious to both of them. It was two o'clock later that day. Peter and Franz were back at the *Seawolf*. They were disconsolate. The water was calmer than either had ever seen it. There was no way they could sail anywhere, let alone the long distance to the island. The prospect of the wind picking up later was remote.

'We'll try again tomorrow. Let's go,' Peter said.

Both knew that they could not abandon the family of three and they would have to reach the island, if not today, then by tomorrow at the latest. Having seen the island for himself, Peter was now convinced it was a poor place to hide and they would soon be discovered.

The boat was just five metres long and had oar attachments in the middle, with no oars. In the past they had never needed them. If they could not sail, they simply did not go out on the water. Now that travel on the water was a necessity, the lack of oars was extremely frustrating. One person might struggle to row to Peacock Island; two strong young men could surely manage it. Their first priority after Wolfi was to find some oars. They walked away in silence.

Back at the Professor's flat, Peter helped with the latest forged documents. It filled the time, but he could not stop thinking about Wolfi. Franz sensed this and every so often would utter words of reassurance.

'We shall find out how he is tomorrow at two,' he kept saying. They especially looked forward to seeing Lotte again.

When the next morning came Peter and Franz were very happy to discover the wind had picked up. Their planned trip was on once more. They walked to the boat's moorings laden with a rucksack each. There was equipment for building a more weather-tight camp: an axe, hammer and nails and some tarpaulin. Although Peacock Island was a bad hideout, it was the only place available to them at that time. They knew they needed to find somewhere else, and soon. They thanked their luck that they had not left all their tools at the old camp. The family would be dry for the few days they stayed in hiding on the island.

One of the rucksacks was almost filled with the supplies of food that Peter had hidden at the camp. It was risky. They had decided that they could not simply waste all those provisions. As it transpired, the soldiers had burnt any items they could and smashed the earthenware stove. The canopy of branches that provided such decent shelter formed the base of their impromptu bonfire. The fire had been fuelled with the books Peter had left behind, from which he had sensibly torn any inscriptions. It was not the first time the Nazis had burnt books. It was distressing to see and more so when they came across the patch of blood where Wolfi had lain for so long. It was a wonder they had not burnt Peter's jumper as well, for it was all that the poor dog had to comfort him for such a long time.

On board the *Seawolf* Peter guided the boat towards Peacock Island. It was still quite early with few people about. The boys were in their navy uniforms. It was a good disguise as what could be more natural than two young sailors sailing the waters of Lake Wannsee. The lake was virtually empty, apart from the odd person or couple in a rowing boat close to the bathing beach and one or two brave souls swimming near the edge of the water.

As the bow broke through the water, they discussed the merits of finding a new hiding place for the boat, somewhere closer to Lotte, the Professor and Peacock Island.

'I know it's a long way to travel Franz, but the boat has not been found so far. We can't risk losing it.' Peter was keen that his pride and joy should not be discovered.

Once on the island Peter was impressed to see that the violinist and his two children had not been idle. They had reinforced the 'temporary shelter' with rocks and fashioned a type of barbeque. They had explored the island and utilised whatever discarded equipment they could find. It was all unexpected from a musician. More satisfying was that they did not complain in any way that they had been left for so long.

'I knew we would not see you when the wind dropped,' the father said casually. 'We managed all right any way.'

Having said this, he took Peter by the arm and led him to one side. In a low voice he said, 'I think there is some kind of secret army installation on the other side of the island. I spotted some soldiers guarding an underground bunker. They don't leave the site. Still, we need to be careful. On an island this size they are bound to come across us soon. Don't mention it to the children.'

Peter nodded. Franz, Peter and the violinist sat on the ground out of earshot of the children and considered what they should do. For the time being a camp on the side of the lake was not safe. The authorities may still be combing the woods for 'undesirables'. They had no more permanent accommodation to offer them. The family would have to stay there at least for the next few days.

'Be careful about lighting fires. During the daytime the smoke can be seen a long way off, unless you cook everything in a pit underground. At night the glow of the flames may be visible, so you need to construct an oven of some sort. My advice would be to cook at night and not in the open. Sleep during the day. Keep a lookout for day trippers. Best stay hidden in the trees in daylight,' Peter said, passing on his invaluable experience from life in the woods.

On the point of leaving the island Franz broached a new topic. 'We understand your concern about using fake identity cards,' he began sympathetically, 'but you cannot continue to live like this. We know from experience that very few can survive outdoors without regular help. You really must reconsider.'

Peter shook his head vigorously in support, adding: 'Your greatest fear is that someone will recognise you from the concerts you gave? We can help disguise you so that even close friends will not know you.'

The violinist stood up. His movement made it clear he could not believe it was possible, no matter how much he wanted it to be true. Peter glanced at Franz for his agreement before he broke one of their cardinal rules.

'The man who brought you and your children to us for help?'

'The Professor, as you call him?' the violinist interrupted.

'Yes, the Professor,' Peter replied, 'He is someone you have met on many occasions yet you did not recognise him. He is Professor Blumenthal. He has had drinks with you several times after your concerts.'

'That was Professor Blumenthal?' the violinist asked.

'Yes,' Franz replied, 'and if he did not recognise you and you did not know him for who he was, does that deal with your worry?'

'I should have guessed when you called him 'professor',' the violinist responded. 'How stupid of me! It is a good disguise.'

Persuaded, the concerned violinist determined that as soon as practically possible, they would adopt a new identity.

Pleased with the morning's work Peter and Franz left the island, mooring the boat at its usual place.

Back at the Professor's apartment they impatiently awaited Lotte's arrival. Peter paced up and down the small living area. It was almost three o'clock and Lotte had not appeared. She was sometimes late. Many people were these days, though not this late.

'She's probably not able to get away from her husband,' Franz said in a vain attempt to calm Peter. 'Or there are problems with the trains,' he added unconvincingly. Lotte was not very familiar with public transport and had taken time to adjust.

'One of us will have to ring her. We must know what is happening.' In spite of his close run in with Lotte's husband, Peter was prepared to take a chance once more.

It became clear very soon in the subsequent discussion that it was best if the Professor rang. He had the voice of the older man and might attract less suspicion from Lotte's husband. With this purpose in mind the Professor went in search of a public phone box. It took a while. The first had been bomb-damaged. The second one was not functioning. Finally he came across a working telephone. Unfortunately it was in a post office where no doubt the operator would listen in. He had no choice other than to make the call.

To his relief, Lotte's voice crackled across the poor line. The Professor had only just said the word 'Lotte' when Lotte interrupted.

'I'm sorry my husband is out at the moment and will not be back until later this evening. I have another visitor at present. If it is about the dog that is apparently recovering so well I have already told someone else that you have the wrong number.'

With this short passage she had cleverly conveyed certain vital pieces of information. Firstly, and most importantly that Wolfi was getting better. Secondly that her husband was not at home and would not be back for several hours. Finally, that she had a visitor and an unwelcome visitor at that, judging by her tone. The Professor left the telephone booth and hurried back to Peter and Franz with the news.

Lotte replaced the receiver on the telephone on her desk and turned to face her visitor. Herr Klein, the hated warden, was grinning contentedly. He was sitting on the largest sofa with his legs crossed and arms stretched out as if relaxing in his own home.

'Well, dear lady. Do we have a deal?' his smile widened and displayed his tobacco-stained teeth.

'I will need time to think it over. It is a lot that you ask,' Lotte said, trying to hide her contempt for her blackmailer.

Herr Klein got up from the sofa and walked over to her. He raised his hand towards her long blonde hair as if to touch it. She brushed his hand aside and moved away.

'You have twenty-four hours. If you do not agree to my terms then I will tell your husband about the many male visitors. I am sure he would be very interested.' Herr Klein grinned once more and left the apartment.

Lotte sat down. She was glad he had gone, the odious man. She smiled to herself at the idea that he thought her late night visitor, Peter, and the other men, were lovers. If only he knew what they were really doing. In spite of her amusement, she knew that this was a serious problem and required careful consideration.

Later that day, the Professor arrived at the apartment. Lotte had wanted to leave. She now feared that she may be followed, and the last thing she desired was to disclose the Professor's address. When the little man appeared at the door she was delighted.

Without stopping to either greet him or offer any hospitality, Lotte put on her coat and taking him by the arm, led him down the steps from the building. She put a finger to her lips to indicate the need for silence at that point. Herr Klein might still be around.

They need not have worried for at that very time Herr Klein was celebrating his good fortune in a nearby pub. This was the opportunity he had craved for so long. The residents under his care were all very wealthy and mostly snooty. Especially that Lotte! What had she done to deserve so many privileges? He had worked hard all his life and had nothing to show for it. As he sipped his pilsner beer and gulped the schnaps chaser, he planned what he would do with all the money he was going to extort.

Meanwhile Lotte and the Professor walked towards the Brandenburg Gate where they met with Peter and Franz. Lotte greeted them in her usual fashion with a peck on the cheek.

'We have a lot to discuss,' she said. 'Come to my apartment in twenty minutes. If the coast is clear I will signal to you from the window. My husband is not due back for another two hours.'

Lotte and the Professor returned to her apartment. The only way that she could think of to ascertain whether Herr Klein was at home was to brazenly knock on his door. There was no reply. She prayed that he was indeed out of the way.

When Peter and Franz arrived on the pavement outside, she pulled back the curtain slightly and waved to them. Once inside she came straight to the point.

'Herr Klein is trying to blackmail me,' she said calmly.

'Then what are we waiting for we have to clear out and take everything incriminating with us,' Peter replied.

'No it's nothing to do with our work, Peter. He thinks that you and Franz are more than just my friends,' Lotte said.

Peter and Franz were surprised, though a little pleased, to learn that they were suspected lovers.

'He might have thought I was a lover,' the Professor said, feigning upset. They laughed.

They debated the best response for some time, eventually agreeing on a plan. It was perilous, although in the circumstances necessary. Having questioned Lotte further about Wolfi, Peter and Franz left, satisfied that tomorrow Wolfi would be with them once more. Shortly after they left, the Professor said his farewell, taking the same route as his friends, only at a distance so that he could observe whether they were being followed. They were not. By now Herr Klein was slumped on the bar, his drinking companions bemused as to the source of his exceptional good humour.

CHAPTER TWENTY

The next day Peter was awake long before his friends. He was a little apprehensive about their plan, but mostly excited to see Wolfi again. Lotte had offered to collect Wolfi from the vet's surgery and deliver him to Peter. In spite of the danger involved, Peter had insisted that he wanted to be there when he was discharged from the vet's care. None of the others begrudged him this indulgence. He would meet Lotte there. Her husband was as busy as ever and was unlikely to be home all day. She had made him promise though that whatever happened he would return by five that afternoon.

Outside the vet's practice Peter stood waiting for Lotte. She was just a few minutes late, and as a result he was already impatient. When she did arrive it was in her husband's car and she was at the wheel.

'Lotte, how did you manage to persuade Eric to let you have the car?' Peter was intrigued and delighted.

'Oh I can twist Eric around my little finger,' she said, not entirely truthfully. 'And we couldn't let Wolfi walk home, could we?'

'What about the damage to the runner board? What did he say about that?' he asked.

'They left so early that it was still dark. Neither he nor

the driver noticed and when they did they thought it must have been caused by another vehicle.'

He wondered whether to bother about his next question as to how she had covered the shortage of petrol in the tank. She knew what he was thinking and said, 'I told him it had probably been siphoned off.'

Lotte rang the bell. Dr Messner was a sole practitioner and had long ago dispensed with his receptionist and nurse and so answered the door himself. Times were very hard, especially in his profession.

Inside the vet took them straight through to the back of the building where Wolfi was resting in a cage. His ears pricked up as soon as he saw Peter and he began pawing at the door. His thick tail was beating the metal sides. Peter could hardly believe the difference from the half-dead animal he had brought there a few days ago. Outside the cage Wolfi washed Peter's face as the boy bent towards him and rubbed his head.

'Not too much excitement. He still needs rest,' the vet cautioned. 'He was fortunate. Without the blood transfusion he would not have made it.'

'What? I thought you didn't have any blood?' Peter said, confused. The vet was about to respond when Lotte interrupted.

'Let's not worry about that. Let's just get him home.' Her face and manner told Peter that she had been responsible.

'Who else?' he thought. Peter reached into a pocket and produced a diamond ring set in gold.

'It is my mother's,' he said and held it out to the vet. 'This should cover the bill.'

'No need,' the vet said, 'I have been paid enough already.' He looked adoringly at Lotte. 'You have brought back the only woman I ever loved.'

Unusually Lotte blushed. Lotte and the vet embraced and then with Peter and Wolfi she left the premises. They drove straight to the Professor's flat. In other circumstances they would have parked a few streets away. This time they wanted to shorten the walk for a weakened Wolfi.

Peter carried his dog up the stairs to the Professor's apartment. Once inside Wolfi was fussed by both the Professor and Franz. They spent the rest of the day inside, Lotte having returned home in the car. She did not want any more awkward questions about her whereabouts.

Wolfi slept most of the time, snoring with his head in Peter's lap. When three o'clock came the Professor and Franz left together and walked to Luisenstrasse. They waited outside on the pavement, slightly out of view of the apartment until Lotte signalled that Herr Klein was not in. Peter had desperately wanted to accompany them, but he was persuaded to stay and look after Wolfi.

At Lotte's apartment they discussed their plan once more and made their final preparations. They drank coffee until at exactly twenty minutes to five there was a knock at the door. Franz and the Professor hid in the master bedroom. Lotte opened the door, having first hidden the coffee cups.

'Come in, come in Herr Klein.' She beckoned him. He still wore the irritating and stupid grin. He had come prepared for an argument and was therefore surprised when Lotte seemed to greet him almost warmly.

'Before we get down to business, would you like a

cognac?' she asked. The alcoholic Herr Klein struggled with Herr Klein the cold, calculating blackmailer. The alcoholic Klein won. Only one. He would keep his wits about him.

'Sit down. Sit down,' Lotte said, gesturing towards the smaller sofa.

To his surprise she sat down beside him, uncomfortably close. She was in a tailor made, close fitting blue and cream dress with buttons up the front and as always looked very alluring.

'Come Herr Klein, drink up. It's good cognac'. She knocked back the contents of the glass. He eyed the glass suspiciously, until seeing her drink, he did likewise.

'Now about the money,' he began. He got no further as Lotte leaned forward and placed her index finger on his lip.

'Shush,' she said, 'let's not talk about money just yet. It's so common.'

Herr Klein was now even more suspicious. He was about to move away when she grabbed him by the lapels and pulled him closer to her face. It was so unexpected he ended up sprawled on top of her.

'Click! Click!' The noise of the shutter was accompanied only by the bright flash of the camera. The photographer had sneaked up behind and with Franz's camera photographed the incriminating scene. Or at least that was the impression given by the flash.

Hearing the camera click and seeing the light, Herr Klein sprang to his feet. As he did so there was a further flash and he turned just in time to see Lotte with her hair tousled and half the buttons of her dress torn off.

'What the hell are you doing?' Herr Klein was shaken and angry.

Lotte was by now quite composed. 'It's simple,' she said. 'My husband is due back in a few minutes. As you know he is a very powerful man and very jealous. Unless you drop this blackmail I will tell him that you attacked me and we have the photographs to prove it.'

'That's ridiculous,' Herr Klein said, almost spitting out the words. 'He will not believe that you happened to have a photographer standing by.'

'Oh but he will, Herr Klein.' She emphasised the 'Klein' and went on to say: 'He was asked to be here at five precisely for a surprise. The surprise is that I have arranged a family photograph. My friend, the photographer, was in the bathroom when you arrived and you proceeded to assault me. He saw I was able to defend myself and so thought, quite properly, that first he should capture the evidence. It will certainly speed up the trial at the People's Court. I hear Dr. Freisler has an eye for the ladies.'

'He'll never believe that,' Herr Klein said with venom in his voice, seeing his great opportunity slipping away. He was unable to hide his terror at the mention of the dreaded People's Court and its even more dreaded President, Dr. Freisler. Lotte could see her words were taking effect and so she continued.

'My husband has already commented on the way you have been looking at me. He will not find it difficult to believe that you tricked your way in under some pretence and then assaulted me. As for my friend's action in photographing the event, rather than trying to save me, he will applaud him for his common sense and cool thinking under pressure.'

Herr Klein did not respond so she played her trump card. 'Do you want to risk it? Take a look at that letter on the desk.'

Herr Klein walked anxiously to the desk and picking up a piece of writing paper began to read.

*'In the Name of the German People, it is hereby ordered that the following are deemed enemies of the People and are to be transferred forthwith to the concentration camp Sachsenhausen without trial. They will remain in protective custody.'*

There followed a long list of names which appeared quite authentic. They were genuine victims of the regime known to the Professor. The typed name and signature at the bottom was that of Lotte's husband. The letter heading was from the 'Reichs Security Headquarters'. The signature was stamped with the eagle clutching the swastika. The same stamp Franz had used so often. This was a masterpiece of forgery and Lotte was convinced even Himmler himself would have accepted it as genuine.

'Well Herr Klein. Do you want to gamble with your life? Your name can easily be added to the list. In the meantime you can be questioned by the Gestapo for a number of days, maybe weeks.' By now Lotte could see the ploy had worked. Herr Klein was for an alcoholic, unusually white. To clinch the deal she pointed to an envelope on the mantelpiece and told him to take it.

'In that envelope is a considerable amount of money.

It is less than a quarter of what you asked for. No doubt you planned to ask for more, again and again. It is still much more than you deserve. This is the deal. You leave Berlin and do not return. You can easily start a new life with that money. We will hold onto the photographs. If anything happens to me or any of my friends, or my husband hears of my little 'indiscretions' we will assume it was you and you will be arrested. Agreed?'

Having outlined the terms of the offer, Lotte stood back and waited for a short time, finally saying, 'Do we have a deal? My husband is due any minute. Do we have a deal?'

Sheepishly Herr Klein mumbled 'yes'. He had been outwitted.

'Then get out! You have until tomorrow lunchtime to disappear for good. When you do you will leave a letter to your superiors, recommending this person to replace you, as suggested by my husband.' She handed a piece of paper to the defeated caretaker and indicated with her eyes that he should go.

Herr Klein did not wait any longer and virtually ran from the apartment. When he had disappeared out the door, the photographer ran to Lotte and hugged her.

'Bravo! Bravo! Simply magnificent,' he enthused and began to remove his disguise. Fortunately Herr Klein had not recognised the Professor.

In days gone by she would have taken a bow and bathed in the limelight. Her husband's arrival was imminent. It was essential that he arrive soon to confirm Lotte's story. They needed to destroy the fake letter and any sign of Herr Klein's presence. The Professor and Franz must get out as soon as possible. Lotte was exhausted. It was a trying role. She was grateful that it had not turned nasty and Franz's assistance had not been required. They could never know if Herr Klein would stick to the deal. At least, for now, the problem had gone away.

The annoying difficulty of Herr Klein and his failed blackmail attempt turned out to be a blessing. Not only had their chosen solution rid them of the prying eyes of Herr Klein, Lotte's ingenuity had permitted them to install the caretaker of their choice. Usually the appointment of a new caretaker and block warden would have followed official procedures. Herr Klein's apartment was quite small, but desirable, being located in a magnificent block in a prime location in the city. As such there would have been many willing candidates for the post, and many eager to bribe the appropriate person. Accommodation throughout the city was very scarce.

Lotte's candidate was an excellent choice. A member of the Party, with two young children to support, he was skilled at domestic maintenance and had recently been bombed out of his home. The fact that he was a violinist and not a caretaker, and the fact that he was a Jew in hiding, she did not disclose.

At first the violinist had been hesitant. Lotte's apartment block was full of the very people who had often attended his concerts. If he had regular maintenance tasks to perform he would come into contact with them much too regularly, he had argued. The major flaw though was that he was neither a skilled plumber nor electrician.

'Not to worry,' Lotte reassured him, 'Herr Klein could do none of those things either. His main function was to spy on the residents.' At the mention of spying the violinist had gone pale.

'Oh don't worry. If you have to report on someone I will give you the names of the ardent Nazis in the block. You can say they were listening to foreign radio. Most of them do. Or, better, you can report that the presence of my husband means no-one dare step out of line. Perhaps that would be safer.' Lotte was teasing a little.

When she had finished giving the new caretaker his disguise, he finally relented. 'Where better to hide a prisoner, than in prison,' he said.

And so, days after the hated Herr Klein had departed so abruptly, the new caretaker, 'Herr Riesen' was installed. Naturally a few noses were out of joint that such a plumb job had been filled so quickly. When Lotte's husband made the phone call at her request, the minor officials involved did not dare to protest. Lotte had stifled a giggle as her husband bellowed on the phone, 'Of course he's in the Party. He's a good Nazi. I can personally vouch for him. There's no need to check him out. I have interviewed him myself and examined his papers and he is definitely one of us. Now that is the end of the matter.'

Herr Riesen had been interviewed by the great man, in person. It was a frightening ordeal, though helpfully the concert violinist was used to performing. He had not flinched as the newly acquired identity card and Party membership card were scrutinised. He had hidden his disgust as he was questioned as to the merits of the concentration camps. He had even impressed his interrogator with his obvious hatred of the Jew. It was a fine performance. The interview had ended quite abruptly with Lotte's husband saying, 'Good man. Make sure the boiler works. I hate a cold bath. I suppose my wife is safe from you?'

Without waiting for a reply he left the room. Part of Lotte's persuasion had been to contrast the lecherous, bachelor Herr Klein with the family man, Herr Riesen. It had done the trick.

The group of friends were much more relaxed that evening as they sat with Wolfi in the Professor's apartment. They had rescued a family of three and provided them with accommodation and an income. In the same move they had a friendly lookout, capable and willing to assist.

Although relaxed, they still knew that caution was required. In each apartment block or house anyone might report suspicious goings on to the Gestapo, either for revenge or financial gain or even from jealousy. With their own resident spy their ability to come and go had been greatly eased. As a further precaution they agreed that Lotte would place a large white vase in the bay window, if the coast was not clear.

Lotte's husband was due to leave for the East in a few days and they would be able to congregate at the apartment again. Lotte had one more plan to simplify things before he left and they were to put it into action the following day.

It was three o'clock on the next afternoon. Lotte was perched on the edge of the sofa, pouring coffee and handing out slices of cake. The cake was made with replacement flour and some of its contents were a little suspect, but it was edible in spite of it.

Lotte had two young visitors, handsome in their naval uniforms. Both their faces were weather beaten and sun-tanned from their time at sea. One face was in fact genuinely brown and healthy from a spell in the outdoors, the other required a little rouge to achieve the desired effect. Next to the naturally sun-tanned sailor was a large black dog which lay attentively at his feet, hoping for a piece of cake. It had stitches in its hind quarters.

The three friends chatted happily about old times and distant relatives. In the middle of memories of their own childhoods, the door of the apartment was flung open and the master of the house strode in. He did nothing in a calm or normal manner.

'What's this? Who are these people? What's that mutt doing in my house?' he fumed.

Lotte was by now in front of him and kissing him on his cheek. Peter and Franz, as befitted naval ratings, were on their feet standing to attention.

'Oh darling. Don't be so rude. These are my cousins from the country. You remember? I have told you about them. Ah yes, of course, you never listen. Typical man! They are on leave. Then they are departing on active service. The dog is a war hero. Peter has adopted him. Look he was injured in the service of the Führer,' she said, handing him a cup of coffee.

'Oh. Yes. Of course. I forgot,' he replied meekly.

The accusation that he never listened had hit the mark. He had met few of Lotte's relatives. They were strict Lutherans and had not approved of her choice of career. Nor had they approved of her marriage to such an older man. As an afterthought and by way of appeasement he said, 'I'll see the dog gets a medal.'

Peter and Franz looked at each other a little concerned. They were uncertain whether he was serious. He might want to know the dog's story of heroism.

Lotte promptly saved them any concerns: 'The dog does not need a medal. It needs a home while Peter is back at sea. It can't go on ship with him. Why don't I look after him? You are away so often and I get lonely. He's well-trained and he can protect me,' she pleaded.

Without much more persuasion, the powerful man, who boasted he could smell a Jew, had agreed that they could stay for dinner and sleep in the apartment. Better than that, Wolfi could stay whilst Peter was at sea. He, however, would be out that evening at a business engagement. Lotte wondered what her name might be, the 'business engagement'. She no longer cared. Her husband's work and his attitude had sickened her for some time. She wanted to divorce him, but he was too important to their rescue attempts. Recent events proved this fact.

In the space of a few days this significant cog in the Nazi war machine had unwittingly safeguarded the fate of three Jews and not only accommodated another, wined and dined him to boot.

As Peter and Franz, honoured guests now, ate and drank the especially fine meal, Peter thanked his good fortune. Wolfi was recovering quickly and he was now officially resident at Lotte's apartment. If the dog was pleased he gave no sign as he dozed noisily under the table, after a large dinner of lamb bone and gravy.

# CHAPTER TWENTY-ONE

'There's something we need to discuss.' Lotte's tone was unusually pessimistic and immediately caught the attention of her companions. Wolfi sidled over to her and lay at her feet.

It was a warm afternoon in July. The close knit group was in the woods, gathering berries and enjoying the sunshine. Unusually Lotte had joined them. She appeared embarrassed as she spoke.

'We are broke.'

They were shocked. Lotte had always seemed to have an unlimited supply of money.

'My husband is extremely wealthy, but he looks after his money very carefully. Everything I buy for the house is from an allowance. Everything I own is actually his, even the jewellery.'

'What about all the petrol to travel to Switzerland with Berta? The money for the stolen identity cards? Peter's chauffeur outfit? All the other things you have paid for? How did you mange that?' Franz asked.

'Oh that was my savings from my time in the movies. I had hoped to use them one day to leave Eric.'

Peter stood up and walked over to Lotte. He took her hand in his and said, 'Thank you. Thank you Lotte.' He already knew that she had paid for the blood transfusion.

Only now did he know it was her own money she had used to save Wolfi. The bribe to Herr Klein had wiped out most of the little money she had left.

'I'm sorry,' she said. 'I have been trying to hide it from you. I hoped something would turn up.'

'Nonsense my girl. It's our fault for never asking.' The Professor's words were echoed by Peter and Franz.

They set to thinking of ways to raise funds. Without money they would be severely limited in the number of people they could help.

Peter spoke first. 'I still have my mother's jewels. They are worth quite a lot, I should think.'

'No Peter,' Lotte replied, 'you will need them for after the war. Besides I am sure that the Professor will confirm that there is so much jewellery, especially gold in the market, that the prices are not very high.' She winked at the Professor, determined that Peter would keep the one thing that he still had of his parents.

The Professor confirmed what she said. It was not in fact a lie. So much property had been 'confiscated' from the millions of Jews transported and stolen by soldiers, officials and employees of the Reich, the market was indeed flooded with gold, silver, diamonds and other precious stones.

'Whatever money it raises, it could be enough to save another life.' Peter was determined that it was his turn to make the sacrifice. The end of the war could still be a long way off and he knew that his parents would approve of the intended use of Mama's jewels.

'That may not be necessary,' the Professor interjected. He was pacing up and down playing with the ends of his

271

moustache. His audience was intrigued as he warmed to his theme.

'One of my contacts was telling me just recently that there is still a thriving market in rare stamps. Collectors apparently are so obsessed that they will pay top prices. Especially abroad. Now I know we may not have any rare stamps, but I imagine the same applies to works of art, such as old masters. Most people are worried what will happen to our currency if we lose the war and so anyone with money prefers to invest it elsewhere. In your dining room Lotte I noticed an oil painting. It is the one of the hunting scene. I examined it recently and if it is genuine it could be worth a lot of money.'

Lotte's face brightened. 'Oh it's genuine. No doubt of that.'

She knew the one he meant. She had no interest in art whatsoever, although she could recall the day her husband returned with the painting, wrapped in paper. It was about a year before the war after the annexation of Czechoslovakia. He had been very pleased with himself. When she had expressed her dislike of the painting, he had simply agreed. It was hideous to him too. No matter, it was their financial future in the event of war. And it was not the only picture he had plundered from the occupied territories. He had tried to keep it from her, no doubt as he suspected she intended to leave him. She knew he had more pictures stashed away somewhere. She just did not know where.

'We can't take the painting in the dining room, but if we can find his cache, we could sell those. As long as he does not trace it to us we should be safe. He can't exactly go to the police to report it.' Lotte was excited as she spoke, seeing a way out of their financial difficulties.

Peter stood in silence. He looked pensive. When he eventually spoke, his words surprised all except the Professor.

'Those paintings have almost certainly been stolen from Jews like my parents. They are family heirlooms and should be returned to their rightful owners.'

'Peter my boy,' the Professor said, placing his hands on the young man's shoulders. 'Of course you are right. However, the original owners may not even be alive. If they are, they can be reunited with their property when this war finishes. Until then is it better to use them to save many more lives or leave them to those who have stolen them in the first place? We *must* make use of them.'

Peter did not argue. He was no longer thinking of family heirlooms as reluctantly the idea that his parents may no longer be alive dominated his thoughts.

'What will we do about money in the meantime?' Franz said. 'It could be months before we sell any paintings, if we ever find where they are?'

'Don't worry. We'll survive for a few more weeks. If we are careful,' Lotte replied, 'In the meantime I will write to Aunt Berta. I am sure she will help.' Lotte was suddenly much happier. She was thinking about those paintings.

Thankfully, within a week of sending her letter, Berta had responded and with a very generous cheque, written on her Swiss bank account. She had understood the hidden meaning when Lotte had written that the boys were 'doing well if a little undernourished; that is only to be expected with the shortages. We struggle on regardless.'

The clandestine rescues could continue as normal for many months to come. In spite of the new wealth, Lotte did not forget the prospect of finding the hidden works of art.

As the summer months of 1943 passed, Peter and Franz continued to fish the lakes and trap game. Whenever possible they would pick fruit or mushrooms and gather chestnuts. They became so successful that some of the produce was bartered for other items they needed. They still had printing paper to make many more identity cards and they had since obtained a new supply of ink. Franz was particularly careful not to waste either paper or ink and scolded himself ferociously if he ever made a mistake. His skill was such that these occasions were few and far between. The chemicals for developing photographs were close to running out, though they hoped to barter for more.

'Herr Riesen' was much more comfortable in his new abode. He soon gained the admiration of the residents by remaining in the building, even during air raids. It was to protect their property from looters, he had claimed. It was actually to avoid close scrutiny of his children and himself in the confined space of an air raid shelter. The devotion to duty even prompted some of the residents to make gifts of extra food for the children and the occasional bottle of schnaps for him. One even wrote to the authorities praising this 'fine patriotic Aryan, a great example of National Socialism'. His original worries as to his abilities in maintenance were unfounded as he quickly adapted to the new skills required. The children's non-attendance at school he explained away by saying that they were being privately tutored at home. It was costing him a fortune, but it was worth it. This selfless sacrifice for his 'darling children' attracted yet more praise. The only danger now facing Herr Riesen was his popularity. Everyone loved him so much he was seldom left alone.

In the period since Wolfi's injury the chance to rescue anyone had seldom presented itself. In the main their actions had consisted of providing forged papers to those who required them. Most fugitives were cautious and slow to trust anyone. It was sometimes the most they could do to submit to being photographed. None were permitted to leave without some sort of food parcel, some money and whatever clothing was available.

To reduce the chances of detection and arrest, Franz had located a new venue for their forgery and photography. It was ideal. It was in the basement of a nearby block. The majority of the building had been destroyed and outwardly it appeared that only a pile of rubble remained. It took a very close inspection for anyone to discover the entrance through the huge pile of concrete and bricks. It was so well disguised they had contemplated whether to use it as a hideout for some of those they were attempting to rescue. In the end, their forgery activities were so important to their plans they decided to keep it separate from their other work.

'This is perfect Franz. Completely uninhabited with plenty to hunt. And no chateaus or peacocks to attract the tourists. Plus an old stone ruin that can easily be rebuilt. Best of all, it is so difficult to land a boat that very few will even try.' Peter was pleased that their long search for a new camp was over.

They were standing on top of their newly discovered island paradise. It was a small island in the Havel, where the river widened to form a lake. It lay a short distance below the island of Schwanenwerder and was only to be reached by private boat. It was situated away from any of the ferry services that conveyed day trippers to the other islands of interest.

Apparently inaccessible, they had found the one approach to the island that allowed a small boat to land. As the water flowed swiftly down one side, on the other, it moved at a more sedate pace. On the southern tip of land where the two bodies of water met, a whirlpool was created. Provided a boat approached at the right angle to the swirling water, it was in fact possible to turn inwards to the shore and moor out of view in a small inlet of rock. Only by crossing the whirlpool and continuing on this one course was the inlet of rock visible from the water. On the other side of the small island the land fell sharply to the water and the banks were guarded by heavy foliage, that from the water appeared impenetrable. This foliage served to hide the activities of anyone living on the island from the outside world.

Where possible Peter and his friends would try and provide the 'u-boats' with new identities and hence the prospect of ration cards and accommodation. With the new papers and proper lodgings there was some chance of survival, although the daily search for food would continue.

Not everyone could be helped in this way. Some poor

souls were so dejected and dispirited and physically weak, that they had no realistic hope of surviving in everyday Berlin society. Some like 'Robin', were convinced that their 'Jewish' appearance was such a giveaway, they would not risk using even the most genuine of papers and so were forced always to remain in hiding. For this category of u-boat, those permanently hidden from view, life was especially hard. Never being able to wander freely outside; always disappearing when the doorbell rang or the door was knocked; constantly whispering for fear neighbours might detect their voices; the never diminishing fear of discovery; the uncertainty as to whether and when it might end: all of these restrictions led to an overwhelming feeling of imprisonment and hence depression and despair. For all u-boats two matters constantly occupied their minds: when will I next eat and how long can I stay here?

'At least we can stop worrying about anyone wandering off and getting caught,' Franz commented.

'Yes, I suppose that is an advantage. I just hope they don't feel trapped here,' Peter replied.

They were conscious that those living on the island might have the feeling of swapping one type of prison for another.

Whilst Peter and Franz were checking the new hideaway, Lotte was making an important phone call.

'Of course it's urgent. I wouldn't ring otherwise. Tell him it's his wife. I am not going to tell you what it is about. Now just put me through to my husband.' Lotte was on the verge of losing her patience with the operator. Eric was in a meeting and not to be disturbed. She wondered what her name was, this 'meeting'.

'Yes! What do you want now?' Eric balled down the telephone line, 'More money no doubt?'

'Sorry I bothered to ring,' she replied. She tried to sound concerned. 'I just thought you might like to know about the visitor earlier. He was asking about that horrid painting in the dining room. You know? The hunting scene. Anyway goodbye.'

'Wait darling Lotte. Wait!' Eric pleaded, his manner suddenly altered. 'Tell me about this visitor. Who was he?'

'Oh I can't remember his name. Actually there were two of them. They were both wearing those hideous black leather coats and hats, you know that the Gestapo like.' Lotte was beginning to enjoy her husband's discomfort.

'Don't speak to anyone. Anyone! You understand? I will be home tomorrow.' Eric slammed down the phone. Lotte smiled. He had taken the bait. Peter's idea had worked. So far.

# CHAPTER TWENTY-TWO

'It can't be, can it?' Peter asked, uncertain of what he was looking at.

Peter and Franz stopped and stared. Wolfi strained on his lead, barking noisily. The Nazi seizure of power and the subsequent war had turned life upside down to such an extent that many bizarre sites seemed common place in Berlin. Even for these strange times, this was something unheard of. The two boys were in the Tiergarten, just off the Charlottenburger Chaussee. The area brought back happy memories as it was close to Aunt Berta's house.

In the centre of the park was a large ornamental fountain. In the water surrounding the fountain was a giraffe drinking and splashing water. The water was obviously much colder than it was used to, as it coughed from time to time. It was November and very cold. A few metres away, and eyeing up the giraffe, was a lion. It appeared as if the lion was uncertain whether the giraffe had the physical advantage and so was unsure whether to strike.

Behind the lion was a keeper with a net and a long pole. On the end of the pole was a loop of rope, presumably to restrain the lion. Behind the keeper was a crowd of Berliners egging the unfortunate man closer and closer. He would creep a few steps towards the lion and then a few steps back, as the lion periodically turned towards him.

Some of the crowd were wondering what giraffe or lion might taste like as it was so long since proper meat had graced their tables. For most however, it was the best entertainment they had enjoyed for many long months. It was a welcome respite from the tribulations of everyday life, especially the terrifying bombing raids that had destroyed much of Berlin, including the zoo that very day.

Peter and Franz left the park smiling. Wolfi was still keen to herd the escaped animals. Like most of the crowd they were supporting the lion and the giraffe. Unfortunately they did not have time to dawdle any further for they were on their way to the new island camp. Currently it was occupied by just two people, a young married couple who had taken to their new surroundings very well. After life in a cramped cellar, the couple found life on the island much more bearable, especially as they had decided to treat it as the honeymoon they never had. Peter and Franz were making the weekly visit with supplies of everyday items they could not obtain, most importantly salt.

There was another purpose to their visit. They were going to live on the island for a few days. Peter relished the prospect. He enjoyed the comfortable surroundings of Lotte's apartment and the companionship of his friends. There were times however when the simplicity of life in the outdoors appealed to him. Especially at this new camp where less caution was required. He particularly enjoyed spending the whole day with Wolfi.

The reason for their temporary exile was the impending return of Lotte's husband, Eric. He now believed they were Lotte's cousins, but it would arouse suspicion if they were once more on leave.

Lotte's telephone call the day previous day had the desired effect. In spite of his position in the Party and in government, even Lotte's husband feared the consequences if his boss Göring were to discover he had been hoarding looted treasure for himself. Any rewards for subordinates were to be granted by Göring alone.

And so as Peter and Franz journeyed to the island hideaway, Lotte's husband was pacing up and down inside the apartment. Ever since his arrival he had appeared nervous. He had barely greeted his wife and had sneaked out of bed in the night to whisper a phone conversation, to whom, Lotte knew not.

Eventually he stopped his pacing and putting on his overcoat and hat, then left the building with a large brown parcel under his arm. He said nothing to Lotte about where he was going, but she noticed that, unusually, he did not take the official car, preferring to walk. This was unheard of and aroused even greater suspicion in her mind. On the wall above the sideboard in the dining room, a white rectangular space, framed by dust, stared back at her where an oil painting had once hung.

As he left the building, the distracted Eric did not notice the elderly well-dressed man behind him. Both walked for about twenty minutes then descended to the platforms at Potsdamer Station. The Professor watched from a distance as Lotte's husband purchased a ticket to Friedenau, a wealthy upper-middle class district. The

Professor calmly bought his ticket for the train and soon, the two men were standing on the platform, apart by some fifteen metres. They entered separate compartments when the train pulled up, five minutes later.

At their destination the Professor allowed his quarry to leave the train first. On reaching street level, Lotte's husband turned left and walked about two kilometres, stopping at a large apartment block set back from the street. Without turning around he climbed the steps and pressed a bell at the top of a row of four. The Professor watched as a very pretty young woman opened the door. She had long blonde hair and in appearance looked similar to Lotte. She was about twenty-five and very well-dressed. The impression that she might be the man's niece was quickly dispelled by the apparently passionate kiss that she gave him.

When the pair had disappeared inside, the Professor mounted the steps and tried the door. It was locked. As he contemplated his next move he read the name from the doorbell: 'Miss Elise Ritter'. He was about to take a chance and ring another of the doorbells, when a postwoman arrived at the top of the steps. She was tired and undernourished and fed up with feet that had blistered again. The soles of her shoes had long since worn through.

'Anything for my granddaughter, Elise, Elise Ritter?' the Professor said, before adding helpfully, 'I can take it up to her if you wish.'

The weary postwoman was surprised, if pleased by the offer and readily handed over the small brown envelope. There were no other deliveries to the building that day.

By this means the Professor established not only the name of the young lady, but her precise address too. When the postwoman was out of view he slid the envelope under the front door, having first memorised the address.

Back on the pavement he remained at a safe distance from the front door and watched. Twenty minutes later he observed as Lotte's husband stood on the doorstep and kissed the young Elise then made his way down the steps and back to the station. He no longer had the parcel under his arm.

The Professor did not follow him, instead stayed in position a little longer. Not knowing what to expect or hoped to discover, he decided that a further half an hour's surveillance might be useful. In the event he did not have to wait half an hour until Elise came out the front door, a large canvas bag under her arm. He could just see the top of a brown paper parcel protruding from the bag.

He followed Elise to the station where she caught a train to Zoo Station. From the Zoo Station he watched from afar as she walked towards Kurfürstendamm, one of Berlin's most prestigious shopping streets.

Passing the memorial church on the right, she hurried westwards along the Ku'damm until she stopped in front of a shop window. The Professor was stationed on the other side of the street. Even in wartime the Ku'damm was crowded and therefore no-one paid him any attention. Once the young woman had disappeared into the shop, he crossed the street. As he was stepping onto the opposite pavement he saw the sign in the door to the shop turn around to read 'closed' and heard a bolt pulled to one side. He leaned towards the shop window and peered inside. The shop was full of mostly junk, and some genuinely valuable antiques. At the back there were a few oil paintings of reasonable quality.

Positioned to one side of the window the Professor appeared to be admiring a particularly fine, antique cuckoo clock. From his vantage point, however, he could just see the torsos of two people, Elise and a much older man. On the floor was the oil painting from Lotte's dining room with the brown paper covering partly torn away. The hand of the man reached out towards the girl and the Professor was able to distinguish a large bundle of Reichsnotes, which were passed from one to the other. The Professor was slightly embarrassed as the girl pulled aside her overcoat and hitching up her skirt, deposited the notes in a pocket.

The Professor was on the verge of turning around when he felt a tap on his shoulder.

'Interested in young ladies are we Grandpa?' a stern voice said. The Professor spun around on the spot to see a policeman, thankfully from the criminal police not the secret police. The policeman was smiling to himself.

'No. No!' the Professor blustered. 'I was admiring that clock. A cuckoo clock from Switzerland. There are only two things that Switzerland has to be proud of. The cuckoo clock and chocolate. They are cowards for not supporting us in the war.'

'Okay! Okay Grandpa!' the policeman replied, almost laughing. The vehemence of this funny old man's denial had surprised him. But he was right about Switzerland.

'On your way then. And don't let me catch you admiring too many more cuckoo clocks.' As he said this the policeman winked. The Professor did not wait and tipping his hat hurried away. He was a little red in the face.

At her apartment Lotte had removed the white vase in the window to show the Professor that it was safe to enter.

'A peeping Tom, eh, Professor?' Lotte teased. She had not been surprised to learn of Elise's existence. She had long suspected as much.

'At least we know where the paintings are kept and where we can sell them,' she said, thinking out loud. 'We must act quickly. Eric may only have sold the one painting as it was a clear link to him. Or he may have taken fright and decided to sell the lot, one or two at a time.'

The Professor did not speak. He was still thinking about peeping Toms.

'I wonder,' Lotte said, and failed to finish her sentence. The Professor looked at her. He was intrigued. Another scheme was being hatched.

Two days later Peter and Franz were back at Lotte's apartment. Her husband had stayed for just one day and so, Lotte reasoned, he was not intending to sell any more paintings. She had not been idle since the discovery of Elise's whereabouts. Pretending that her car had broken down, she had rung the doorbell to Elise's apartment and asked whether she could use the telephone. It was no surprise to learn that her husband had not paid to have a phone installed at his mistress's address. He no doubt begrudged paying the rent for her and was certainly not going to stretch to the cost of a phone, in spite of his enormous wealth. Anytime he wanted to see her he would simply turn up and expect her to be there.

'Eric's secretive late night phone call must have been to the antiques dealer,' she reasoned.

Furthermore, it was clear that Elise did not go out to work, something confirmed by the Professor, who kept watch outside the address.

Lotte knew she was taking a chance by undertaking this excursion, but she had been keen to see her rival. It shocked her somewhat to discover that she was very similar to her in appearance, just a little younger. Her main purpose had been achieved. They now knew that Eric was unable to phone his mistress either at home or work.

Upon returning home, Lotte sat down with Franz to draft a letter. The contents were brief, yet it took some time to write as Franz patiently copied samples of handwriting and practised the same signature, over and over.

Finally, after hours of hard work the completed letter was sealed in an envelope and addressed to Elise Ritter, in Friedenau. Lotte took the letter to the post office herself and was pleased when the clerk confirmed it would be delivered the following day.

Three days after the Professor had discovered Elise's existence and the purchaser of the paintings, Herr Riesen was waiting outside the antiques shop in the Kurfürstendamm. He was uncomfortably attired. It was not the cut or the fit of his clothing that made him uncomfortable, it was what he was wearing. The Gestapo did not have an official uniform for its detectives, but they wore one nonetheless. It consisted of leather hat, boots and long leather coat, all black. Everyone knew the Gestapo when they saw them. He wondered at how his circumstances had changed, when just a few months ago he carefully avoided bumping into anyone wearing this garb, now here he was clad head to foot in black leather. He could feel people's eyes hastily turning away from him, unable to hide their fear.

Herr Riesen had been more than happy to help Lotte when she had requested his assistance. Now he wished he had been more circumspect. He owed his life to Lotte and her friends. He understood they needed funds to continue their activities, but could he really pass himself off as an inspector from the Gestapo? He could see that the Professor was too old to play the detective, and Franz and Peter too young. He had been the only possible choice. What worried him most was the knowledge that he was about to 'arrest' the mistress of the powerful man who had recommended him for his post as caretaker.

As Herr Riesen debated the merits of the situation with himself, he heard the jingle of bells as the door to the antiques shop opened and the pretty young girl emerged. She had acted upon the letter written apparently by her lover and was in the process of selling more paintings. As per instructions she had not contacted him since receipt of the letter.

Across the street, Peter nodded to him and some twenty or so metres from the shop, Herr Riesen approached the girl. Holding up his false identification card in its leather wallet, he spoke sternly saying: 'Miss

Elise Ritter? I am arresting you for handling stolen art treasures. Do you have anything to say?'

Elise Ritter went pale and Herr Riesen feared she was about to faint. Thankfully in her shock it did not occur to her that the Gestapo always arrived in pairs and this man was alone. Nor did she notice that apart from flashing an identity card, he had not said his name.

'Now Miss Ritter, I know you have a large amount of money on your person. Either you hand it over to me or I will have to remove it from you right here in the street.' Herr Riesen prayed she would indeed hand over the money there and then.

With little fuss, the young woman reached inside her coat and produced an envelope containing an enormous bundle of notes which she handed to him. He quickly secreted them inside his own leather overcoat. The fact that this Gestapo agent was holding an enormous sum of money did not register with any of the passers-by, so intent were they on avoiding his attention.

'Good Miss Ritter, I am glad to see that you are cooperating. We of course know where you live. It will save time if you confirm that there are more paintings hidden there. And do not think you can protect your accomplice, we know who he is.'

The unfortunate Miss Ritter could not hide her distress when her accomplice was mentioned. Her only response was to nod. The next part of the plan was potentially the trickiest. In most circumstances the unlucky victim of the Gestapo would have been transported to the 'Alex' or Albrechtstrasse in a staff car. It was often the last comfort they would experience. On this occasion Herr Riesen did not have a car to use and would have to rely on a taxi, if he could find one.

The effect of the Gestapo outfit was such that the normally disinterested taxi driver could not ignore Herr Riesen as he hailed a cab. If Miss Ritter was surprised that there was no official transport, she did not show it.

When the cab driver pulled alongside he was unhappy with his potential fare, but knew there was nothing he could do. The Gestapo hardly ever used his car and when they did they never tipped. Sometimes they wanted a free ride.

'Friedenau! The young lady will direct you,' Herr Riesen ordered.

The taxi driver's upset grew. The destination was not in the city centre. Miss Ritter was surprised that they did not go to the Gestapo headquarters first. She knew, like most Berliners, that they would normally search an address whilst the owner was in custody.

Herr Riesen seeing her concern, reassured her: 'We shall go to your apartment first and then let's see where after that.'

The cab driver was looking in the rear view mirror. It was not the first time he had seen this happen. 'Poor girl,' he thought, 'she will probably wish she had been taken to Headquarters.' Reluctantly he drove the detective and the frightened young lady to Friedenau.

On arrival at the address, the driver was paid and dismissed. Whatever was going on he was not going to interfere.

Elise Ritter was so nervous she could not insert her key in the door. Herr Riesen felt a pang of sympathy and regret. He took the key from her and having opened the door, stood back to let her enter.

Once inside the apartment the girl went straight to an old settee upholstered in burgundy velvet. She began to tip the settee on its side when Herr Riesen rushed forward to assist. Once upended and the lining underneath removed, the settee gave up its bounty of three large and six smaller oil paintings. One of them Herr Riesen held up to the light.

'Beautiful, very beautiful,' he cooed, forgetting his alter ego. It was a painting he knew well and often admired.

Miss Ritter sat down on an armchair and began to cry. Herr Riesen could see her suffer no longer.

'Now Miss Ritter you have been very cooperative. We are not so interested in you. You are young. It is your partner we are concerned with. No doubt he pressurised you into doing this?' he said.

Sensing a glimmer of hope, Miss Ritter stopped crying and said, 'Yes. But not only to do this. We only got together because he threatened what he could do to me otherwise. I was a secretary in his office. I either did what he wanted or he would have me sent away.' She sobbed even more. Herr Riesen's sympathy was genuine. There were many victims in these terrible times.

'Don't cry my dear,' he said tenderly. 'Here is what we will do.'

At this point he departed somewhat from the previously agreed script. Afterwards no-one held it against him. He made it clear to Miss Ritter that she must destroy any evidence of her involvement. She sat down and he dictated her last letter to Eric. She wrote that her flat had been raided by the Gestapo and turned upside down and that they were asking for his whereabouts. They had taken everything of value, and emphasised the 'everything'. She was to be allowed her freedom as they were satisfied she had been used and that the real culprit would soon be caught. She could no longer stay at the flat and was to leave for the country.

'That's that, my dear. Now one last thing, have you relatives or friends you can go to? And have you any money?'

'I have friends in Austria. Eric knows nothing about them. I have a little money saved, enough for a train fare,' she said.

Herr Riesen reached into the envelope and pulled out almost a third of the notes.

'Take this. Now pack your cases quickly, before my sergeant gets here. Do not ever communicate with either Eric or my office again. Understood?'

A week later Lotte, Franz, Peter, Herr Riesen and the Professor were toasting success with real champagne. They had allowed themselves a treat as the whole venture had turned out much better than imagined. Upon receipt of the letter from Elise, Lotte's husband had panicked. He was well-connected and very senior, yet even that would not save him from Göring's wrath. Göring had been building an art collection for some years and one of the most prized items had been stolen by Lotte's husband. Now that he believed the Gestapo were onto him he had no alternative. He had to flee. He had lost the paintings but had a considerable fortune that he had transferred abroad, in case the war went badly.

He had communicated all of this by a brief call to Lotte: 'I am going abroad. You will not see me again. You will get your divorce eventually.'

With that he had hung up the receiver and indeed Lotte did not see him or hear from him again. After so many years she was free. She had the apartment to herself and no worries about her husband returning. His influence and contacts had been helpful at times, but on the whole, his departure meant greater freedom for all of them. They now had a collection of valuable artwork, enough money from the sale of the other paintings to fund their activities for another year and yet another source of income. Whilst her husband had been planning his escape Franz had forged a transfer of funds from his account to Lotte's. She was an independent, wealthy woman once more.

# CHAPTER TWENTY-THREE

It was the end of November 1943 when Lotte's finances were restored to their original position. The money could not have arrived at a better moment. Winters were harsh at the best of times. With rationing of just about everything, including fuel, it was even harsher. Even those who could live legitimately in the open found it difficult to maintain a full and healthy diet. Ration cards did not guarantee supplies. Often shopkeepers would only sell to those they knew. A long wait in a queue often resulted in disappointment. There was nothing left to buy. For many the only means to supplement their meagre rations was through the black market. Not only was it dangerous, it was very costly. For those living underground it was almost impossible to survive without outside help. Fortunately, and to their great pleasure, Peter and his friends were able to do this many times over. By now their resistance group had helped almost twenty Jews to a new identity and a new chance of life. Through their distribution of food, clothing and ration cards they had aided many others. With the provision of shelter on their island, many more had found a temporary haven.

Those they assisted shared many similar characteristics. By the time they had come to the attention of the group of friends, they were desperate and despairing. Some had been on the verge of taking matters into their own hands to bring an end to their suffering and that of their family.

Peter and the others were careful to try and avoid preferring one desolate person over the other. However, it was only human nature that they should have their favourites, even if they were fastidious to avoid letting this show in the way they treated others. This rule that they normally adhered to steadfastly was broken only once.

It was just over mid-way through December 1943, about a week before Christmas. Peter was waiting on the famous museum island, close to Berlin Cathedral, a remarkable and impressive piece of architecture. Wolfi lay at his feet. It was cold, but dry and he was growing impatient. That he was waiting to meet a 'person in need' was all he really knew. The time and place had been agreed through the Professor. Close by Franz acted as lookout.

'No-one is coming,' Peter muttered. Franz had come to Peter's side. The meeting should have been half an hour earlier. Peter tried not to show any annoyance. It was often difficult to keep appointments. If the threat of the Nazis did not interfere, the reality of the Allied bombers might.

'We'll wait just ten minutes longer,' Franz replied. It was close to seven and they were hungry and cold.

At least this was one Christmas they would spend in comfort and warmth. Lotte had somehow managed to buy a rare traditional carp for Christmas Eve. There was even a splendid tree in her sitting room, decorated with ginger bread men and chocolate bells. The bells were substitute chocolate but the gingerbread was genuine. The ever resourceful Lotte had procured all the ingredients to make a festive mulled wine.

Lotte's final touch was to place presents under the tree for each of them. The boxes and packaging were impressive enough, irrespective of the contents. Of course Herr Riesen and his children had not been forgotten. Nor of course, had Wolfi.

Franz was looking forward to this Christmas in a way that had been unimaginable just a year ago. The only problem he faced was what to buy Lotte? Even if he had the money what would be available?

As Franz recalled the many happy Christmasses he had spent with his parents, and looked forward to the next, he failed to notice Peter as he drifted away from the rendezvous point, followed by Wolfi. Peter was normally very disciplined, but on this occasion he looked like a boy hypnotised.

In fact he was not hypnotised, he was simply enchanted. From the nearby cathedral the sound of angel's voices floated through the air. The words of 'Silent Night' sung in beautiful harmony escaped the solid walls of the cathedral. Peter and his family, although Jewish, had always enjoyed the celebration of Christmas, particularly the hymns. Peter could not help himself as the music and the harmony of the perfectly united voices drew him closer and closer, until he entered the cathedral, telling Wolfi to wait inside the large front doors.

Franz followed, both concerned and intrigued, and sat down beside him in a pew at the back. The gold candlesticks on the altar sparkled with the flickering lights of the candles, as wax dripped slowly down the stems. The choir boys in their pristine white vestments stood proudly at the front, conducted enthusiastically by the choir master. The whole scene reminded Peter of the last time he and his parents had worshipped at the synagogue in Oranienburger Strasse.

'There really is so much in common with the faiths,' he thought.

They sat in silence for the next half an hour as more Christmas favourites were performed. The recital finished with another rendition of 'Silent Night', this time with the congregation joining in. Peter and Franz, two friends of different religions, united in adversity, sang as loudly as their lungs would allow.

As the words echoed around and outside the cathedral, the inhabitants of Berlin gave thanks that for the moment, no bombs were being dropped and the heavens were clear. Peter gave thanks that he had survived another year since separating from his parents and prayed that he would one day see them again. Franz, who did not believe in prayer, gave thanks for the day that he met Peter and Wolfi, and the day they had both met Lotte.

The recital finished, they left through the main entrance, greeted enthusiastically by Wolfi. The rest of the congregation filed out hopefully behind.

'Let's just check the meeting point one last time,' Peter suggested, cheered by the Christmas service. By now it was much later than the agreed rendezvous. They returned to the arch of the bridge where they had arranged to meet. There was no-one there.

'No-one. Let's go home, Peter.' Franz was thinking of the warmth of the Luisenstrasse apartment. Peter turned to follow his friend, calling Wolfi to him. Wolfi did not move. The dog was sniffing at a gap in the parapet of the bridge. Then he began to paw at the brickwork. As he pawed more rapidly he began to whine.

'What is it boy? What's the matter?' Peter said, walking back towards Wolfi. Suddenly he stopped. 'What's that?' he whispered to Franz.

'I can't hear anything,' Franz muttered, growing impatient.

Peter held up his hand, telling him to be quiet. `Sit Wolfi!' Wolfi sat obediently, remaining silent. 'There it is again!' Peter said, overcome with excitement.

This time Franz could not fail to hear it. It was a gurgling noise, like a well-used cistern. They stood still momentarily and then both heard it again. It was coming from behind the parapet of the bridge where Wolfi had been pawing. Wolfi whined.

'All right Wolfi! All right!' Peter said and leaned over the wall.

He could just see a figure scurrying away in the darkness beneath. As he stood upright, in the corner of his eye he spotted a small bundle of rags. It was wedged between two columns, precariously close to dropping into the river. He leaned over and pulled back a dark woollen blanket.

'What on…?' Peter exclaimed. 'It's a child!'

He could scarcely believe his eyes for on closer examination he realised it was a young girl of no more than four or five years old. She was tiny. The gurgling noise was her laboured efforts to breathe in the cold air. She was virtually unconscious. Her cheeks chilled his hands as he felt for any signs of warmth. Wolfi was now by Peter's side, sniffing the bundle and periodically licking the girl's face.

'Well done fella! Well done!' Peter said.

Picking the girl and blanket up, Peter cradled her in his arms and began walking away, before anyone could see what he was doing. He carried her easily for she was very underweight.

Although they had long since stopped taking anyone to the apartment, this was different. Without any discussion Peter knew that Franz was in agreement.

Back at the apartment the bundle including the small child was lying on the sofa, wrapped in a warm blanket. She had been bathed in very hot water and some of the colour had returned to her cheeks. Lotte had held her close to her chest and having warmed her, managed to feed her some soup. The child had not spoken a word and was sleeping, at times fitfully. Her tiny overcoat was on the chair next to her with threads hanging from one lapel where Lotte had torn off the Jewish Star in disgust.

'What sort of person tattoos a number on a child's arm?' she asked.

For the first time ever her friends had seen her really incensed. Lotte had bathed the young girl and was dumbstruck when she had come across the long series of numbers tattooed on the child's forearm. Until this point the horrors of war had largely passed her by. Of course she had heard Franz's horrible tale and all the details of Peter's survival. She knew of terrible acts perpetrated by the regime from many of the very people she had helped to rescue. All of this she had managed to put to the back of her mind, as much for her own sanity as for any other reason. This was different. This one act of mutilation to a girl so young and innocent had a profound effect on her.

After nursing the young visitor most of the evening, Lotte placed her in her own bed and took up position in a chair by the bedside, wrapped in a horsehair blanket.

When Lotte woke the following morning she leaned forward to examine the patient. 'She's gone!' Lotte said anxiously.

Throwing the blanket from her shoulders she rushed out to the sitting room. Her young charge was standing in front of the Christmas tree holding Peter's hand. She was looking at the gingerbread men and the chocolate bells.

'In a few days you will be able to eat them. When Father Christmas has been.' Peter was crouched down with his head touching hers as he spoke. Next to both of them lay Wolfi. Lotte was pleased as the only real reaction they had observed from the girl was to try and hide when Wolfi had approached. Now she was wedged against him with his head resting on her foot.

The first full day with the girl was spent trying to encourage her to talk and disclose her name. As yet no-one had heard her speak and it was to be another full day before she uttered a word. Her means of communication was to nod or shake her head.

She was very underweight and pale looking. Her black curly hair flopped over her forehead and her dark eyes radiated sadness. It was difficult to guess her age as she was so small, but she could clearly understand what was being said to her.

For all the adults, the first full meal that she ate on her own gave them great pleasure. It was only a vegetable soup, thickened with flour and served with bread and a little cheese. As she ate she looked around her in all directions, as if expecting someone to steal it. Lotte constantly reassured her.

'Don't worry my darling. No-one is going to take it away,' she repeated over and over. Still the young girl looked around her.

Once she had eaten the girl wandered around the apartment, taking in her surroundings. She had big dark eyes which widened when she saw something unfamiliar or impressive. When eventually she did speak it was to say just one word 'telephone'.

Lotte tried to encourage her to say more. It was to be another twenty-four hours until any new words were forthcoming. That evening Lotte tucked her up in her own bed once more and kissed her on the forehead. Within minutes her small chest was rising up and down and she entered into a deep sleep.

The following day they made much better progress. The girl ate very well but still looked around her suspiciously. When she had finished breakfast, Lotte tried to ascertain her name.

'I am Lotte. That is Peter and that is Franz,' she said, pointing at each in turn. 'And that man there is the Professor.' As she said the word 'Professor', the little girl looked very intrigued and replied with a single word 'Papa'.

The next major advance did not take long to follow. 'What are you called, little one?' the Professor prompted.

'I am called Hannah and I am five years old.'

Over the next few days Hannah grew stronger and more curious. As her trust grew in her surroundings so did her gregariousness. Unsurprisingly she knew little of how she had come to be on the bridge and had obviously blocked out memories of whatever camp she had been in or how she had been rescued from it.

'It's probably for the best,' the Professor consoled them.

Five days after little Hannah's arrival it was Christmas Eve. The apartment was almost as lively as the pre-war and pre-Nazi years. There was Lotte, the Professor, Peter, Franz and Wolfi and Herr Riesen with his two children. And of course Hannah. Despite being considerably older, the violinist's children played noisily with the new guest.

When they sat down to eat it was a real feast. Lotte had spent a fortune on the black market. All the traditional favourites were there as well as the promised carp with three different types of vegetables. For pudding they had a real Stohlen, a special German Christmas cake, served with real coffee from freshly ground beans.

'To my husband Eric.' Lotte raised her glass as she toasted the founder of the feast.

After dinner they gathered around the tree and swapped Christmas presents. For all of them, even the older children, the highlight was the smile on Hannah's face as she unwrapped a wooden doll, made for her by Franz. She hugged everyone politely, then sat down on the rug to play with it.

Lotte was not forgotten. Peter and Franz had somehow scraped together the money to purchase bath salts for her. It was a long time since she had soaked in a hot bath with proper salts.

'Right, time to sing some carols,' Lotte enthused and made everyone stand around the tree. Franz was about to begin a favourite carol when Lotte held up her hand.

'This will not do,' she said. 'Something's missing. I know. Music!'

'We have no music,' Peter protested. Lotte was already out of the room. When she returned she held a large box wrapped with paper and a red bow on top.

'Merry Christmas,' she said, handing it to Herr Riesen. He hesitated. He had already opened a splendid present from Lotte, a lovely, warm, lambswool scarf. 'Please open it,' she said.

Without further encouragement Herr Riesen gratefully unwrapped the present. He stood silently for a few minutes. This one gift meant more than any other he had ever received. It was a violin.

'It's no Stradivarius, but I guess it will do,' Lotte joked. Herr Riesen was choked with emotion.

After a few minutes of effusive thanks, he took the violin in his skilful hands and plucking each string several times, tuned his instrument. Then he played. The violin may not have been a Stradivarius, yet it sang nonetheless, as the bow smoothly caressed the strings, allowing the notes to dance into the air. When finally the musician took the violin from under his chin, little Hannah surprised everyone.

'Mendelsohn! Mendelsohn!' she said, over and over.

She was clapping enthusiastically at the same time. They now had another clue as to her true identity.

For the rest of the evening the gathering was entertained by one of the world's premier violinists. He was no longer Herr Riesen, the caretaker, but the great concert violinist once more. Elsewhere in the building those who heard the music assumed that Lotte had acquired a gramophone. None realised that the music being played was forbidden by their rulers.

# CHAPTER TWENTY-FOUR

'We *must* get her abroad somehow. We *must*!' Lotte said. It broke her heart to say it, but she was suggesting that little Hannah, to whom she had become so attached, should leave them.

'We just cannot keep her here. The risks are too great. I can't pass her off as my daughter as everyone knows I don't have a daughter. Besides her colouring is much too dark. Most of all, we can do very little about that thing on her arm. What if someone sees it?'

Peter, Franz and the Professor had to reluctantly agree with Lotte. They had all fallen for this remarkable little girl and none could bear to see her suffer again.

'Look,' Lotte repeated, 'she cannot stay here. Who knows how this war will end, but it looks more and more likely that Germany will be defeated and we could soon be under Russian rule. Hannah cannot hide inside for the rest of the war. She must have the chance to play like normal children and not worry about the future. We cannot jeopardise her safety by keeping her here.'

Although little Hannah had become a carefree child, with barely a hint of her past suffering, she often looked longingly out the window. She was happy playing inside most of the time, but every morning as Peter and Wolfi left for their daily walk, she would rush towards them and ask to go too. Peter put her off as best he could saying that for the time being it was not safe. He found it hard to bear the disappointment in that otherwise happy face and more so when the same explanation was required in the afternoon. Peter had never had a sister and this little girl had, in just two weeks, become so important to him. Nonetheless as much as he would miss her, he understood Lotte's insistence that she should be able to play, just like any other child.

The conversation continued along these lines for some time. It was the second week of January 1944. Since little Hannah had been discovered they were still no closer to knowing what exactly had happened to her and by what miracle she had escaped from the camp. Nor did she identify the person Peter had seen running away from the bridge.

What was undoubtedly clear was that she had lived in a house or apartment with a telephone and that her father had been a professor of some type, probably music, and that she was accustomed to the sound of all the classics. She even knew how to hold the violin properly and the correct angle for the bowing action, as well as being able to play some of the chords. Herr Riesen so longed to teach her. It was too risky. It was one thing to give a concert at Christmas, it was yet another to play in Lotte's apartment on a regular basis. His whole disguise was to hide his origins as the great concert violinist and he knew that once he had the instrument in his grasp, he could not resist playing. When he played, the passion, the emotion and the skill would betray him at once. He simply could not endanger the others in that way. Instead he vowed that the first thing he would do when the war ended would be to give a concert.

After a long period of discussion, the agreement was reached that somehow, Hannah would be smuggled out of Germany. They did not need to consult as to where. There was only one person they would trust to love and care for Hannah and she now lived in Switzerland. A visit to Aunt Berta was in order.

'Yes, but how do we get her there?' Peter asked. 'A car will cost a fortune even if we can find petrol supplies. We cannot risk being stranded half-way to Switzerland.'

Lotte had long since been required to give up both limousines for the war effort and the official car had been taken away. Even with a car, petrol was now so tightly rationed it seemed impossible they would ever buy enough.

'We shall go by train,' Franz announced.

'We can't it is too dangerous, especially for Hannah.' Peter was exasperated. 'And we will need permits for the journey.'

They had already considered travelling with Hannah openly. Franz could easily prepare false papers for her including the necessary travel permit. Lotte could partially disguise her distinctive colouring. With makeup the tattoo could be hidden from all but the closest inspection.

The problem was Hannah. She was so pretty, with her lovely dark eyes, dark hair and dark complexion she was bound to attract attention. Hannah was clever and they could easily teach her to adopt a pretend name and persona. Yet she was so beautifully Jewish and very proud of it. Whatever her origins, and in spite of her age, Hannah had no doubts as to her own identity and was prone to telling anyone who cared to listen, even quoting well-known parts of the Torah. These were usually prefaced with the words 'My papa always says as it states in the Torah.' Apart from the obvious dangers of an inadvertent slip, deep down Lotte, Franz, Peter and the Professor did not want Hannah to lose this quality. It was part of her and one of the reasons they all adored her.

'I have an idea about that,' Franz smiled. By now his friends knew what that smile meant.


'Excuse me. Excuse me, please.' After several hours queuing Lotte was beginning to lose her patience. Everyone in Berlin seemed to be in Potsdamer station trying to leave the capital. And then her luck changed dramatically. 'Excuse me,' she repeated and tapped the man on the shoulder.

The object of her attention was middle-aged, in an expensive hand-made Italian suit and good quality leather shoes. His overcoat and hat also spoke of the highest quality and therefore significant wealth or power, or both.

'What? What the hell do you...?' The man did not finish the sentence. His annoyance vanished as soon as he saw Lotte.

'I'm so sorry to trouble you,' she said coyly. 'I couldn't help overhear. You have a ticket that you want to refund along with a reserved compartment. I want tickets for my two boys. One is badly wounded and I am taking them south to recuperate in the mountains. I can pay the full price. Oh please help.'

'The gentleman's compartment is available only to the most senior party officials or ministers. Civilians are not permitted to use it. And his ticket is non-refundable.' The ticket booth attendant's interruption only served to renew the gentleman's fury.

'Shut up or you will take a different train journey and it will be one way only,' he bellowed at the attendant. The effect on the attendant was clear to see.

'Well I suppose if, if, if…' he stammered.

Fifteen minutes passed and Lotte had more than just her tickets. She had a reservation for a separate compartment, all the way to Munich.

Back in the Luisenstrasse apartment Lotte was making a phone call.

'Gertrude? Aunt Gertrude! How good to hear your voice.' Lotte heard the click which confirmed the Gestapo were tapping the conversation. They tapped virtually every phone call these days.

'Yes Gertrude, I miss you too. Good news! I am bringing the boys for a visit. Franz needs some recuperation. His submarine was torpedoed. They can hardly wait to see you. We have a special gift for you.'

Aunt Berta or 'Gertrude' as she was known when the Gestapo were listening, was of course in no doubt that Franz could not have been wounded in a submarine. She was not worried. She was excited at the prospect of the 'special gift'. She once confided in Lotte that her only regret was that she had never had children. Never received that 'special gift' as she described it.

Just five days later a very glamorous former actress and a young man in naval uniform were travelling first class through the countryside of Southern Germany. The young man had his arm in a sling and walked with a limp. They were in a sleeping compartment with the bed folded up on one side and down on the other. The modesty curtain was pulled across in front of the bunk that had been opened up. On the luggage rack was a large trunk and two smaller suitcases. The guard had helpfully offered to store the trunk in the baggage compartment. Lotte had been most determined.

'Those are the few clothes I still possess. I want to keep them close to me,' she had insisted. As she had paid for the use of the whole sleeper compartment and tipped handsomely, he did not complain.

Out in the corridor another young man stood in his pristine naval uniform. He was stockier and taller than the first sailor and was staring distractedly out the window. Or at least that was the appearance he gave. He was in fact keeping a very close lookout for any unwanted visitors. He was ably assisted by his large black shaggy dog. Wolfi was a useful addition to the party. His size and powerful jaws and teeth kept many people at bay, frightened by him. He did not need to snarl, something he seldom did and only when the occasion really required it. Anyone who did venture close to him was more likely to be greeted by a wagging tail and a flip onto his back, paws in the air.

The Professor had stayed behind in Berlin to look after the apartment and their various charges. Wolfi would have been happy to stay with him, but Lotte had a particular reason for hoping that Peter would insist that Wolfi travel with them. Deep down she hoped that both Peter and Franz would finally agree to stay in the safety of the Swiss Alps, looking after Hannah and looked after by Berta. Lotte knew that this would never happen if Wolfi remained in Berlin. Peter would never allow himself to be parted from his faithful pet.

Closer examination of the large trunk that Lotte was so keen to keep by her would have revealed many tiny holes bored into one side. When opened it was a little smaller inside than the outside suggested. The false bottom created a space just big enough for Hannah to hide in. They had hated the moment in Lotte's apartment when they had asked little Hannah to see if she could squeeze inside. She had managed it easily as she was so very small and underweight. She had accepted confinement in the trunk without any complaint, happy to treat it as a game. It was a game in which she must remain still and silent until they told her otherwise.

The reserved sleeper compartment was a godsend, for it meant that for long periods, little Hannah could lie on the bed behind the curtain or even occasionally sit by the window. At night she was able to lie with Lotte and sleep, well-concealed. And as they were relatively hidden from view the journey could be completed in one go as Hannah did not need to stow away in the trunk.

Best of all, as the sleeper they were in was normally only for the use of top officials it had a notice on the window declaring this. In the circumstances it was unlikely that anyone, except one of those high-ranking officials, would disturb them.

For Lotte their great good fortune in obtaining this compartment had another significance. It was to her a sign that this rescue was destined to succeed. Whatever God was looking down, of whatever persuasion, he or she was looking after Hannah.

For the first day the journey was smooth and uninterrupted. On the few occasions the steward entered their compartment Lotte requested that the bed remain down as she often suffered dreadful headaches and may need to lie upon it.

In peacetime the journey to Munich should have been completed in a day. As the railways were a major target for the Allied bombers there were substantial delays as trains were rerouted and tracks repaired. Trains travelled at much less than full speed in order to conserve fuel. Additional stops were made, sometimes unscheduled to pick up freight for transport. These days there was no clear distinction between the freight and passenger train.

They had one tricky moment when a very frail and elderly lady had got on to the train at Jena.

'Please madam. This lady is too frail to stand. The rest of the train is jam-packed. She needs to sit. Surely you would not deny her that? She is only travelling a few stops and you have plenty of room.' The steward's plea was entirely reasonable. With Hannah on board it was dangerous to allow her in. If Lotte refused it could attract comment and unwanted scrutiny. Lotte had no choice. She had to agree.

Fortunately, the woman was almost blind and very hard of hearing so that she did not see Hannah on the folded bed. Nonetheless it was a relief when an hour after joining the train she got up and left, courteously assisted by Peter.

Lotte was tense as the miles rolled slowly by and they gradually got closer to their destination. They passed through towns and cities with names that were familiar, places she had never desired to visit. Some of them she had seen in her time as a film actress and mostly forgotten.

She marvelled at the devastation in Dresden, almost as bad as Berlin it seemed. Likewise in Chemnitz. Other smaller towns seemed completely empty and sad. Some names reminded her of the trip to the border with Berta and Albert. It was ten months since they had parted at Bodensee, the last time they had seen each other. It had been good to speak to her on the telephone. Thankfully Berta had been astute enough to understand the hidden message in her phone call.

The next day the train rumbled out of the station at Nuremberg. The significance of the name did not escape any on the train. 'Such a beautiful city and such terrible laws named after it,' Peter complained bitterly.

Soon they were well into their journey and approaching their final destination of Munich. At least that was their purported destination for now. Once in Munich they would have to change trains to travel to Innsbruck and then find a way to Switzerland. That was a part of the trip they did not look forward to, for it was probable Hannah would have to hide in the trunk for the whole of the journey. With luck in a few hours they would at least reach Munich, as they were now approaching Ingolstadt, the penultimate station.

Suddenly and without warning the train braked sharply. Peter fell against Franz and elsewhere on the train passengers bumped into each other. Peter and Franz ran back into their compartment to check on Lotte and Hannah.

'What's wrong? Why have we stopped?' Lotte asked. 'We are not at a station.' They were still several hundred metres from Ingolstadt.

Peter pulled down the window of the train and leaned down to look out along the tracks. There was nothing ahead of them, except other trains. 'I can't see anything blocking the way,' he shouted back through the open window.

As the familiar roar of the Hurricane engine erupted above him, the cause of their sudden stop became clear. A bomber had been spotted. It was a surprise to them all as daytime raids normally concentrated on more important industrial targets and this was ostensibly just a passenger train. As Peter leaned out of the window a train conductor knocked on the door of the carriage.

'Everyone off the train immediately! Quickly out! To the shelter! Follow the other passengers!' he ordered. As soon as the train had stopped Hannah had quickly and expertly climbed into the trunk for the first time since being carried onto the train at Berlin. Peter could see the look of panic in Lotte's eyes. They could not just leave Hannah in the trunk. It could only be opened from the outside and an air raid was in progress.

'I can't leave,' Lotte pleaded. 'Please let me stay here.' For once she seemed to be losing her composure.

Her mood worsened when the conductor replied, 'It is much too dangerous. I have authority to order you off the train and I do order you to leave.'

Before Lotte could respond with any other argument, Peter had stepped away from the carriage window and said authoritatively:

'Listen, Herr Conductor. My cousin, the lady will go with you, I will stay with Franz. As you see he has been wounded. He was in a submarine at the time and so is terrified of confined spaces. If you force him out with other passengers he will go beserk and panic everyone else. I will stay with him and make sure he is safe.'

'But, but I...,' the conductor attempted to reply.

His sentence was unfinished when Peter added: 'Look he is a war hero. If you wish to endanger both him and all those women and children, then do so. Remember you will be held accountable.'

'Okay. But you are responsible for your own safety.' The conductor relented and escorted Lotte off the train and into the air raid shelter at the nearby station.

The air raid was brief but terrifying nonetheless. The bombers had indeed been making their way to another target. One had been struck by a hail of bullets from a German stukka and lost fuel. On its return journey it had come across the train station, always a worthwhile target and decided to drop its load.

For Lotte, the half hour she spent in the dingy, cramped air raid shelter was the worst of her life. The prospect that Peter, Franz and Hannah could be killed by the Allies was too much to bear. Especially after everything they had already been through. She struggled to stay calm when finally the all-clear sounded. She was so anxious to get back to her family she almost knocked over several other passengers in her struggle to exit the shelter. She raced back along the tracks, cursing her stylish, if impractical shoes all the way.

As she neared the train she was relieved to see that it was seemingly undamaged.

'Oh my darling girl! You're safe! Thank God!' Lotte held Hannah close to her. She was back in the compartment. The little girl had been secure in her trunk, completely unaware of the danger.

The train had sustained no direct hits, although ahead one side of the tracks was warped and misshapen. The station was virtually destroyed. There were no casualties and so the journey could continue, though more slowly now as trains would have to take turns at passing through the station in opposite directions.

After another three hours the train pulled into Munich station. A relieved Lotte alighted along with Peter and Franz. On a luggage trolley they pulled two suitcases and a large trunk. Inside the trunk Hannah played her new game perfectly. If she could stay absolutely still and remain silent, Lotte had promised her a big chocolate cake. She made no sound.

Lotte approached a guard. 'When is the next train to Innsbruck?' The reply was unexpected.

'I am sorry Madam. There are no more trains to Innsbruck today. You will have to try tomorrow.'

'No we must get to Innsbruck today!' Lotte said.

'I am sorry madam there are no more trains today and I am certain you will not get there by any other means. I suggest you find a hotel for the night, before all the rooms are taken.'

There was nothing else for it other than to find a hotel.

Hannah could not stay imprisoned overnight. After a few enquiries they located a small establishment a short distance from the station. It was quite run down, but clean and more comfortable than the station. Lotte wondered why it was so empty as so many trains had been cancelled or delayed. She discovered the reason when asked to settle the cost of the stay in advance. It was almost four times the normal price, well beyond most Germans' means.

'I'm sorry we have no porter at the moment. Why not leave your trunk here at reception? It will save the young men lugging it up all those stairs.' The hotel receptionist's suggestion would ordinarily have been most welcome. Lotte did not reply. Peter stepped forward.

'Thank you. We can manage.'

The receptionist looked on in surprise as the other heavily wounded sailor lifted the trunk with ease.

As soon as they were in the bedroom they opened the trunk and let out Hannah.

'Do I get my cake now?' she asked, a big grin on her face.

'Not just yet darling,' Lotte replied. 'We must all keep very quiet tonight and tomorrow until I say. Aunt Berta will buy you lots of cakes. All right?'

Hannah jumped onto the bed and placed her head in Lotte's lap. Lotte stroked her hair as she fell asleep. For the rest of the night Hannah was quiet.

# CHAPTER TWENTY-FIVE

Once Hannah had settled into bed, fast asleep and in the watchful care of Peter and Wolfi, Lotte went downstairs to make a phone call. She was relieved to find a phone in the lobby and more relieved to find it was working.

The telephone line burred as Berta's phone rang. Within seconds Berta's welcome voice spoke on the other end. They had to be careful what they said.

'We are in Munich at present,' Lotte explained, 'and we do not know when we can get a train to Innsbruck. We are staying in a hotel for tonight and we shall see what we can do tomorrow. We hope to pick up a train then and deliver the special gift I have for you.'

'My husband is not able to get away at present. He will not be able to collect you from Innsbruck. Perhaps we can meet in Oberstdorf?' Berta replied.

'Oberstdorf?' Lotte said, struggling to hide her devastation. 'I will see what I can do. I shall ring again tomorrow.'

Berta could hear the disappointment in her voice. In her mind too she could picture Lotte standing in the hotel lobby, phone in hand and a sense of dread on her usually cheerful face. Obesrtdorf was a small village in the Allgäuer Alps and at least eighty kilometres from Munich. Lotte knew it very well. It was sometimes known as the

317

'last village in Germany'. It was close to the Austrian border, if still some distance from Switzerland and most worryingly it was still within Germany. Berta knew all too well the town's significance to Lotte and hoped that her suggestion might be taken up by her good friend, in spite of her reluctance.

The plan had been that Berta's husband would travel from Switzerland to meet them in Innsbruck. That was for some reason no longer possible. Since they had last spoken Berta had become aware that she was not the only one wanted by the authorities in Berlin. Now they were after her husband as well. He simply could not leave Switzerland.

As Lotte replaced the receiver she heard a second click. As usual she assumed it was the authorities listening in. It soon became clear it was the receptionist.

'Miss! Miss! May I speak with you?' the receptionist said, her voice barely audible. 'I could not help overhearing your conversation,' she said. Lotte was about to explode in a rage at the absurdity of this statement, when the receptionist's words caused her to check.

'My brother has a truck, a lorry that he uses to deliver supplies to the army. If you are able to pay towards his petrol and other expenses, I am sure he can take you, your friends and your luggage to Oberstdorf.'

Lotte was unsure how to respond to this offer. It seemed the perfect solution. Yet she was wary as the receptionist had lied once already. What choice did they have? Perhaps though they could get a lift to somewhere else, anywhere but Oberstdorf.

'You may find it difficult to get a train there or

anywhere else,' the receptionist added. Lotte was certain they would eventually get a train. The prospect of poor Hannah stuck in the trunk while they awaited a train that might never arrive was too much to contemplate.

'I will speak to the others and let you know this evening.' Lotte wanted time to think it through.

The next morning at first light, Peter and Franz were rocking to and fro in the back of a canvas covered truck. Lotte was on the front passenger seat, eyeing the roughly dressed driver suspiciously as the vehicle bumped along the potholed road. Wolfi was strategically placed between Lotte and the driver, something which had caused an argument to begin with.

In the back, and out of the eyeline of the driver, Lotte's two suitcases and her large trunk were wedged between Peter and Franz and heavy oil drums. The lid of the trunk was partially open and Hannah lay perfectly still, smiling at her friends from time to time. Peter had wrapped her in a blanket as it was winter still and the rear of the truck was open to the elements.

The cost of the journey was much more than even Lotte had anticipated. It was the equivalent of a year's income for the driver. She had wondered whether they might not have found a driver to take them all the way to Switzerland for that. She had the good sense at least to pay only half the amount at the start.

After an uncomfortable journey of an hour and a half, they pulled into a side road. It was clearly not the way to Oberstdorf.

'Where are we going? This isn't the way,' Lotte protested.

'I have deliveries to make,' the driver grunted, not stopping to remove the cigarette from his mouth. Lotte began to feel uneasy.

'He's taking us into army barracks,' she said to herself. They approached the gates to a camp. There was nothing she could do at that moment except hope. She sat quietly, wondering if they were about to be betrayed. After a cursory check the sentry at the barrier waved them through. His lack of interest only increased her worry. 'They are expecting us,' she thought.

They were indeed expected. The driver delivered oil regularly to the base. It was quite common to see passengers with him. Everyone was trying to make a little on the side.

The short time the fuel drums took to deliver was torturous for the group of friends. Peter distracted the driver from Hannah's trunk by helping to roll the heavy drums off the tailgate. Lotte tried not to show her nerves, nerves that only increased when a guard approached the rear of the lorry.

'Excuse me corporal,' she shouted over the noisy drums. 'Excuse me!' As planned the soldier stopped walking to the back of the truck and turned to the much more enticing Lotte. 'I have been travelling for some hours now. Is there a bathroom I can use?' she asked coyly.

'Of course Miss. If you care to follow me into the guard house?'

From that moment on every soldier in sight of Lotte followed her pronounced walk into the guardroom and her return to the vehicle. Noboody was interested in the back of the truck anymore.

Fifteen minutes later they were back on the main road, having deposited four barrels of the oil. It had been very tense. Luckily, thanks to the distractions, no-one had examined either their papers or luggage. Once more Hannah had performed magnificently and remained motionless and silent in the trunk.

Soon they were approaching the outskirts of Oberstdorf. Virgin snow lay on the ground and the wooden chalets with their steeply sloping roofs looked very pretty. Even the woodpiles were neatly arranged. The village was largely deserted, apart from a few skiers making their way up the slopes. The last time Lotte had driven into this village it was in the luxury of a leather upholstered Mercedes limousine. Now she was the passenger in a beaten up lorry. She didn't care as long as they were successful.

'Follow the main street to the hotel Bayrischer Hof. On the market square.' Lotte's directions were blunt without any formality or customary German courtesy.

The lorry stopped outside a large hotel on the main market square. It was typically Bavarian in style with wooden verandahs and balconies and a large overhanging roof. The name 'Bayrischer Hof' was just legible as the paintwork had been neglected in recent times.

The driver parked at the main entrance and sprang down from the driver's seat. Lotte held out the rest of the money he was owed. He ignored her, went straight to the back of the lorry and lowered the tail gate.

Franz jumped onto the frozen ground, and was met by Wolfi and the driver. Peter remained in the back of the lorry and began passing the two suitcases to Franz, one at a time. Neither boy could prevent the lorry driver climbing into the back of the vehicle. He moved quickly to the rear of the cab and grabbed the trunk.

'It's all right I can manage that,' Peter said concerned.

'Not at all. It's no bother,' the driver replied.

He was dragging the trunk roughly along the floor of the cab. Nothing would stop him. He pulled the trunk to the edge of the tailgate. Franz stepped forward to take one end of the trunk. Without any warning the driver dropped the leading end onto the hard ground.

'Ow!'

A high-pitched noise, but soft, like a puppy's yelp came from the trunk. At the same time the frame of the trunk made a cracking sound. If the driver heard Hannah's cry, his face did not betray him. The deafness that had kept him out of the war had temporarily saved little Hannah.

The driver was genuinely surprised. The trunk weighed more than he expected. From the outset he had been suspicious, supposing the trunk to contain contraband goods or maybe large quantities of cash to be smuggled over the border. By its weight it was not currency, nor was it cigarettes. Maybe it was gold or diamonds? This snooty cow clearly had money to burn looking at her fancy clothes. Whatever was in the trunk, he was going to find out.

'Let's see what you are all so concerned about,' the driver said and leaned over to prise open the locks.

'Grrrr!' Wolfi had other ideas and pushed past Franz in front of the driver, growling and flashing his fangs at the same time.

'Leave that, or the dog will attack!' Peter said. The lorry driver hesitated. There must be something really valuable in there, he thought. For a brief second his greed almost overcame his fear.

'Look, he already has the souvenirs of war,' Peter said, pointing to the still visible scar from his run in with the Doberman. On queue Wolfi reared up so that he almost looked the man in the eyes. This final display of strength convinced him that for now he could do nothing and he stood up, leaving the trunk alone. Lotte stepped forward.

'Obviously the only thing you respect is money,' she said, not even attempting to hide the contempt she felt. 'Here is the rest of the money I owe you. If you take us to a point near the border, I will pay you the same again.'

The man scratched his untidy beard. This was not the outcome he expected. To further tempt him she added, 'I don't mean now. Tomorrow tonight when it is dark. About midnight would be best. I cannot go before then because I am waiting for a particular delivery, another trunk.'

The prospect of a second trunk filled with diamonds grabbed his attention. Taking him to one side Lotte quietly dictated the arrangements and the fee.

'Bayrischer Hof. Tomorrow at midnight. We will be here. Do not be late.' Her tone was stern and threatening. He could have no doubt she would not tolerate any deviation from the plan. The lorry driver drove off, still contemplating his imminent wealth.

Once the lorry had disappeared from view, Lotte turned to the others and said in an urgent tone, 'Quick I'll carry the suitcases. You two bring the trunk.'

They did not stop to ask any questions, following her along the street a further 300 metres. Protruding from the snow Peter could just read the street name, '*Prinzenstrasse*' on a sign at the side of the road. Lotte stopped outside a smaller and more attractive hotel, '*The Wittelsbacher*'.

'Wait here!' she said, and disappeared through the main entrance. As she vanished from sight Peter was tempted to bend down to the trunk and check Hannah was still all right. He dared not, however, as he could not take the chance of Hannah being seen. Just ten minutes later Lotte came back out through the entrance. She had a door key on a wooden fob in her hand.

'Come with me,' she said and walked off around the side of the building. At the back of the hotel was a separate chalet rented out to special guests. As soon as they were inside Peter quickly opened the trunk and helped Hannah out.

'My poor darling! My little Hannah! Are you okay? Are you hurt?' Lotte said and hugged the little girl tightly to her.

'I'm sorry, Aunty,' the little girl said, 'I made a noise. Now I will not get any cake.' She had recently taken to calling Lotte 'Aunty'.

'Don't worry, darling. You were so good Aunty will buy you a whole cake shop!' Lotte beamed, delighted her little girl was still in one piece.

'I was worried about the lorry driver as soon as I saw him. Especially when Wolfi reacted to him,' Peter said.

'Me too. I thought it was all over when we entered the barracks, but clearly he is expecting a bigger payoff. That was why I directed him to the other hotel,' Lotte replied.

Seeing the confusion in the boy's faces she continued: 'It will take him a while to realise we are not there. If he thinks I am expecting another trunk, he will wait until it is safely here. That should give us a day's start.'

'Unless he heard the noise. He must have done,' Peter replied.

'Well if he did, and he recognised what it was, he will have gone straight to the police,' Lotte added. 'He seemed a little deaf, so maybe he really did not hear.'

Peter and Franz were almost at the door, urging Lotte to leave immediately.

'We are safer here for the moment. Even if they do house to house searches it will take them some time to find us,' she said calmly.

'And what if the people here betray us?' Peter said. He was unwilling to trust his fate and particularly Hannah's fate to the hands of strangers.

'We will not be betrayed,' Lotte replied. Peter was still uncertain.

'They will not betray us because I grew up here. They are my family. They may not have approved of my choice of career, nor my choice of husband and my lifestyle, but they would never hand over anyone, let alone a little girl, to the Nazis. '

Peter and Franz looked in wonderment. This sophisticated glamorous woman, former film star and society lady had grown up in this small village. She had not even a hint of the strong Bavarian accent.

'Elocution lessons,' she said, reading their thoughts.

Lotte's forced arrival at her family's home had brought an unexpected bonus. She was familiar with the mountains, though nobody knew them like her father, a former mountain guide. He would lead them across the border by one of the more difficult and least observed routes. How she wished she had swallowed her pride sooner and approached her parents for help.

They rested in the chalet for the remainder of the day, mainly sleeping and occasionally eating. Lotte left them for about an hour and when she returned she had a treat for little Hannah. It was a small chocolate cake and a glass of milk. Rationing had not been so harsh in this area close to the Swiss border. The others were not disappointed with small bread rolls cut in half, with cheese and sausage in the middle and a slice of rye bread holding them together on the other side. This was washed down with hot soup, better than anything they had tasted in Berlin. To keep the cold at bay they had a bottle of Jägermeister, the heavily spiced liqueur, popular in the area.

Finally the hour of their departure arrived. Peter was pleased that at long last they could move on. He trusted Lotte and her family, nevertheless he was worried the lorry driver had gone to the police. For most of the day he had kept watch at the window. Not even Franz was able to persuade him to sleep for a while.

It was dusk, but there was sufficient light to move around when the knock came at the door. Lotte looked out through the window and confirming it was her father, walked to the door and opened it.

Her father was a slight man, yet obviously strong and fit. His weather-beaten face glowed with health and he had the same bright blue eyes as Lotte. His grey hair was still quite thick and seemed to shimmer in the light. He was dressed for the outdoors with sturdy leather boots, warm wool trousers, an oiled wool jumper with matching hat and a waterproof coat. On his back he carried a grey canvas and leather rucksack from which dangled several lengths of hemp rope, two ice axes and sets of crampons. In his hands he carried a large canvas sack. On seeing the crampons Peter hoped they would not be necessary on the forthcoming hike.

'This is my father, Jürgen,' Lotte said. She introduced her friends one at a time. Jürgen simply nodded his head and began to remove boots and coats from his canvas bag. He was a man of few words.

Normally Lotte and her friends did not disclose their names. It was safer that way for all concerned. This occasion was different. This was her father and these were her friends. She was proud of all of them and hoped he might in a small way be proud of her.

'And this is my little Hannah,' Lotte said. With that Hannah ran forward and taking his rough hand in her tiny fingers, pumped it up and down.

Jürgen could not hold back a smile. 'So this is the little girl who needs rescuing,' he thought. 'Put these on. We leave in five minutes,' Lotte's father said in a business-like manner, handing out coats and boots. 'These mountains are dangerous, especially for city folk. Do exactly what I say, when I say and do not wander off the path.'

In looks Jürgen was like Lotte, but not in temperament. She was the party girl, always ready with a witty comment, easy in company and with strangers. He, on the other hand, preferred to listen than to talk and only spoke when he had something that needed to be said. On this occasion his abruptness was reassuring. His manner exuded confidence and composure.

Having quickly donned their walking gear they set off on their journey.

'Why don't you walk with me? You can help me show the way.' Jürgen smiled at Hannah who smiling back, placed her mittened hand in his and walked off without saying a word. Lotte was pleased, remembering similar experiences so many years earlier.

As the sun disappeared behind the mountains, the temperatures dropped dramatically and their breath crystallized in the freezing air. There was little light, but the partial moon reflected off the snow so that they were at least able to see their own footsteps. The silhouette of the high mountain range was imposing and impressive at the same time.

The snow was deep in places and the effort of lifting their feet began to tell. Hannah had managed to walk some kilometres until the route began to climb steeply and Franz lifted her onto his back to carry her. Apart from Jürgen, Peter and Lotte had a rucksack each. The hated trunk had been discarded at the chalet and the two suitcases stored away. Peter had remembered the problems with Wolfi's paws in previous winters and had protected them from ice with four pieces of cloth.

As they ascended into the mountains Peter thought of his hiking trips with his papa. They had always intended to visit Oberstdorf with the famous Breitachklamm, the longest and deepest gorge in Europe with its beautiful waterfall. For some reason or other they had never made it this far.

'One day Papa, you and I will come back here,' Peter promised himself in silence.

For the first few hours the weather favoured them. It was still bitterly cold, but clear and free from snow. Lotte surprised everyone in her speed and agility up the rocky path. Then they remembered she had spent her childhood in these mountains, no doubt accompanying her father on his rambles with tourists. She surprised them even more when she took one of the rucksacks from Franz and easily threw it over her shoulders. She seemed so different from the Lotte they knew who appeared so awkward in the woods of Berlin.

Of all of them, Wolfi coped best with the terrain. He was off the lead and stayed at the front, bounding up the path, periodically stopping to wait for his pack. Even at the points where they needed to climb, he easily scrambled up the rocks.

Their progress was gradual, if slow. The path was icy and in places treacherous, with steep drops on either side. Hannah was by now oblivious to her surroundings, having fallen asleep as she was carried by Jürgen at his insistence. Franz was now shouldering one of the three rucksacks. With each step their breathing became more laboured and noisy. Stopping for a short rest, Franz admired a high peak in the distance.

'That's the Nebelhorn,' Lotte said. 'Luckily we can go around it.'

Her father beamed happily. 'You remember the way then? You haven't completely forgotten your roots?'

'No, Papa. I have never forgotten you or Moma or these mountains,' she replied, and placed her hand on his arm.

It was close to midnight and they had been climbing for five hours. Their route was to take them south onto the ridge of peaks that separated Austria from Germany. Then they would turn towards the West and walk across the mountains towards the Bodensee and the Swiss border. In total it was about thirty kilometres with several thousand metres of climb. On his own, Jürgen could make the journey in a single day, weather permitting, and without a small child and his fellow travellers.

For now they were safely out of the town and beyond the ski slopes which were most in use. He would have preferred to carry on, but reluctantly decided that they should stop for the night. As if to confirm his decision, a snow shower began and the wind picked up. He pointed to a small hole in the face of the mountain and waved to the others to follow him.

Twenty minutes later they were in a mountain hut, a refuge for climbers, sheltering from the elements.

# CHAPTER TWENTY-SIX

The mountain hut was dry and warm and pleasantly comfortable. Jürgen brewed a beef drink over a little portable stove. Hannah snoozed away in Lotte's arms, as she and Franz slept. Peter kept guard at the door as usual, with Wolfi by his side.

'Don't worry son,' Jürgen reassured him. 'If anyone comes here it will not be until tomorrow morning and we will already be under way. I will get you there.'

Peter was happier and began to relax a little. As neither he nor Jürgen were able to sleep they chatted a while. Mainly it was Peter who talked. He spoke lovingly of Lotte and all the sacrifices she had made, the people she had helped rescue, including Peter. Lotte's father said little in response. Peter could tell he was beginning to see a different side to his daughter.

'You should be very proud,' Peter said, as he finished relating her adventures.

'I am proud and always have been,' Jürgen responded. In the darkness of the cave Lotte smiled to herself and hugged Hannah tighter.

As soon as dawn broke, Jürgen roused everyone, including Peter who had slept for the first time in days. They wasted little time as Jürgen had prepared a breakfast of more beef tea and bread rolls. Quickly consuming the delicious beefy liquid, they hoisted the rucksacks on their backs and set off once more.

Hannah was excited and walked to begin with. All around the snow-capped peaks, hundreds of them, glistened in the morning sunshine. In the daylight the terrain underfoot was still difficult, but less than at night time as they could see more clearly where they were going. The path was hard to discern in places as so much fresh powdery snow had fallen overnight. Without their guide they would have struggled to stay on the correct course.

For the rest of the day they ploughed relentlessly through the snow, stopping only once at midday. At this altitude they were beyond the ski pistes and so met no-one else, not even climbers. Since the advent of the war most able-bodied men and women were otherwise occupied. As the holiday period was over there was little prospect of a chance encounter.


Back in Oberstdorf a furious lorry driver was standing at reception in the *Bayrischer Hof*. He had arrived almost ten hours early as a precaution, yet he was still too late.

'You must know where they are!' he demanded. 'I dropped them off outside yesterday.'

'I am sorry sir, no-one of that description has checked into this hotel.' The young girl was becoming a little afraid.

'There was a very pretty, young lady, blonde. She was with two sailors and she had a large trunk, about so tall.' He held his hand out to demonstrate.

'I am sorry I have not seen them,' the receptionist

repeated. The more often the young girl at reception denied that she had seen this group, the angrier he got.

Realising at last that she was not lying, he stormed off to check all the other hotels in the village, all thirty of them. He vowed he would soon find them.

'They cannot have left as she still has to collect the second trunk,' he consoled himself.

Only when he had indeed been to each and every hotel did he finally accept he had been tricked. He did however have a lead. At one particular hotel the owner, a middle-aged local woman, had some valuable information.

'Oh yes. I remember. They left in a large black car. A woman and two young men. That's right. They were struggling to lift both trunks into the boot. They went off on the road to Munich.' Lotte's mother could not help him anymore.

As they were no longer in Oberstdorf she must be telling the truth about them, he reasoned. If he hurried he could catch them on the road.

And so it was that as the group of friends, guided by Jürgen, made their way ever nearer to the Swiss border, the traitorous lorry driver was speeding in the wrong direction.

A full seven hours after they had set off from the mountain hut the party stood in silence. All save Jürgen looked dejected. They were at the foot of an almost vertical slab of rock stretching for almost 100 metres. The granite was icy and damp and would be a difficult ascent, even in normal conditions. Peter had climbed a little, as had Lotte. Franz should be able to reach the top. In places there were a few iron rungs to which they could attach ropes. The problem was Wolfi. He was quite a large dog and the prospect of hauling both him and Hannah up the rock face was daunting indeed.

'We can't take the normal route. It is blocked by an avalanche,' her father explained. 'There is a much easier route, past a checkpoint manned by soldiers. We have to climb.'

Peter's face fell. 'I must find another route with Wolfi,' he said. 'I cannot abandon him.'

As so often, Lotte had a solution. This was more welcome than most. 'I can take Wolfi by the road. I have a legitimate visa and travel permit to Switzerland. I will say that the train was bombed and so I decided to cross the mountains from my home town. It should convince them as it is essentially the truth.'

She had reverted to her original heavy Bavarian accent, demonstrating thereby how convincing she could be. Noboby hearing it would doubt that she was a local girl.

'Thank you Lotte. Thank you,' Peter said, stroking Wolfi's head at the same time. Wolfi tilted his head to one side unsure as to what was going to happen.

'Will you be able to make the climb?' Lotte asked.

Peter nodded keenly. Franz's agreement was less convincing.

'I will manage it Lotte, don't worry,' Franz replied.

She did not need to ask her father. She knew Hannah would be safe with him. It was a climb he had made with her when she was about the same age and in the same way. She confirmed the route she must take with Wolfi and waited until they began their ascent.

'Now Hannah,' she said. 'This is a new game we are going to play. My papa is going to strap you onto his back. You must keep your eyes closed until he tells you to open them and you must not move. I am going to take Wolfi for a walk and tomorrow we shall meet you for that chocolate cake.'

Lotte embraced Hannah and squeezed her tightly, planting a kiss on her cheek. Meanwhile Peter said farewell to his beloved dog. Lotte hugged both Peter and Franz, urging them to be careful and to look after Hannah, then swung around to speak to her father. She hesitated, momentarily unsure as to how she should say goodbye. The split second of awkwardness vanished as he moved quickly towards her and looping his arms around her waist, held her close.

'I will look after them,' he said. 'Please come and see us again when this is all over.' Lotte stayed in his comforting embrace for a few precious seconds longer. She kissed him on the cheek and then taking her rucksack in one hand and Wolfi's lead in the other, she walked away. She thought about waiting to see the boys safely up the rock, but knew that might distract Hannah. By now her father was already at the foot of the rock.

Peter watched as his good friends disappeared from view. Any worries he had about Wolfi leaving him were unfounded. Once more the clever dog had seemed to know what the situation required.

'Good luck both of you.' Peter's hopes remained unspoken.

'No time to hang around,' Jürgen said brusquely.

Peter and Franz looked on nervously as Jürgen reached up to the first hand hold with his left hand and lifted his right foot onto the rock. With no apparent effort he gracefully moved higher and higher, stopping periodically to place a piton in the rock, and then attach the rope with a carabiner. Hannah was firmly strapped to his back and as instructed, her eyes were tightly shut. Peter and Franz had suggested that she be hauled up once Jürgen was safely in position, but he had refused. There was a danger the rope might snag and it would be difficult for him to do anything about if from above. Climbing down was much more difficult than climbing up.

In an amazingly short time, Jürgen was standing on a ledge halfway up the face, lassooed to the rock, encouraging Franz to start the ascent. Peter was to follow up last as he had some experience. Hannah was still strapped securely to Jürgen's back with her eyes closed.

Franz hesitated. He looked up at the wall of rock. How he wished they could have used the crampons, but there was insufficient ice to dig in the metal spikes. He had been nervous not scared when he had rescued Peter from the Gestapo. Now he was terrified. He had been unable to admit it: he was scared of heights. Peter sensed his fear.

'It's all right, Franz,' he said, laying his hand on Franz's trembling shoulder. 'If you want you can go with Lotte and Wolfi. You will easily catch them up.'

Franz had contemplated this course, but knew it would be harder for Lotte to pull off her deception. He also had a visa for Switzerland, though as a forgery it might be unwise to submit it to too close an inspection in the circumstances. Especially as the reason for his trip was given as 'recouperating from his war wounds'.

Telling himself to stop being so cowardly, Franz gingerly touched the cold surface of the rock. Tentatively he felt for a hand hold. As he began to climb he shouted up to Jürgen, 'Climbing.'

'Just remember,' Peter said, 'nothing can happen as the rope will hold you.'

Franz moved at a snail's pace up the face until he was almost three quarters of the way to the belay point. At times he struggled to grip the rock with the soles of his boots, yet he persevered. At one point his feet gave way from under him. Jürgen had a tight hold of the rope and had taken in the slack and a nervous Franz found his footing again. His whole body shook as he moved first one limb then another and the adrenalin raced around his body. Forty minutes after he had begun, Franz clambered onto the ledge.

'Well done lad. Now stand over there.' Jürgen pointed behind him.

It was now Peter's turn. In spite of the long years since early childhood when he had last climbed, he remembered the moves and techniques his father had taught him. In about the same time as Jürgen, he had reached the ledge.

'Great climbing Peter.' Jürgen was clearly impressed with this boy from the city.

The second pitch was a little easier and considerably faster. Franz was still nervous, but managed to keep his footing and his head. In a surprisingly short time all four were at the top. Jürgen coiled the rope and fastened it to the straps on his rucksack. Franz had finally stopped shaking. He was sitting well back from the cliff edge.

'Good girl Hannah. Good girl,' Peter said, bending over to see her. Her eyes were now wide awake and taking in everything around her.

'I hope Lotte and Wolfi are safe.' Franz expressed the sentiments of them all.

They need not have worried. It was still some distance to the road that led to the border crossing. The weather was sunny and bright and Lotte and Wolfi simply enjoyed their surroundings. The walk was really quite pleasant. They made excellent progress, in spite of the snow and just before dusk they arrived at the first check point.

'Hello boys. So pleased to see such fit young men guarding us.'

Lotte was at the Austrian side of the border. The checkpoint was manned by three young soldiers, not even out of their teens. Their uniforms drowned them and their rifles looked enormous. They gave every appearance of toy soldiers. Lotte was used to wooing a crowd and had little difficulty in convincing the three boys about her story. They barely examined her visa and she was soon in the nomansland strip, walking towards the Swiss checkpoint.

Here she had a little more difficulty. The sentry was a balding, middle-aged official who was fed up sitting in a cold sentry box. Lotte's charms had little effect on him. He was more interested in the end of his shift and his evening meal. 'These mountains are no place for a woman on her own,' he said, shaking his head.

'I am not on my own. I have my dog and he is a better companion than any man,' Lotte replied. Unimpressed the official stamped her passport and without further comment, she and Wolfi marched across the border.

That evening they dined alone in a small hotel on the side of the Bodensee. After a dessert of coffee and delicious cream cakes, with Wolfi watching, she dialled Berta's number.

'Berta? Berta? It's Lotte. I am at a hotel in Switzerland. Just over the border.'

'Lotte! Lotte darling! Tell me the address and we will drive over and pick you up straight away. Have you got my special gift?'

'No the others are travelling separately. I must wait here for them as arranged, darling Berta. Be patient! If all goes well we shall see each other tomorrow.'

'Oh! All right, but make it soon, dear Lotte.' Berta was disappointed, but she knew it was the wisest course of action.


Having reached the summit of the rock face it was a further four hours of almost constant trudging until Peter and the others found themselves looking down upon a welcome sight. It was the shimmering surface of Bodensee. They were in the hills above Lauterach. Fortunately there had been no more climbing required and the crampons had not been used. From their position they had a clear view of the lake and the surrounding countryside.

Jürgen pointed into the distance towards the lake. 'Just to the left of the large crag with the single tree on top is where you should cross the border. It will be dark soon. Make your way there as close as you dare and as quickly as possible. Wait until dark and then cross over where I have shown you.'

He bade farewell to Peter and Franz before bending down to speak to Hannah. 'Look after my Lotte for me. And don't worry you will see her again soon.' He reached out to take Hannah's hand in his and as he did, she clasped her arms around his neck and kissed him. For the first time in years Lotte's father blushed.

Darkness fell quite early and just an hour after leaving Jürgen, Peter, Franz and Hannah were crouched behind a rock, looking towards the lake's edge. The little girl was perfectly still and silent. For her the game had continued.

In the distance some half a kilometre away the dim lights of a sentry's hut were visible. It was a cold night and so far the guards had shown little desire to leave the warmth of their shelter. Moonbeams reflected on the lake which lit their way forward.

'Now Hannah. If you can keep quiet until I tell you, you will be the winner. Okay?' Hannah moved her head up and down in response to Peter's question. Somehow she knew not to speak.

'Good girl. Now let me carry you. Don't worry Franz will be right behind.'

As Peter and Franz sneaked slowly closer to the lake's edge he wondered at how light the little girl was. That would hopefully soon change. They edged forward one cautious step at a time. Peter's heart was racing. He was certain the others, including the sentries must be able to hear it.

After what seemed an eternity the two boys and their young charge were right by the water's edge. The only sound was the gently lapping water in the slight breeze. Peter crouched low to the ground and signalled to Franz to follow suit.

'Listen Hannah,' Peter whispered, this is the last part of our game. Do you see that big boulder over there?' Hannah nodded vigorously.

'Do you think you can crawl to that rock without making any noise and without being seen?'

Again Hannah nodded and without waiting further, she began to crawl quickly, but quietly. When a few minutes later she was safely behind the large boulder, Peter began to crawl after her. Just moments later Franz began the same scramble along the ground. Metres from safety Franz stopped.

'Grrr! Grr!' The German shepherd's growl carried across the open space from the sentry box. Franz froze. As he pondered what to do next a sentry's voice made the decision for him.

'Ach you stupid dog. It's only moonlight. Inside now.' He turned and pulled the dog away, still growling.

'You should listen to your dog,' Peter thought, glad at the sentry's stupidity.

Franz clambered the last few metres to his friends and fell behind the rock exhausted. They rested for just ten minutes. Peter lifted Hannah in his arms and the three walked quickly away from the border. At last they were in Switzerland!

By ten o'clock that evening Franz, Peter and Hannah had safely arrived in the village where Lotte was staying. Fortunately the last stage of the journey was much easier than they had anticipated. The guards were unable, and in many cases unwilling, to try and patrol the whole of the border, let alone anywhere more than a kilometre from the border itself. They had not seen anyone else. A short walk and the three fugitives were outside a hotel room. Peter knocked on the door. On his back Hannah had fallen asleep. Inside the room Wolfi barked and bobbed up and down boisterously.

Lotte opened the door and flung her arms around Peter and Hannah. Hannah stirred momentarily, then fell asleep once more.

'Oh thank goodness you're safe,' Lotte cried, tears in her eyes. Wolfi had wedged himself between Peter and Lotte with his tail thumping against their legs. She hugged Franz before ushering them all into the room.

Peter and Franz rented a second room. The owner, unused to such late night arrivals, was grateful for the extra business. Hannah was still hidden from view. Even though they were now in neutral territory, it was too close to the border for her to be seen. As they were due to go back to Germany they could not afford to be spotted with a smuggled Jew, as return might then be impossible.

The reunion with Berta the next day was very emotional. She and her husband arrived by car almost as soon as they had finished breakfast. Aunt Berta almost suffocated her two boys as she pressed them tightly to her.

'Oh, my boys. How you have grown! How handsome you are!' she repeated over and over. All the while Wolfi bounced around her impatiently. In her enthusiasm Berta had almost forgotten about the 'special gift'.

When the hubbub had died down, Berta and Lotte

embraced warmly, saying very little. Lotte stepped to one side to reveal the tiny Hannah. Hannah was uncharacteristically shy. Berta stooped down to her level and said, 'Hello my little treasure. I am Aunty Berta. What's your name?'

'Hannah,' the little girl replied and stepped behind Lotte.

With some encouragement from Lotte, Hannah allowed Berta to cuddle her. Within minutes she was sitting on her knee in the back of the car as they drove to Berta's house. Wolfi was stretched out on Peter and Franz's lap and Lotte sat in the passenger seat. Much though she loved her good friend Berta, Lotte could not help feel a bit jealous. Something inside her still longed to protect 'her little girl'.

They spent a full month at Berta's house. Lotte was able to travel to her parents at Oberstdorf as it was so close. With Hannah safely in Switzerland she could travel openly as a German citizen. Peter was reunited with an object especially important to him: it was the walking stick with Wolfi's head carved on top that Franz had made in their camp. Berta had kept it for him. Peter took it with him on all their long walks in the hills, something which pleased Franz immensely.

After her initial hesitation Hannah was as smitten with Berta as Berta was with her. In just the few weeks of freedom the little girl had changed. She behaved much more as a young child should. She played outdoors with Wolfi where they made snowmen and went sledging. She never missed a walk with Peter's dog. She quickly learnt how to ski and terrorised the others with the speed she flew down the slopes. Most pleasing of all, she started to put on weight with her improved diet and the treats that Berta lavished on her: ice creams, cakes of all descriptions, especially chocolate and real Swiss truffles. As her weight increased and her happiness grew she also became more talkative. She still could or would not disclose what had happened to her in the past, but otherwise she was a chatterbox.

Aunt Berta had never been happier. She had been dispossessed of her fine home in Berlin. Much of their wealth had been lost. She and her husband were living in exile and seldom able to see old friends. In spite of all of this Berta was overjoyed. Of course she was thrilled that her friends, including Wolfi, were there. There was one single overwhelming cause of her happiness: Hannah. Never had she believed that someone so young and so small could have such an impact. Berta wanted to adopt her, but knew she would have to wait. And of course there was Lotte. She had never shown the slightest maternal instinct in her life. The short time she had cared for Hannah had changed her. Lotte and Berta were very good friends and neither would allow that to alter. For the time being the issue would not arise as Lotte was returning to Berlin. She had agonised for many weeks, finally deciding she could not leave Peter and Franz.

'At least I will visit Hannah regularly,' she consoled herself, 'and for months at a time.' Even the ever optimistic Lotte knew this was impractical.

On the 10th February 1944 Peter and Franz were leaning out of the window of a passenger train bound for Berlin. They were at the station in St. Gallen, Switzerland.

They had said an emotional farewell to Hannah and Berta at Berta's home. Now they must say goodbye to Lotte, if only for the next month. As usual Lotte's appearance attracted the attention of many people, especially men, but she did not notice. She was focussed on Peter and Franz. Against her wishes they were returning to Berlin alone and with a number of important items hidden in their luggage: more ink for forging documents and chemicals for developing photographs, disguised as bottles of alcohol. They both had their forged travel permits and identity documents and passports. Carefully secreted in the lining of one of the cases was a genuine document, a Swiss passport. Franz had a new idea how to rescue more people and he could not wait to put it into operation.

Lotte reached up to the open window as the guard blew his whistle and waved his red flag and the train moved off. 'Be careful boys. I will see you soon,' she said, waving to them.

## CHAPTER TWENTY-SEVEN

'Oh thank heavens. Thank heavens!' Lotte said over and over. Peter and Franz were silent. Wolfi looked on, happy to be with his friends. The Professor stared at the radio, taking in the news. The old valve radio set in the corner of the room was barely audible. It had to be that way. No-one must know that they were listening to the BBC. Again the broadcaster repeated the news that was so welcome.

'Early this morning Allied forces landed on the beaches of Normandy and have progressed inland.' The Allied invasion had begun. The Nazi war machine was on the retreat in Europe.

Peter and Franz had been back in their Berlin apartment for three and a half months. In that time their frustration grew almost daily. For both of them it had become even more difficult to travel openly. They were clearly of military age and apparently fit. The war was going badly for Germany. They should be at the front or at sea. The excuse that they were on leave would only succeed so many times. They even had to avoid contact with Lotte's neighbours, any one of whom was capable of reporting them to the authorities.

As a consequence the Professor made most trips around the capital, normally by bicycle. The resistance consisted mainly of distributing ration cards or money to a network of u-boats. Most were in hiding with friends. Many moved every few days to lessen the risk of detection. For all of them life was extremely hard. At least with money to buy food on the black market they had some hope of survival. For now there was still a thriving black market, although all of them knew that could not last forever.

'Do you think it will work?' Franz asked Peter. Both were delighted with the news of the invasion. But they had learned to be cautious in their optimism, lest this be just another false dawn. Meanwhile their work must continue.

On the coffee table Franz had spread out a pile of passports, Swiss passports. All of them forged. Unable to venture outside on a regular basis, Franz had been very busy. His skills as a forger had only improved with practice.

'They are very convincing. But how do we get the new owners to the border? The train is too dangerous. We can't hide them all in trunks.' Peter's pessimism was not unfounded. On their journey back from Switzerland a talkative train conductor had been asking about the ships they had served on. His son was also in the navy. It had been too close for comfort.

As Peter examined the passports more closely he noticed something quite unusual. 'They are nearly all children and quite young children,' he said surprised.

'That's right. All of them are in hiding with one parent or both. Even though it is hard, the parents agree we should help them escape to Switzerland,' Franz explained, 'the Professor has been in contact with all of them.'

For the u-boats that were lucky enough to have shelter with other citizens the greatest difficulty was ensuring that young children, confined indoors for all the daylight hours, did not make a noise and give them away.

Lotte moved away from the radio set, wiping away a tear with her handkerchief. It was time to get back to the business in hand. She had that look in her eye that they had seen so frequently.'The Professor and I have an idea,' she said. 'And if we are going back to Switzerland we should take these with us.' She reached into a tall art deco porcelain vase and removed several rolled up canvasses.

'So that's where you hid them!' said the Professor. They had decided that it was safer for all concerned if only Lotte knew their hiding place.

'If my plan is to work we will need a lot of money.' Lotte was pacing up and down, the priceless canvasses still in her hand.

'All tickets, passes and travel permits please,' the conductor shouted as he walked the length of the train. It was two weeks later. As he approached the two nurses and eight children he wondered why they were virtually alone in this compartment. The rest of the train was overflowing with many passengers forced to stand. The train was bound for Geneva. All the children wore warm hats and coats and their necks were wrapped tightly with scarves.

'Tickets, passes and travel permits please,' the conductor repeated his request, this time less forcefully.

A very pretty nurse, with bright blonde hair just protruding from her nurse's cap, handed him ten passports, ten tickets and a letter. As she did so she appeared to wink towards the children. The conductor did not notice. On cue, two of the children coughed and spluttered. The other nurse stared steadfastly at the floor, avoiding his gaze.

The conductor's face rapidly changed from officious to horrified. The letter bore the official stamp and heading of the Reich's Security Office. It was countersigned by the Reich's Minister for Transportation.

*'In the interest of the security of the Reich, the Minister has granted travel permits to the children named below. All are Swiss nationals and are presently resident at the Berlin Hospital for Infectious Diseases under the care of the world's foremost expert, Professor Dr. Eitlinger. Their presence in the Reich is deemed too great a risk to the war effort and the well-being of the People. As such they are undesirables and are required to return to their homeland'*, the letter declared.

The conductor read no more. He did not even check the passports and tickets, simply handing them back to the nurse.

'I can't dawdle here I have work to do,' he blurted and, having made his excuses, he hurried out of the compartment.

Several uneventful hours passed until later that evening the train stopped near the border. It was not a scheduled stop, however, and the passengers grew anxious. The pretty nurse stood up and pulling down the window poked her head through the gap. She watched nervously as the conductor spoke with a Major in the SS, a Major Krieg. She could not hear precisely what was being said, although she did manage to decipher a few key words, including 'infectious' and 'children'. The officer raised his hand dismissively to the conductor and walked towards the train. In spite of the warning from the conductor, Major Krieg boarded. Worse still he boarded closest to the two nurses and their wards. He made his way straight to the nurses' compartment. The pretty nurse sat down in her seat and waited for the inevitable. The second nurse was less calm.

'We have been betrayed,' she said, standing up.

'Sit down!' the pretty nurse scolded, 'And stay calm!'

'Papers!' Major Krieg made no pretence at courtesy. In the long years of the war he had witnessed a lot of suffering. A few sick children would not deter him from his work.

The pretty nurse passed all the necessary paperwork to Major Krieg. He carefully read the letter from the Ministry, tutting now and then. Next he examined the passports carefully one at a time. Meanwhile the other nurse subdued her panic, but was barely able to breathe. Although worried the pretty nurse forced herself to look the soldier in the eye, feigning a friendly smile all the while. Avoiding eye contact would only increase suspicion.

'You are German?' Major Krieg seemed surprised.

'Yes,' came the pretty nurse's single word reply. Her voice was faint as her nerves began to get the better of her.

'My men are bravely fighting the enemy. They are dying daily or worse they are badly wounded. We are short of everything, even ammunition. And you waste valuable resources taking children who are going to die anyway out of the country. Swiss children! Not even good Germans!'

She could not think of a suitable response and so the pretty nurse said nothing. Until now the Professor's brilliant idea had worked wonderfully. He had noticed on the underground train how everyone moved compartment when an extremely ill-looking man had begun coughing. Major Krieg was battle hardened and entirely unsympathetic and the ploy had not worked on him. The pretty nurse, wondered whether he was going to throw them off the train there and then. Or worse.

Major Krieg moved towards her. She flinched, fearing he was about to slap her. His hand was raised. He did not strike. Instead, stepping towards her, he tossed the papers at her angrily.

'Clump!' Major Krieg's worn leather boot caught the large suitcase resting at her feet. To her horror he paused a moment, stooped and bent down to examine it. She gulped as he asked, 'What's in here? Open it up. The penalty for smuggling is very severe.'

Lotte, the pretty nurse, leaned forward as slowly as she dared. For once her looks and charm had not succeeded in distracting the enemy. If he felt in the lining of the case he would surely find the precious paintings. Much more frightening, he might arrest her and her travelling companions. It would not take long for the truth to come out.

'Why oh why did I bring the paintings with me?' she reproached herself. In reality she was being very harsh in her self-condemnation. There had been little choice. The antiques shop owner, purchaser of the other paintings, had left the city, fleeing the oncoming allies. To sell to anyone else in Berlin was too dangerous. The only safe market was in Switzerland.

Lotte was struggling with the straps on the case. Her tense fingers had lost their usual dexterity and she was fumbling.

'Give it here you imbecile! I will do it!' Major Krieg screamed. He grabbed at the handle of the case and tried to wrench it from her. She was unusually panic-stricken. She did not care less about the paintings. They were simply a means to an end. She cared greatly, however, for the young children she was smuggling.

'Herr Major! Herr Major!' a voice shouted from the other end of the compartment. Major Krieg swivelled on the spot, still holding the case.

'Thank goodness,' Lotte sighed. It was a moment's distraction, a welcome distraction nonetheless. Or so she thought until she spotted the cause.

The SS officer, a very young lieutenant, only a boy, came rushing along the train, still shouting, 'Herr Major! Herr Major!' On reaching Major Krieg the young boy clicked his heels together and, offering the Nazi salute, stole a glance at the pretty nurse, all the while facing his commanding officer. Lotte looked away, distractedly studying the floor.

'Don't look this way! Please don't look!' she prayed.

Major Krieg did not salute in response to the boy

lieutenant, instead asking in a clearly irritated voice: 'What now? Can I not have a moment's peace?'

Out of breath and somewhat concerned the boy soldier leaned forward and whispered something in Major Krieg's ear. Suddenly and without warning, Major Krieg dropped the case on the floor, pirouetted abruptly on the spot, then dashed back along the corridor. The boy lieutenant still breathless, turned to follow. He took a last look at Lotte, his gaze remaining on her for longer than was comfortable. She did not lift her eyes from the floor.

With one final glance, the boy lieutenant clicked his heels in salute and hurried along the corridor before jumping onto the platform. At last Lotte could relax a little as Major Krieg and his trusted and eager young Lieutenant Kurt drove away at speed in a staff car.

Lotte did not hear what had been said between the two men. She did not care. Once more Kurt had played a role in events, except this time he had unknowingly helped to save several Jewish children. The thought made her want to laugh out loud. She resisted. Thankfully the little contact she had with Kurt was not enough for him to recognise her, helped by her basic disguise. She had recognised him at once. He had gained his wish and was part of the 'struggle'. In spite of everything Lotte hoped he might survive the war, if only for Berta's sake.

'Come on! Come on!' Lotte implored. In spite of Kurt's disappearance the tension was unbearable. The Major had gone, but he might delegate someone else to check the contents of her trunk. Finally, after a few agonisingly slow minutes, the train wheels creaked into motion, and with the engine belching out smoke, the locomotive pulled slowly away. Lotte was so grateful. The children were almost safe, as was the mother of one of them, the other nurse. The paintings had not been discovered and she would soon see Hannah again. Surely nothing else could hinder their journey.

Meanwhile Peter was in Berlin in the park near Lotte's apartment. He studied the man carefully. His face seemed familiar. He could not quite place him. He was certain however that he was a friend of his father's. More importantly he was a Jew and therefore must be in hiding.

Peter was in the Tiergarten with Wolfi. He was in his naval uniform. Since he had first acquired it he had grown again and it was a little tight. That was not uncommon in Berlin as many boy soldiers were forced into the service of the Reich and even material for uniforms was scarce. Unwanted questioning was a gamble he had to take. Wolfi needed his daily exercise.

Peter was toying with the idea of approaching the Jewish man when he halted in his tracks. Gestapo agents! How could he have missed them? Two were reading or pretending to read their newspapers and one was sitting on a bench eating a bread roll. It was plain they were Gestapo men from the usual uniform of black leather. They were just ten or so metres away from the Jewish man who was walking through the park away from Peter.

'He's going to be caught,' Peter said to Wolfi under his breath. Wolfi looked back at his master, stick in his mouth. Peter began to follow in the direction of the Jewish man. He was desperately trying to think what to do when he came to a dead stop.

'Did I just imagine that?' he whispered to Wolfi. The Jewish man had looked right at the two Gestapo officers, pretending to read their newspapers. Rather than turn away from them he appeared to nod his head in their direction. As if to confirm it, the Jewish man nodded very quickly once more. The Gestapo men lowered their newspapers and one quite clearly tipped his head forward in response.

All of this occurred in seconds and Peter was still undecided how to react. He could not be their target. His own father would scarcely recognise him now. In particular he was healthier looking and better nourished than most fugitives. He was on the point of running away when he saw the real quarry.

He was sitting on a bench marked 'Aryans only'. His appearance looked quite smart, apart from his shoes. 'Always the shoes,' Peter winced. Understandably the little money they had was spent on food to survive rather than expensive shoe repairs.

Peter was closer to the target than either the Gestapo or the Jew catcher, for that was his occupation. To save himself the Jew catcher helped the Gestapo locate and arrest Jews by befriending them. He would pretend to be living underground as well and the fellow Jew would thus happily confide in him, before being betrayed.

'Not this time,' Peter said to himself. He called Wolfi to him and took the stick from the dog's mouth. He leaned over and stroked the dog, all the time saying very loudly, 'Good dog. Good dog.' As quietly as possible he ordered Wolfi to take the stick to the Gestapo's target. Wolfi obeyed perfectly and ran towards the man on the bench.

'Wolfi come back. Leave the man alone,' Peter shouted after him. Without the customary whistle from his master, the words 'come back' meant nothing to Wolfi who continued on his way.

Wolfi was a large dog, black and sometimes ferocious looking. Even other dog lovers sometimes found him intimidating. The appearance of a dog rushing towards him was enough to grab the man's attention and he looked up, not just scared, terrified.

By now Peter was near the bench. With his back to the Jew catcher and the Gestapo, Peter mouthed the words, 'Jew catcher and Gestapo behind me! Get out of here!'

The man's look of surprise was mixed with his genuine fear of Wolfi. He hesitated on the bench. 'If you don't leave now you will be arrested,' Peter mouthed again, this time a little louder. He was becoming very anxious. Perhaps he had made a mistake?

The man leapt from the bench and started to run from the park. Two of the Gestapo men gave chase. The Gestapo agents were obviously fitter and healthier for they had regular nourishment and regular sleep. Unfortunately for the Gestapo they could not outrun Wolfi who particularly liked this game, especially when he could run in front of the pursuers. The man may have been weakened by hunger, but he ran for his life. Every time an agent seemed within grabbing distance, Wolfi somehow weaved between their legs.

'No! No! Don't shoot!' Peter shouted, 'You will hit my dog.' One of the agents, the fattest of the three, had given up the chase. In his hand he held a revolver, his arm outstretched and one eye closed to aim at the fugitive u-boat.

'Phew!' Peter said, rather too loudly. With two agents blocking his view the fat Gestapo man could not fire. Hitting a civilian was one thing, hitting another agent was a disaster.

'Besides the paperwork would be too tiresome,' he consoled himself. As the revolver was slowly lowered, Peter was just able to see the target jump onto a passing tram as the other two Gestapo agents struggled to reach him. The agents waved their arms frantically at the driver as the tram moved on defiantly. Not even the Nazis could delay German public transport.

'That was close boy.' Peter patted Wolfi on the head, all the time aware of a person behind him.

'What did you say to that Jew? You warned him didn't you?' the person demanded. Peter ignored the question. He was aware of the shadow of someone standing over him. 'And why were you so happy he got away?' the voice continued. 'Answer me when I speak to you! Papers! Papers now!'

Once more Peter ignored the demand. Instead he stood up and feigned surprise when he turned to face the person. It was the third Gestapo agent.

'Papers now!' the agent screamed. He was now so close to his face, Peter could smell his tobacco breath. 'And why aren't you on board ship at the people's hour of need?'

Peter calmly handed over his papers. Included was an official document from the war ministry. 'Sorry. I can't hear very well,' Peter indicated apologetically, tapping his ear at the same time. 'Thank you for not shooting my dog.'

The Gestapo agent calmed slightly as he read the official confirmation. Peter had been injured by an explosion. As a result he was virtually deaf and unfit for war service. This was now so common even amongst the civilian population that the agent did not doubt the truth of it. The agent folded the letter from the Ministry and handed it back to Peter along with his identity card.

'Okay you can go. Be careful who you speak to in future.'

Peter did not wait around. Both he and the target were lucky that day. In the subsequent days, instead of avoiding the park Peter deliberately went back to the same place, hoping to see the escapee. He did not see him again.

# CHAPTER TWENTY-EIGHT

Making his way along a badly damaged and potholed street, an elderly, but well-groomed man was wending a path through the ruins. So many craters had opened up that the Professor found it faster to walk than cycle. Under his arm he held a small, tightly wrapped, brown parcel. It was not much, though the few provisions he had managed to purchase were substantially more than most Berliners could ever hope to buy.

As the Professor negotiated the rubble and the potholes, elsewhere in the city a haggard and battle-worn grey man was handing out medals to boy soldiers, their uniforms coated in dust. The boys were frightened and the man disconsolate. On his fifty-third birthday the great warmonger and murderer, Adolf Hitler was decorating the last line of defence outside his bunker. It was his penultimate official act before marrying his long term mistress, Eva Braun and then committing suicide.

Berlin was on its knees. The population were at their wits' end. Suicides amongst the population were commonplace as many feared the reprisals of the Soviet forces as they marched on the capital. Marshall Zhukov's forces outnumbered the Germans by fifteen to one. The bombardment of the city was incessant, with scarcely a single building untouched. Most streets were impassable. Boys as young as fourteen and fifteen were conscripted to serve alongside the pensioners forced to defend the city. Some were simply too small or too weak to lift the heavy anti-tank guns. Most wore uniforms twice their size that would not save them from the advancing hordes. On the Kurfürstendamm the SS hanged anyone brave enough to fly the white flag on the outside of their home. Throughout the city, special SS units executed deserters and anyone else with the courage to defy the Führer's last wish: Berlin would fight until the end. Food was scarce, morale was low and fear pervaded every part of the city.

Just a few days later, in Luisenstrasse, Lotte and her friends were celebrating. It seemed an odd celebration as they were officially going to be on the losing side, but for them the war was virtually over. The Soviet Forces were bombarding the city constantly and it was only a matter of days until the end must surely come. Apart from the news of Hitler's death rumours had spread that the Nazi leadership were negotiating an armistice. For all that, the streets of Berlin were as dangerous as ever. For Franz and Peter in particular, as many Russians sought revenge for the atrocities committed by the Nazis in their homeland and these two young men were of military age. Lotte, like many German women, was all too aware of the particular danger that she faced from the invading troops.

In spite of the fear of reprisals and the uncertainty as to their future, Lotte was optimistic. She raised her glass and toasted their freedom in champagne. 'My dear friends. It is hard to believe it will soon be over. You can start living your lives again.'

She lifted her glass to her lips and began to sip. Her best friends were with her. Peter, Franz and the Professor. And not forgetting Wolfi. Each of her companions raised their glass and repeated her toast, 'To dear friends!'

'Boom! A loud thunder clap shattered the near silence. And then another. 'Boom!'

With no further warning an enormous explosion shook the building. The force of the blast was so powerful that Lotte and Peter were thrown to the floor. The Professor and Franz were still sitting on the sofa, covered in plaster and dust. Wolfi's usually dark black coat was white with a covering of the powdered plaster. This was not a thunderstorm of nature's making.

'Lotte! Lotte! Are you all right?' Franz was the first to react and was frantically digging for Lotte under a pile of plaster and debris. Peter checked the Professor was uninjured and began to help Franz. Wolfi shook the dust from his coat and began to dig in the rubble where once the wall had stood. As they flung bits of masonry to one side, the rapid fire of machine guns came ever closer, accompanied by more mortars exploding. The Russians were close to the Reichstag just a few streets away.

After a few tense minutes Peter and Franz helped Lotte to her feet. She was dazed and apart from a few scratches, unharmed. She had been blown under a mahogany side table that had taken the force of falling masonry.

'I'm fine,' Lotte said again and again, as the boys fussed around her. 'Pity about the champagne.' Peter and Franz smiled at one another. They knew she really was fine.

'Hands in the air! Now!' The order was in German, with a distinct Russian accent. It came from a young soldier in Soviet Army Uniform. He was pointing his weapon at Peter. To either side of him were standing two other soldiers. A fourth soldier in what appeared to be an officer's uniform pushed past them. None of them had heard the rifle bolt as it was pulled back, such was the ringing in their ears from the explosions. Peter, Franz and Lotte stayed completely still, moving only to raise their hands. Just moments before they had been celebrating the imminent defeat of the enemy.

'Jews! We are Jews!' Peter said desperately.

'No Jews, all dead!' the soldier said in broken German.

'No! We are Jews! It's the truth,' Peter pleaded.

After everything they had been through the prospect of dying at the hands of the Russians was too cruel. He held Wolfi back by his collar as he strained to get to the intruders. One of the soldiers looked menacingly back at Wolfi and grasped his rifle tightly.

Behind Peter an unfamiliar sound could be heard. The Professor was speaking in a language he could not understand.

'It's Russian,' he said to Franz, 'the Professor speaks Russian. He will be able to persuade them.' But their hopes faded as the aggressive faces of the soldiers remained unchanged. Their guns were still threateningly close to their faces. None but the Professor could understand the soldiers' gruff responses. The manner of delivery left little doubt however.

'It's no use,' the Professor explained. 'They have this address as the home of a top Nazi. They refuse to believe there could be any Jews here. Everywhere they go, everyone is claiming to be Jewish.'

'Tell them I still have my original identification card with 'J' for Jew stamped on it,' Peter replied. His desperation was heart rending.

'It won't help Peter. They have seen so many forged passes they will think it is just another one. Especially as we are all carrying forged passes at the moment.' The Professor spoke again in Russian. They did not understand, although the anxiety in his voice was clear. The officer said something in Russian and pointed towards Franz and Peter.

'Niet! No!' the Professor shouted, moving towards his friends. The officer prodded his chest with his machine gun. Walking towards Peter and Franz, the three soldiers held the muzzles of their guns just centimetres from the boys' faces. Wolfi reared up at the soldiers barking all the time, his fangs bared and gnashing. Peter struggled to restrain his dog.

'Down Wolfi! Down!' Peter said. One of the Soviet soldiers had aimed his rifle at Wolfi's head and was about to shoot.

Wolfi did not understand, but obeyed nonetheless. Thankfully the soldier did not shoot and momentarily lowered his weapon, before raising it to shoulder height once more.

'Come with us,' one of the soldiers said in German and roughly grabbed Peter's shoulder.

'No! Leave him! Let him be!' Lotte's shout was so loud it caused everyone to stop. Peter and Franz were no longer scared of their own fate. The officer was looking at

363

Lotte and both were terrified of what might happen to her. Worse still the other soldiers were now fixated on her.

The Professor began to babble in Russian once more. He had said just a few words when a strange sound pierced the air. Even with a background accompaniment of gunfire and shells it was unmistakable. And it was getting closer.

Herr Riesen climbed through the hole the soldiers had used. He was no longer Herr Riesen. He was the concert violinist once more. Even as he clambered over the rubble his hands expertly played the violin. Peter had heard it before, but could not name the piece. It did not matter. Whatever the music was the Russian soldiers stopped and listened.

After a few minutes the great violinist took the instrument from under his chin and began to sing. The words initially meant nothing to Peter.

'*Hava neranenah ve-nismeha, hava nagila,*' the violinist sang. His voice was loud and clear. Soon the violinist's voice was joined by another. It was the Professor. It had been years since either he or Peter had used this magical language. A third voice joined in the singing as Peter recalled the words he had learnt so long ago.

'Let us sing and be happy. Let us rejoice.' That was the meaning of the song. If they were to die they would die defiantly.

'*Hava neranenah ve-nismeha,*' the words rang out, this time in a deep bass voice. A voice with a strong hint of a foreign accent. It was a miracle! The officer had joined in.

'He is a Jew! He is a Jew!' the Professor shouted. It had been twelve long years since anyone had been able to shout these words in public in Germany. After several magical minutes the song came to an end and silence fell. At first no-one moved. Then the Professor spoke pointing at the violinist and at each of his friends in turn, first Lotte then Peter and finally Franz. The violinist bowed as his name was spoken.

The officer issued a command in Russian. The soldiers immediately lowered their weapons. The officer spoke to the Professor and as he did he took a small notepad and a pen from his breast pocket. He scribbled several sentences. They did not understand, but Lotte, Peter and Franz recognised their own names. The Russian officer stopped and spoke to the Professor in Russian once more. The Professor replied briefly in just a few words. Finally their new found friend signed the document and handed it to the Professor.

The two men shook hands. The officer said something to his soldiers in Russian and, saluting all those present, left the way he had arrived.

'We have safe conduct around the city,' the Professor beamed. 'And when things are settled we can exchange it for official passes. Our war is over!'

The piece of paper in his hand bore not only his name, but those of his friends.

'It says that we are all enemies of the Third Reich and friends of the Soviet Union,' the Professor translated. 'Anyone who harms us will be treated as a war criminal.'

The five companions embraced in a circle. Not one of them could hold back the tears. Wolfi sat right in the middle barking his approval.

Almost a year after the Soviet forces entered Berlin and tore down the Swastika from the Reichstag, Peter and Wolfi were in the Tiergraten. Peter was sitting on a bench that not long ago had been denied to him. In the year since the war in Europe had ended, Peter and Franz had remained at Lotte's apartment. The wall had been rebuilt at enormous cost. Fortunately, even though close to the Russian sector, Lotte now lived in the British zone. The Professor, a regular visitor, remained at his old apartment, free from the fear of denouncement. Berta had returned from Switzerland with Lotte and somehow managed to reclaim her old house. Remarkably it was undamaged by either bombing or shelling. Lotte bravely accepted the strong attachment that Hannah had formed in the months with Berta and resolved to play the loving aunt, rather than mother. Herr Riesen, as he was once known, had very quickly been able to emigrate to the USA with his children where he played to packed concert halls.

On this particular day Peter had just returned from the synagogue in the Oranienburger Strasse. Each day for almost the last year this had been his first port of call. It was the headquarters of the *'Organisation for Displaced Persons'*. Each day, like so many others, he had sought news of his mother and father. As usual there was none. Franz had long ago accepted that his parents were no more. Peter was still unwilling to give up hope. From time to time he travelled back to his first hiding place in the woods where he had left clues for his father. He found nothing. For the first time in a long while he was overcome by an unfamiliar feeling. Despair. During the war his fight for survival had largely occupied his mind.

Now that the full horrors of the camps had emerged he knew the prospect of seeing his parents again was very remote. As he contemplated this terrible reality for the first time he failed to notice Wolfi and the man playing with him.

'What a great dog you have. I knew a dog like that once. What is his name?'

Peter looked up at the figure in front of him. It was an old man. His face suggested he was about seventy, his eyes somewhat younger. He was very thin, which was not uncommon, even so long after the war. His hair was very grey and receding and his hands looked frail. Peter could just see the last few numbers of a long tattoo on his left arm. Wolfi was bouncing up and down excitedly. More excited than Peter had seen him for years. His tail was wagging and he was barking. The bark was not aggressive. It was the sort of bark he gave when Peter returned to Lotte's apartment. The sort of bark that used to greet his father when he returned from the city.

Wolfi's reaction to this man confused Peter. Other than the Professor he had greeted no-one else with the same enthusiasm.

'Wolfi. His name is Wolfi and he is a great dog,' Peter said proudly.

The old man looked up. 'Wolfi, Wolfi,' he murmured. The excited dog was pressing against the old man's legs.

'Down boy! Down!' the man commanded. Wolfi sat immediately, though his tail still made semi-circular sweeps across the ground.

'I followed my son's clues. I have found his dog, but not my boy,' the man said sadly.

Peter's mouth had gone dry and he struggled to speak. He had hoped for so long, but now the reality refused to sink in. 'Papa? Can that really be you?' He was standing holding the elderly man by the elbows.

'Papa?' he repeated in disbelief. This could not be his father. He was a large man, very tall and stocky with a paunch. Now Peter towered over him. Whereas Peter had grown tall and athletic, his father was stooped and weary.

The man was also confused. The dog was certainly Wolfi, but the boy was unlike the son he remembered. The son he had dreamed about all those years in the camp. Of course that boy was only fifteen when they had lost each other. And that was five years ago. This was his son and he was a fine young man.

'Peter? Can it really be you? My Peter?' the man asked again, barely daring to hope.

Peter stood back and examined the man carefully again. He wanted to believe it was his father, he was still uncertain.

'And Wolfi! What a dog you are! I knew you would look after my son,' the man said. 'That night when you jumped off the boat, I saw Wolfi save you.'

'It is you Papa!' Peter cried out and hugged his father to him.

They held each other tightly for several minutes, neither saying anything. Moments later Peter stood back a little. 'And Mama?'

Isaac did not speak. He simply shook his head and pulled Peter to him once more. Wolfi lay at their feet looking up.

At the edge of the park, Lotte and Franz watched as father and son, reunited after so long, clung to each other, weeping.